Praise for *The* [Veil]

'[*The* Veil was full of action, a steady t[...] slight romance element, and an interest[...] world building. Any and every urban fantasy fan out there needs to read this'
Vampire Book Club

'*The Veil* was truly a fantastic read and most certainly one of my top reads for 2015 thus far. If you're a fan of Chicagoland Vampires, you will fall in love with *The Veil* . . . and Claire and Liam'
Literary Escapism

'The world building was fabulous; the characters were likable; the plot and tension provided a great 'what's going to happen next?' feeling that kept me engaged. . . . I loved it and basically devoured it in only a few sittings'
Paranormal Haven

'A great start to a new paranormal series from an author I love! If you don't have this on your to-read list, make sure you get it there ASAP! I think it's going to be an amazing ride!'
Fiction Fare

'Action-packed and fast-paced, with enough sexual tension to keep a girl hoping. And with a cast of characters that I couldn't have picked better myself. This book was exactly what I needed to restore my faith in the paranormal. Yes! There can be a new series that catches my interest and gets me giddy again!'
Under the Covers

'Neill is truly a master storyteller!'
RT Book Reviews

'A fast-paced read that you won't want to put down once you pick it up'
A Book Obsession

'A fabulous beginning . . . filled with nonstop action and drama'
Fang-tastic Books

'This was absolutely enthralling, entertaining, and completely original. . . . This truly was a wonderful start to what promises to be a standout series'
My Guilty Obsession

THE
SIGHT

A DEVIL'S ISLE NOVEL

CHLOE NEILL

First published in Great Britain in 2016 by Gollancz
an imprint of The Orion Publishing Group Ltd
Carmelite House, 50 Victoria Embankment
London EC4Y 0DZ

An Hachette UK Company

1 3 5 7 9 10 8 6 4 2

A CIP catalogue record for this book is
available from the British Library.

ISBN 978 1 473 21536 8

Printed in Great Britain by Clays Ltd, St Ives plc

www.chloeneill.com
www.orionbooks.co.uk
www.gollancz.co.uk

And the nations were angry, and thy wrath is come . . .

— Revelation 11:18

CHAPTER ONE

New Orleans, Louisiana
Late November

We rode in a truck that had seen a lot of miles—more than two hundred thousand of them, according to the odometer. The windows were open to the heat and humidity and sunshine, all of it powerful even in the early morning. But that was New Orleans for you.

I piled my red hair into a topknot and futzed until the bun was secure, then leaned my head against the door. Even the hot breeze felt better than none. The truck rocking beneath us, the city nearly silent around us, my eyes drifted closed.

"You gonna fall asleep?"

I slitted a glance at the man in the driver's seat. Liam Quinn was tall and lean, built of hard, stacked muscle. His hair was dark and short, and matched the scruff along his jaw. His eyes were a shockingly bright blue, with lashes dark and thick enough to make a fashionista jealous.

He was undeniably handsome, undeniably sexy, and undeniably off-limits.

And I was getting loopy from lack of sleep. I could have used a ten-minute power nap. Or a four-hour power nap. But since I still had something to prove, I sat up straight, blinked hard to force my eyes to focus. "Nope. Totally awake and eyes on the road and checking my six."

He looked amused. "You're just stringing words together. Bounty hunters don't sleep on the job."

"I'm a bounty hunter in training," I pointed out. "And I wasn't sleeping. I was . . . silently debriefing."

Liam was the actual bounty hunter, and we'd spent hours searching the Lower Ninth Ward for a wraith, a human infected by magic. We hadn't found him, which was a bad result for everyone. Containment wouldn't be happy, and the wraith was still on the loose, still a threat to the public and himself.

"You did good tonight. We didn't get a great result, but you did good." He paused. "And I'm still thinking about that football."

I nodded. "Yeah. I'm still thinking about the baseball cards." We hadn't found the wraith in the several abandoned houses we'd searched, but we had found a former bachelor pad with a man cave and plenty of sports memorabilia.

"I know the owners could come back," I said, letting my fingers surf in the wind outside the truck. "It's unlikely, but it's possible. It's just—somebody really loved those cards, and they're getting moldier by the day."

Liam smiled a little. "And you want to put them in the shop."

The "shop" was Royal Mercantile, my store in the French Quarter. Or what was left of it after the war with the Paranormals. They'd come through the Veil, the barrier separating their world from ours, and spread destruction and chaos across the South. New Orleans had been ground zero.

"For display and for safety," I said. "Not for sale." I glanced at him, his muscles taut beneath the short-sleeved shirt, strong hands on the steering wheel. "You like to sports?"

He lifted an eyebrow. "Do I like to sports? You sound like a woman who's never said that word before."

"My dad didn't care about sportsball."

"You know that's not a thing."

"I do," I admitted. "But I like the sound of it." I looked at him, the long, rangy body with a powerful chest and arms. "I'd say quarterback—possibly receiver. Maybe pitcher, maybe power forward in sportsball." It wasn't difficult to imagine him muscling in for a layup.

He shook his head, but a corner of his mouth was still quirked in a grin. "I played sportsball in high school. Power forward."

"Nailed it."

"What about you?" he asked.

"I ran track for a couple of years in high school, until I realized I didn't really like running."

"You do plenty of running now," he said, turning onto North Claiborne.

"That's because I'm chased. If there'd been Paranormals and wraiths chasing me in high school, I'd have put more effort into it."

When the truck began to slow, I glanced up. The street was clear; ours was the only vehicle. "If we've run out of gas, you have to carry me back to the Quarter."

Liam just shook his head. "Look," he said, pointed to the side of the road.

A billboard in front of an auto repair shop had been covered in eye-searing yellow paint. DEATH TO PARANORMALS had been painted in enormous red letters across it.

"I came down this street yesterday," Liam said, squinting into the sun as he leaned over to look through the window, his cologne lingering faintly behind him when he sat up again. "That wasn't there."

"It's new," I said, gesturing to the buckets, brushes, and cans of spray paint that littered the parking lot around the post.

"I don't suppose you sold that stuff. Know who bought it?"

I shook my head. "The supplies didn't come from my shop. The only paint I have is white, and I don't have any spray paint."

"The brushes?"

I shook my head again. Whoever had painted the billboard had used foam rollers to color in the large letters. "Only bristle brushes. They're not from Royal Mercantile."

The supplies could have come from anywhere—and from anyone with an ax to grind. The war with the Paranormals had started seven years ago and ended a year later, but the billboard proved the animosity hadn't completely faded.

"We should tell Gunnar," I said, thinking of one of my closest friends, and the second-in-charge at Containment, the division of the Paranormal Combatant Command that managed everything in the former war zone, including Devil's Isle, the prison where Paranormals were incarcerated—or were supposed to be. There were fugitive Paras who'd managed to evade imprisonment and fugitive humans newly infected by magic who hadn't yet been rounded up. That's why bounty hunters like Liam had jobs.

His gaze still wary, Liam drove on, taking us closer to Devil's Isle's towering walls, which enclosed the Marigny neighborhood. "Tell Malachi and the others, too. They should know someone's got an attitude problem."

Malachi was an angel and a friend, and a member of Delta, a group of humans and Paras dedicated to changing the treatment of Paranormals. Their existence proved that not all Paranormals were enemies, just as the billboard proved that not all humans were allies.

The tricky part was telling the difference.

It was a Saturday morning in the French Quarter, and there wasn't a single person in sight. My shop—the first floor of a three-story town house on Royal Street—was one of the lucky buildings that hadn't been destroyed, although we sold a lot more MREs and bottled water these days than antique sideboards.

Liam sputtered to a stop in front of the store. Our victory flag—a gold fleurs-de-lis on a field of purple—flapped in the breeze from the second-floor balcony.

I climbed out of the truck and into heat that was already oppressive at eight in the morning, then leaned down to look through the open window. "You want to come in for some iced tea?"

"Yes," Liam said without hesitating, and turned off the truck, followed me to the door. I picked up a scrap of paper and a dead leaf from the tiled threshold, unlocked it.

Anticipating a hot day, I'd left the shop closed up. I'd found a small air conditioner at a swap meet a few weeks before, and I'd managed to get it running. The power had stayed on long enough to cool the air by a few degrees, wring out a little of the humidity.

"Oh, that is nice," Liam said, pausing inside the door with his eyes closed, black lashes dark against his cheeks and his hands on his lean hips.

Longing, hot and strong as fire, burned through my chest.

I was a Sensitive, one of the few humans exposed to magic who'd developed magical powers as a result. That meant I was a nearly wraith, an almost wraith, a could-be wraith. Liam was supposed to hunt people like me, to lock them safely away in Devil's Isle. Instead, he'd introduced me to people convinced I could control my magic, that becoming a wraith wasn't inevitable.

But it was always between us, the possibility the magic would overpower me and he'd be forced to take me in. He believed that would be cruel and unfair to me. And despite the chemistry between us, that wasn't a gap he'd been able to bridge. So I'd worked to ignore the heat, the connection. It took a lot of conscious effort on my part. And even then, I wasn't very good at it.

I flipped the CLOSED sign to OPEN, forced myself to put space between us, to walk through the front room past bins of duct tape and bags of Camellia red beans and into the small kitchen. I opened the refrigerator, let the air chill my burning cheeks, then pulled out the pitcher of iced tea. I could've used a stiffer drink, but that would have to wait.

I poured two glasses, found Liam standing at the counter's far end, where I'd spread the shards of a cuckoo clock that had hung in the store. I settled myself on the stool behind the counter, slid his tea over.

"New project?" he asked.

I looked over the piles I'd already separated into wood and metal fragments, the figures of Little Red Riding Hood and the wolf that had traveled across the clock's front. "This is the clock Agent Broussard's cronies smashed. It was a gift from my father, so I'm going to put it back together."

"You know how to put together a clock?" he asked, sounding impressed.

I smiled. "With enough time and patience, you can figure anything out. I'm ignoring the mechanisms for now—the gears are so small. I'm going to fix the case first."

The bell on the door rang as two Containment agents walked in wearing their dark fatigues. I didn't exhale until they offered small waves, headed for the canned goods. I was still waiting for the shit to hit that particular fan again.

"You want to help?" I asked Liam, offering a bottle of wood glue.

He frowned over the pieces. "I'm not sure this is my crafting sweet spot."

I snorted, poured glue into a small dish, dabbed a brush in it. "And what would be your crafting sweet spot?"

"Chopping wood," he said as I daubed glue on the back of a wood sliver. "Changing oil. Fighting marauders."

"I don't have any wood that needs chopping, and I don't have a car. Marauders are more likely. Glad to know you're prepared for that."

Liam made a sarcastic sound, then glanced up at the wall of clocks still functioning. "I should get back to Devil's Isle, say good morning to Eleanor."

Liam's grandmother lived in Devil's Isle, but by her choice. Only a few knew that she could *see* magic, the result of a blow during the war from a magical weapon.

The door opened and my other two closest friends walked in. Tadji Dupree waved hello as they walked into the store. She wore dark fatigue pants, a flowy tank, and enormous earrings of gold and silver discs that shone against her dark skin.

Gunnar Landreau was tall and militarily fit, with dark, wavy hair, pale skin, and a trickster's smile. He wore dark Containment fatigues, but he was very decidedly on our side. Whatever "side" that was.

"You two nearly match today," I said, gesturing at the fatigues as they came forward. "Pulling a Cagney and Lacey thing? Or Abbott and Costello?"

"Did their clothes match?" Liam asked, head cocked.

"No," Gunnar said dryly. "Those were the only duos she could think of. Did you know she didn't have a television growing up?"

"Deprived child," Liam said, looking back at me thoughtfully. "Although that does explain 'sportsball.'"

Tadji snorted, put her messenger bag on the counter with a *thud*.

"We had a television," I corrected. "We just didn't watch it very often." I gestured to Tadji's bag. "What do you have in that thing?"

The Containment agents approached the counter with an armful of water and MREs, so I put down my brush and moved to the metal cashbox and receipt pad to deal with their purchases.

"My notes," she said. "I'm hoping to write up some of my outline today." Tadji was working on a degree in linguistics. "And I've heard a rumor there's a coffeehouse in Tremé."

We all went still, looked at her.

"There's a coffeehouse in New Orleans?" one of the agents asked, hope in her eyes.

"That's the rumor," Tadji said. "Woman set up a little café in her living room, sells muffins and coffee. I'm going to check it out."

"And report back," I requested, putting the agents' purchases into a bag and offering their change. I closed the cashbox again, looked at her. "Like, Folgers, or what?" Coffee was relatively rare in the Zone—a high-priced luxury.

Tadji's eyes gleamed. "I don't know. But I'm going to find out."

As the Containment agents left, I looked at Gunnar. "And what's on your agenda?"

"Keeping the Zone running smoothly, as per usual." He glanced at Liam. "You find that wraith in the Lower Ninth?"

"We didn't," Liam said, and Gunnar looked at me speculatively.

"'We'?" he asked. "You went with him?"

"Bounty hunter in training," I said, offering him a salute. "It still makes for good cover." And gave me a chance to be sure that any wraiths taken into Devil's Isle were treated as well as possible. We owed them that much, at least.

"No sign of the wraith," Liam repeated, "but we found something else. Giant billboard on Claiborne. 'Death to Paranormals' painted over it."

"Lovely," Gunnar said. "I'll have someone take a look."

"Who has that much free time on their hands?" Tadji asked.

"There are plenty of people out there with delusions about Paranormals," Gunnar said. "Plenty of people who believe in conspiracies, or who think the government owed them something after the war."

In fairness to those people, the government did know about the Veil. But it hadn't known who'd waited for us on the other side.

Speaking of angry humans, loud voices began to fill the air with what sounded like chanting.

"What is that?" I asked, glancing at the door.

"Maybe protestors?" Liam asked with a frown.

"Could be," Gunnar said. Liam, Tadji, and I followed him outside, then to the corner and down Conti.

About a dozen men and women, most in their twenties or thirties, but a few older, a few younger, stretched across Bourbon Street. They all wore nubby, homespun fabric in bulky and shapeless tunics and dresses.

Their arms were linked together, and they sang as they walked, their voices woven into an eerie, complex harmony. I didn't recognize the song, but it sounded like a hymn, with lyrics about death and smiting and Calvary. If this had been a different time, they might have been congregants walking to a country church. But I hadn't seen many churchgoers carrying bright yellow signs with CLEANSE THE ZONE OR DIE TRYING in searing red paint.

Leading the group was a man with pale skin, dark hair, medium build, and a heavy beard. He was flanked by two women—one pale, one dark, but both with dark eyes that looked across the French Quarter with obvious disdain.

It wasn't the first time there'd been protestors in the Quarter; there'd been plenty during and shortly after the war, when it was popular to complain about how the war was being fought, or how it had been won. But the war had ended six years ago, and as a Sensitive, I wasn't feeling very sympathetic to antimagic arm waving.

Liam shifted, moving a protective step closer to me while watching the group with narrowed eyes.

Gunnar's expression was cold and blank. That was a particular skill of his—that level stare that showed authority and said he wouldn't take shit from anybody.

The man in the front glanced in our direction, stopped, and lifted his hands. Like an orchestra following a conductor directing his symphony, the protestors stopped behind him, and silence fell again.

He walked toward us. He wore an easy smile, but there was something very cold behind his dark, deep-set eyes.

"Good morning," he said, in a voice without a hint of Louisiana in it. "Can we talk to you about the Zone?"

Gunnar didn't waste any time. "You have a permit?"

The man's eyes flashed with irritation, but his smile didn't change. "I don't subscribe to the notion that citizens of this country require a permit to exercise their First Amendment rights."

Gunnar didn't even blink.

"Of course," the man said, "we also respect human laws. It's just that we believe those laws should be enforced to their logical conclusion." The man pulled a folded piece of paper from his pocket, offered it to Gunnar.

"Any law in particular?" Gunnar asked.

"The Magic Act," the man said. "All magic is illegal. And all magic should be removed from our world . . . by any means necessary."

CHAPTER TWO

I t was actually the MIGECC Act—the Measure for the Illegality of Glamour and Enchantment in Conflict Communities. But he was right about its effect.

Eyes narrowed, Gunnar looked at the man for a moment—like he was memorizing the lines and shadows of his face—before shifting his gaze down to the paper in his hand. Gunnar reviewed the document, handed it back to the man. "Thank you, Mr.—"

"I am Ezekiel." He gestured to the men and women behind him. "We are trumpeters, and we carry our message through the Zone."

Gunnar gave the signs a suspicious look. "Which is?"

"Bringing clarity. Sharing the truth." Ezekiel scanned the faces of those who'd gathered around us to check out the commotion. "The Paranormals destroyed our world, our lifestyle. They're now incarcerated, but have things improved? No. We're told the Zone can't be saved, the soil can't be treated, can only be replaced, that magic is now part of our world. But no one tells us the truth—that the world is polluted by the presence of Paranormals, stained by the obscenity of their existence."

Liam's gaze moved from the protestors and signs to Ezekiel's face. "The billboard near the Lower Ninth—that's yours?"

Ezekiel's smile was chilling. "That depends on which one you're referring to. We have many allies in the Zone."

"And how," Gunnar asked, pointing to a sign, "do you and your allies intend to 'clean' the Zone?"

"By removing all magic from the world."

"And arguing with humans in the French Quarter is how you're going to go about it?" Gunnar asked. "That doesn't seem productive."

"Spoken like a Containment mouthpiece. You have a financial interest in keeping them in our world."

"I have an ethical interest in treating prisoners of war appropriately, and keeping them secure and away from humans. What would you rather us do? Line them up and take them out?"

Ezekiel's gaze went ice-cold. The loathing in it sent a chill down my spine. "The Magic Act demands the eradication of magic."

He didn't seem to care that not all Paranormals were the same—that they hadn't all come into our world willingly, or fought willingly in the war.

"Class act," Liam muttered, and began to turn away.

Ezekiel's eyes flashed with anger. "You'd rather do nothing? You'd rather stand by and watch our culture evaporate?"

"I don't see anyone's culture evaporating." Liam turned back, gestured to the people who'd gathered behind us—a few agents, a few customers. "These people are working to make a living in the Zone, to keep New Orleans alive."

"And that's not always easy, is it?" Ezekiel looked accusingly at Gunnar. "Containment tells us the monsters are all in Devil's Isle, but that's a lie as well. Monsters roam this land. Wraiths kill innocents." Ezekiel narrowed his gaze at Liam. "I know your face."

Liam was close enough that I could feel his body go rigid with sudden anger. "You don't know anything about me."

"Oh, but I think I do." Ezekiel's smile went smug. "I know your sister was killed by monsters." That was true. Either too arrogant or stupid to understand the risk he was taking, Ezekiel stepped forward, eager to push the point. His eyes searched Liam's face as if looking for weakness.

"I know they found her broken and bruised. I know she'd been torn and ripped by their claws, by their poisoned bodies. And yet you *live* in Devil's Isle, don't you, among our enemies? That doesn't sound like a way to honor her memory. It sounds like you bed with them."

"You're going to want to step back," Liam said.

Ezekiel ignored him, his eyes gleaming with purpose. The other protestors moved into formation behind him. "I'm not here to make you or anyone else comfortable. I'm here to testify, to protect what remains."

"We don't need protecting," Liam gritted out.

"I bet your sister's opinion would differ. If she was still alive, that it. Pity we can't ask her."

Before any of us could move, Liam's fingers were tangled in Ezekiel's shirt, and he hauled Ezekiel up to his toes. Liam's eyes, vibrantly blue, shone with fire. "Tell me again what you bet my sister would do. My sister, who was innocent, and was killed because assholes like you who refuse to acknowledge the complexities of the real world."

Ezekiel's gaze flicked back and forth across Liam's. "They killed one of yours, and still you protect them. Why? Was your sister not enough reason for you to acknowledge the truth?"

Where Liam's eyes showed fury born of pain, Ezekiel's showed satisfaction. He was out to make a point, and damn those he hurt in the meantime. And although it would have meant immediate imprisonment, I wanted to squeeze magic from the air and wring his neck with it.

"Claire." Tadji must have seen the intent in my eyes. Her voice was quiet, her fingers strong around my arm, jolting me back to the street, to the crowd, to the fact that magic monitors—armed and ready—would be triggered if I so much as ruffled Ezekiel's hair.

I forced myself to relax. This wasn't the time or place for my big, magical reveal.

Ezekiel's smile grew wider, more satisfied. "Are you going to hit me, Mr. Quinn, because I do tell the truth? Because you're uncomfortable admitting you contributed to your sister's death?"

Ezekiel was still in Liam's grip, sweat beading on his forehead, but his eyes utterly calm. He'd done exactly what he'd meant to—gotten attention for his particular brand of vitriol.

"My sister was murdered," Liam said, every muscle taut and ready for action, a warrior ready for battle against the advancing enemy. "Would you like to feel even an iota of her pain?"

"Is that a threat?" Ezekiel asked. "And in front of a Containment agent. Has magic made you a barbarian?"

"Idiocy has made me a barbarian," Liam said, baring his teeth.

"Liam," I said quietly, calling him back just as Tadji had called me.

For reasons too simple and complicated to think about, that seemed to be enough.

Liam opened his hands, so Ezekiel dropped back to the ground, stumbling before his followers reached out, helped him regain his balance.

"You deny the truth!" Ezekiel said, lifting his hands to conduct his protestors into another round of chanting.

This time, I stepped forward. "Do you think this helps you prove some kind of point? Using a family's tragedy, a young woman's death, to get attention? Go back to the hole you crawled out of."

Before Ezekiel could respond, Gunnar took a step forward. "If you want to protest, go protest. No more harassing residents, or you'll get an up close and personal view of the Cabildo."

Ezekiel's jaw worked. "Another denier," he said, then cast his glance around at those who'd gathered to watch. "The day of reckoning will come. A new Eden is planned for our world, and those who stand in the way of it will be cast aside. It will be our reawakening. We are Reveillon, and we will see it come to pass."

Ezekiel's eyes went cold, and his smile was just as frigid. If he believed in damnation—and I'd bet that he did—he'd long ago decided he was on the right side of it.

He walked back to the front of his line and began the march again.

When they'd put two blocks between us, I turned back to look for Liam, to offer what comfort I could. But he was gone.

Gunnar went to the Cabildo to report on the billboard and the protestors. I walked outside, found Liam sitting on a wrought-iron bench in the small brick courtyard behind Royal Mercantile.

The building was scarred from the war, the courtyard marked by the pigeons we used to send messages to Delta.

Liam looked up at the sound of my footsteps, his blue eyes shadowed. I offered a bottle of water. "You all right?"

He nodded, took the bottle, flipped it in his palm. "I don't like my family being used as a weapon in someone else's war."

"Total dick move," I agreed, and sat down beside Liam as he uncapped the bottle of water, took a drink.

"And calling themselves 'Reveillon'?" he said, disgust coloring his voice. "That's a slap at New Orleans. At our traditions."

Reveillon was a holiday dinner served in New Orleans, a tradition with French and Cajun roots that lasted through the night and into the early morning. The word meant "reawakening."

I nodded. "They're after reinventing the city. Destroying what's left, and building it up in some kind of new image. They're dangerous."

"Yeah," Liam said. "I imagine they are." He flipped the bottle again. "I made the decision to stay here, in the Zone. To keep our connection to this place. To who we were. Home sweet home and all that. If I hadn't . . ."

"Along with the rest of your family, you made a choice to stick it out. To give New Orleans another life. I didn't know Gracie. But the pictures I saw of her—she looked like a very happy person. She didn't look unhappy. She didn't look like she felt out of place, or like she didn't belong here.

"Sometimes horrible things happen, and they're no one's fault. Sometimes they're just horrible things. The world keeps on spinning; we just try to stay on our feet."

I let my head fall back against the brick and looked up at the blue sky, the enormous white clouds. Liam tilted his head back, too, and we watched the sky together in silence.

For a moment, there was peace.

And then the world shattered, the earth shaking with concussions that rattled the windows.

Liam grabbed my arm, and still held it when the world stilled again. And for a moment, everything went perfectly, horribly silent.

We ran to the street, found Tadji watching smoke rise from Devil's Isle. Air raid sirens began to wail.

"Shit," Liam said, then looked at me. "I'm going."

I glanced at Tadji.

"Go," she said. "I'll stay here with the store, keep an eye on things while you see what's happened." The grim certainty on her face said she knew, and had accepted, what might happen if we ran toward the sound of trouble.

She reached out and squeezed my hand. "Be careful, Claire. Magically and otherwise."

I promised I would and took off.

We weren't the only ones heading toward Devil's Isle. There weren't many civilians left in the Quarter, but the former Marriott was a Containment barracks, and they were running, too.

Devil's Isle was a prison, and looked like one. Tall concrete walls with guard towers at each corner, the front marked by a massive wrought-iron gate from a River Road plantation and checkpoint. That gate was now gnarled fingers of scorched metal, a monstrous claw revealed by the apparent explosion that had rocked it.

I stopped short, arms jostled by the people running past me, and stared.

There was smoke, shrapnel, debris—and worse—everywhere. There were protest signs on the ground—some still burning, some singed around the edges. People were screaming, agents were running and shouting orders, chasing back Paranormals who saw their opportunity and ran for the gate.

"Reveillon bombed the gate," Gunnar said, each word colored with awe and shock and fury.

"Their tunics," Liam said. "They were bulky. Some of them must have worn explosives under the tunics—vests or something. Jesus." He ran a hand through his hair. "Jesus."

Silently, Gunnar moved into Devil's Isle, to the remaining splinters of the guardhouse, features hardening as he crouched beside the agent who lay there, half in and half out of what remained of the guardhouse, his face and hair bloodied. Gunnar checked for a pulse, looked up.

"I need a medic in here!" he called out, then gestured to a set of agents with a stretcher.

I tore my gaze away, looked back at Liam. "Your . . . your grandmother," I said. Eleanor Arsenault lived only a few blocks away.

His eyes flared with concern as he considered, but looking around, he shook his head. "The attack looks contained, and there's no reason to think she'd have been a target. I'll do what I can here, then check in on her." He looked at me. "You could go back to the store."

He didn't make it an order or a question. It was a mild suggestion at best, and one I appreciated. But I couldn't just walk away, however horrific this was. I looked around for something to do, some way to help.

There was a clinic inside the prison, where Sensitives and Wraiths were held—would continue to be held until Containment allowed Sensitives to manage their magic and avoid becoming wraiths in the first place.

Lizzie, one of the clinic's nurses, was on her knees beside a bloodied woman whose white linen clothing gave her away.

Streaks of fire shifted beneath Lizzie's skin and burned in her orange-red irises. She was a Paranormal with an intimate relationship with flame. And despite the fact that the woman she was treating had wanted Lizzie and those like her eradicated from the earth, she still helped. That was something Reveillon wouldn't understand—or wouldn't admit.

As I watched her work, memories of the war surfaced. The body, bloated with death, that I'd seen floating down the river. A soldier killed by friendly fire, his comrades on their knees beside him, faces slack with horror. A man, skin singed black from the flame of a magical beast whose wings still darkened the sky above us. Her wings had been nearly black, and had looked like leather sculpted around bone and vein and tendon. The air had smelled of smoke and burning meat that soured the stomach.

I swallowed hard. "I'll see if I can help Lizzie," I said. "I have to do something. If I go back to the store, I'll just . . ." I'd have memories. I'd think about this. And I didn't want to think about it.

I shook my head. "I have to do something," I said again.

His brow furrowed over eyes dark with protectiveness that sent heat through my chest. "You'll be careful?"

I nodded.

Liam watched me for a moment, then put a hand behind my head, made sure I met his eyes. "If you need a break, find me. I'll walk you back."

I nodded again. I didn't have the words for anything else.

Lizzie had already moved on to her next patient—a Containment agent with dark skin and shorn hair—when I reached her. His eyes were closed, a gory and angry-looking wound in his shoulder.

"I could help."

Lizzie looked up at me, and it took a moment for recognition to dawn in her eyes. When it did, she gave me a frank appraisal. "You can handle it?"

"I was here during the war, the Second Battle." Every word out of my mouth sounded awkward. "I helped some. And I can follow directions."

She considered it for a moment. She nodded, dipped her chin to gesture to her hands, which applied pressure to a pack of bandages covering a gaping wound on the man's shoulder.

"The civilian medics aren't here yet. Pressure here," she instructed, and when I'd scooted beside her and replaced my hands with hers, I felt the officer's blood—warm and pulsing—beneath my fingers.

"I could cauterize it with a fingertip," Lizzie said, fire dancing on her neck as she pulled off one pair of gloves, pulled on another, and moved to his leg. "But they'd consider that a felony."

Lizzie pulled a wad of gauze from a pocket of her tunic and wrapped it around his thigh, just above the knee, where the violence had torn another gash.

"Over here!" she shouted, to a man and woman who drove a small utility vehicle with a stabilizing board strapped to the back.

"Get him to the clinic," she said as they followed her orders, stepped in to whisk him up and away. The only functioning civilian hospital in New Orleans was on the north side of the city—too far away to be helpful now.

The skin on my hands felt tight, and I glanced down. Blood—his blood—had dried on my palms, stained my nails.

"I was hoping I wouldn't have to be in this position," she said, pushing streaked hair from her face. "That I wouldn't have to pretend my allegiance."

"To humans?" I asked.

"To idiots who refuse to accept reality." She looked around. "Something is beginning."

"Something is beginning," I agreed.

We'd have to hope it ended quickly.

CHAPTER THREE

We worked for hours.

Six years of peace had weakened my ability to deal with death and gore, wiped away the desensitization that had been necessary all those years ago. But dealing with blood and horror again made me numb to the sight and smell of it quickly enough.

Not counting the protestors, four people had been killed, twelve more injured. Those closest to the gate had caught the brunt of the explosions. Two of the dead were Containment agents who'd done nothing more than show up for work. The other two were Paranormals. Sunday in Devil's Isle wasn't unlike Sunday outside it, and families had been gathered on the long strip of green that reached into the prison from the gate, enjoying the fresh air, maybe pretending they were somewhere else.

Containment moved the dead, and we helped move the injured. But the ground was still littered with debris and evidence of carnage. Containment's forensic unit picked through it now for evidence, although it seemed pretty obvious who'd done the damage.

Containment counted fifteen protestors who had engaged us on their trip down Bourbon Street. And when they'd reached Devil's Isle, they'd gone to war. Containment believed seven of them had been killed, either because they'd carried the explosives or had been fatally injured in the explosions. In the chaos, Containment hadn't arrested any of them, and believed three had escaped back into the Quarter. That left five unaccounted for . . . and still in Devil's Isle.

I watched Lizzie peel off a pair of latex gloves, toss them onto the ground. She uncapped a bottle of water, poured it over her hands to clean away powder from the gloves.

"Was fighting like this in the Beyond?" I asked.

She dried her hands on a clean spot of fabric on her pants, then took a drink.

"Life in the Beyond was very structured," she said. "Society was tiered, regulated, hierarchical. It was stable, peaceful, refined, orderly. But not flexible."

Paranormals had roared into our world with golden armor and weapons, many dressed for battle in brilliant, flowing fabrics with braided accents. Some had ridden horses through the Veil, and they'd been bridled with gleaming, tooled leather and golden armor of their own. It wasn't hard to imagine the rest of their society was orderly and refined, too.

"The Consularis was strict," I said.

She nodded. "There had been war in our world for a very, very long time. Our Dark Ages—when the Beyond was led by warlords, and civilians were cannon fodder. The Consularis changed that. They brought peace, and they brought rules."

Which the Court of Dawn apparently hadn't liked, since they'd split the Veil in search of a new land to rule, bringing magically impressed Consularis Paranormals with them to serve as soldiers. When the war was over, humans had bundled Court and Consularis together into Devil's Isle. Few humans knew the truth. I'd only just learned, and I'd lived in New Orleans my entire life.

"That's why the Court rebelled."

She nodded. "The leaders of the Court believed they were entitled to more than their stations allowed them. More possessions, more respect."

Screaming split the air behind us. We looked back, watched as three Containment agents dragged a sobbing Paranormal back inside the walls. She was petite, her skin brilliantly crimson. Small, iridescent wings fluttered in panic at her back. They'd pulled her arms behind her, and there were dark smears of blood across her face, her knees. Probably where she'd fallen while fighting back.

I watched them carry her away, feeling equally guilty and impotent. I looked back at Lizzie. "You could have run today instead of helping. Tried to make it out, into the bayous." That's where the fugitive Paranormals generally hid to avoid Containment.

She shook her head. "I swore to myself that when it was time to leave, I'd walk out of here with my head held high. I wouldn't crawl, I wouldn't be carried, and I wouldn't be dragged. No manhunts, no canine searches." Her voice softened as she watched the Paranormal struggle against the agents. "She only *nearly* made it out. Now she's on their radar."

Lizzie turned away, dark shadows beneath her eyes. I knew there was nothing I could say, so I tried to think of something I could do.

"What can I do to help you and the clinic?"

She looked at me for a long minute, embers burning in her eyes, as if the flames had tired and cooled from her efforts on the battlefield. "You can get supplies?"

The question surprised me, although it shouldn't have. Why would I be surprised that a clinic for Paranormals had needs Containment wasn't satisfying? There'd have been no public support for that kind of spending. "What do you need?"

"Salt," she said without hesitation. "Sea salt, if you can get it. It's an antiseptic for most Paras. I can only get table salt from Containment, and not much of it."

I nodded. "What else?"

"Clove, thyme, lavender. Any or all of those."

"Are they medicinal, too?"

She smiled. "They are, and thyme's good for turtle soup. Turtle shows up in our food allocation with regularity. And can you get some suckers? Lollipops, or whatever you'd call them? Something like that? Moses used to get them for me, but . . ."

Moses was the first Para I'd met in Devil's Isle. He was short of stature and big of attitude, and had totally saved my ass. He'd owned his own fix-it shop, a sliver of a building full of discarded electronics. But that was before he'd blown it up to keep his gear out of the hands of Containment and the defense contractor who'd worked for it. There weren't many who knew he'd survived the fire; I think he was enjoying the subterfuge.

"Yeah. Hard candies are easier than chocolate. They don't melt as easily."

Lizzie nodded. "That would be good. Wraiths like them."

The statement, which was so frank and simple, made me start. "What?"

"They have a calming effect. Maybe it's the sugar, maybe it's having something to focus on, something pleasant. Whatever the reason, they work. I'd appreciate getting more."

I nodded. "I'll put it in my next order."

She lifted her eyebrows. "It's that easy? You'll do it because I asked you?"

"I'll do it because I can, and because it's the least I can do. And I'll do it because someday I might end up in the clinic, and it matters that you care. It matters that you help people when it would be really easy to hurt them."

She looked at me, evaluated. "You're in a unique position, Claire. You've got friends with skills who are willing to teach you, to ensure that you stay on the right path. To ensure that you don't become a wraith. Most aren't so lucky. Most don't know any better, and others just want to use it, to feel good."

I nodded. "I'm working on balancing."

"Good," she said. "Because I like you. You've got sense and you seem to have some gumption. But do me a favor?"

"Sure. What?"

"Stay that way. Stay balanced, and stay out of here."

I'd do everything in my power.

With Lizzie gone, and Gunnar and Liam helping, I found a spot out of the way, and watched as Containment and its contractors worked to put the prison back together.

Shrapnel was tagged, photographed, and bagged. The damaged gate was measured and assessed, and contractors began the work of sawing away broken spindles and rails, welding in temporary replacements. The government could move quickly when it wanted.

Fifty feet away, behind the make-do barricade Containment had erected with chain-link fence, stood the wary Paranormals who watched the cleanup. I didn't doubt there'd be some Containment agents who sympathized, at least a little, with Reveillon, and who believed the world would be better off without Paranormals. I hoped the Paras wouldn't suffer for their beliefs.

"When the levee breaks, it breaks."

I looked back, found Gunnar beside me. His hair was furrowed into rows where he'd raked his fingers through it, and there were streaks of grit and grime across his clothes and face. He looked physically tired and still plenty pissed off.

He offered me a bottle of water. I thanked him with a nod, opened the cap, and drank deeply.

"You okay?" I asked.

"I'm managing," he said, but sounded like a man on the verge of not managing. "Reveillon has officially claimed credit. They say they want to clean the Zone, but they mean cleanse it. Every Para is the same to them, and they should all be wiped off the face of the earth. They've promised to continue to destroy any vestiges of magic left in New Orleans—and the 'systems that support them.'"

"Containment," I guessed, and he nodded. "Who did the claiming?"

"Ezekiel, I understand."

"So he wasn't wearing explosives. I guess that doesn't surprise me."

"Me, either." Gunnar's eyes darkened. "They have their mission, and I by God have mine." His gaze followed the agents who carried someone out on a stretcher, a dark sheet draped over the body. "Every bit of this was intentional. A war they're determined to wage against the lives we've built here."

"Ezekiel called Liam out," I said, sickening as I remembered our interaction on the street. "Knew about his sister, and thinks he supports them."

Gunnar looked at me, sympathy in his expression, and nailed it in one. "That doesn't mean he's a target."

It didn't *necessarily* mean that, I thought, but it might.

"Any more longing in your eyes and I'll think you're a basset hound."

"It's not longing. It's . . ." I sighed. "Fine. It's longing. But calling it what it is doesn't make me feel any better."

"Sorry," he said, and ran a hand through his hair, which deepened the furrows. "That was an unsuccessful attempt to lighten the mood."

"I'm not sure that's possible," I said, glancing at the slender woman with almond-shaped eyes who stared at us from the other side of the fence.

Her pale hair fell in waves around her narrow and equally pale face, which was marked by the line of crimson that colored her skin from nose to chin, and marked the fingers that were tightly twined in the chain link.

She was a Seelie Paranormal, a member of the Court, and a woman I'd seen in Devil's Isle before. Human mythology said Seelie fairies, like so many other Paranormals, were mostly "good."

Human mythology had been wrong.

She met my gaze with a look of unadulterated hatred. She had the bearing of a queen, but instead of sitting on a throne, she languished in a war-torn neighborhood behind chain-link fence with her enemies.

And yet, a dozen yards away, another Para passed what looked like a piece of bread through the chain link to an exhausted-looking Containment officer, who took a bite, thanked him with a nod.

The Seelie caught the action, tossed her head in disgust.

Two worlds, thrown together in prison. Probably not the outcome the Court had predicted, and certainly not one they'd wanted.

Gunnar caught the direction of my gaze, watched the Seelie turn, her long dress spinning around her as she moved, and disappear into the crowd.

"Do you think Reveillon would care about the difference between Consularis and Court?"

"I don't know why they would," Gunnar said. "Based on the hand they've shown so far, everything is black-and-white for them. Consularis and Court are both magic; that makes them the enemy."

He sighed.

"You look tired."

"I am exhausted. Why don't I meet you at the store later? We can debrief." He rubbed his temples. "Maybe I can find a bottle of booze in the Cabildo in the meantime."

"I wouldn't say no to booze," I said.

"What the hell are you doing here?"

And the pro-booze feeling grew stronger.

We both turned to find Jack Broussard. A Containment agent, Broussard had been the one to tell me my father was a Sensitive, and he'd trashed the store to find proof I'd been hosting illegal meetings of Sensitives. He'd been wrong, and didn't know the truth about me, but that hardly mattered. Like Reveillon, he'd already decided who the bad guys were—and Liam and I both fell into the category.

Broussard was a tall man with brown hair and green eyes. Not an unattractive face, except that it was usually pinched by anger and irritation. Or maybe just weighed down by the giant chip on his shoulder.

"Not that we need to explain anything to you," Gunnar said, "but we're helping with the response. We were in the Quarter and heard the explosion."

Broussard's gaze, which lit with anger, stayed on me. "Do you really think she should be here? In Devil's Isle?"

"*She* can speak for herself," Gunnar said. "But since you're asking me, yes. She has a pass, and she's done her service today working triage. Unlike some of us," he added, with a disdainful look at Broussard's clean clothes.

"I was out of the city."

"And now you're here," Gunnar said. "If you want to work, talk to Smith." He gestured toward a tall man with dark skin and a white clipboard. "He's handing out assignments."

"You aren't my superior."

"And you aren't mine, nor am I interested in wasting time arguing with you. If you're here to help, then help. If you're here to make trouble, do us both a favor and save the paperwork: go back to the barracks and stay the hell out of the way."

Broussard stepped closer to Gunnar. They could have bumped chests if Broussard had been dumb enough to start something.

"You know what, Landreau? One of these days, you're going to get knocked off your high horse. You're going to lose all that social cachet, those special privileges, and you'll be treated like the rest of us."

"You're an idiot, Broussard, if you think I have my job because of my name. I'm good at what I do. Very good. Why don't you do everyone a favor and back off? It's been a helluva day, and we've lost good people."

"Because of Paranormals," Broussard spat.

Gunnar rolled his shoulders like a man preparing for battle. "Jesus, you aren't going to stop, are you? Can you not see this was caused by humans? Can you not see this has nothing to do with magic, but with idiocy? And can you not see past your own stupid prejudices—your own issues, which are legion—and just get to fucking work? This isn't the time or the place for your myopic politics."

"Gentlemen."

A man in camouflage fatigues—tall, built, and blond, with eyes the color of good bourbon—stepped forward. I knew plenty of Containment agents in the Quarter; I'd never seen this man before.

Irritation flared in Gunnar's eyes again. The man looked totally relaxed, even as he'd positioned himself to stop them from beating the shit out of each other.

"This is a very bad time and place to act like teenagers," he said.

"I couldn't agree more," Gunnar said. "I was suggesting to Agent Broussard that there were several ways he could contribute to the cleanup efforts, and he should select one of them or get back to the barracks."

"I think that's a very good idea," the man said. "Still a lot of work to be done before the light's gone. Agent Broussard, if you can't find something to do, I've got reports you could collate."

Broussard's face reddened with anger as he looked between the men. "This is on your heads. This, and whatever worse follows. It's on you."

He stalked off in the direction of a clutch of uniformed Containment agents.

"John," Gunnar said, "this is Claire Connolly. Claire, John Reece. He's with the army. He's investigating Containment in light of the Memorial Battle."

A former defense contractor had wanted to open the Veil at Talisheek, where the Veil had first been torn and a memorial had been erected. We'd managed to keep it closed, but it took magic and effort—and I'd inadvertently split open the earth trying to channel the sheer amount of power in play.

I guessed the Joint Chiefs had lost some faith in Containment and its contractors. And I assumed that was what had put the flint in Gunnar's eyes.

"Not investigating," Reece said. "Reviewing." He looked at me. "You own Royal Mercantile."

"I do."

"And what's his story?" Reece nodded toward Broussard.

It took Gunnar a moment to answer. Hard to pick which devil to trust, I imagined. "He's ambitious and shortsighted. There are three kinds of people in the world. Those who believe humans are always right. Those who believe Paranormals are always right. And those who know the truth."

"And Mr. Broussard takes his 'always' a bit too literally?" Reece asked.

Gunnar nodded.

Reece's gaze lifted to the gate. "Not unlike our enemies on the outside."

"We were just noting that. Blind loyalty is dangerous, regardless the side."

Reece nodded. "The cleanup has been relatively well organized, all things considered."

"We run a tight ship," Gunnar said brusquely. "Feel free to take that back to Washington."

Reece looked back at him, gaze still cool. "I will, and more. I haven't seen the Commandant around."

Gunnar, who respected his boss, managed to keep his tone steady. "He's monitoring from the Cabildo until things are clear here. It's safer for him there, and it's better for Containment, for the Zone, for stability, if he's safe."

Reece nodded, as if processing the information, recording it for later. "In that case, I'll let you get back to ensuring its safety."

He nodded at me, then Gunnar, who bristled as the soldier walked away. Even if he might have liked Reece, might have respected him, he didn't look like he trusted him.

For his part, Reece didn't walk toward Broussard or the other clusters of Containment agents and Devil's Isle staff. Instead, he walked deeper into Devil's Isle in the direction of the clinic. Maybe to visit the wounded, check on their care. Maybe to see how well the rest of Devil's Isle—the rest of New Orleans—was protected from them.

"He seemed okay," I said as Gunnar watched him walk away, eyes slitted, expression tight with concentration. "Not nearly as big an asshole as Broussard, anyway."

"Yeah, but he doesn't have to be." He looked back at me. "He's got power, authority, and a mission. Broussard wants those things, so he creates his own landscapes of conspiracy." Gunnar sighed. "As if this cluster fuck isn't enough to keep him busy."

"Maybe having a new enemy—someone human, not Paranormal—would actually be good for Broussard."

"Ever the optimist," Gunnar said, then pressed a kiss to my cheek. "And because I'm one, too, I'm going back into the fray. Be careful."

I nodded. "Take care of yourself," I said, and watched my best friend walk away. Because sometimes that was the only good option.

Liam found me at the fence, helping pass out bottles of water to the Paras who watched Containment work. He looked as dirty and tired as the rest of us, and grim resignation was set on his face.

I passed him a bottle of water. "Are you all right?"

He drank deeply, wiped grime off his brow. "I made it through the war because I told myself war was only temporary. Might last a long time but would end eventually. That's the nature of human history. But this? This is disheartening."

"Yeah," I said.

He shook his head. "My Quinn grandfather was sixty-four when they broke through the Veil. He refused to leave the Zone or move into the city so he'd be near the family, medical care." Liam picked at a corner of the water bottle's label, peeled off a strip. "Went out to the Quinn place at Bayou Teche and stayed there. He'd been a shrimper, and he swore like a sailor." He grinned. "He said he was a filthy sailor who'd been raised hard, which was true. You remember about a month before the Second Battle when everyone was saying New Orleans would be hit?"

I nodded. There'd been more air raid sirens, more evacuations, more stocking up on water and batteries.

"Gavin and I went out to Bayou Teche, made one more attempt

to get him out of the Zone. We didn't want him in the city—not if things were about to go bad. But we also didn't want him completely cut off, which would have happened if New Orleans fell."

"What happened?"

Liam pulled another strip of paper from the bottle, and it fluttered to the ground like confetti. "He said his time was coming, and war wasn't going to take him away from home in the meantime. Gavin and I had been geared up for a fight—for arguments, for reasons why he should leave. But he was at peace with it, and that was the one thing we couldn't argue with."

"So what did you do?"

"We stayed the night, watched the sun go down. He loved to cook, made chicken fricassee. We ate on his back porch, watched turtles on cypress stumps, pelicans floating over water, drank some very good, very cold beer."

"He died?" I asked, after a moment of silence.

Liam nodded. "Three weeks later. Right before the battle, as it turned out. We still own that property, although I haven't been out there in a few years." He shook off the melancholy. "I guess the point of that story is that sometimes you just have to find your place, your home, and accept what's happening."

He looked at me, gaze drilling down into the truth of me, and I felt my soul's answering shudder. "And how are you, Claire Connolly?"

"I'm holding up. I helped Lizzie, talked to Gunnar. Lizzie asked for some supplies. I told her I'd get what I could."

"Good," he said. "Although I'm not sure a fire sprite and redhead working together will be good for the rest of us."

Everyone needed a lighter mood, it seemed, even Liam.

I gestured to the fence. "I also watched the Seelie give us all the evil eye."

"That woman is very good at the evil eye. And she's not the only one." He gestured to a man on the other side of the fence, eating what looked like pistachios as two Paras beside him talked animatedly.

He was a big man. Wide, with broad shoulders and a gut that popped beneath his brightly colored tunic and matching pants. He had a wide, round face and eyes as black as pitch, his skin an olive green. Glossy black horns like Moses's, but his were longer, spiraling upward a few inches above his head.

"Who is that?"

"That, Claire, is Solomon."

Solomon was the self-proclaimed Paranormal godfather of Devil's Isle. I hadn't met him yet, but I knew he wasn't a fan of Liam's. His thugs had stopped us before. Then again, Liam had gone to him before when Eleanor needed protection.

"He looks like Moses."

"They're cousins."

That stopped me short. "No kidding?"

"Both Consularis, although on different sides of that particular fence."

At first glance, Solomon looked bored by the commotion, the Containment activity, as he popped one nut after another, let the shells drop to the ground. But there was something very shrewd in his eyes. Something wary and focused. And when his gaze landed on us, it contained a little of the evil eye I'd seen before.

I gave him a little wave, which set his minions on a tirade I was probably glad I couldn't hear.

"Better not to antagonize him."

I glanced at Liam. "Should I be afraid of him?"

It didn't comfort me that it took Liam a moment to answer. "No. But be wary. As you've seen, he mostly blusters. But his ego is large, and he's surrounded by yes-men who think he's their ticket out of Devil's Isle."

I wondered if today, if this new threat, would change his attitude, too. Maybe we'd all become too complacent, too used to the status quo, to the chain of command.

Liam finished the water in his now naked bottle, tossed it into the box set aside for recycling, looked at his watch. "It's nearly five o'clock. I think we're winding down here, at least for now. Containment will work the forensics, the analysis." He glanced at me. "Is it all right for you to still be away from the store? I mean, I don't know what your profits are . . ."

Honestly, I hadn't even given the store a thought. Tadji might have put the CLOSED sign in the window, held off anyone who wanted to buy stuff until I got back.

"Nobody makes much of a profit in the Zone," I said. "I doubt there are many people shopping now. Most are either locked up in their homes or outside the gate, trying to figure out what happened."

Liam nodded. "You think Tadji will keep an eye on things a little longer?"

"Probably. Why?"

"I still haven't made it to Eleanor's. You wanna take a walk?"

When I nodded, we walked to the spot in the temporary fence where guards allowed agents to walk through and were waved inside. I didn't have my pass on me, but the guards had seen me working, helping with the wounded. They'd decided I wasn't much of a risk.

Marigny had been heavily damaged during the war. Some of the Creole cottages and shotgun houses had survived, and some of the empty spaces had been filled by cheap government buildings. Along with the concrete walls, magic monitors, guards, and overhead electric grid, they made the neighborhood feel like the prison it was.

It was a short walk to the side-by-side houses where Liam and Eleanor lived. He had the columned, two-story town house on the right. Her building was on the left, surrounded by a low black fence and ringed by a balcony.

"Maybe you should think about staying at Eleanor's for a while," I said. "Just to make sure you're both safe."

Liam glanced at me as we took the sidewalk to the house. "Both?"

"She's got magic, which makes her a potential target. And Ezekiel knew who you were."

"He doesn't know about Eleanor," Liam said as we reached the front porch, and he stuck a key in the brass lock.

She didn't live in Devil's Isle because others knew she had magic, but because she'd wanted to be near those like her. And because Liam had wanted her close.

"I'd rather Ezekiel take a run at me directly. I'd welcome it, and not just because he wouldn't be using people, killing them, like the coward he apparently is." Liam pushed open the door and we walked inside, locked up again.

The door opened onto a central hallway, with rooms to the left and right. The first floor was empty, the hardwood floors old and bare, the walls marked by the smoke and pits of battle. The town house would have been a single-family home when Devil's Isle was still the Marigny. As far as I'd seen, the only room that was used and occupied now was Eleanor's, which sat at the top of the stairs. There must have been a kitchen, since she liked to bake, but I hadn't seen it yet.

The house was quiet, but I braced for the attention of Eleanor's very happy yellow dog, Foster. But after a moment, there was still no sign or sound of the Lab.

"Who goes there?" asked an unfamiliar voice in a very bad British accent, and not one that I recognized.

Liam glanced at me. "Liam and Claire."

"Liam and Claire who?"

Liam rolled his eyes. "Is this a knock-knock joke?"

The voice paused, the speaker apparently confused. "No?"

"You know who we are, Pike," Liam said, hands on his hips. "Just get out here and say hello to Claire."

The voice had been deep and booming and male, and I'd expected a very big man with broad shoulders and a chest that resonated sound.

I did not expect the small, skinny man who walked into the room. His skin was pale, his hair coal black, his eyes the same shade. His hair was straight and fell to his shoulders but didn't hide the pointed tops of his elfish ears. Pike hadn't been here the last time I visited Eleanor's home in Devil's Isle. I guessed Liam had increased security in a particularly Devil's Isle way.

"Claire, this is Pike," Liam said, holding out a hand. "Pike, Claire Connolly, purveyor of Royal Mercantile."

"So," Pike said, putting his hands on his hips. "This is Claire, the Sensitive."

"In the flesh," I said.

Pike's eyes narrowed suspiciously. "Mmm-hmm. Has she been through any kind of security clearance?"

I lifted my eyebrows. "I'm pretty sure Containment has done its due diligence. I'm friends with the Commandant's chief adviser, and I run the biggest store in the Quarter, where a lot of agents shop. Other than that, Liam can vouch for me."

"Liam's a troublemaker," Pike said with total seriousness, but I couldn't help a smile.

"No argument there."

Pike narrowed his gaze. "If he's a troublemaker, and you're his friend, you might be a troublemaker, too. One false move," he warned, pointing a finger at me, "and you're out of here."

"I consider myself duly warned."

"Well, you have been."

I nodded. "Then we're on the same page."

"Glad to hear it."

The sound of canine trotting emerged from the other room, quick steps to the door, then halting ones as a yellow dog stuck his head through the doorway, investigated.

Liam crouched. "Come on, you baby."

Tail wiggling like it might fly off, Foster waddled toward us and sat at Liam's feet—or more accurately, *on* Liam's feet—to accept his obligatory pets.

I wouldn't have called myself a dog person, but when Foster padded over, I went instinctively to my knees, wrapped my arms around him. He whimpered once, pushed his soft muzzle against my face.

"Yeah," I said, scratching a spot beneath his collar. "Today really sucked."

As I scratched, his back leg twitched against the floor in uncontrollable pleasure. His happiness made me feel better about the entire day. When he offered up a full body shake, then padded over to Pike, I rose again.

"Foster seems to like you," Pike said, trying to scratch Foster's back, but doing a really weird job of it. His long, pointed fingers waved across the dog's fur, like Foster was a piano to be played rather than a dog to be petted. Maybe there weren't dogs in the Beyond? To his credit, Foster sat placidly and endured it.

"That's quite a technique you have there," I said.

"I enjoy animals," Pike said, that deeply booming voice such an odd contrast to his small form.

"Pike, we're going to check on Eleanor. Keep things safe down here."

Pike offered a crisp salute as we headed to the stairs.

"I guess you got a new security guard," I whispered. "Is Pike a friend of yours or Eleanor's?"

"He's a friend of a friend," Liam said cagily.

"He seems like a very interesting type."

"Some Paras adjust to our world faster than others. I think Pike's still working on it. But he's as loyal as they come."

"That's something," I said.

The second-floor landing led to several closed doors and one open, which we headed for. This was Eleanor's room, full of the décor that was absent from the rest of the house. The walls held dozens of paintings in gilded frames, the floor was covered by fine, overlapping carpets, and gorgeous antiques—probably the few things salvaged from the Arsenaults' former mansion—were dotted around the room.

The lovely Eleanor sat at a round table near a window on the other side of the room. She wore a long-sleeved shirt in a silken fabric and a taupe wrap that set off her medium skin and short silver hair. Her eyes, blue like her grandson's, were sightless, at least to the material world. But she could see magic, the kaleidoscope of colors reflected by everyone with magic.

It was nice to see Eleanor. But it was even nicer to see the man who sat across from her at the table, the one who'd probably brought Pike into Eleanor's and Liam's lives.

He was probably three feet tall, with pale skin and short black horns protruding from his head. I'd have called him a demon, but that was a human word that I was nearly certain didn't capture whatever he actually was. And since he'd saved my ass before, it couldn't have been less relevant.

"Took your sweet damn time," Moses said.

I smiled, really and truly, for the first time in hours.

I hadn't seen him in a few weeks. Apparently, he'd been spending more time with Eleanor, which made me feel better. Safety in numbers, maybe.

Moses hopped down to the floor onto short and slightly crooked legs, then walked toward us with a swinging gait. When he reached us, he looked me up and down, then Liam.

"You look whole enough," he said, then looked back at Eleanor. "They look whole enough." His voice was a shade too loud, as if he thought the volume was necessary to accommodate her blindness.

But Eleanor just smiled at him. "Thank you, Moses."

He bobbed his head in acknowledgment, a move she certainly couldn't see.

"You're all right?" she asked to confirm, eyebrows raised in hope.

"We're fine," Liam said. "You heard what happened?"

"Heard it, felt it, smelled the smoke," she said. "The block captain came by, but he wouldn't tell us anything."

"Asshole," Moses muttered, moving back to the chair opposite Eleanor's and hopping onto it.

"Then we might as well start at the beginning." Liam offered me the other free chair, but I waved him off, sat down on the floor before he could argue.

"I'm grubbier than you are," I said. "I don't want to ruin the cushion. Please go ahead."

Liam folded his tall frame into the chair. He and Moses were physically different, but there was something about them—call it their spirits or souls—that was similar. They were both on the right side of good.

"They call themselves Reveillon," Liam said. "They believe magic is the root of all evil, so all magic, all Paras, Containment, everything, has to be eliminated to bring the Zone back to life. To bring about a 'reawakening.' They think killing the remaining Paranormals will usher in a better New Orleans."

"They said all that at the bombing?" Eleanor asked.

"They were protesting on Bourbon before they reached the gate. Came at me with nonsense about Gracie."

"Oh, Liam," Eleanor said quietly, and put a hand on his, squeezed.

"They don't have boundaries," I said.

Liam nodded. "They're led by a man named Ezekiel. Could be as much cult of personality as cult. I don't like it. The lack of respect for life, this 'kill 'em all and damn the consequences' mentality."

He sat back in the chair, ran long fingers through his hair. "I'm a bounty hunter. I get there's an irony in my saying that—"

"Nonsense," Eleanor said, swatting away the idea. "That's nonsense, and you know better. You know the difference between what's legal and what's good. You know what it means to be Paranormal in this world, and you choose your bounties very carefully."

While Liam's eyes widened at the ferocity in her voice, Eleanor—clearly not done—made a haughty sound and pointed a skinny finger at him. "I know you don't take every bounty. Bounties are a prime topic of conversation in Devil's Isle. Who's been brought in, who the Paras believe is still out there. We know who you bring in—and we know who you don't bring in." She aimed her gaze in my direction. "Case in point."

"And thanks for that," I said, smiling at him.

Eleanor smiled approvingly. "But all that, my dears, is neither here nor there, just an issue I'm a bit sensitive about. Do not come between me and my grandchildren." She settled in her chair again, and her expression sobered. "You're saying this won't be their only act of violence."

Liam looked at her squarely. "They had enough explosives to break through the gate, put a crater in the ground, and kill people in a hundred-foot radius. And they had enough time and wherewithal to get all that done and convince each other that death—theirs and others'—was worth it. That the cause was worth dying for. They won't stop until they're satisfied."

"Will they ever be?" I asked.

"Maybe not," Liam said. "At the very least, there's more destruction to come." He leaned forward, linked his hands on the table, and looked at his grandmother. "I think it may be time for you to leave Devil's Isle."

"No." Eleanor's answer was quick and brooked no argument. "Absolutely not."

"It's dangerous here," Liam insisted. "And now with Reveillon—"

"It's dangerous for *everyone*," Eleanor finished. "As much as I appreciate your looking out for me, this is where I belong." She looked at Moses. "I am magic, just like every other Para, wraith, and Sensitive in here."

Moses nodded. "Damn right you are." It was clear he meant it as a compliment.

"Besides, there's no reason to think I'm any more of a target than anyone else."

"Everyone is a target," Liam insisted.

"And are you going to get everyone else out?"

That question hung in the air, stained with guilt.

"No," Liam said. "I don't have that power."

"Then I stay where I belong." Eleanor crossed her thin arms, set her jaw. There was determination in her eyes that belied her age, her apparent delicacy.

Liam breathed in and out for a moment, staring down his formidable grandmother. Two generations, testing their wills against each other.

"All right," Liam said, sitting back again. "But I don't like it."

Eleanor grinned. "You don't have to, dear."

"Hardheaded," he muttered.

"Damn right," she said, chin lifted. "I am no simpering miss."

"I would certainly never accuse you of that."

"Maybe we could come at this another way," I said. "Educate Reveillon about how they're wrong." I looked at Moses. "Getting rid of Paranormals—even if they walked right back through the Veil again—wouldn't really change anything, would it? Clean the soil, for example?"

Moses rubbed one of his horns. "No. Magic doesn't belong in this world; I don't think anybody would argue with that. But whether the magic comes from the Veil or the Paras, it's already out there. Killing us isn't going to change anything. Now, if these Reveillon assholes were smart, they'd talk to Paras about fixing the soil, the power grid. Making the damaged areas usable again."

My eyebrows lifted. "Do Paras know how to do that?"

Moses shrugged. "I don't know that anybody has tried. I'm guessing you'd have to use magic to fix magic, and that's not something Containment wants to talk about."

Considering, Liam leaned back. "They also won't talk about treating Paras as temporary allies, even against a group with an arsenal."

"We have friends in Containment," I pointed out. "Maybe they could use their influence, try to get Delta involved." After all, Delta had been crucial to keeping the Veil closed at the Memorial Battle. And giving me hope that becoming a wraith wasn't an inevitability.

Moses snorted. "Red, I know you've only been recently indoctrinated to the church of the actual fucking truth, but to do that, they'd have to admit Paras aren't all enemies, and Devil's Isle is fundamentally unfair. They won't do that."

"Sooner or later," I said, "they'll have to. That's just history. Kingdoms don't last forever. People change, attitudes change. Maybe we can speed that process along."

Liam looked at me. "You're sounding very optimistic."

"We've got a prison full of Paras who shouldn't be in there, a magical curtain that could split at any time, and a group of humans who think the way to fix the Zone is to kill everyone and everything in it." I looked at Liam. "It's almost certainly going to get worse before it gets better, so might as well hope for the better to get here sooner rather than later."

Moses's eyes narrowed. "There may have been logic in that, but if so, it was buried deep, deep down."

Liam smiled at me. "That's a redhead for you."

"Don't be such a stranger," Moses said, when we said our good-byes. He looked up at me with those gleaming green eyes. "But also don't be killed by xenophobic idiots."

"I will try to not do both of those things," I promised.

"You should probably send a pigeon," Liam said when we walked downstairs. "Tell Delta what's happened, and what might be coming. Like you said, it will probably get worse before it gets better."

In the Zone, things seemed to work that way.

'd expected to walk into Royal Mercantile, find the store dark and empty, Tadji behind the counter reading a book, waiting impatiently for me to come back.

Instead, she stood in front of a counter that was now dotted with displays and racks of product. In her beautiful, waving script she'd made pretty signs that now hung from the ceiling and pointed customers to different areas of the store.

And that wasn't the only difference. Business had always been steady; the customers knew me, and there just weren't a lot of options. But even as the sun set, when most remaining NOLA residents would be returning home for the night, there were a dozen people milling around the store, carrying wicker baskets to hold their goods—baskets I recognized from the storage room.

In the half dozen hours that we'd been gone, she'd turned Royal Mercantile into a bustling retail establishment.

"Damn," Liam said quietly as the bell strap on the door rang our arrival. "Even Mos would be impressed by this."

I was sure Liam was right. I had clearly not been giving my best friend enough capitalistic credit. So why did I have an angry clench in my belly, irritation at the sheer number of people in the store, and anger that she'd rearranged it—and better than I ever had?

Tadji's head lifted at the sound of the bells, and she said something to a customer at the counter, then hurried around it to get to us.

"Thank God," she said, looking us over. "I was frantic. You're all right?"

"We're fine," Liam said when I didn't answer.

"I've been getting reports from people about what happened." Her eyes darkened with anger. "It was Reveillon, wasn't it?"

"That's what it looks like," Liam said, "but Containment's still investigating. It's going to take time to piece everything together."

"Your grandmother?" Tadji asked.

"She's fine. Thanks for asking."

Tadji nodded, shifted her gaze to me, and I could feel her eagerness, which only made me more irritated.

"I hope you don't mind," she said, waving a hand at the store. "I was antsy, and I needed something to do, and this was the least destructive thing I could think of." She looked around. "I tried to think like a customer and, I guess, take everything up a notch." She looked back at me, her eyes gleaming with enthusiasm. "I've got some more ideas, too, actually."

"Uh-huh," was all I said.

She frowned at me, the enthusiasm shifting to concern. "Are you all right?"

I wasn't. I was suddenly itching with irritation, with anger, and I had no idea why. And considering what I'd just walked away from, that made me feel ridiculous and petty.

She put a hand on my arm. "If I overstepped, I can move everything back. It's no big deal."

"It's not a big deal," I lied, because I didn't know why it *was* a very big deal. I couldn't process it.

The only thing I could think to do was get away, try to figure out what the hell was happening inside my head.

"I need to go upstairs," I said and, without waiting for an answer, tromped up to the second floor like a kid who'd taken her ball and run.

The storage room on the second floor of Royal Mercantile was a warren of antiques and furniture. I'd tried to organize it roughly into departments, but that effort had failed when I was nearly pinned by a metal gas station sign and discovered—at a rusty point—that I had magic.

I walked through the maze to the wall of windows that faced Royal Street, pushed back the silk curtains, and stared into the falling darkness. And then I tried to figure out exactly why I'd just been bitchy to my best friend.

Liam let me stew for fifteen minutes before wooden floors signaled his entrance. Darkness had fallen completely, and I hadn't thought to turn on the light. He did so, and I blinked into the shock of it.

He found me in an oak rocking chair in front of the windows, the floor creaking beneath me.

"This is a horror movie waiting to happen, *cher*—you sitting in the dark in a rocking chair, making that sound."

Silence stretched between us. "You want to talk?" he asked.

"I don't know," I said honestly.

"The bombing, or what she did to the store?"

"Both, I think." I sighed, not entirely sure I wanted to bare my soul. But I knew I'd have to get it out sooner or later, because I was going to have to apologize to Tadji. Maybe if I talked through it, I'd understand it. I'd understand myself.

"Before the war," I began, "I had this plan for my life. I had pretty good grades, and that mattered back then. I was gonna go to Tulane, live in a dorm, be an irresponsible college student. I was going to get roaring drunk at parties and find a boy and make the dean's list."

"And then war came," Liam said.

"And then war came," I agreed. I sighed and rose, feeling suddenly antsy, and not a little bit trapped. Maybe that's how I'd felt then, too.

"Dad started selling provisions," I continued, "started moving more of the antiques up here, started spending more time at the store. By that point, it was dangerous to stay alone in the house. Better to be here with him, even if the Quarter was a bigger target. So I stayed here most of the time, and I worked. I didn't have a lot of choice, and I didn't feel like I should complain about the choice I did have." I looked down, picked at a spot of dirt on my jeans with a thumbnail. "I was alive, I was safe, and I had a way to make a living. That was rare in the Zone."

"Why not leave when your father died?"

I looked back at him. "Because I'm the last of the Connollys. If my father had lived, he'd have stayed here forever. Maybe I'd have kids, and one of them could have taken it over. Still could, I guess. But in the meantime, I couldn't let it just fade away."

I walked to the windows, pointed at the pale green building across the street. "That's the Prentiss Building. Built in 1795, I think. It's one of the first structures in New Orleans." I traced the building's lines on the glass with a fingertip.

"The thing is, that building held an operating business from 1795 until the war. And then the war came, and the Donaldsons—they owned it at the time—left." The windows and door had been broken, the store rummaged and hollowed out, blackened with war. But the building had still survived.

"I was just trying to keep going," I said. "And it turned out, being here was the best way to remember him. People came by all the time.

Mrs. Proctor, Mrs. Jones, Tony. People who'd known my father. They checked on me every day. They were brave enough to stay, to hold on to what we had. So I did the same."

"But maybe," Liam said, joining me at the window, "you'd have liked to have had another option."

I nodded. "I've worked hard on the store, and I love it. But as much as it's a part of me, I've never had that look in my eyes—the eagerness Tadji had."

I paused, trying to put my churning emotions into words. "After the bombing, after all that today, I was really looking forward to getting back here. Getting into my space—my place."

"Your comfort zone."

"Yeah. After all this time, yeah. The place where I'm in charge, where I make the rules. And instead, I find her in tornado merchandising mode." I looked up at him. "She's been in retail for five hours . . . and she's done a better job of it than I have in the years since my father died. And it suddenly felt like this wasn't *my* place."

"Come here," Liam said, voice filled with compassion. Then he pulled me against his body, wrapped his arms around me.

Want rose so quickly, so powerfully, that it might have been a tangible thing. To be so close to something I wanted so badly but couldn't have. But I let myself have what I could. Not because I was a Sensitive, not because I could someday become a wraith, but because I was a woman, and he was a man, and something had sparked—bright and hot—between us.

I dropped my forehead to his chest and rested there, let myself be, let my hands rest at his lean hips.

I could have tipped up my head and offered him a kiss; I had the sense he was waiting for it, would welcome it. But I knew where it would lead. As sure as he felt the spark, he didn't want to hurt me. We'd both walk away, but I'd get bruised in the process.

I gave it a minute, then two. And I dropped my hands, pulled back. Liam gave the embrace a last bit of strength before letting me step away.

"Claire." My name fell softly, part exhalation, part frustration, part grief.

I just looked at him. After a moment he tore his gaze away, looked over my head to the windows behind us. There was stubble around his jaw, tiredness in his eyes.

"Probably going to rain tonight," he said.

Yes, let's please talk about the weather. Let's talk about anything but need and want and feelings. It hadn't rained in two days, and this was New Orleans, so a downpour soon was pretty much inevitable. "Yeah."

We stood in that room of memories, the breach between us as big as the one I'd created at the Memorial Battle. And then the lights above us buzzed, went dark as the city's power grid was overcome once again by magic.

The sudden darkness was as good a metaphor as any.

Liam went downstairs alone to give me a chance to compose myself. That took me ten more minutes.

By the time I made it downstairs, Tadji had switched the OPEN sign to CLOSED. She'd also lit two pillar candles on the counter, which flickered shadows across the room.

I heard shuffling in the back—probably Liam—but Tadji was the only one in the front of the store. I rounded the corner, walked to the counter. She sat on a stool behind it and looked at me, our positions reversed from the usual.

"I'm sorry," I said.

Her dark eyes narrowed.

I cleared my throat. I hated apologizing. "I'm not really ready to talk about all of it. It has to do with my father, with the store, with what we saw today, and I'm still working through it. But I wanted to say I'm sorry."

She opened her mouth to speak, then closed it again, her eyes growing wide. "I didn't even think about your dad, Claire, about how this was his place, his stuff. I just wanted to be helpful. I'm—" she said, preparing to apologize, but I cut her off.

"You did absolutely nothing wrong. It just brought up some stuff that I guess I haven't dealt with." I made myself turn around, let my gaze move from sign to sign, display to display, until I'd surveyed the entire store.

I glanced at the nearly empty carton of boxed matches on the counter, the showy sign above it. "Fire sale?" I asked.

Tadji grinned. "I appreciate a good retail pun, and since that box was full when I put it out, I'd say I'm not the only one."

"Who knew you'd be so good at merchandising?"

"I know, right?" she said, smiling with pleasure at the compliment. "I think it's because of my research, because I've spent so much time talking to people in the Zone. You talk to them, you begin to figure out what they want."

I nodded. "Have you seen Gunnar since we left?"

She nodded. "He dropped by earlier. Didn't talk about what happened. Just said he was going to catch a nap at the Cabildo, then head back in. He looked exhausted, but you know how he is—he'll work till he drops."

"As long as he drops, and no one drops him."

Tadji went peaky at the comment.

"Sorry," I said, rubbing my eyes. "I'm sorry. Grim humor. I meant the sentiment, though. Containment's on Reveillon's radar."

"I can't think about that," she said, and cast a glance at the door. I wondered if she thought of Will Burke, a PCC Materiel agent, a Sensitive, and a member of Delta. He was a friend and ally, and had serious eyes for Tadji. Being Containment, he'd have been on Reveillon's radar. Unfortunate in a number of ways, and not just because he was recovering from a gunshot wound he'd gotten at the Memorial Battle.

For the second time tonight, I'd put a distressed expression on her face. I was not going to win any awards for friendship today.

She hopped off the stool, pulled her messenger bag over her head. "I'm going to get going. I'm starving and tired, and I've had enough chaos here today." She walked around the counter, hugged me. "You've got food? Something to eat?"

"I'm sure there's something back there, yeah. Thank you—really. For everything."

She nodded. "You're welcome, Claire." She paused. "I'd like to come back tomorrow—I'm working on my outline, and it helps to get out of the house, to think about something else. Unless that would bother you?"

I looked around the store, at the cheerfulness she'd brought into it. The sense of humor. "If it does, it shouldn't," I said, and we exchanged hugs again. "I guess you didn't get to the coffeehouse today."

"I did not. I think I'm going to stick close for the time being. But for now, I am out like the power in the Zone." She waved a hand and walked out the door, the bells jingling behind her.

Liam walked out of the kitchen, bottle of water in hand, and looked around. "Did you run her off?"

I yawned, covering my mouth with the back of my hand. It wasn't far past sunset, but I was ready for bed. "No. She'd had enough."

"Long day for everyone," Liam agreed.

I couldn't stop another yawn. "We need to update Delta."

"I'll do that," Liam said. "I think you've done enough for the day." He looked back at the front door. "You'll be safe here?"

"As safe as I ever am. The doors will be locked, and I'll be upstairs with magic."

He looked understandably dubious at my assessment.

"I can handle myself if I need to. And Ezekiel called you out, not me. He probably doesn't know who I am." And even if he did, what could we do about it short of leaving the Zone or my having a twenty-four-hour bodyguard? Neither of those was an option.

Liam nodded. "I think I'm going to take a drive. I want to look for billboards, maybe check out the Lower Ninth."

"You're going to look for the wraith again? You shouldn't go alone."

He grinned. "*Cher*, I hunted alone for many years before I met you. I'll be all right. I just want to pass through, see if I can get an indication of where he's been, where he's holed up. If I find it, we can pick him up tomorrow in daylight. Maybe Delta will have settled on a location for their new HQ, and we can talk to them, too."

"About Reveillon."

Liam nodded.

"That sounds good. Be careful when you go home, Liam." He would, after all, be heading back into Devil's Isle, and he'd already pissed off Ezekiel once today.

"I will, Claire. You take care of yourself."

When I nodded, he slipped into the darkness, back toward Devil's Isle. I closed and locked the door behind him, then stood there for a moment, watching until he was out of sight, as if that would keep him safe.

It didn't hurt to try.

I needed sleep and a new day, so I poured a glass of cold water and took the staircase to the third floor, to my long room of hardwood floors and plaster walls bookended by floor-to-ceiling windows.

I put the glass on the bureau and opened the front and back windows a crack, hoping a breeze would work its way upstairs.

A pigeon cooed on the courtyard side, so I checked for a message from Delta, found nothing. The mottled pigeon tilted its head at me in the halting, robotic way of pigeons, so I shook some seed into the small cup attached to its post and left it to its dinner.

When I reached my daybed, I unbuckled my boots, let them drop to the floor. My jeans and shirt followed, until I was left in "answering" clothes. (Just enough clothing, a customer had once told me, that you could still answer the door.)

I fell back onto the bed, exhaustion seeping into every bone and muscle. Some was physical, some was emotional, the cost of seeing horror, of remembering it, of dealing with its aftereffects.

I closed my eyes, tried to relax into the darkness. But even as weariness made my bones feel like lead, my mind continued to spin. It wanted to obsess, to wander, to repeat images of death and violence, to replay my conversations with Liam, to recite the things I'd need to do tomorrow—talk to Delta; order goods for Lizzie; apologize to Tadji again, just in case.

When the list rolled on and on, I opened my eyes and looked at the ceiling, forced myself to slowly trace through the constellations formed by glow-in-the-dark stick-on stars. I followed Orion's shoulders, belt, dagger, the long line of the scorpion, the lion's powerful body.

Halfway through, my mind tripped to Liam, and I had to drag it back again. When I'd traced all ten of them, I was still awake.

So I counted backward from one hundred. I got to nineteen . . . and I thought of Liam. *"Stop it,"* I ordered myself.

I imagined I was walking through the storage room, tried to remember each piece of furniture in order. I made it through to the windows, could feel my body relaxing into sleep . . . and thought of Liam's arms around me.

And so the cycle continued, over and over again. An hour and a half later, I was still awake.

"Son of a bitch," I muttered, then sat up and scrubbed my face, staring angrily into the dark.

There was no point in tossing around, so I swung my feet over the edge of the bed and stood up. I pulled on a pair of boxers to match the tank I already wore, shuffled to the doorway, and headed for the stairs.

I flipped on the light in the second-floor storage room, testing it. The power was back on.

I'd always liked to stay busy—fixing broken things, organizing the storage room, restoring an antique I'd found or traded for other things in the store.

And since learning my father had been a Sensitive, I'd been going through the building—the records, the antiques, my father's personal effects—looking for some clue about when he'd become a Sensitive and what he'd done about it.

Had he learned to cast off his magic, to keep his magic balanced? Was that why the store had been shielded from the magic monitors outside? And the most important question—the only one that really mattered: Why hadn't he told me?

"He just hadn't told me *yet*," I mumbled, repeating the mantra I'd decided on.

I'd been too young—only eighteen—when he was killed. He had meant to tell me, maybe when I was older. He'd had every intention of telling me but had been killed before he was able to take that step. Because the alternative made my chest ache—the possibility that he'd never intended to tell me, he'd never considered the possibility that I'd end up the same way—but without his help or guidance.

I sat down in front of two barrister's bookshelves in the storage room and opened the glass door on the bottom shelf. This week, I was working my way through the books my father had collected. The spines were gorgeous, all tooled leather and gilding, and they'd have sold for a pretty penny once upon a time. There were French Quarter tourist favorites—*A Confederacy of Dunces* and William Faulkner's *New Orleans Sketches*—along with plenty of classics I hadn't been allowed to touch as a child. Those tables had certainly turned.

"I'll take a letter," I said, pulling a book off the shelf, flipping through the pages. When no hidden note or secret message appeared, I replaced it again. "A sticky note. A receipt. A recipe card. A torn page from an old phone book."

Anything that would help me understand who he'd really been.

I pulled a copy of *The Secret Garden*, my heart momentarily speeding when I spotted faint scribbles in the front of the book. But it was just a penciled price from some long-ago sale.

With more discoveries like that, night slipped away. Five more books followed, then ten. Then twenty. And then I was down to the final shelf.

"*The Revolt of the Angels*," I murmured, reading the gold letters on the red leather spine. I didn't know the book, but I'd bet the author hadn't correctly imagined what a revolt of angels actually involved. I ran my fingers over the pressed metallic designs in the cover, the blue and red points of a radiating star.

"And how long ago were you written?" I wondered, opening the cover to find the publication information on the first page.

But there was no publication page.

The book's interior pages had been hollowed out, carved into a rectangle but for a border of pages about an inch on each side. And there, resting inside the book, was a set of papers.

My heart pounding, palms suddenly sweating with anticipation, I carefully unfolded them, pressed them flat.

They were old legal documents—a deed issued to a name I didn't recognize and what I thought were supporting documents, all of them yellowed with age.

They weren't my father's, I realized, flipping through half the pages. Just documents someone had put in a book for safekeeping, probably thinking they were being clever about it. My father had likely gotten the book as part of a larger lot, hadn't even opened it.

I put them both aside, lowered my head to my knees. Maybe I'd never figure out anything else about my father. Maybe I'd learn to live with what I knew and what I didn't.

"And maybe hell will freeze over, and angels will populate the earth," I muttered. "Oh. Wait."

I rose, taking the book and papers with me, turned off the light. Upstairs again, I put them on top of my bureau. Maybe I could find someone to send the papers back to. Maybe I'd keep the book for the irony.

And maybe, if I was lucky, I'd manage to get some sleep.

CHAPTER SIX

I t was early. So early that darkness still spilled unmolested into the room. Sound had woken me, but it was too dark, I thought, for *Reveille* to have rung over the Quarter from the Devil's Isle.

The song trilled again.

I blinked into darkness, the bed and walls and ceiling coming into focus. And eventually, the mottled gray pigeon singing an aria on the window ledge.

I considered pitching a shoe at it, but since it was probably a message from Delta, I dragged myself out of bed. I winced as I crossed the room, trying to force my legs to work together in sequence, my brain still foggy from the few hours of sleep I'd managed to grab.

"It's five-damn-thirty in the morning," I said, reaching for the pigeon, which danced back and forth. "Quit playing hard to get." When I managed to grab him, I pulled the slip of ivory paper from the leather band on his foot. The script on the curled paper, long and elegant, read: *Algiers Point. Practice. Now.—M.*

"M" was Malachi, my Delta colleague and today, my new magic teacher. This was a summoning from an angel at five-damn-thirty in the morning.

Grumbling, I put some seed in the pigeon's feeder, closed the window again, and resigned myself to my fate. I wasn't sure how long Malachi had already waited, and being even later wasn't very mannerly. Especially since he was helping me not to become a wraith, which I was totally on board with.

When angels called, Sensitives listened.

I showered, dressed, and noshed on one of the bananas a note from Tadji explained had been traded for powdered milk the day before, then slipped on a quilted PCC surplus jacket.

I locked up the store and went outside, headed for the river.

The Quarter was still dark, corners lit by gas streetlamps and the red glow of untriggered magic monitors. As Liam predicted, it had rained overnight, leaving the city damp and unusually chilly for this time of year. Another effect of magic—startling weather changes in our typically tropical corner of the world.

Even now, years after its peak, the Quarter smelled like the Quarter. Dampness, alcohol, garbage. It was like the boozy essence of Bourbon Street in its heyday had been trapped in the humidity that now misted through the city. Or maybe daiquiris, pralines, and their aftereffects had soaked into the asphalt and brick.

I should have been nervous, wary that Reveillon members were patrolling the neighborhood, looking for objects of their anger. But there was something magical in the darkness. Once upon a time, early morning in the Quarter meant garbage trucks, produce deliveries, joggers, businesspeople preparing to open stores and restaurants, tourists out and about before the heat became too oppressive.

Now the city was quiet, mist fuzzing the edges of the buildings and giving the gas lamps an otherworldly gleam. Devil's Isle still glowed to the north, but the humidity softened its even lines.

I walked toward the union of Canal Street and the Mississippi River. The Crescent City Connection, the bridge on U.S. 90, had been destroyed during the war, and the new crossing was several miles downriver. There'd been a ferry terminal here once upon a time, but it was gone, too, destroyed right after Mardi Gras World had burned to the ground.

You wanted to visit Algiers now, you paid Mr. Bernard.

His ferry had been cobbled from a section of barge, the seam sealed and made watertight. Rings were welded to one side, which were intricately laced to the bottom half of a long ellipse of rope that spanned the river.

A man, thin as a rail with lived-in skin tanned by the sun, stepped out of his tent on the edge of the riverbank. "Mornin'."

"Good morning, Mr. Bernard." I held out a few dollars, which he accepted with a nod and then tucked into his worn backpack. "Can I get a ride across?"

"Sure. Early."

I nodded. "Not my choice. Friend needs me."

He nodded, gestured to the barge. "Climb aboard."

I stepped onto the dock, then onto the long, flat barge, and watched as Mr. Bernard untied the hefty ropes that moored it to the muddy shore.

Rumor was, Mr. Bernard had been a pediatrician at a posh clinic in the Garden District when the war started. His office was hit in a fierce day of fighting during the Second Battle of New Orleans, and the loss of life—the loss of children—changed him. He walked away from what remained, joined the war, and then become the ferryman. Instead of battling illness, he battled the churning Mississippi day in and day out.

He tossed the ropes onto the barge's deck. Now loose, it shifted into the current, pulling tight against the cable that kept it from washing downriver and eventually into the Gulf of Mexico.

He walked to the middle of the barge, hands in heavy leather gloves, his arms tanned and corded with muscle. He began working hand over hand, pulling the upper rope to move the ferry into the river.

I grabbed a rail as the barge bucked against the current. We needed to move east; the river, which boiled brown in the early dawn, wanted very much to push us south.

The barge shuddered as a tree limb jarred us, nearly ripping the rope out of one of its stations. Mr. Bernard grunted but kept his hands on the rope.

"I can help," I said, and offered to do my part. But he motioned me back, beads of sweat popping on his face, and continued pulling.

He fought the river inches at a time with teeth bared and forehead furrowed until we'd crossed the half-mile span. Maybe this was his penance, fighting back against Old Man River because of the fight he hadn't been able to win.

He moored on the east side of the river, focusing on his task while I walked to the other end of the barge and across the dock. He'd wait there until he had a return fare, so if someone came along before I came back, I'd have to swim or wait him out.

Or catch a ride from an angel.

My legs unsettled, the ground seemed to wobble beneath me when I stepped onto dry land again.

Algiers wasn't the tourist spot it had once been; neighborhoods had been flattened by human shelling. The walls of the Mardi Gras World warehouse had crumbled long ago, and enormous faces—the heads of creatures that had once populated Mardi Gras floats—still stared out from what remained of the enormous building like idols to a different age.

Because it hadn't taken much magical damage, the things that grew in Louisiana grew here in abundance. The land had become a creeping meadow, with flora and fauna that helped feed those of us who lived in the Quarter.

Just as he had the first time I'd seen him, Malachi stood in a copse, wings retracted. He wore jeans and a thin navy pea coat, his tousled blond curls just brushing his shoulders. He was tall and broad-shouldered, with golden tan skin. His eyes were golden as well, his nose straight and leading to lips that were fuller on the bottom than on the top.

If it wasn't for the mantle of authority that he wore as well as the clothes, you'd have thought he was a human. But that mantle was difficult to ignore.

I'd known Malachi for a month now, and I still wasn't sure of him. He'd been a general in the Consularis army, and his manner was almost always formal. I wasn't sure if that was because he was Consularis and we were human, or he was a commander and we were, if anything, soldiers. Or maybe that was just his personality.

He glanced back, met my gaze, and pressed a finger to his lips. Nodding, I crept through the grass to stand beside him.

A deer and a fawn stood in a clearing fifteen or twenty yards away, their bodies lit by the early light that slitted through the trees and spilled across the fog. They gnawed at grass that had grown where a parking lot once stood, then lifted their heads. Jaws working, ears alert, they chewed in the growing dawn.

The moment lengthened, and crickets resumed their chorus around us. The fawn, its haunches dotted with white spots, pranced forward merrily, tail switching to brush away gnats or mosquitoes.

Malachi's sudden whistle split the air and the silence. The deer jumped and ran, disappearing into the mist.

"Why did you do that?"

"It's better they remain afraid," he said. "They become too used to humans—or anything else—and they're more vulnerable."

"To being dinner."

"There's no reason to make the hunt too easy."

I cocked my head at him. "And are humans more vulnerable for becoming too used to Paranormals?"

He seemed pleased by the question, but that didn't change his manner. "Do you think I am your ally?"

I gave the question honest thought. "I don't know. But I don't think it matters."

He lifted his brow in surprise. "Oh?"

"We have a common enemy. That makes us allies enough for right now."

He smiled. "On that, we agree."

"You heard what happened yesterday?"

He nodded. "Yes. Liam and Burke both got messages to us."

"We'd seen a billboard near the Lower Ninth that morning. Then they marched down Bourbon Street. The leader, Ezekiel, said they had lots of allies, lots of signs. Have you seen anything like that? Recruiting messages? Other signs of them?"

"I've seen several billboards. But no indication of who painted them, or the size of their group. They'd have to be big enough not to worry about the loss of seven members in an orchestrated explosion."

"Yeah." And that was disturbing enough. "Is that why we're here so early?"

He smiled. "It isn't early for me. But generally, yes. You will not always have the opportunity to choose the conditions under which you use magic. You need to be prepared to use it in less than optimal situations."

I glanced around. It was cold, dark, and foggy, and I was still groggy from a night spent tossing and turning. "Less than optimal," I agreed.

Malachi smiled. "Give me your jacket."

My shoulders slumped. "I don't suppose you could trade it for a white chocolate mocha with soy and whip, could you? And maybe a croissant to go with it?"

He just looked at me.

"Never mind," I said, taking off the jacket and handing it to him. "Did you make Burke do this?" I wondered, goose bumps rising on skin chilled in the brisk air.

"I didn't train Burke. Let's see what you can do."

I glanced around. "No one will see?"

"No. I've shielded the woods."

I lifted my eyebrows. "You can do that?"

He nodded, and I watched him for a moment. "Did you shield Royal Mercantile?"

"No," he said with a smile. "I didn't know your father. And that is not a skill I have. I can bring you within the aegis of my magic—as I've done now. But that aegis requires a certain physical proximity."

Malachi walked twenty feet away from where I stood, into the clearing where the deer and the fawn had munched on grass minutes ago. He linked his hands in front of him, feet spread as wide as his hips. He looked vaguely Viking-esque there in the meadow, the mist pooling at his feet.

"I want you to pick me up," he said.

Like in a bar? was the first thought that came to mind. "I— excuse me?"

"Pick me up." He raised a hand, pointed a finger to the sky. "Lift me into the air."

"Could I point out you have wings?"

"You could, but that would be a waste of time. Pick me up."

"Just call me Skywalker," I muttered, and took a good, hard look at the object of my magic.

Malachi was tall, broad shoulders, strong body. He probably weighed somewhere between one ninety-five and two twenty, not counting the wings. And I had no idea how much they weighed. I hadn't moved anything that heavy before—not on purpose, anyway—but didn't see why I couldn't do it now.

I gave him a nod, centered myself, blew out a breath. And then I lifted a hand, palm out, and began to gather the invisible magic that surrounded us. I couldn't see that energy, but I could feel it with some sixth sense, the perception that marked me as a Sensitive and—if I wasn't careful—would make me a wraith.

I pulled the magic together, building filaments of magic, and circling it around Malachi like a rope. When I'd built up enough magic that I was nearly dizzy with it, I slowly lifted my hand to raise him off the ground.

He didn't budge. Not even an inch.

"Problem?" Malachi asked casually, as if still waiting for me to start.

"No," I said, and narrowed my gaze. I'd be damned if I couldn't do this—because there was no reason I couldn't do this. I had telekinesis. I could move things. He was a thing, so I could move him.

Maybe I hadn't calculated his weight well enough, I thought, and began to gather more than enough magic to account for his muscle and mass. Lifting my hand again, I wound more and more magic around him, until he seemed to glow with it, like he'd only just stepped through the Veil in the golden armor Paras preferred.

I drew my fingers into a fist and raised that fist to the sky, pulling the magic with me, and pulling him with the magic.

Not even a lock of his hair moved.

Frustration boiled over. "Son of a bitch."

"You aren't trying."

I made a sound of doubt, shook out arms that were trembling from effort. "If I try any harder I'll pop a blood vessel." I narrowed my gaze at him. "You're doing something—something that makes you heavier."

"If I was human, I might be offended by that."

"But you aren't. What's the deal?"

Malachi looked at the ground, ran a palm over the nubby grass, pine needles, and sticks that littered the ground. He picked up two pinecones, then walked back to me. He held out his palms, one in each hand. "Open your palms."

I did, mirroring his position.

"Example one," he said, and dropped the pinecone in his left hand into my palm.

It felt like a pinecone, pointy and nubby.

"Example two," he said, and released the other pinecone.

My hand fell like he'd dumped a concrete block onto it, and I had to catch myself before I stumbled forward. I had to use both hands to pull the pinecone up again. It looked like a pinecone, but it weighed at least twenty pounds.

I thought of the box I kept in the store's second floor, which held the magic I cast off to keep my levels in balance. It had become heavier over the past few weeks from the accumulated weight of that magic.

I looked up at Malachi. "It's heavier—because you put magic in it."

"Good," he said. "You can drop it now."

I considered hefting it onto his toes but let it fall to the side, where it hit the earth with a thud, no bounce, no roll. I cocked my head at him, put my hands on my hips, and gave him an up-and-down appraisal. "Okay. I get that. But what about you?"

"That is the advantage of having innate magic—it complements our anatomy. I wasn't making myself heavier—my mass stayed the same—but I used the magic to forge a bond between myself and the earth."

"Which made you harder to lift."

Malachi nodded. "You have to be prepared for the unexpected."

"If I can prepare myself, that means I can adjust to it? Like, by gathering more magic?" Although I wasn't certain I could do that without passing out.

"No," he said. "That's the point, and a lesson it took humans a very long time to learn. There is no fighting it. There is no combating it. Is cold iron any more deadly than steel?"

It had taken us long to realize the myth was mostly correct; our use of cold iron had been a turning point in the war.

"No," I said. "As metals go, it's softer."

He walked forward. "Correct. But it interrupts magic. That is its particular quality."

"So I have to figure out what something is in relation to magic, and use my magic accordingly."

"Just as you did at Memorial when you locked the box that held the Veil's encryption keys. You identified its particular magical qualities, and you worked the locks accordingly."

I opened my mouth to brag, but he beat me to smugness.

"You still split the earth," he pointed out.

Damn it.

"Do you know why that happened?"

"I assumed it was magic from the Veil snapping back into place—when the energy of its movement was forced out."

He looked vaguely impressed. "Good. How could you have done better?"

A cricket literally chirped in the silence that followed. I tried to pick up the leash I thought he'd been leading me on. "Maybe I could have, given more time and experience, gauged how it was likely to react and adjusted my magic accordingly?"

Malachi smiled broadly. "Good."

"I was a little rushed at the time."

"You were. And likely afraid and angry. Next time, use that."

I blinked. "How?"

"I can't be inside your head, Claire. That's the lesson you must learn." And with that, he walked forward, picked up my jacket, which he'd laid carefully at the foot of the oak tree, handed it to me.

I guessed the lesson was over. "You're going to tell me all that, and not tell me what to do with it?"

Malachi looked down at me. "If you want to learn to wield the magic, you must *learn* to wield the magic."

"Wax on, wax off," I muttered, and watched him disappear into the trees.

CHAPTER SEVEN

By the time I made it back to the store, the lights were on. Since I hadn't turned them on before I left, I assumed Gunnar had used his key. Sure enough, he was pacing back and forth in front of the counter when I opened the door. Since it was nearly opening time, I flipped the OPEN sign on the door and walked inside, the bell ringing my arrival.

"Where the hell have you been?" he asked, boots polished and fatigues perfectly pressed.

"Practice with our aerial friend."

"Practice—oh." Gunnar closed his eyes for a second. "I may have panicked when you weren't upstairs."

I walked into the kitchen, pulled a bottle of water from the fridge, which was still running, thank goodness. "And you didn't assume I spent the night with a gorgeous and witty man?"

"Since the only man you have eyes for—gorgeous, witty, or otherwise—has issues, no. I didn't."

I took a seat on the stool and uncapped the water, took a drink. "I can't really argue with that. How are things at Devil's Isle?"

"It was a late night," he said, which was confirmed by the dark shadows beneath his eyes. "But we're making progress, if that's what you want to call it." He pulled a piece of paper from a folder, slapped it onto the counter.

"What's that?"

"They have a manifesto. Assholes," he muttered, walking behind me toward the kitchen. I was going to start charging my friends for using it like their own personal store.

I scanned the paper. The letters were tiny and neat, marked by faint marks probably made by an old-fashioned typewriter. The language was old-fashioned and sounded biblical, except there weren't any actual mentions of religion other than the references to Eden. There were, however, a lot of implicit threats.

"'Only through blood will our land be redeemed,'" I read aloud. "'Only in blood will our land be revived.' That's pretty telling."

"Yeah. In my opinion, the letter is a bunch of self-important, masturbatory nonsense. We've got profilers looking it over for an official analysis. I can already tell you what they'll say—that the author is egotistical, narcissistic, possibly paranoid, and generally an asshole, as I predicted."

"You think Ezekiel wrote it," I concluded.

"He didn't sign it, but it's got 'cult leader' written all over it."

"There's nothing specific about next steps," I said. "I mean, generally they want to destroy Containment and anyone who's ever done anything in support of Containment, but they don't go into specifics. Do you think they have more explosives?"

"If they could get access to the components once, they can probably do it again."

After that conclusion, I nearly jumped when the bells on the front door jangled.

Liam and Tadji came in, chatting amiably. Royal Mercantile was becoming the meeting space for our group of humans-in-the-know.

Today, Tadji wore leggings and a thin, dark poncho over combat boots. She looked ready for battle, even if I hoped the retail battle was the only one she'd wage. Liam wore his uniform—fitted jeans that pooled over boots, and a snug gray Henley with the top buttons unfastened, the fit showing his body with cruel definition. He hadn't shaved this morning, and the dark stubble across his cheeks only made his eyes glow bluer.

"What are you two doing here?" Gunnar asked.

"And good morning to you, too," Tadji said, pressing a kiss to his cheek before pulling off her messenger bag. "I'm here to continue my efforts to bring this store into the twenty-first century."

"And you?" Gunnar asked, glancing at Liam. "What's your excuse?"

"Well, there's the outstanding bounty for the wraith, or we could discuss the bounties Containment just issued for Reveillon members." He looked at me. "You want in?"

"Maybe," I said, thinking about the store, the fact that I'd basically dumped it on Tadji yesterday.

"Claire has a full schedule," Gunnar said. "She had magic practice this morning."

Tadji and Liam both looked at me.

"And how did it go?" she asked. Liam didn't speak, but his gaze was steady and intense.

"Fine," I said, giving Gunnar a look. I felt like I was being set up. And since his gaze was on Liam, it wasn't hard to guess the plan. He was trying to bait Liam, or make him jealous I'd spent time alone with Malachi. Which was a waste of everyone's time.

"We went to Algiers Point, which was very pretty. We saw two deer. The river was rough. Magic is difficult."

They waited for more.

I shrugged, leveled a stare at Gunnar. "Nothing more to tell."

Liam looked at Gunnar. "What's happening with Reveillon?"

"They have a manifesto," I said, and slid the paper to Liam with a fingertip.

"There are still five Reveillon members unaccounted for," Gunnar said while Liam scanned it. "They scattered in the chaos. Right now we believe it's most likely they're in Devil's Isle. We've got extra patrols on the streets looking for them, and we've asked the block captains to spread the word among the Paras." He looked at Liam. "I made sure your grandmother was told."

"Appreciate it," Liam said. "What's Containment's strategy outside the prison?"

"Stop them," Gunnar said simply. "The Joint Ops unit—half PCC and half FBI—had our first briefing last night. We'll be coordinating to identify, locate, and stop Reveillon."

"You're talking about a manhunt," Tadji said.

Gunnar nodded. "As soon as we reported the bombing, PCC dispatched troops from Pensacola. One of the convoys was ambushed on the road. All but two were killed."

We went silent.

"Damn," Tadji said, sadness punctuating the air.

"Yeah," Gunnar said. "Ezekiel couldn't have known where the troops would come from."

"Which means, if that attack and the Devil's Isle bombing are related," Liam said, "he's got people spread out across the borders, or at the Zone's entry points, at least."

Gunnar nodded. "Joint Ops considers Reveillon a hostile militia."

Tadji frowned. "Wait, you think he's got an organization that's spread across the Zone?"

"It doesn't necessarily have to be big if it's agile, mobile," Liam said.

"But it's not hard to recruit people who are already pissed off," Gunnar said. "If we arrested everyone who said nasty things about Paranormals, most of the U.S. population would be in chains."

"I've heard from people in the Zone who are still angry," Tadji confirmed. "Not paint-a-billboard angry, but angry."

I found that kind of baffling. "Seven years later? I'm not saying you can't feel what you feel, but holding on to that anger, obsessing about it—I don't get it. It seems like such a waste of energy. Of limited time."

"Some people don't have a store," Tadji said gently. "They lost loved ones like you but don't have livelihoods. They live hand to mouth, and they stay here because they don't think they have anywhere else to go. That leads to bitterness, to anger."

"And like-minded individuals find other like-minded individuals," Gunnar said. "Or that's Joint Ops' working theory. Either way, he managed to orchestrate the bombing of a federal facility without anybody catching on."

"Operational security," Liam said. "His people are smart enough not to talk."

"Yeah," Gunnar said. "PCC will be sending more convoys in— but in smaller, elite units that are prepared for guerrilla-style warfare. Still, the Zone is a very big place. There's a chance they'll do more harm before it's all over. That they'll kill again before it's all over."

Silence fell again as we all faced the possibility of war. This time by our own people.

"They'd have to have resources," Liam said. "Money, contacts for the explosives."

"And enough expertise to know what to buy, how to build them," Gunnar agreed.

"I've seen a lot of the Zone," Tadji put in, arms stretched and palms on the counter like a general considering strategy. "There's no money in it, or not much, anyway."

"We had money," Gunnar said. The Landreaus had an enormous

house in the Garden District, had been an important part of the city's society class. "We put most of it into restoring the house, putting in generators, keeping it up. Keeping it as a memorial to the money we used to have," he added dryly. "But I take your point."

Liam crossed his arms, which made the muscles shift and flex. "So, outside funding?"

"Or members who stockpiled resources. There are still weapons from the war to be found across the Zone."

"Could the members be ex-military?" Tadji asked, frowning. "There were stories during the war about disgruntled soldiers with a 'kill all the Paranormals' attitude. Maybe they were recruited."

"Could be," Gunnar said. "Or maybe Ezekiel—or whatever the hell his real name is, 'cause I'd put money on it not being Ezekiel—"

"Tad," I suggested. "Or Chip. He could be a Chip."

"You had it with Tad," Liam said, leaning against the counter, eyes shining with humor. "I knew a Tad in high school. Total douche."

"Tad the cult leader," Gunnar said. "We'll see if it holds. Anyway, maybe Ezekiel brought his own cash."

"From outside the Zone," I said. "He didn't have an accent."

Gunnar blinked. "You're right. I didn't catch that." He penned a note on his small, ubiquitous notebook.

"We talked to Moses about his theory that magic has ruined the world," Liam said.

"What did he say?"

"Basically, that it was bullshit. Magic leaked through the Veil when it was opened, and magic weapons saturated the soil in some areas. The ongoing effect of Paras is miniscule compared to that. Whatever effects magic has had won't be fixed by killing Paras. But they might be fixed by more magic."

"And that won't happen until Congress is willing to enlist Paras to help," Gunnar said. "That's not going to happen any time soon, since it would require admitting the difference between Consularis and Court Paranormals, among other things."

The door opened again. A few agents came in, including Burke. He stepped beside Tadji, nearly dwarfing her slender frame with his broad shoulders. Tall, with dark skin and dark eyes, and a generous mouth that always seemed to be smiling, he directed that smile at Tadji. "Tadji."

"Burke."

There was heat to be sure. I needed to grab some time with Tadji and quiz her on the rest of it. Nosiness was an honored New Orleans tradition.

"Hey, Burke," Gunnar said while Burke's gaze danced busily around the store.

"Looks different in here. I like it."

"Thank you," Tadji said with a smile. "Claire's still getting used to it."

"Change can be difficult," Burke said.

"What's the good word?" Liam asked.

Burke cast a glance around, making sure the other agents were out of earshot. "Our friends have a new house and would like to discuss and coordinate."

"Our friends" meant Delta. They'd been infiltrated and betrayed by a Paranormal who wanted to reopen the Veil, so a new HQ had become a necessity. That Para, Nix, had also betrayed Liam's younger brother, Gavin. He'd left New Orleans right after on some secret mission.

Burke held up a set of keys. "Who wants to go for a ride?"

Liam nodded. "I'm in," he said, and looked at me. "You?"

I glanced at Tadji. "Can you merchandise while we commune?"

"Maybe," she said with narrowed eyes. "If I get full details on the practice."

"Nothing to tell," I assured them. And I pinched her arm on my way to the door.

Burke had a jeep, a spare, military model with no doors and no top. The day had become hot and sticky, so the breeze was glorious. I braided my hair on the way out of the Quarter to keep it from flying around, and stretched out on the bench seat in the back after Liam called shotgun.

We took St. Charles, which was divided in half by the neutral ground where streetcars once ran. We drove through the Garden District, where the houses of the wealthy were stacked like boxes along the street. Most had been abandoned. A few, like Gunnar's parents' house, had been brought back from the brink of destruction. His large family still lived there, biding their time until . . . Well, I wasn't really sure what they were waiting for. Maybe, like Reveillon, they were waiting for something different, something they hoped was inevitable.

"Look," Burke said, slowing down.

A sign formerly identifying someone's business—smaller than the billboard we'd seen on Claiborne—now read DEATH TO PARANORMALS.

"Spreading the hate," Burke said.

"Like a virus," I agreed. But there was no mention of Reveillon, Ezekiel, or anything else on the sign. "How do you think they're actually recruiting?"

"Word of mouth," Burke said. "You help someone chop some wood, you both talk about how pissed you are that you're trying to eke out a living on bad soil. Junk man comes through, selling junk, picking up junk, and you talk to him. He's heard about a meeting of like-minded individuals in the next parish, and you decide to go."

Liam glanced at him, eyebrows lifted. "That's pretty specific."

Burke nodded. "One of our caravan drivers heard some talk out near Natchez. We put Containment on it, but we didn't find the meeting."

"Maybe they're mobile like the junk man," I said. We didn't see junk men often in the city. It was more common for someone to bring something in to the store to sell—from heirloom silver to busted-up electronics—for a few dollars or Devil's Isle tokens. "Reveillon, or at least those outside the city, stay nomadic so they don't attract too much attention."

"Very possible," Liam said.

Burke made a note of the sign's location on a scrap of paper stuck beneath the sunshade. "Let's keep moving," he said, flipping up the shade and putting the jeep in gear again.

We moved down the street, the sign growing smaller behind us, but still big in our minds.

Burke pulled the jeep in front of a simple, white church, APOSTLES the only word that remained on the peeling wooden sign in the small yard in front of it. The white clapboard building, situated in Freret, was small and narrow, with a door between two windows on the front. A steeple reached into the sky above the arched doorway.

"Interesting choice," Liam said as we headed up the sidewalk.

"It's an historic property," Burke explained. "The building's on the National Register, so the state won't touch it. The feds don't have money to deal with all the abandoned buildings under their author- ity, which makes it a political no-man's land." His tone softened. "And there aren't enough people in the neighborhood to use it."

The war had treated every neighborhood differently. Battles had striped devastation into the Garden District, leaving blackened blocks beside pristine ones. The Lower Ninth, so damaged by the storm surge from Hurricane Katrina, had been mostly spared, probably because there weren't as many houses there.

Freret had been terrorized and picked apart by a group of Paras who'd nested nearby during the war. A group of neighbors on a nighttime patrol had been slaughtered, and the neighborhood had been mostly abandoned after the attack. Who could blame them?

"We've been watching it for a while," Burke said, "just to make sure we'd have the place to ourselves. Helps that the church is in a neighborhood, off the main roads."

Burke rapped on the front door. Seconds later, the locks snapped. A curvy woman with pale skin and dark hair opened it. She wore cropped black pants and a short-sleeved sweater, her hair curled into soft waves around her face, tortoiseshell glasses perched on her nose.

This was Darby Craig, a former scientist who'd been kicked out of her research unit when she learned the truth about Paranormals.

"Hey, Claire, Liam. Welcome to the new Delta HQ." She stood aside so we could enter.

The door opened into a small, empty foyer, and a double doorway leading into the chapel. It was a space my father would have appreciated—antique in the extreme, with rough-hewn wooden floors and bare beams across the steeply pitched ceiling. There were marks on the floor where benches had once provided seating for congregants, but they were gone now. Probably used for kindling during the war, when magic sent cold snaps through New Orleans with chilling regularity.

An enormous stained glass window spilled light across the other end of the room. In front if it, wings outstretched, stood an angel. Malachi turned, his wings folding behind him with the soft *whoosh* of moving feathers before disappearing completely.

"As you can see," Darby said, closing the door behind us, "the place was mostly gutted, but there's a receiving room in the back and a small office." She reached us in the middle of the aisle, smiled. "There's a rookery in the steeple. The bell's gone—probably melted down for weapons during the war. Pigeons took over the space, and we've started training ours to roost here. That's one of the reasons why we picked it. Oh, and there's this."

She walked to the low stage at the front of the church, knelt down, and pressed her fingertips to the wood. A panel of the floor popped up beneath her hands.

"What is that?" Liam asked, moving closer.

"Trapdoor," she said, pulling the panel up, which brought the scent of damp earth into the room. "Leads down to the crawl space. We're guessing it was used during Prohibition given the age of the church. And during the war," she added, her expression sobering as she dropped the door again and rose. "We found some empty soup cans down there, water bottles, that kind of thing. Folks probably hid during air raids."

Paranormals with wings didn't need electricity to fly above the Zone, which made the peal of air raid sirens all too common during the war.

"There was an office in the refinery above the factory floor," Darby continued, glancing at me and Liam. "I don't think you ever saw it," she added, and we shook our heads. "Anyway, we kept basic supplies there—food, water, flashlights, batteries, a small genny. We moved them into the crawl space last week."

Liam looked up. "Good to know we have it, if we need it."

"Wanna see the back?" Darby asked, and Liam and Burke agreed, followed her through a narrow paneled door on the right-hand side of the stage.

While they walked to the back of the church, I stayed behind, met Malachi's gaze. He'd been standing on the other side of the stage, arms crossed, his gaze intense on the stained glass, his thoughts partly hidden by the tousled curl that fell over one eye.

"And so we meet again," I said.

"And I still have no coffee."

I smiled, appreciating the humor. "I won't hold that against you. We got an update from Gunnar."

He nodded, and we stood there awkwardly for a moment. I still wasn't entirely sure what to talk to him about. There was something very formal about him—maybe because he'd been a general in the Consularis army. "So, do you have any hobbies?"

His gaze slid slowly my way. "Hobbies?"

"I mean, what do you do when you aren't working with Delta, or handling Para issues, or, well, working out?" I added, considering his physique.

"I read."

"Oh? What do you read?" I thought about *The Revolt of the Angels*. If the text hadn't been chopped out of it, I could have given it to Malachi.

"Military texts, primarily. Books on tactics and strategy."

"Understandable," I said. And when silence fell again, I was more than a little relieved that Darby, Burke, and Liam walked into the church again.

"And now that the tour's over," Darby said, "let's get down to business."

We gathered together, and Liam put his hands on his hips, gave his report.

"Four killed in the bombing by a group called Reveillon. Seven Reveillon members killed. The leader calls himself Ezekiel and contends the only way to fix the Zone is to rid the city of magic—Paranormals, Containment, and the works."

"Imprisoning Paranormals isn't sufficient?" Malachi's voice was tight with anger. If humans knew what he was—and had been able to catch him—he'd be in Devil's Isle with the rest of them.

"Apparently not," Liam said, and reviewed what we'd learned about the group, the bombing, Containment's investigation.

"How many from the bombing are still on the loose?" Darby asked.

"Outside Devil's Isle," Liam said, "unknown in numbers and spread, although a PCC convoy out of Pensacola was hit. Inside the gates, Containment thinks there are five fugitives."

"Preparing for the next attack?" Burke asked. "Or planning a different one?"

"We don't know yet," Liam said. "Containment has people searching the prison, and I understand they're warning the Paras."

"There are too many places to hide," Malachi said, walking to one of the church's side windows and staring pensively outside. "Paras will be watching, and they may very well report what they find. But the prison, the neighborhood, is enormous."

Liam nodded. "I think Containment is aware of the scale of the problem. They're considering Reveillon an armed militia."

Malachi turned back. "Good. I'm glad they recognize the severity." He paused, seeming to choose his words. "There are clearly humans who, like yourselves, are sympathetic to our situation, our circumstances. But not all feel that way. Frankly, I wasn't certain they'd take the threat with enough seriousness."

"They're after Paranormals, so who cares?" I asked.

"Exactly."

"If Ezekiel had wanted Containment to be lackadaisical about the threat," Burke said, "he picked exactly the wrong way to do it. He killed humans, soldiers, families. That guaranteed Containment's involvement and attention."

"Agreed," Liam said. "What's our response?"

"There are Delta members outside New Orleans," Malachi said. "Paranormals, primarily. Not many, but enough to gather intelligence about Reveillon's activities outside the city."

"I'll assist with that," Burke said. "Check in with the caravans, our suppliers, see what they can tell us."

Malachi nodded. "I can help search inside the city, and we'll get the information to Burke or to you," he said, looking at me and Liam. "You can get it to Gunnar?"

"We can," I said.

"Containment issued a bounty for Reveillon members," Liam said. "I'll be working that." He glanced at me. "With Claire, as time and patience permit."

"I do find patience is required," Malachi said.

I gave them haughty looks. "I assume you're both referring to my needing patience to deal with you."

Beside me, Darby worked to bite back a smile. "And speaking of things requiring patience, I'm working on the slower side of things. I've managed to find a place—a former biotech building near the airport—that still has some pretty good supplies in it."

"We're helping her set up a lab," Burke said, smiling at Darby. "She might as well be using all those letters behind her name."

"Damn right," Darby said.

"What will you be working on?" I asked.

"Soil samples," she said. "I want to figure out a way to reverse the effect of magic, to make it usable again."

"That would change life in the Zone," Liam said, obviously awed.

"Yeah, if I can experiment without running afoul of Containment, actually get it to work, figure out a way to scale it up if it does, and get Containment to buy into it." She smiled. "That's why I said it would require patience."

We'd covered New Orleans, the Zone, and the soil. But that left one big gap in the plan.

"If this gets worse," I said, "it's going to get worse for the Paras inside Devil's Isle first. They aren't allowed to have weapons, they can't use their magic, they can't leave, and from what Lizzie tells me, they have trouble getting basics from Containment. So how do we help them?"

Malachi smiled knowingly. "Instead of asking me, and presuming I can speak on behalf of a thousand very different people, why don't you ask them?"

I did not have a good response to that. "Point taken," I said, and Malachi nodded. I guessed I'd be going back to Devil's Isle. Maybe Lizzie or Mos could help with the introductions.

Before we could discuss it further, the door opened with a slow creak, and we all turned toward it, hands and bodies ready for trouble.

And trouble walked right in.

CHAPTER EIGHT

Gavin Quinn, Liam's younger brother, was just as tall, just as dark-haired, and just as blue-eyed. His body had been honed differently; he was finer-boned and leaner than Liam, but no less handsome. And like his brother, he knew it.

Gavin exuded that confidence despite the black eye, the cut lip, the faint bruising around his jaw. His heather gray T-shirt and jeans were dotted with blood and smeared with what I hoped was mud.

"What the hell happened to you?" Liam asked.

Gavin glanced at his brother. "Work."

"And yet you're alone," Malachi said, and he didn't seem happy about it.

"Give it a minute," Gavin said, walking forward. "She's probably putting her face on."

The door opened again, and a woman—tall and willowy, with tan skin and coal black hair, walked in. She wore a red tank top and a long skirt, her long hair pulled into a braid that rested on her left shoulder. Her eyes were wide and dark, and there was a half-moon shadow beneath her left eye. And when she put her hands on her hips, her knuckles were split and bruised. She looked like a goddess, which might very well have been true if she was a Para.

Malachi smiled grimly. "Hello, Erida."

It took her a moment to answer, and in that intervening silence, she looked at all of us. Her eyes widened slightly when she looked at me, but the apparent surprise faded before I could make anything of it. It was probably because I was the only human in the room who didn't have some previous connection to Delta, to Containment, or to Paras.

"You called?" she said, sliding her gaze to Malachi again, her voice fluidly accented.

"It's good to see you home again," Malachi said.

"This isn't my home."

"Neither was Lake Borgne," Gavin said.

She cast a narrowed glance at him. "I was doing just fine until you showed up."

"And now you'll do just fine here," Malachi said.

Darby moved closer to me. "You think humans are dramatic?" she whispered. "You've never seen Paras bicker. Watching them is one of my favorite hobbies."

I glanced at her, eyebrows lifted. "It's possible you need some healthier hobbies."

"You wouldn't be wrong," she said, but kept her gaze on the pair.

"It looks like you both worked out some aggression," Malachi said, glancing between Erida and Gavin.

"Not enough of it," she said, leveling a stare at Malachi. "Why am I here?"

"Excuse us for a moment," he said, and drew her toward the back of the church, where the stained glass window spilled blue and red light over them.

While they chatted, and Burke and Darby did the same, Gavin walked over to us. "Claire, Liam. A pleasure to see you again."

"And how was your vacation?" I asked pleasantly.

Gavin snorted, pointed to his face. "This sums it up pretty accurately."

"Are you going to punch your brother hello?" I asked. That was how he'd done it the last time he reunited with Liam, and right in the middle of Royal Mercantile, giving me and my customers a pretty entertaining show.

He grinned, winced at the pain. "No."

"I'd ask how you got the shiner," Liam said, sliding his glance to Erida, "but I'm pretty sure I already know the answer."

"It looks like you were pretty evenly matched," I said. "I mean, given your injuries."

"Agreed," Liam said. "How'd you get her to come back?"

Gavin grinned, lighting dimples at the corners of his cheeks. "I'm very good at persuasion."

"Bullshit," Liam said through a cough.

"She's a goddess of war," Gavin said quietly.

I looked at her again, the perfect posture, the slim but toned shoulders and arms. She looked to be lecturing Malachi, gesturing wildly, and not very happy about it.

"She wasn't fighting to avoid coming back," Liam said. "She was fighting because that's what she does. She's one of Malachi's marshals—his soldiers. Let me guess," he said. "She challenged you, and you stupidly accepted?"

"Hey, I'm still walking. She didn't break anything." But he winced when he rolled his shoulder. "This is an old baseball injury."

"Sure it is," Liam said, and clapped him hard on the arm.

Gavin's face went a shade paler. "Asshole."

"Back at you," Liam said. "I'm glad you're back. We've got trouble."

Gavin nodded. "I heard about the bombing. You remember that piece-of-shit marina on the north side of Lake Borgne?"

Liam closed his eyes and nodded, as if trying to remember. "Owned by an asshole with a domestic violence habit?"

Gavin nodded. "Beat the shit out of his wife in front of his kid and a Containment agent." He looked at me. "Real class act."

"Sounds like it."

"The kid, Jasmine, is all grown up now," Gavin said with a grin. "She runs the outfit. Pretty nice operation, actually." He smiled. "Pretty nice Jasmine."

Liam rolled his eyes. "I'm shocked you'd use a contract as an opportunity to get laid."

"I'm no monk. And the point is, the marina's a way station. It's the only operating marina for twenty miles. They want gas, food, water, they go to her." Gavin looked at me, grinned. "It's the power of the hot girl in retail."

"My duct tape brings all the boys to the yard," I said dryly, and both brothers smiled.

"I bet. As to the marina, you get shrimpers in and out, the occasional Para in and out. I used the marina to find Erida, and to find out about the bombing. Word had traveled from New Orleans."

Malachi and Erida moved back to us.

"Erida," Malachi said, "this is Liam Quinn and Claire Connolly."

She looked at me, nodded. There was nothing unfriendly in the gesture, but nothing particularly friendly, either. Maybe she was the all-business type.

"We should stay in touch," Malachi said. "Particularly now. Sharing information about Reveillon may be the only way to stop them."

Liam nodded. "We'll let you know if Containment learns anything else. And send a pigeon if there's trouble."

Malachi nodded. "We should assume Reveillon will attack again. We try to stop them if we can, and minimize casualties if we can't."

He looked at me. "We'll train again," he said, which made Liam shift ever so slightly beside me.

"When?" I asked, ignoring the movement.

He smiled lightly. "When I show up."

I shouldn't have bothered asking.

"In that case, we're going to get back," Liam said. "Claire needs to at least make an appearance at the store today, or people will start getting suspicious."

"And we're taking you back to the store," I said, pointing at Gavin. "We'll get you fixed up."

"I'm fine," he said, but winced and touched his lip. "But I wouldn't say no to a drink."

Burke drove us back. Because Gavin called shotgun before Liam and me, we shared the bench. Gavin almost immediately dropped his head back and closed his eyes. He looked, now that I was looking for it, completely exhausted. Maybe finding Erida had been harder than he made it sound, notwithstanding the bumps and bruises.

We updated Gavin on the way back to the store; then he, Liam, and Burke talked through the ins and outs of Containment bounties, strategies for locating Reveillon members in a city as big as New Orleans—with a million places to hide.

"Thanks for the ride, Burke," I said when he pulled up in front of Royal Mercantile. "You want to come in?"

He smiled, shook his head. "Thanks, but I need to get to the Cabildo. We've got shipments coming in and convoys heading out, so I need to get my people prepared."

"Stay safe out there," Liam said, tapping the side of the jeep.

Burke gave a salute and headed down Royal.

Gavin stretched his arms over his head, showing just enough abs to prove he and Liam also had good definition in common. "I am starving. Who's got eats?"

Liam looked at him. "Your apartment is down the street. Why don't you go get something?"

He grinned. "Because I haven't been home in two weeks, there was boudin in the fridge, and the power's probably gone off more than once."

Liam and I both made faces of disgust.

"Your apartment is going to need fumigating," I said.

"It's going to need an exorcism," Gavin said, opening the door to Royal Mercantile, and holding it open so Liam and I could go inside. "Which is why I'd love to share a meal with two of my favorite people."

I shook my head, glanced at Liam. "As his older brother, you should have done a better job teaching him how to lie."

Liam snorted. "Consider who he just escorted to New Orleans. It's unlikely he'd take advice from me, no matter how good."

Gavin turned, walked backward through the store. "Technically, she challenged me. No respectable man could say no to that."

"Since when are you respectable?" Tadji said, stepping in front of us.

"Long time no see," Gavin said, giving her a hug. He walked into the store, took a look around. "Claire, I like what you've done with the place."

"That's all Tadji," I said. The store looked the same as it had last night, which relieved me more than it should have. I guessed I still needed my comfort zone.

There weren't any customers in the store. "Slow day?" I asked Tadji.

"No," she said with a smug smile. "Check the receipts."

That was an offer I couldn't refuse, so I walked to the counter and flipped through the stack, calculating them mentally.

Then I stared at her. "Are you serious?"

She put a hand at her waist, made a bow. "I am good."

"You are a freaking genius." I held up a receipt. "You even sold two walking sticks!"

She nodded, her expression sobering. "People are nervous about the attack on Devil's Isle. I reminded folks they made good weapons in a pinch."

"They'd be great weapons with a little training," Gavin said, leaning on the counter.

"Maybe you could offer a class," Liam said.

"Maybe I could."

"Should I ask about . . . ?" Tadji began, and drew a circle in the air around Gavin's face.

"It speaks for itself," Liam said. "He got himself beaten."

"I chose to fight an incredibly sexy and skilled woman for the challenge of it."

Tadji looked dubious. "And how did she fare?"

"Better than him," Liam said, and pointed to the paper bag on the counter. "Let's move to other topics. I brought that in this morning."

I hadn't noticed him bring it in, but I knew what bags like that usually held. "Is that what I think it is?"

He uncurled the top, pushed it toward me. Two rounds of crusty bread sat inside. Eleanor's bread, if I was any judge. The woman had an amazing hand with flour.

"Oh yes," I said, realizing I hadn't eaten anything all day. "Please tell me this is lunch."

"And that you're willing to share?" Tadji asked, hands pressed together in hope.

"Of course he is," I answered for him. "I think I have some pea-nut butter. We could make a meal out of that."

Liam made a sound of disgust. "This bread is not for peanut butter."

"There's nothing wrong with peanut butter," I said, heading to the kitchen. God knows I'd eaten and sold enough of it.

Liam followed me. "Bread this good deserves more than chewed-up peanuts."

There was a lot of conviction in his voice. "That doesn't ade-quately capture the glory that is shelf-stable peanut butter. And you sound a little bitter."

I walked to the refrigerator, pulled out the bottle of iced tea. Sniffed, just in case it had gone bad in the night. It smelled fine, which was our primary food safety test these days.

"I once spent two weeks on a run near Monroe in August, ate peanut butter every day," Liam said. "Can't even look at it now."

"I could eat it by the spoonful."

"That's because you're a redhead."

I gave him a look. "I'm pretty sure there's no correlation there." I pulled open the nearest cabinet, took out a bulk jar of peanut butter, and scanned the shelves. "Now, what else do we have?"

Ever helpful, Liam opened another cabinet, produced a roll of duct tape. "Why is this in a kitchen cabinet?"

I took it from him, put it back in its spot, closed the cabinet again. "It's in every room in the building, as it should be. Duct tape cures all ills." I found a jar of anchovies, held it out.

Liam looked absolutely disgusted. His being naturally gorgeous, the expression still looked pretty good on him. "No."

Frowning, I looked over packages of MREs, dried beans, rice, cornmeal. A slender jar of sun-dried tomatoes hiding in the back of the cabinet got a thumbs-up, so I put it with the pile. "Someday I'd like to have a big kitchen. All the bells and whistles."

"Is that because you cook, or you want to have a pantry full of food?"

"Mostly the food."

Liam could cook. We'd shared roasted chicken one night at his place in Devil's Isle.

"Feel free to take a look," I said, and waved game-show-style to invite him to review our options.

He stepped in front of me, his big body leaving that cologne lingering behind him. His Henley was fitted enough that it snugged against the taut muscles of his back, then curved into a perfectly bitable ass. I wanted to put my hand in the hollow of his back, feel strength and muscle shift and contract beneath my fingers.

"Don't you think?" he said.

I blinked, realizing I hadn't even heard what he'd asked me, and yanked back my hand.

Liam glanced over his shoulder. "You okay?"

"Fine," I said, turning to face the other side of the kitchen while my blush faded. "Just thinking about apples. I should have grabbed a few when I was in Algiers." It was a cover, but it happened to be true. Next time Malachi and I practiced, maybe.

I grabbed a butter knife. "Why do you think Erida's here?"

"I don't know. Things are getting dangerous. Maybe he's calling his people home."

Tadji pushed the curtain aside. "You two ready? We're starving out here."

"On our way," I said, and we gathered our bounty.

We had iced tea, amazing bread, decent peanut butter, and a surprisingly delicious tomato spread that Gavin put together from the sun-dried tomatoes, salt, and olive oil. The latter was one of the few "gourmet" ingredients I could get relatively easily onto the Zone caravans. And thinking of that, I made a note to myself to add Lizzie's orders to my next request.

But first, the mystery.

"So, what's with Erida, and your mission to bring her back?" I asked, slathering on tomato spread.

"She's a soldier; he's her commander," Gavin said, pouring iced tea into a glass. "He made it worth my while not to ask questions."

"He paid you?" I asked, frowning. How did an angel get money?

"He did. I'm guessing there are human sympathizers with funds," he said to my unspoken question.

"I bet Malachi has something specific in mind," I said, picking a piece of bread from the shard in my hand. "Maybe he's planning for what I saw on the other side of the Veil."

The Veil had passed over me at the Memorial Battle, and I'd seen an army of Paranormals with their golden armor and shields, including a warrior on her steed, clearly eager for battle.

"Maybe," Gavin said. "I left before the bombing, so it's likely not related to Reveillon."

Tadji frowned. "But the Veil's closed, right? So why would that matter?"

I didn't know the answer to that, which was probably for the best, I thought, slathering peanut butter on bread. Unfortunately, while peanut butter was great, and Eleanor's bread was great, peanut butter and Eleanor's bread were not great together. They somehow managed to bring out the worst in each other. Like Gavin and Liam, I thought with a smile. And the joke almost made the gluey texture worth it.

"Why are you smiling?" Liam asked, eyes narrowed.

It was a good minute before I could unstick my mouth to answer. "Because this is delicious."

Liam's gaze was direct. "Liar."

"It's practically Christmas dinner," I said without much enthusiasm, picking up another slathered hunk.

"I wish we still had Christmas," Gavin said, crossing his ankles on the empty chair beside him.

"We do have Christmas," Liam said, and kicked his feet off. "Get your feet off the furniture."

Gavin put his feet down but slouched in his chair to get comfortable. "I know we still have the day, the holiday. But it doesn't mean the same thing anymore. Call it consumerism or whatever, but there was something magical about Santa Claus, stockings, presents."

"There was something literally magical," Tadji said, counting them off on her fingers. "Magical elf sweatshop. Flying reindeer. Corpulent bearded man who fits in chimneys. Ability to visit every house in the world in the span of a single night. Automatically knows who's been naughty and nice."

Gavin snorted. "Maybe he had magic monitors, 'cause that sounds like Containment."

"Amen," Liam said.

I smiled at them. "Did you celebrate with Eleanor?"

"Our entire family," Liam said, crossing his arms on the table. "Eleanor spoiled us at Christmas. She was frugal for an Arsenault— as far as that goes—but when the holidays came around, she'd have boxes of presents for me, Gavin, Gracie." Grief shadowed his face at the mention of his sister, but he shook it off. "Did you ever drive by the Arsenault house?"

"Everybody drove by the Arsenault house," Tadji said.

That was Eleanor's home on Esplanade Ridge, which had burned to the ground during the war. Every Christmas, Eleanor put on a monumental holiday display—thousands of lights, animatronic animals, a live Nativity scene, and a visiting Santa Claus. Neighbors fussed about the traffic, but that didn't stop her. She said Christmas was for kids, and she made the displays bigger every year.

"Did y'all see the polar bear in the bikini?" Gavin asked.

"That was hard to forget," Tadji said. "Didn't some morals council throw a fit about it?"

"Yep, did," Gavin said with a slow and satisfied grin. "Eleanor had asked us for ideas for the display that year. I drew Paulette the Polar Bear, complete with bikini and"—he held rounded hands in front of his chest. "Sure enough, she had a light board made."

"Part of me wants to ask why you drew a polar bear in a bikini," I said. "And part of me already knows the answer."

"Polar bears live in the snow," Gavin said. "If they want to relax by the ocean, they're going to do it in a bikini just like anyone else."

I narrowed my gaze at him. "I can't find the hole in that logic, although I'm pretty sure there is one."

The bell on the door jingled and I sat up straight, remembering we were sitting in a retail establishment.

"It's just Gunnar," Gavin said, glancing lazily over at the door and then back again.

"Good to see you, too," Gunnar said, walking toward us. He looked a little less polished than he had that morning, his hair a little more rakish, fatigues a little more lived-in beneath a camouflage vest he hadn't worn that morning. "When did you get back?"

"Today," Gavin said, hand half covering his mouth as he chewed another piece of bread.

"You look like shit."

"Aw, now you're just being rude," Liam said, reaching out to ruffle his brother's hair. "He can't help the way he looks."

Gavin looked at me. "Is he always this funny?"

"Yes. The laughter died long ago."

"Har-har," Liam said this time, reaching past me to grab a piece of bread from the tray.

"And you're having dinner without me." Gunnar pulled off the vest, which was heavy and lined, and put it on the back of the chair.

It was a flak vest, I realized, and couldn't tear my gaze away.

"It's just a precaution," Gunnar said, looking around the table before his gaze landed on mine. "We haven't yet found the Reveillon members who escaped the bombing, so we're being careful."

"You're searching door to door?" Liam asked.

"Every door in Devil's Isle," Gunnar said, taking a seat. "Quadrant-by-quadrant searches, but we haven't found anyone yet. Evidence they've been hiding—empty water bottles, protein bar wrappers— but no people yet."

"Are they waiting for an opportunity to escape," Liam asked, "or an opportunity to strike?"

"Either. Both." Gunnar scrubbed his hands through his dark, wavy hair, then linked them behind his head. "We don't know if they ran into the neighborhood to avoid capture, or because that's what they were supposed to do. If it was on purpose, they haven't done anything yet."

"What would they do?" I wondered.

Gunnar glanced at me, dread in his eyes. "If they bomb indiscriminately, pretty much anything." He looked at Liam. "At the risk of sounding like a total fucking hypocrite, considering who I work for, have you considered moving Eleanor out?"

Liam nodded. "I broached the issue. She wasn't interested."

Gavin made a sound that was half laugh, half rueful sigh. "And one doesn't tell Eleanor Arsenault what to do."

"Pretty much." Liam pushed the tray of bread toward him. "You need food?"

Gunnar held up a hand. "No, thanks. I was teasing. We spent the morning reviewing physical evidence. It doesn't do much for the appetite."

"Any new developments there?" Liam asked.

"Not as of yet. The forensic experts are running tests, doing the things they do." He glanced at Liam. "Do you want to look through the photographs?"

"No," Liam said. "But I will." He looked at me, and I shook my head.

I could be brave when necessary. But since I didn't have any particular forensic skills, didn't know anything about explosives, I'd sit this one out. There were some things I didn't need to see again.

Gunnar pulled a green folder from his messenger bag, passed it to Liam. The folder was marked with the Containment logo, TOP SECRET, stamped in red across the front.

"You have clearance?" I asked.

"I do," Liam said, flipping through the folder. I kept my gaze on his face, on the shifting expressions. Disgust, pity, fear, sadness, rage. Each time he turned over a new photograph, the course of emotions crossed his face.

And I saw it the moment he stopped, frowned, squinted at one of them. And then he looked up at me. "Do you have a magnifying glass?"

I blinked at the request. "Um, yeah." I'd set it out for the clock repairs. I walked to the counter, grabbed the brass-handled tool, and offered it.

"Thanks, Sherlock," he said, eyebrows lifted as he looked it over. "Do you have one of those earflap hats?"

"It belonged to the store," I said, knowing perfectly well that he'd said it to lighten the mood.

He turned back to the photograph, centering the magnifying glass over a bit of skin on the deceased's arm. "There's a mark here."

"What kind of mark?" Gunnar asked.

"I'm not sure. It's on"—he looked up at us, then down again—"it's on one of the bombers' arms."

My stomach rolled. The arm had clearly been separated from the rest of him or her. And it hadn't been a good separation.

"A tattoo?" Gunnar asked, moving closer.

"Maybe?"

Tadji edged in behind them, her eyes widening and lips thinning at the shot, the violence and gore. But she kept her composure. "That's not a tattoo. Or not just."

Gunnar looked up at her, frowned. "What do you mean?"

"It's a Couturie code."

"Camp Couturie?" I asked. Camp Couturie had been the largest refugee camp in New Orleans—hundreds of acres of tents in what had once been City Park. People still lived there; it had become its own neighborhood.

"Is it?" Liam asked, leaning down to check the mark again.

The ink was blurred with time, and looked hand-drawn on top of that. The tattoo probably hadn't been very crisp even when it was new.

"It's the Couturie X-Code," Tadji said, tracing a fingertip over the uneven lines.

Like during Katrina, X-Codes had been used during the war to mark a house that had been searched for survivors. They'd also been used to create an address system in the camp, which took up a lot of real estate. Containment thought it helped give a sense of stability to the refugees.

"Huh," Gunnar said. "That's a damn good catch. Maybe Reveillon's been recruiting at the camp."

Gunnar took the folder back from Liam, scribbled a note inside it, closed it again. "I'm going to have to talk to the Commandant. Take a trip out there, get a look at the camp and a feel for what's going on."

"You can't go," I said.

Gunnar turned back to look at me. "Why?"

"You can't just walk around Camp Couturie. You're too conspicuous. Everyone in town knows who you are, and they'll know why you're there, why you're poking around. If there are Reveillon members at the camp, you won't be able to get any information about them."

"She probably has a point," Liam said.

Gunnar narrowed his eyes. "And what are you proposing, mistress of strategy?"

I smiled, walked to the aisle of the store where food and produce were organized, and picked up a basket of beets and greens I'd grown in the community garden on top of the former Florissant Hotel.

I walked back, put it on the table. "I'll go. Because I'm in retail."

Gunnar went quiet, eyebrows drawn together as they did when he was considering. "The camp has a farmers' market."

I nodded. "Every day of the week. It's open to the public, and to whatever vendors want to set up shop. I've only been there a couple of times. It was a lot of bartering, and I'm not really in the market for more dry goods." I gestured to the store's interior. "I'm full up, so I haven't been in a while. But I can go now, take some extra vegetables, do a little trading, and do a little recon."

"You're a civilian."

I smiled. "No, I'm a bounty hunter in training, with a Devil's Isle pass to prove it."

Gunnar was quiet for a moment, tapping his fingers together. Then he looked at Liam. "You'd go with her?"

"Not that I need an escort," I muttered, but I wouldn't have gone without Liam. It's not like I could just whip out my magic, especially when facing down magicphobes.

"I could do that," Liam said, glancing at the basket. "We play retailers trying to get rid of some stock, make some cash. See what we see."

"And if the opportunity permits, ask some very subtle questions," Gunnar said. "I'll have to talk to the Commandant, the Joint Ops team. We've got all available resources deployed, so we're running lean until PCC can get more troops across the border."

"How's that going?" Liam asked.

"Not great. Outfit out of Branson was attacked last night. They were attacked coming into Arkansas. PCC hoped a mountain pass would be an easier approach. There was a band camped out on the border."

"They can't have people along the Zone's entire border all the time," Tadji said. "That's impossible."

Gunnar nodded. "Exactly."

"You think they've got somebody on the inside," Liam said.

"I do think," Gunnar said. "And I think it has to be someone in Washington, someone at PCC who's sympathetic, who has access to troop movement information. Or, if not on the inside, a very talented hacker or spy. But that investigation is several pay grades above mine. We're assured they're looking into it."

Liam snorted. "That sounds like bureaucratic bullshit."

"I don't disagree. But it's another reason why your taking a look at Couturie would be beneficial."

"They won't be prepared for it," I said, and Gunnar nodded.

"What about me?" Gavin asked.

"You have an apartment to fumigate," Liam said, and Tadji and Gunnar both wrinkled their noses.

"Do I want to know why?" she asked.

"You do not," I promised.

Liam glanced at me. "Are you going to make me sell beets?"

"And collards." I waved a bunch of leaves at him. "Delicious, delicious collards."

"Ham hocks are the only good things about collards," Liam said, but fished his keys from his pockets, put them on the table. "Get what you need, and let's head out."

It took a little more than an hour to get the okay from the Commandant. Technically, we didn't need permission to drive across New Orleans and sell some beets, and the Reveillon bounty was still in effect, which made its members fair play for Liam. But we also didn't want to make things worse for Containment—or spook Reveillon.

"Joint Ops thinks it's a long shot," Gunnar said. "That the tattoo only indicates one of the Reveillon bombers lived at Camp Couturie previously, not that it's now the Reveillon HQ. They also think the odds of actually finding something in the 'canvas labyrinth' are low enough that it's not worth the effort to move an active team from their search quadrant into the park."

Liam smiled. "But we're expendable?"

Gunnar's features went stony. "Not even funny as a joke. Joint Ops is playing the odds, and the camp isn't the priority." He looked from Liam to me. "But that doesn't mean you shouldn't be careful."

"When have I ever been less than careful?" I asked.

The look on their faces was less than flattering.

"So," Liam began, when we climbed into his rickety truck. "Tell me about this practice with Malachi."

I guessed Tadji and Gunnar had been able to bait him.

"We practiced," I said. "Hence the name."

"What?" he asked, driving through French Quarter streets that would have once been full of people shopping, drinking, and dancing in Second Lines.

"Generally, anticipating the unexpected. And he gave me homework."

Liam pulled onto Rampart. "What kind of homework?"

"The kind during which I practice my magic." I slid him a glance. "Why are you giving me the third degree?"

His jaw worked as he eased the truck around a tree that had fallen into the street. There was no road crew in New Orleans these days. We'd have to tell Gunnar about the obstacle, if he didn't already know.

"Because he is who he is."

"Because he's a Paranormal? You sound like Reveillon."

"You know that's not what I meant. Because he is who he is. And because you are who you are."

Slowly, I turned back to him, eyes narrowed. "What is that supposed to mean?"

"It means you should be careful. He's powerful." He paused. "And he looks at you . . . like he covets you."

That had me staring at the street again with enormous eyes. It wasn't that he didn't like Malachi—he didn't trust him, at least not with me.

Good, I decided, when I'd processed the feelings. Liam was wrong—dead wrong—but I didn't mind if he felt as unbalanced as I did. I was unbalanced, after all, because of him.

"He doesn't covet me," I said. "He thinks I'm a novelty—a human with totally green magic who he can teach and observe. And he'll keep teaching me until I'm not a threat to him, myself, or anyone else."

Liam tapped his fingers on the steering well. "All right, then."

"Damn right it's all right," I muttered. "I'm the boss of me."

He snorted. "You should probably tell Gunnar that. He didn't get the memo."

He was quiet for a moment, then groped blindly for something beneath the front seat, pulled out an old beige cassette tape. For the first time, I realized he'd added an old tape player to the truck.

"I see you share my love of antiques," I said.

By way of answer, Liam popped the tape into the slot. "Born on the Bayou" spilled into the car.

"All right, then," I said, and relaxed back against the seat. "Apology accepted."

And with heat and music and sunshine, we drove.

City Park was enormous, more than a thousand acres of meadows, trees, trails, and ponds. It had once housed the New Orleans Botanical Garden, the New Orleans Museum of Art, an amusement park, and a wooded area known as Couturie Forest—but that had been before the war.

Liam drove around the park to get the lay of the land. Nothing much had changed in the months since I was here, except that everything looked a little more worn. The white canvas tents—seven years since they'd been put up by FEMA, the military, the Red Cross—were still in neat rows, but the canvas was patched and dingy. The ground between the tents had been worn to dirt, and electrical wires skipped from tent to tent. Someone had figured out how to tie the tents to the grid, for what good that did.

In contrast to the still-straight rows, nature had crept in at the edges of the park, softening the lines of what had been a long rectangle of ponds and meadows.

Liam had turned off the music, the world outside quiet as we drove through. "The camp has a mayor," I said, gestured to the small stone cabin where he lived. "I met him the last time I was here, and I don't see him as being involved with Reveillon. He's a belly laugher."

Liam chuckled. "A what?"

"A belly laugher." I put a hand on my stomach, offered a round, hearty laugh. "He has a belly, and a very big laugh."

"So Santa Claus runs Camp Couturie," Liam said. "Appropriate, since we were just hoping for Christmas."

He pulled the truck off into the edge of the grass near the circular Popp Fountain, which had become the formal entrance to the camp. It didn't run anymore, and someone had stuck a hand-drawn WELCOME TO CAMP COUTURIE sign into the dry pipe in the middle.

We got out of the truck, walked around to the tailgate. I waited while Liam untied the rope to lower it. I pulled a pencil out of the cigar box I'd brought to make change, wound my hair through it.

"Hot," I said as Liam's glance skittered from my hair back to the truck.

"Very." He pulled the boxes toward us. "You know where we're going?"

"I do. And it's my store, so I'm in charge."

"Yes, ma'am," he said, with a drawl.

I just rolled my eyes. "There's a different attitude here. Follow my lead."

"Don't take ridiculous chances."

"We live in a war zone by choice," I pointed out, hefting a box. "We take chances every day."

The market was held at the fountain, between the columns that surrounded it. Tables filled the gaps where some of the columns had been, which make it look a little like Stonehenge. We walked around to look for an empty table, passing collections of old clothes, electronics, vetiver leaves and roots, plastic junk, and pretty much everything else.

On the other side of the fountain, where the lines of tents began, the curious and suspicious watched us from doorways and plastic patio furniture. Not unlike Devil's Isle, but I doubted they'd appreciate the comparison.

I nodded at those we passed, but I didn't smile. I hadn't been here often enough for them to recognize me, and smiling strangers walking through the compound would look suspicious. I tried to look uninterested in the tents and focused on finding a spot.

We found a table with a few inches of shade, at least for a little while. I put my box on the table, gestured Liam to do the same.

"Afternoon," said the woman at the next table, suspicion narrowing her dark eyes. She sat on a folding stool, a ball of purple yarn in her lap and two busy knitting needles in her pale hands. She wore jeans and a faded LSU T-shirt—definitely not the tunics worn by Reveillon.

I almost dismissed the knitting, but the bright gleam of metal had me looking again. They weren't needles—they were arrows, long and golden. She'd turned Para weapons into craft tools. I'd read Dickens in high school before the war, and there was something very Madame Defarge about that.

I took two Royal Mercantile aprons out of the box, passed one to Liam. I pulled the top canvas loop over my head and doubled the long straps around my waist.

"Good afternoon," I said, then glanced around. "Rule used to be tables were first come, first served, but it's been a few months since I've been here. Do I need to check in with someone?"

"You find an empty table, it's yours."

"Good," I said, and began taking beets and bundles of greens, the stems tied with twine, from the box and spreading them across the table.

She took in the Royal Merc logo, put down her knitting. "I'm Lonnie. Lonnie Dear."

"Claire and Liam," I said. "We came up from the Quarter." I put my hands on my hips and looked down at the spread of vegetables. "I haven't been able to convince the Containment types that collards are good for them."

"Collards are good eating," she said, nodding with approval that I'd been trying to spread the gospel.

I glanced at her table, which was loaded with rows of cassette and video tapes. "Hey, Liam," I said, and gestured. "You can find something different for the ride home."

"You criticizing my taste in music?" he asked, smiling at Lonnie and walking around her table to get a look at the merchandise.

Lonnie watched him, her expression slightly awed, like she was viewing a fine piece of sculpture for the first time.

Been there, sister, I thought.

Liam picked up a tape. "What's an Ace of Bass?"

"It means you should stick with CCR," I said, and smiled as a girl emerged from the tents, crossed the twenty or so yards between us to look over the vegetables. She was thin but well toned, her body in that not-quite stage between woman and child, her hair in braids across her dark shoulders. No tunic for her, either. She wore cutoff jeans and a worn tank top.

"How much for the beets?"

"Two for a dollar," I said with a smile.

She nodded soberly, pulled a dollar from her front pocket, offered it to me.

"You need a bag?" I asked.

She shook her head, picked up two beets, and scampered back to the tents.

First purchase a success. Now we just needed some information.

"The Eagles," Liam said proudly, putting his new purchase carefully in the box.

I couldn't help laughing. "If it survived the war, I think it could survive a trip home from the market."

"No harm in being careful," he said, coming to stand beside me again, hands behind his back. "I'm ready for the retail onslaught."

"Good to know," I said with a smile.

"You hear about that trouble in the Quarter yesterday?"

I glanced at Lonnie, heart tripping. That was the kind of question that opened doors. "We were there," I said, and let her see the truth of it—the horror of it—in my eyes.

"Folks are talking about it," she said. "Everyone's got an opinion."

A leading question, but an understandable one.

"That's New Orleans," Liam said noncommittally.

"What kinds of opinions do folks have?" I asked. "Seems like what happened was pretty cut-and-dried. Lot of folks died."

Her arrow needles clacked together. "Well, but none would be dead if it weren't for the Paranormals."

"You mean if they hadn't attacked us? Sure. That was the catalyst."

She seemed satisfied by my answer.

"I'm surprised word got out here so fast." I wasn't really surprised; Gavin had found out about it in the hinterlands, after all. I wanted to know how she'd found out. Had reports traveled, or had folks in Camp Couturie known what was going to happen?

"People talk," Lonnie said, and this time, there was a hint of suspicion in her eyes. "I mean, it's good you have a solid communication network. It just takes a while even in the Quarter to get news about anything."

"Except Containment," Liam added, his voice carrying a perfect, subtle edge of disgust. "With the Cabildo, barracks, Devil's Isle, we always know what they're about."

"We hear things," Lonnie said. "News gets here eventually. As for living in the Quarter, I certainly couldn't do it."

"Why's that?" Liam asked.

"Being monitored all the time. It's practically martial law being so close to the prison. To Containment."

Weren't there magic monitors in Camp Couturie? I glanced around, and didn't see the familiar black boxes. But Containment had installed them even through rural areas, so maybe the Campers had taken them down. Or maybe the camp had simply been forgotten.

The woman executed what looked like a very complicated loop and twist of the yarn, then put it down again. "I'm a good Christian woman and I don't take with magic. But humans weren't to blame for what happened, for the war, and we aren't children. We don't need cameras on us twenty-four-seven. That's fascism."

She was saying the kinds of things someone who wanted to take up arms against Containment might say. But they weren't the types of things Ezekiel had said, or the manifesto had discussed. Reveillon didn't care about privacy. They didn't care about the Constitution. They cared about annihilation.

"Can't argue with that," Liam said, stepping beside me and looking out over the camp. "It's hard to live under the scrutiny. To feel normal. I guess you have more freedom out here. To live the way you want."

"We don't have much," she agreed. "But we have our freedom, and we have our community. Don't need much else than that."

So Lonnie was content with her lot. Did everyone in Camp Couturie feel that way?

People milled around the table, probably as much to get a look at us as to inspect the things we'd brought to sell. I sold a few more beets and a few bunches of collards, and traded some for two Mason jars of cane syrup, a spool of handmade hemp twine, and a small paper bag of deer jerky. You never knew what you'd find in the country.

As they inspected me, I inspected them. None wore tunics, but maybe those had just been "special occasion" outfits for Reveillon. These people looked like they lived off the land, and that land was hard. Lean bodies and faces that worked hard for what they had, to make a life in a place that had only been meant for temporary living.

They whispered about the bombing as they moved from table to table, but no one confessed to knowing about it before the fact, or knowing anyone involved. On the other hand, no one spoke out against them, either.

Still . . . I had a feeling something was brimming here, something under the surface that we couldn't see. Something had made the Campers tense. Maybe the attack had made people nervous, afraid war was coming again. I didn't think that was the only issue—I had a sense emotions ran much deeper than that—but we'd given it three hours, and we hadn't seen any hard evidence.

I got a brainstorm and dug my fingers into the center of a beet I'd cut open as a sample, coating my hands in dirt and juice. I made a show of wiping my hands on my apron, holding up stained fingers and dirty fingernails.

"Damn it," I muttered, frowning as I looked at them. "I should have brought a scrubber." I put my hands down again, looked apologetically at Lonnie. "I don't suppose there's a place I could wash up? Maybe a spigot where I could rinse off my hands before we head back?"

She looked at me for a minute, then pointed toward an alley between tents that led deeper into the camp. "Wash station's down that road. Four lanes in, and take a right."

"Thank you," I said, showing plenty of relief. I looked down at my hands. "Looks like the first time I dyed towels. That was a big, bloody, beety mess."

Lonnie chuckled lightly, and I turned back to Liam, so only he could see my face.

"I'll be fine," I mouthed. His face showed clearly that he didn't like the idea of our separating. I understood the sentiment, but I had a purpose, which I was sure he'd figured out. A trip to the wash station would at least get us a look inside the camp—maybe the only one we'd get today. And we'd invested too much time to walk away with no information.

"I'll go ahead and pack up what's left," Liam said.

"I appreciate you," I said cheerfully, then headed for the labyrinth of canvas.

The "road" was about fifteen feet wide and lined with canvas tents that faced one another. The tents were the same—square canvas with a pitched roof and a roll-up door in the center. But most of them had been fixed up or customized. Many were "shingled" with pieces of plywood; a few had wind vanes. Plywood had also been propped upright between some of them, probably to add at least a little privacy. Tarps were thrown over a few tents that had been connected together, their side panels cut and sewn open into hallways to make bigger spaces. Tidy rows of bricks peeked beneath some of the tents, where people had paved over dirt floors.

I kept my eyes peeled for anything unusual, tried to stay alert to any suspicious sounds—anti-Para chants, bomb-making supplies, general plans for mayhem and chaos. Instead, I heard the sounds of normal life—babies crying, people laughing and arguing, music, snoring. People probably borrowed sugar or eggs, fought about noise and smells and space, worried together about heat and food and hurricanes.

It seemed impossible to be alone in Camp Couturie, while most of the Zone had the opposite problem. But no one seemed to take any notice of me.

I counted down the lanes, turned when I reached the fourth. The tents should have had X-Code addresses, but they'd long ago faded.

A few yards down, the space between the tents had been widened into a square. A contraption of steel and pipes stood in the middle, with spigots of varying heights. A boardwalk kept the ground from getting too muddy.

I stepped onto the boardwalk, dunked hands into water that was ice-cold despite the heat. I washed my hands slowly, taking care to scrub under each fingernail, while I looked around, scanned the tents around me for any sign of Reveillon. Once again, I saw nothing. I turned off the water, dried my hands on the back of my apron.

A large rubber ball rolled past, and a boy of six or seven came running behind it, a grin on his cute, freckled face. He had brown hair and pale skin, and a gap between his two front teeth. He wore dirty jeans and a short-sleeved Saints T-shirt. He picked up the ball, smiled instinctively when he turned my way . . . and then froze.

I could practically see "stranger danger" written on his face.

"Hi," I said, and waved a little.

The boy stared at me like I was a monster from a foreign land. If his world was limited to Camp Couturie, to familiar faces in close proximity, I might have been.

He turned, grabbed up the ball, and sprinted back in the direction he'd come from.

I was here with permission, but if he sounded the alarm, I might not have much time. I kept an innocent smile on my face, turned, and walked back in the direction I'd come—and "missed" the turn that would have led back to the fountain.

I passed one lane, then two, then three. If Reveillon had a presence in Camp Couturie, they weren't advertising it. Maybe we'd been wrong about the tattoo's meaning, or Ezekiel was smart enough to recruit and spread his gospel quietly. Loud enough to pull in members. Not so loud that he could be easily found by Containment.

And then I stopped short, glancing into the open flap of the tent I'd just passed. It was a rectangle of space with a wooden-plank floor, a big rug thrown over it. Ladder-back chair in one corner, simple bed in another. No blankets on the bed, nothing personal in the tent. It didn't look like anyone lived here, but if that was the case, why hadn't the neighboring tents taken the floorboards? The rug? The chair?

After ensuring that the coast was clear, I stepped closer, peering deeper into the shadowed darkness . . . and spotted blood on the floorboards. Large drops and long streaks, as if someone had been dragged across the floor. And on the opposite wall, smeared in blood or mud or both, was a single word: EDEN. Ezekiel had said Reveillon would bring about a new Eden. Was this supposed to be a reminder?

"You shouldn't be here."

I jerked back, turned to find a woman behind me. She was pale and thin, with delicate features and brown hair pulled into a topknot. Her bangs were long, and almost covered the bruise around her left eye.

And she wore the same homespun fabric as the Reveillon members.

I pasted on a clumsy grin. "I'm sorry—a lady at the market showed me where to wash up, and I am completely turned around. I'm trying to get back to the fountain?"

She watched me for a moment, fear and wariness in her eyes. I didn't think I was the one she was afraid of, and I put money on the possibility Ezekiel—or those like him—might have been. But then she nodded.

"I'll walk you back."

"I'd appreciate it," I said, and fell into step beside her. Her movements were swift, every step delicate, like she was used to being quiet, trying not to make a sound. Trying not to be noticed.

The road she'd picked, probably on purpose, faced the back sides of two rows of tents, so I couldn't see into them.

"There are roads and lanes," she said. "Roads run north-south. Lanes run east-west." That was undoubtedly a federal system created by someone who wasn't from New Orleans. Otherwise they'd have been lakeside-riverside, and downtown-uptown.

"Right," I said. "I think I came down a road, then turned right onto a lane? But I got turned around."

"Yeah, you passed your turn."

"How do you remember where you're going?" I asked. "All the tents look the same."

"They aren't the same when you've been here long enough."

I guessed the plywood and tarps became markers, signaling where you were.

"Why not move into empty houses around the city?" I wondered, thinking how little privacy they had, how unprotected they were from bad weather—or anything else.

"Houses belong to other people," she said simply, turning again onto a wider road, this time faced by the fronts of several tents. "Camp C belongs to us."

A thin man with dark, weathered skin and deep lines around his face looked out from the tent flap, nodded as we walked by. The woman nodded back.

I couldn't really argue with that. What was Royal Mercantile but something—the one thing—that truly belonged to me? "I understand. Have you lived here long?"

"Since it opened. I was part of the First Wave."

They were the first group of New Orleans evacuees. They'd lost their homes in Uptown in one of the first attacks of the war, when a flight of Valkyries burned a path through the neighborhood. The attack was only a couple of days into the war, which meant she'd been here since the beginning. I guessed her age at twenty-four, the same as mine. And I guessed our last seven years had been very, very different. Tadji had been right about that.

I blinked as we emerged into the space near the fountain. I was relieved to be in the open again. Community or not, there was something unsettling about being in that labyrinth. I wasn't the only one who felt relief—it was clear in Liam's expression.

"We made it!" I said cheerfully, and turned to the girl. "Thank you for the help. I was getting a little claustrophobic in there."

She smiled lightly. If she worried that I'd seen too much, she didn't show it. "It can be disorienting at first. It gets easier."

I was happy to take her word for it. "You know, I've got some extra greens we didn't sell." I walked the rest of the way to the table, giving Liam a little nod of acknowledgment, and picked up the last bundle. I turned and held them out to her, looked pleadingly. "I don't suppose you'd be willing to take them off my hands? There's not really much of a market for them in the Quarter."

She'd done me a kindness. And she looked like she needed them, and didn't have the resources or confidence to ask.

"Okay," she said more confidently. "If you're sure you won't use them."

"I won't," I assured her as she took them. "You're doing me a favor."

"Greens are disgusting," Liam said, stepping behind me, offering her a smile. "That's why nobody will touch them."

"No," she said with a smile. "A piece of ham, maybe, and some pepper vinegar. They're delicious, and the pot liquor that's left over will cure pretty much anything."

"I'll just trust you on that," Liam said with a grin.

"Hey!"

The girl's expression turned blank, and she cradled the greens against her chest, looked back toward the tents at the woman who'd called her name—one of the women who'd accompanied Ezekiel in the parade.

Fingers hidden by the table, I tapped Liam's leg. He nodded.

She looked back at us, then dropped her gaze and jogged back to the tents, disappeared inside them.

"And that would be our cue to exit," he whispered. "She recognizes us and reports back, and we're going to lose our window to get out of here."

Spurred by the comment, I stood and yawned, stretching my arms over my head. "All righty," I said, glancing at Liam. "I think I'm ready to head back to the Quarter. You ready to go, or did you want to look around? Find some more forty-year-old music?"

"'Fraid I'm broke," he said with a smile, then loaded the few last vegetables into the box.

I wanted to leave them on the table for folks who needed them but who didn't have anything to trade. But even assuming the residents' pride would have allowed them to take what was left, I was playing retailer. Giving away the goods would have looked suspicious.

We untied our aprons and put them into a box. I looked at the woman beside us. "Thanks for your help. Hope you had a productive market day."

"They always are," she said, gaze wholly on her knitting now as she added a stripe to her project in yarn the color of blood.

CHAPTER TEN

"**W**hat did you find?" Liam asked, nodding collegially at a couple we passed on the way back to the truck.

"Whole lot of nothing. The tents look mostly the same, except one that had blood on the floor, streaks like someone had been dragged out. It had been left there—untouched. And 'Eden' was written on the wall. In blood."

I hadn't been afraid when I looked at it, but the memory sent a trickle of cold sweat down my back.

"A reference to the Eden that Reveillon wants to build in the Zone?"

"That was my thought," I said. "But why empty? Why blood?"

"Maybe it's a shrine," Liam said, brow furrowed as he considered. "Maybe a Para killed someone there, and they keep it to remind people."

"Or it's a warning," I said. "The person who lived in that tent was killed, dragged out, for being opposed to the Eden plan. And the tent was left as a warning."

"There's a vibe to this place," Liam said. "Something under the surface that we aren't seeing. Something that makes them suspicious of strangers—even humans—and tense. Like they're waiting for something."

"I couldn't agree more." And it had to be a vibe, because other than the girl's homespun clothing, there was nothing here that marked it as Reveillon territory. Not that they'd be advertising it now, considering they'd killed four people, not counting their own. They had to know Containment was hunting them.

We reached the truck and put the boxes on the still-open tailgate, slid them toward the back.

I turned to Liam, looked up at him. "The woman who led me out of the tents, and the one who called her back. They wore the Reveillon clothes. We could go back in, grab them, try to take them back to the Cabildo."

Liam slammed the gate into place and slipped knots through the rope like a seasoned sailor. And then he rested an arm on the top of the tailgate.

"We could," he said, looking back at the rows of tents. "But there are almost certainly more in there. And while I'm glad you're confident in our skills, we're seriously outnumbered."

"Spoilsport."

He gave me a sardonic look. "You planning to take them out with magic? Because other than the gun in the glove box, we don't have any weapons. First lesson of poker and bounty hunting: Know when to be aggressive, and when to call in the standing army."

"I . . . am confused by the metaphor. But I take your point."

"Good. Because if I take you home with so much as a scratch, I'll have Gunnar on my ass for a week."

"Gunnar isn't my father."

Liam made a noise. "No, but he's assigned himself as your protector."

Voices lifted a few feet in front of the truck, where two men in jeans and T-shirts had begun pushing each other with hand-to-shoulder jabs. I put them in their mid-twenties, with tan skin and dark hair, both in casual clothes.

"No, fuck you," said the shorter of the two, a stockier man with a sturdy, square body.

Liam, in full alpha alert, looked up and over, watched them shout and shove, and turned his body at a slight angle, positioning himself— his body—between me and the threat.

The taller man threw up his hands, started to walk away, but apparently couldn't resist bumping the other guy with his shoulder.

"You asshole!" the shorter guy screamed, and threw the first punch.

"Morons," Liam swore, then looked at me. "Stay here." He strode forward, easily a head taller than both men. "Hey! Break it up."

I turned back to the door, and that's when Liam's voice rang out. "Claire!"

There was alarm and fear in the word, but before I could turn again, I was slammed against the truck, the door handle catching my solar plexus.

I fought for air, kicking back against the perpetrator, but he kicked the inside of my knee, and I stumbled. He grabbed my hair, pushed my face into the door window as my wrists were bound with coarse rope that bit into my skin like live wires.

"*Claire!*" Liam yelled again, fury boiling in his face as the fighters shoved him to the ground, guns pointed at his head at point-blank range. He didn't blink, didn't offer them even a glance, just kept his gaze on mine—hot and possessive and unspeakably angry.

"*Liam!*" I screamed, before darkness covered my eyes.

The fight had been a distraction, a trap.

And we'd fallen right into it.

I was wrenched backward by my hands and pulled away from the truck, shoved in the direction of the hood. They'd covered my eyes with a black cloth but hadn't tied it very tightly. If I looked down, I could see a sliver of the ground we covered as we walked back to the tents, and down a row.

"Claire!" Liam called out again, but his voice was farther away. They were separating us.

We were in trouble. Panic rose swiftly, tightening my chest so I could hear my breath whistling in and out. I wanted to sink to the ground, to clutch at dirt and grass until I could breathe again, until I was safe again.

Stop it, I ordered myself. *Stop freaking out. That won't help you or him. You have to stay calm. You just need a plan.* I just had to take this step by step, be as careful as I could, and take whatever opportunities I could to get away, to get free.

Notice everything, I ordered myself, and realized the ground was hard-packed beneath my feet, and a baby was crying somewhere nearby.

I was in the tents again. The sounds were muffled, so I was probably on one of the rows that faced the backs of the tents. There were people on each side of me, gripping my arms, guiding me down the row at a speed that had me nearly skipping to stay on my feet.

My toe caught a divot in the dirt and I flew forward, was hauled upright again before I could hit the ground. I caught a whiff of perfume to my right, the heavy and heady scents of peonies and gardenia, and the fingers that clawed into my arm were tipped by sharp nails. Probably a woman on my right. Thicker fingers on my other arm, the grip slightly stronger. Probably a man on my left.

We turned together to the right, and I was marched deeper into the field of tents. This time, we were on the door side, and I could smell and hear people nearby.

"Goddamn troublemakers," yelled an older man who stood only a couple of feet away. "Gettin' in others' business."

"Need to mind their own business," a woman agreed.

That they could see troublemaker and busybody in me—a twenty-four-year-old with beet juice still staining her hands—was remarkable. I mean, I was both of those things, but how could they have known?

Because the woman from Bourbon Street had seen me and passed the word. And like Lonnie said, news traveled. Probably spread like wildfire through the camp. I was beginning to wonder if that was the only thing that traveled. If hatred and paranoia had spread as easily, too.

We stopped, and I was heaved into a tent, the canvas flap brushing my face. I was shoved down onto a hard chair, my arms released, yanked around the chair, and tied again.

There was shuffling around me, and then silence. And then they left me to wait.

Time passed, but I couldn't tell how much. Half an hour, maybe, but it seemed interminable. I couldn't see anything except occasional shifting light, and I couldn't hear anything but occasional shuffling and whispers outside.

I was alone in a tent, probably on the edge of a row, given the relative quiet. I shook my head, trying to dislodge the cloth or shift it enough to let me peek at where I was, but that only gave me a headache.

Since that didn't work, I'd have to work on the rope around my wrists. I pulled against them until my wrists were raw, picking at the edge I could reach with a jagged fingernail. I'd broken through a few strands, but it would take hours—if not days—to make any real progress. That thought only made me panicky again.

Liam was here, somewhere. We'd find each other. And if we

didn't, Gunnar knew where we were. If we didn't come back, he'd send someone. The question was whether he could find us in the spread of Camp Couturie before things got worse . . .

There were footsteps.

I turned my face up and down, side to side, trying to figure out where they were coming from.

And then someone was beside me. Fingers grazed my cheek, and the cloth was ripped away. I winced at the light, squeezed my eyes closed to help them adjust, then blinked them slowly open again.

I was in a canvas tent, sturdy camping lanterns hung at intervals along the walls, casting shadows that jumped in the breeze.

Ezekiel stood in front of me, his face only inches from mine, the blindfold in his hand. His dark hair was damp, as was the neck of his bone-colored linen tunic. He smelled like lavender, had probably just come from a shower.

God forbid he should be unclean, I thought bitterly.

And since he looked completely unscathed, he hadn't been a bomber, and probably hadn't even followed his flock into battle. Maybe he'd watched from a safe distance, or maybe he'd come back here before it began, let them start the war on their own. The coward.

Ezekiel pulled a stool from the other side of the room, set it to face me, and took a seat, hands clasped between his knees. "Hello."

"Where is he?"

Ezekiel's smile was horribly pleasant. "This is your interrogation, Claire. You are here, and Liam is somewhere else."

"Untie me right now," I said, and kept chipping away at the rope. "We haven't done anything wrong, and you don't have any right to assault us, accost us, or hold us. We're here to sell food."

"Yes, I understand that's the story." Doubt colored each of his words.

"We are innocent. You're a killer."

Doubt transformed to outright disgust. "You are conspirators. Enablers. Liars. Traitors. You support Containment and the Paranormals, and you make it harder for real humans."

"'Real humans'? You're an egotistical sociopath."

For an instant, there was a flash of something dark and horrible in his eyes. Something hungry and eager. But it disappeared, leaving behind the shell of false compassion.

"I'm a man who has been given the gift of knowledge, of understanding. Not all believe, of course. But that's true of most of history's saviors."

"Is that what you are? A savior?"

Ezekiel leaned forward, hands on his knees. His clothes were old-fashioned, and even his body language seemed stuck in some other era. It wouldn't have surprised me if he'd accused me of being a Salem witch.

"That's my burden," he said. "To carry this message, this truth, across the Zone. Even if people don't believe me." He looked hurt, as if that lack of belief were a personal insult.

"You tell people magic is the problem, that you're the solution. And yet you stand back while they kill for you." I tilted my head at him. "Why didn't you sacrifice yourself at Devil's Isle? Because you're a coward?"

He moved so fast his hand was a blur, the *crack* of it against my cheek resounding in the quiet. Pain exploded in my cheek, and tears welled and spilled. I ignored them and kept my gaze on him.

"You have no right to show me disrespect." His jaw was tight with obvious rage.

I could taste blood, bright and coppery. "Violence is disrespectful."

He sat back in his chair again. "If you provoke a man to hit you, it's dishonest to call him violent."

I was so baffled by that justification, it took a few seconds to form a response. "And what would be honest?"

"It is necessary discipline," he said. "As for the rest, I'd think that's obvious, too. I'm the leader of this organization. The brains, the heart, the soul." He pressed his hand against his chest, his brown eyes darkening with conviction. "Without me, there is no Reveillon. I'm the vessel through which flows the truth."

Something was certainly flowing through him, but it wasn't truth. But he clearly seemed to believe what he was saying. So I tried a different tack. "Because no one else really gets it," I said, mimicking his seriousness. "Because you are the center of it, the crux."

He nodded, seemed relieved that I'd understood. "Exactly. The Zone has lived in denial for too long."

Might as well follow the train where it led, I thought. That would keep his attention off my wrists and my escape plan. "And the others don't see it. Containment doesn't see it?"

His eyes flashed again. "Without magic, Containment wouldn't exist. Containment would have no funding, no jobs, no uniforms. They have no incentive to admit the truth."

"That magic has destroyed the Zone."

"And continues to destroy."

"We don't have magic," I said. "So why are we here?"

He shook his head, made a sound of disgust before leveling his gaze at me again. "You think I don't see why you're here? What you're doing?"

"Selling beets?"

Ezekiel moved closer, and I instinctively pulled against my bonds. Then he slapped me again, the sting hot as fire.

I looked around at the tent, the shadows of humans who walked on the other side of the canvas. Did they care that I was tied up in here, being interrogated? Or did they agree with it? Think it was necessary for the cause, for "what must be done"?

I didn't know where Liam was, but better not to assume he'd ride to the rescue. I was going to have to save myself, so I had to give myself time to break through the rope. I had to keep him talking.

"You're spies for Containment."

"I own a store. I have a living to make, and produce that's rotting because you scared everyone out of the Quarter. But instead of admitting I'm here to sell that produce, you've decided, what, I'm on a secret mission? Spying by way of root vegetables?"

"You operate a store near Devil's Isle. You serve Containment officers. If your display at our protest was any indication, you're friends with the second-in-command. You are a traitor to your humanity. And your friend is no better."

"He's a Paranormal bounty hunter," I pointed out. "And he's training me to be one."

"You perpetuate the system. You're obstacles to what must be done."

"Cleansing the Zone?"

He didn't answer, but rose from his stool and walked to an old bureau on the other side of the tent, pulled something from a drawer.

I was afraid it would be a weapon, but he brought back a photograph, held it out so I could see it. It was a color shot of dozens of people standing in long rows in front of a sign that read CAMP COUTURIE: OUR TEMPORARY HOME. Parents held babies, older people balanced on canes, and children sat cross-legged in the front. There was hope in their eyes. From what I'd seen of the people who still lived here, that hope was gone now.

"The First Wave," Ezekiel said, turning around the photograph so he could look at it again. "They were left here. Abandoned so that our government and Containment could focus on those who waged war against us. And we are punished for their inaction by destruction, the failure of the soil, the instability of our power system. Those who live here have been forgotten, while Containment wastes money incarcerating those who don't deserve to live. We can solve both problems."

"By having another war? By killing more people? That's moronic. You want to fix the Zone? Get out, and leave us the hell alone. We'll be better off without people like you."

Rage boiled over in his eyes, but before he could hit me again, an ear-piercing whistle cut through the air. Bangs were followed by screams and running. Were we under attack?

Fury flashed in Ezekiel's eyes at the interruption, his head darting up. "Don't move," he said, rising, and disappearing through the door.

I wanted to call Liam's name, to assure myself that he was alive and safe, and the noises hadn't been gunshots—punishment meted out by one of these crazy assholes. But there wasn't time for fear. Not if I wanted to live through this.

Unfortunately, I wasn't entirely sure where I'd been taken, and I didn't have a weapon.

I wanted to use magic. I wanted to use it so bad my fingers tingled, to show this asshole what happened when choice was taken away. But Ezekiel already believed I was a traitor, and magic would only give him another reason to consider me an enemy, for him to send people into Royal Mercantile—amid innocent customers—with bombs strapped to their chests. Surviving Camp Couturie only to emerge with an enormous target on my back didn't seem like much of a win. I'd use magic if I had to, but I had to try my other options first.

It occurred to me that I did have a kind of weapon—the wooden posts currently tied to my back.

I could use the chair against him, but I'd have to time it perfectly . . .

I shifted my body weight back, then forward, then back again, and so on until I could rock forward enough to get my feet flat on the ground. I leaned forward until I could stand, the chair still strapped to my back through my tied hands, but at least I was standing.

I crab-walked to the tent flap, listened for a few seconds. The sounds of chaos—shouting, shuffling—were yards away to my left, at least as far as I could tell. But I couldn't tell much, not hunched over like I was.

Footsteps approached, and I scooted back, just to the side of the doorway.

The canvas flap opened, and Ezekiel moved inside again. His eyes widened when he realized I wasn't where he'd left me, the rest of his face going crimson with anger. "Goddamn it!" he screamed.

Using every ounce of strength, I swung around, slamming the chair into him, groaned, stumbled, and we both hit the ground. I landed on my shoulder, which sang with pain. I tried to maneuver to my knees, to crawl away from him and toward the flapping canvas door, but he grabbed the chair, held me tight.

"You're dead!" he yelled again, climbing to his feet and dragging me backward across the ground.

His cruelty helped me. He yanked the chair back, and the rope that had pinned my wrists together snapped. Ezekiel stumbled back with the chair, knocking a lantern from its hook on the wall. It hit the ground, the glass shattering, the flame sputtering out. Small miracle that the tent hadn't caught fire. The entire camp was a tinderbox.

"You need to learn your place," he said, throwing the chair across the room and stalking toward me. I climbed to my feet, unraveling the rest of the rope from my hands and throwing it out of the way. Keeping my eyes on him, I picked up the lantern that had fallen to the ground. It was heavier than I'd expected—probably military issue. And that was fine by me.

"Put it down!" he ordered, and his tone suggested he was used to being obeyed.

"Not a chance," I said, keeping my eyes on him as he circled me, probably looking for a way to get past my defenses.

"You need a strong hand. You don't understand what's at stake!"

He'd changed his tone, talking to me like I was a stupid child. Probably not the first time he'd used that approach with a woman.

"I don't need anything but to get the hell out of this tent," I assured him.

He took a step toward me, and I swung the lantern. But he dodged, and it grazed his shoulder. He jumped forward to take me down. I shifted just enough to avoid his body weight falling on me completely, but he still pushed me aside. I stepped wrong in a rut in the hard-packed floor, and pain bloomed in my ankle like a hot black flower. I gritted my teeth against it, squeezed my hands around the lantern's handle.

The air filled with noise as warning claxons began to sound. *Liam*, I thought, panic and hope warring. If they were ringing the alarm, either he'd gotten away or the cavalry had arrived.

Ezekiel looked toward the sound, which gave me the chance that I needed.

Lantern in both hands, I lifted it and swung like a golfer on the tee box and hit him on the back of the head. He crumpled, falling forward like a felled tree.

"Asshole," I said, and tossed the lantern aside.

I had to go. And I had to find Liam.

CHAPTER ELEVEN

My ankle throbbed, bringing stinging tears to my eyes. *One step at a time,* I told myself. That was my mantra, my creed in wartime and out of it. It didn't matter what the step was, or how small. Nothing was insurmountable, as long as you could break it into parts, tackle each one in turn.

"One tent at a time" might be a more accurate description. I had to look into each one as I hobbled past, moving as quickly as I could at my stupidly awkward pace. The ground was pounded hard from millions of footsteps, but still mottled with bumps and holes. I hit one, lurched forward. Regained my balance, but winced as my ankle was wrenched.

And then an arm pulled me into the shadow between two tents.

Already on alert and full of adrenaline, I began to scream, but a hand clapped around my mouth.

"*It's me,*" Liam whispered fiercely. "Quit biting my fingers."

I mashed his instep with my good foot, not entirely an accident.

"Are you all right?" I whispered back, relief coursing through me, then went stiff and silent as footsteps approached us. We squeezed farther back into the crevice, his arm still around my waist, as Reveillon members rushed past us, one man shouting out orders to the others to find us.

"I've been better," he whispered, his lips near my ear, his voice a breath of sound. "But I'll live."

"What the hell happened?" I whispered when they passed and the world had quieted again.

"Flares or fireworks, it sounded like. As to where it came from or who did it, your guess is as good as mine. I thought you did it. I managed to get away in the chaos, and then the damn alarms started going off."

If it hadn't been either of us, who'd done it? Someone had created the perfect distraction. Coincidence, or a friend on the inside? Whichever way, this wasn't an opportunity to be wasted.

"We have to get out of here," I said. "Ezekiel wants us dead."

"I'm aware," he said. "We have to get back to the truck. If they find us now, they'll definitely kill us."

"That is not comforting."

"It wasn't meant to be."

"I can't run fast," I said, and felt tears bloom again. "I twisted my ankle."

We went silent again as another group passed, the beam of their flashlight slicing into the shadows at our feet.

"Don't wait for me," I said when they disappeared again. "If you can get away, go."

Anger radiated off his body like heat, and his voice was fierce. "If you think I'd leave you behind to save my own ass, you don't know me at all. No one gets left behind."

We waited another few seconds, until the camp fell quiet again.

"You can hobble, or I can carry you."

"Hobble," I whispered back, and he took my hand, squeezed it.

"Then don't let go," he said, and stepped out of the shadows. We ran in the same direction the men and women had gone.

"Ironic, isn't it, that they think we're the enemy?" he said, then pulled me backward into a tent when a group of people ran past.

Two children playing on a rug on the floor with wooden cars stared up at us with fear and wonderment. Their lips began to wobble, and I knew that was the step before tears.

"I like those cars!" I said quietly, but with as much enthusiasm as I could muster in a whisper. They looked suspicious but proud, and both held them out to me.

I gave them a thumbs-up, but my smile quickly faded. Because they were playing with toys in front of a terrifying sight.

"Liam."

He must have heard the fear in my voice, because he looked back at me, and then at the spot where I'd trained my gaze.

The tent in which we stood had been connected to another behind it, the canvas cut and reconnected to build a narrow hallway between them. In the second tent were dozens of stacked wooden crates, with DYNAMO EXPLOSIVES stenciled in black on the box, beside ominous words: WARNING—C-4—HIGH EXPLOSIVES. I knew what C-4 was, and I knew it didn't take very much to do a lot of damage. From the look of it, they'd amassed enough to take out a good chunk of New Orleans.

Devil's Isle had been only the beginning of what looked to be a horrible campaign.

"Damn," he said, and looked down at the children again.

"We have to—" I wanted to offer a plan, to get these kids away from the crates of explosives, and the explosives away from the terrorists who'd use them against us. But we were trapped in a maze of tents without backup, surrounded by people who clearly thought we were the enemy and wanted us dead. There was nothing we could do right now.

"We can't," I said, feeling suddenly defeated.

Liam reached out, squeezed my hand. "We can't right now," he said, understanding perfectly. "But we will. We'll tell Containment. They'll bring this in."

Before I could argue, voices lifted in the second tent, and Liam yanked me out of the tent again, dodged down another row.

We had made another turn when Liam stopped so quickly I ran into him. Fear struck me, and I assumed we'd been cornered. But when I stepped beside him, I realized what he'd seen and why he'd stopped.

There, in front of us, stood the woman with the black eye—the one I'd given the collard greens to.

She had a clutch of bottle rockets in one hand, a set of long matches in the other. She'd set them off, created the distraction that had given us both the chance to get away.

A chance to live.

"Go!" she said, and pointed to her left, giving us another chance. "Now!"

Liam nodded heavily—an acknowledgment and a thank-you—and we took off.

"To the fountain," he said. "Stay with me, and stay low."

"I'm right behind you."

We reached the end of the row and dashed out of the tents—which was equally exhilarating and terrifying. No more creepy canvas monotony, but no more cover.

The market had cleared out. We ran to the fountain, dived beneath a table, and took a look at the surroundings.

The truck sat nearly alone. One guard stood by, a young woman with a shotgun in hand and oversized boots beneath her poplin dress. I guessed it took all kinds to make a militia.

Liam looked at me, mouth open to give an order, but stopped when he noticed what was probably a blossoming bruise on my throbbing cheekbone.

"Did he put a hand on you?" His voice was low and threatening.

"It doesn't matter."

Liam's eyes fired as he prepared to argue, but I put a hand on his arm to stop him from running back into the labyrinth. "Liam, he's not worth it. He'd have done worse if he had the chance, and that's just a fact. We're his enemies, Liam. All of us—everyone who doesn't follow his line is part of the Containment machine. That's why we focus on getting away." I took in the cut above his right eye, the smear of blood across his forehead.

"And you don't look so hot yourself," I whispered.

"Sucker punch," he said bitterly. "The *Capon*."

His tight features said he was furious, but he reined it in, surveyed the truck, and watched the woman pace in front of it nervously.

From the shaking hands and nervously tapping feet, she didn't look like she'd become a fighter, a soldier, by choice or by necessity. She looked like someone who'd had a weapon shoved into her hands and told to stand guard. Unfortunately for her, that would give us the advantage.

"We do the same thing they did to us," Liam said, scanning the ground and picking up a rock. "A distraction. I'll toss it in front of her, and we'll go around behind to the passenger side. That will give us cover if she sees us."

"When she sees us," I said, wondering if she was a good shot. Not that it mattered, because that shotgun would put holes in anything nearby.

"Probably," Liam said. "Come out behind me on my signal." He held a finger to his lips, then threw the rock into the bushes past the woman. She strolled forward to take a look, and we darted out, half crouching, and ran to the truck, diving behind the rear passenger-side tire.

There were shouts and movement from the direction of the tents, raised voices and instructions. They'd probably found Ezekiel.

Liam crawled to the passenger-side door, face scrunched as he quietly depressed the button on the door's old, chrome handle, began to slowly pull it open.

"There! Stop them from leaving!" Ezekiel called out the order, once again sending people into the fight instead of actually doing any of the fighting himself.

"Fucking coward," I muttered, hustling into the truck behind Liam. Since the noise hardly mattered now, I slammed it shut and mashed down the lock button.

"Nailed it in one," Liam said, and hit the button for the lock on his side of the car just as the woman with the shotgun dived for it. He stuck the key into the ignition, and the truck roared to life. Thank God the power grid was still up, and the truck's electric starter could still fire.

The woman with the shotgun pumped it, raised it.

"This is going to be close!" he called out, and hit the accelerator. The truck jumped forward as she aimed.

"Get down!" Liam said, pushing my head between my knees.

The shotgun sounded, the driver's-side window exploding with glass and shot. "Son of a bitch," Liam said, and jerked the truck to the right, off the road and into the grass. Half-covering me with his body, Liam drove with one hand on the wheel, his head only high enough to see over the dashboard.

She fired again, hit the back window, blowing glass all over it.

"Asshole!" he yelled, threading the truck between two trees. "Do you have any idea how hard it is to replace a window in the goddamn Zone?"

He yanked the wheel to avoid a fallen log. The truck bounced hard enough that my head touched the ceiling. A little late, I grabbed the seat belt, buckled it tight, and held on.

"You know, I think we're both going to have to deal with Gunnar on this one!"

"You think?" he yelled as he swerved the truck around one tree, then another, and off the curb onto the road that wound through City Park again.

We heard the engine at the same time, checked our mirrors. A truck pulled onto the road behind us, a multicolored bastardization that had probably been Frankensteined together from lots of different vehicles. And it was *loud*. A very big engine, or some kind of custom exhaust, or maybe both.

"What's the plan here?" I asked, holding on to the door as the truck bounced again.

"To stay alive, and get the fuck out of City Park!" he yelled over the roar of the truck's engine.

"Good plan," I said with a nod. "Good plan."

"Shit," Liam said, gaze slipping to the rearview mirror.

I didn't want to look but made myself check the side mirror. A man was standing in the back of the truck, aiming a gun at us over the cab.

"I'm beginning to think this movement isn't all about peace, love, and understanding!"

Liam half smiled. "You're cheerful in an emergency," he said, and jerked when a shot whistled above us. "Fucking assholes!" he said, and put a hand at my back, tried to push me down again. "Stay down!"

"Better plan," I said, and from my half-huddled position, I opened the glove box, looking for our advantage.

"What are you doing?"

"You said you had a gun in here." I pulled out the weighty revolver, which I guessed was a .44. "And you were not kidding."

"I know you know how to handle it," Liam said. I'd told him my father had made sure of that. "How's your aim?"

"Good," I said. I looked through the glove box, didn't find any other bullets.

"What's in the cylinder is what we've got," Liam said, gaze skipping between the uneven ground in front of him and the rearview mirror.

I spun the cylinder, confirmed it was full. Six bullets to make this work. No pressure. "Then I better do this right the first time."

I unbuckled and turned backward, sitting on my knees on the bench seat, and used the back to brace my wrists. Their truck was right on our ass, only ten or so feet from our tailgate.

Unless you had a really big weapon, taking out a moving vehicle was tricky under the best of conditions. The truck's back window was gone, but I'd have to climb into the bed to get a closer shot, which would put me directly in their sights and without any cover.

Taking out the driver would be the most permanent fix, but I wasn't going to get a steady shot on this road in fading light, and I was years from the daily practice my father had drilled into me.

I could fire through the radiator, try to hit something critical in the engine, but I'd probably have to go through the bullets first, and that still might not be enough. A few shots might disable the tire, but I'd have to make every one of them count.

We hit a pothole and bounced hugely. My head nearly hit the truck's ceiling. "Not going to help my shooting if you do that."

"Not going to help my driving if you complain about it."

"I think tires are the best bet," I said. "I need you to get me in position."

"And how would you like me to do that? Hold that thought," he said, and swung the car right to avoid driving into the lagoon. I fell backward, slamming into him, and managed not to drop the gun.

"We have to stop meeting like this!" he said while I climbed back onto my side of the car.

"Yeah, this is all fun and games," I said, dropping down when another bullet flashed the passenger side. "They're trying to conserve bullets."

"Probably only one gun in that car, and they'll need it if they stop us. Otherwise they'd have done what you're doing."

Or they wanted us alive, because Ezekiel wanted in on the killing. That seemed equally likely.

"I need a clearer shot. Best way is to let them get beside us."

"You want me to slow down?"

"If you want me to disable the vehicle, yeah." I looked at him. "Or I can drive, and you can do the shooting."

"How close do they need to be?" he asked quickly.

"Close as you can get without getting us killed."

"Fair enough," he said, watching the road ahead. "There," he said, pointing to another long pond in front of us. "I'll slow down like we don't want to hit it, jerk the wheel to the left. That should bring them up on your right."

"Sounds like a plan."

"If this doesn't work, and they stop the truck, run for the trees, run back to the Quarter."

"No, if this doesn't work, we run together."

We looked at each other for a moment, understanding passing between us. We were in this together, and neither would leave the other behind. That was Ezekiel's play, not ours.

"You ready?" Liam asked.

I balanced my elbows on the armrest. I didn't balance the gun yet. I didn't want to scare them off. "Ready."

"Then here we go." He took his foot off the gas, swerved left.

The other truck was still accelerating to our right, which put them on our passenger corner, and then parallel. Their shooter fired, two shots that dinged against the back of the truck.

I saw her face through the window—the young, blond woman with thin arms and big eyes who drove the truck. She didn't look as helpless as the other women I'd seen. In her eyes was the fire of a believer.

Breathe in, breathe out, aim, and . . . *fire*.

The sound was enormously loud, the ricochet singing through my arm. I hit the tire's sidewall. It would lose air, but not fast enough to stop the vehicle outright.

The driver screamed something to the man in the back of the truck, swerved the vehicle away from us. That put me in the perfect position. I fired again, then again, and again.

For a second, I thought I'd lost the gamble.

But I'd hit my target three times over; it just took time for the air to drain. The tire deflated, and the driver overcorrected, swerved to avoid a tree, and fishtailed. The back of the truck slammed into the tree anyway, knocking down the man who'd been shooting over the cab. Everything went still.

Or so it seemed. Fingers shaking with adrenaline, I kept the gun trained on the truck. Two people in linen climbed out of the cab. One kicked at the vehicle. The other aimed with a handgun, but we were out of range, and she wasted her bullets.

Liam headed for the main road again, and the ride smoothed out.

We stayed quiet, but I didn't move, and kept my gaze trained on the darkness for some sign Ezekiel had sent another vehicle, another group with guns to take us out. If they had the arsenal of C-4, it was a pretty good bet they also had an arsenal of guns. But grass and trees and water were the only things that passed behind us, and the truck's engine was the only sound that pierced through the darkness.

"I'm taking a shortcut," Liam said. "Turn around and hold on."

I turned in time to see the chain-link fence looming in front of us. I covered my head with my hands, and Liam roared along with the truck's engine, like his feral yell would be enough to push us through.

Steel rushed over the truck, and we bounced down onto the road below.

We'd made it out alive. We'd made it out together.

Liam pulled the truck to a stop. He put it in park, ran his hands through his hair. "Jesus."

"Yeah." I looked at him. There was a cut on his forehead, glass dusting his shoulders like snow. "Good driving."

Liam nodded, blew out a breath. "Good shooting."

I nodded and put the gun away again, clenched my fingers. "Thanks."

He looked at me, gaze on my swollen lip. "You're okay?"

"I'm fine." I held up a hand. "Plenty of adrenaline to go. We need to get back to the store."

"We will," he promised, then leaned over and pressed his lips to mine.

I didn't have a chance to argue, to remind him who or what we were, or to wonder if he'd dealt with those issues, overcome them.

Or I didn't take that chance. I took the other chance and grabbed locks of his dark hair, pulled him closer until his throat rumbled with satisfied sound. He touched my face gently, then slipped his finger to the back of my neck. The kiss deepened until Ezekiel, the camp, City Park, and all the rest of it disappeared, replaced by a glorious haze across my mind.

Liam pulled incrementally back, lips swollen and eyes closed, before moving back to his seat. "We should get back to the store."

He'd pulled back physically, and he'd pulled back emotionally. But we were alive, and for now I was going to count my blessings.

CHAPTER TWELVE

The lights were blazing when we pulled up in front of the store. Tadji and Gunnar raced to the door, opening it as I climbed out of the truck, glanced in the back.

"Son of a bitch," I said, looking at Liam. "My boxes are gone—they had the aprons in it, the money we got today, the goods we traded."

It took Liam a moment to process. "Including the deer jerky."

"Including the damn deer jerky." I could have worked out some solid frustration by gnawing on deer jerky.

"Why are you limping?" Gunnar asked from the doorway as we walked inside. "And why is there a bruise on your face? What the hell happened?"

"I'm only slightly limping," I said, rolling my foot to test it. "It's better now."

"Camp Couturie happened," Liam said, locking the door and peering into the darkness for a moment before turning back to the rest of us. "Asshole militia bastards."

Gunnar glared at him. "I thought this trip was going to be simple. I thought you were going to be careful and keep her out of trouble!"

"Still in the room," I pointed out. "Which is in the store I own. So."

"You're in the store you own looking like the cat dragged you around a little." Tadji took one of my hands in hers, looked down at my wrists. "You were bound?"

"I was."

"Go sit," Liam said, directing me to the table. "Get off that ankle."

"Sprain?" Gunnar asked.

"Just twisted it," I said, "and during our heroic escape. Really, it's nearly fine."

"I'm going to get you something to clean your wrists up," Tadji said, and hustled to the back of the store.

"There's some salve in a tin," I said, looking at my raw wrists. "Mrs. Proctor brought it." She was one of my regulars. "It smells horrible, but it works on scrapes." My wrists were burning, and the stuff worked miracles. I could stand having garbage wrists for a little while.

"What happened?" Gunnar asked, taking my arm and leading me to the table, too.

"We sold beets, asked very subtle questions, and had a fine time," Liam said. "We headed to the truck, and they hit us. Ezekiel had us dragged into a tent, accused us of being spies."

"Which, in fairness, was accurate," I said.

Tadji came back, handing a dampened cloth to Liam, the tin of salve and a roll of gauze to me. I popped off the lid and took a tentative sniff. Still smelled like hot buttered garbage, but there was no help for it.

"I'll do it," Tadji said, and I held out my wrists. Her touch was careful and delicate, but I still winced at the knife-sharp sting. The cooling sensation that followed it was better. When she'd gentled salve onto the abrasions, she wrapped a couple of rounds of gauze around them, tucked the ends into place.

"Good as new," she said. "And you can sport the latest fashion accessory."

"War bracelets," I said, holding them up so everyone could see.

"Continue," Gunnar said.

"We made it out," Liam said, the cloth pressed to the cut on his forehead. "They gave chase, and Claire disabled their vehicle with a forty-four."

"Engine?" Gunnar asked, glancing at me.

"Tire," I said. "Took a few shots, but we had limited ammo, so I took a chance."

"Good call," Gunnar said, pulling out the chair next to mine, spinning it to face me. "Why'd they decide you were spies?"

"One of the Campers saw us at the Bourbon Street protest," Liam said.

"One of the chicks who walked in the front with Ezekiel," I added. "She only came out of the tents for a second, then disappeared again. It was near the fountain."

Gunnar nodded. "So two confirmed Reveillon members at Camp Couturie."

"That we saw," Liam said. "And that's not all we saw. They have an arsenal." He told Gunnar about the C-4 we'd found.

"Damn," Gunnar said. "That much explosive, they can take out whatever they want. Bridges, buildings, levees."

Liam nodded. "They didn't know we'd found it, but they knew we'd found them, and they only send one car?"

I hadn't considered the possibility they'd let us go, and I didn't really want to consider it now. "I prefer my version of the story."

"You did take out an enemy vehicle," Gunnar said.

"Thank you for that. Although Liam's truck suffered the consequences."

Gunnar nodded. "Containment will repair the damage. You were technically on a mission, after all."

"Appreciate it," Liam said. "Bulletproof glass would not be turned down."

"You think you and Claire will be targeted?" Gunnar asked.

"Ezekiel is now very pissed off at both of us. He doesn't know we saw the explosives, at least not that we're aware, but he knows that we know where he operates."

"He'll come after us," Liam said, "and he might decamp. He can't move all of Camp Couturie out quickly—there are just too many people—but he'll take his core group, the rest of the arsenal they've put together."

Gunnar stood, began to pace. "Joint Ops will want to reallocate now, send teams in. Priority will be finding the bombers and the explosives, getting them out of Reveillon's hands." He looked back at us. "You get any sense of the size of the group? Everyone on their side, a few people on their side?"

"Hard to say," Liam said. "We only saw a few dozen people. Of them, only a few wore those linen garments, but we don't know if that's a requirement or just something the diehards choose to do."

"Some of them are probably just trying to survive," I said, thinking of the men and women we'd seen at the market. They hadn't seemed oppressed, but they hadn't exactly seemed happy, either. Life in the Zone could be difficult under even the best conditions; life at Camp Couturie seemed pretty hardscrabble when you got down to it. "Some don't have time to worry about waging war against Containment. They're focused on making sure they have basic necessities."

"On the other hand," Liam said, "that's probably exactly the thing Ezekiel has used to bring some over to his side."

"Desperate times call for desperate measures," Gunnar agreed.

Tadji looked at me. "I don't want you to stay here alone tonight. Either you can come home with me, or, if you want to keep an eye on the store, maybe Liam can stay?" She gave Liam a pointed look that suggested the "maybe" wasn't entirely optional.

"Good idea," Gunnar said.

"Is anyone interested in my opinion?" I asked.

"Not especially," Gunnar and Tadji said together.

Liam rolled his eyes, looked at me. "You have a place for me to sleep?"

"So many possible answers to that question," Gunnar muttered.

"You're hilarious," Liam said. "Let's make this situation even more awkward."

"It shouldn't be awkward," Gunnar said. "Wouldn't be, if you two would just do it."

You could have heard crickets from Algiers Point in the silence that followed that comment.

"Liam will want to go back to Devil's Isle," I said, ignoring the comment altogether, and looked at him. "Won't you want to check on your grandmother?"

"I can check on her," Gunnar said. "Better yet, I'll put someone on the door. Someone sympathetic."

"I wouldn't argue with that," Liam said.

"I'll need to get a message to Malachi," I said, and lifted my gaze to the stairs. I couldn't fit much in a note attached to a pigeon's leg, and it would have to be cryptic, but it would have to do for now.

"Then it's settled," Tadji said. "Liam will stay here tonight."

"All right," Gunnar said. "Now that we've got that worked out, I need to go. Claire looks like she could use some sleep."

"She could," I said, not stifling an enormous yawn.

"You want a ride back to the Cabildo?" Tadji asked him, rising. "I've got the car."

Calling her tiny box a "car" was generous, but I didn't have the energy to argue. "I'd appreciate it," Gunnar said.

We said quick good-byes, and then the door was locked again, and Liam and I stood alone in the store together. And it was awkward.

I blew out a breath, decided I might as well get some of the awkward over with. I could use a good night's sleep, and the faster I could get to it, the better.

"There's a bed in the back room," I said, gesturing to the room behind the kitchen, where I stored extra merchandise. "I think it's actually pretty comfortable. Gunnar did some time there and only complained about it within usual Gunnar levels. I'll go upstairs and get some blankets."

Liam looked toward the back room, then back at me. "I'll go with you."

My hackles lifted. "I don't need a chaperone," I said irritably. "We're safe from a second-floor ninja attack."

"I want to check the layout of the building. I haven't seen the third floor."

Fair enough, I thought, and was glad I hadn't imagined he'd been curious about where I lived, where I slept. We'd moved past that, I reminded myself. We'd been through trauma together, had come out on the other end of it. We were friends—good friends—and that was fine. There was nothing wrong with having good friends.

We took the stairs, and I stopped at the second floor, gestured to the storage room. "Linens are in here."

His eyes were dark and unreadable. "Mind if I go up?"

I did mind, but that was mostly just personal, so I shook my head. "Help yourself."

While the treads squeaked beneath his weight, I put aside consideration of what Liam would look like in my bedroom and focused on finding sheets. I hadn't been able to salvage any from our old house during the war, but my father had a pretty fantastic collection of linens at the store. With age, the sheets and pillowcases had been worked into a perfect softness. And, I thought, pulling them from the bureau drawer, they now smelled like the rose and lavender sachet I'd packed them with. Hopefully, Liam wouldn't mind smelling floral in the morning, or the mismatched embroidery.

When I put together a set and turned off the light again, the hallway was empty, the third-floor light still on. Still checking things out, or just snooping around?

I took the stairs, arms crossed around the linens, and stepped into the doorway. He stood in front of my bureau, looking over the things I'd gathered there. A silver brush and comb set, a small piece of brick I'd taken from the fallen St. Louis Cathedral.

He looked back at me. "I like the space."

"Thanks. It serves its purpose." I walked to the table by the window, drafted a note for Malachi: "Reveillon at Camp Couturie. Armed and dangerous. Containment going in." Hopefully, that would be enough to keep him and the rest of Delta safe. And maybe they could use the information.

I slipped the note into the bird's leather pouch, ran the back of my fingers down the silky feathers at its neck. If it liked the petting, or didn't, it gave no sign. I let it fly, watch it lift into the air, black wings against moonlit clouds.

Duty done, I closed and locked the window again.

He picked up the stack of documents I found in the storage room, looked at it. "What's all this?"

"Nothing," I said, toeing off my shoes. "I've been looking through my father's things, the inventory, trying to find—I don't know. Something confirming he was a Sensitive, saying how he felt about it. Confessing it to me, I guess."

"Everything I know about him—which isn't much—says he would have been very careful to hide it, to keep you and the store out of danger."

"I know. But I looked anyway. I found the papers in a carved-out book—*The Revolt of the Angels*."

"Ironic." He read through them. "Your father bought a building on Carrolton?"

"No." I said it on a laugh, and looked back at Liam. He'd spread the documents across the top of the bureau, was reading through one of them.

"Did you actually look through these?"

"Not really." I padded toward him.

"There's a deed for a building in Mid-City. Your dad signed it." He held it out to me, flipped through the rest of the documents.

It read QUITCLAIM DEED across the top, and then had a bunch of legalese I didn't recognize. And then there was an address on South Carrolton, my father's signature on the bottom. The entire thing could have been written in German, for all that I understood it—and what it meant.

"Where is this?" I asked.

"Mid-City, maybe?" He looked at me. "You didn't know about it? I mean, he didn't say anything? You'd probably own it now, since he's gone."

I shook my head. "Is there anything else in the papers about it?"

"No," Liam said, looking back at the papers again, pressing some of them flat. "I mean, not the sale. It's all related to the property's history. Looks like it's a commercial property." He flipped through one page, then another, like he was reading a story. "There was a small restaurant there at one time. But nothing about what your father did with it, if anything."

"I want to go see it," I said, and turned for the door. I didn't know what I thought I'd find there; I just knew I didn't want any more mysteries. Any more guesswork.

Liam gently took my arm before I could walk away, pulled me back. "Claire, it's the middle of the night."

My face was throbbing, and my wrists burned, and I was exhausted.

But I had a mission, and I was damn well going to act on it. "My father owned another place that I know nothing about. I want to see what it is."

I could hear the anger in my voice. Anger at my father, anger at Liam.

"It's late, and Reveillon is out there. This could be nothing—just an investment property he didn't have a chance to use."

"Then why hide the papers in a book and never mention its existence?"

Silence. "I don't have a good answer for that."

"There could be something there that I need to see."

"And that building could be rubble on the ground, Claire."

I hated him for that. "Bastard."

"Claire."

"No. You can go to hell, Liam."

"*Claire*," he repeated. "Stop it. All right? Just stop. I know you're angry at him. I can see it in your eyes. Be angry if you need to. Be pissed. But use your brain. You don't need to do this right now. It's too dangerous to run around New Orleans right now."

He was right. Of course he was right. But that didn't make me feel any better. "I just want to know why he didn't tell me." I looked up at him, let him see the misery in my eyes. "He could have prepared me for this, for magic. He could have taught me how to deal with it. How to live with it without feeling like an enemy all the time. Without feeling like a criminal."

"Claire." This time he said it softly. He put a hand at the back of my neck, long fingers sliding into my hair. He pulled me toward him and into his arms. He wrapped himself around me, making a sanctuary of his body.

I dropped my forehead to his chest and rested there, let myself be, let my hands rest at his lean hips. He smelled male—like hard work in sunshine and faint cologne.

Liam had called me reckless, and maybe I was. But I tried not to be completely reckless with my heart—not when I knew how this would end.

I dropped my hands, pulled back. He gave it a last bit of strength before letting me step away.

"I want you to stay with me," I said, looking up into eyes that reflected stormy seas. "And you probably want to stay. But you don't trust me not to become a wraith."

Temper flashed in his eyes. "I do trust you. But it's not that simple."

"I know it isn't. For me, or for you. It's who and what we are. It's who and what the world is." I gathered my courage and found words to speak the unspoken.

"Yes, the possibility exists that I'll become a wraith. That I won't be able to control myself, that I'll become a monster. I'm doing everything I can to avoid that. And I know you don't believe me; you don't think you can believe me. But it's the truth. Either you can accept that, or you can't. But that has to be your call."

He stepped forward, closing the distance I'd put between us, and put a hand against my cheek. I fought back the desire to settle my head into his hand, to find comfort there. "I'm a bounty hunter, Claire. If something should happen, I'd have to be the one to take you to Lizzie. To take you to Devil's Isle. I can't be the one to put you in prison."

"I know," I said. I knew that wasn't enough for him—not for his sense of honor, for the vow he felt he had to uphold. And so I mustered all my courage, and I took a step away from him.

The sudden distance of his body made me feel small and cold. "You should go downstairs."

"Claire."

I looked up at him and his eyes seemed to glow brighter, like he burned from within. And maybe he did. Maybe he burned for me as brightly as I burned for him.

"I want you," I said, and his lips parted, chest heaving with desire that was obvious in his eyes. "But not like this. Not when you'll regret it."

Anger and insult flashed across his face. "I wouldn't regret it, Claire. And that's exactly the goddamn problem."

He turned and walked to the door, and I listened until his footsteps faded away. And when he was gone, I let myself sigh—long and haggard—before closing the door behind me.

He would come to terms, or he wouldn't.

The decision had to be his.

I wanted to kick things, punch things, scream until my voice was raw and hoarse, until this feeling of longing dissipated, leaving nothing but emptiness behind. Emptiness and serenity. I'd be alone, but I wouldn't want for anything.

I wouldn't want *him*.

I wouldn't have an ache in my bones, a tingle in fingertips that wanted to touch and grasp, to pull him against me and finish that kiss—and more. And more. And the wanting made the sense of phantom touch stronger.

Although I was exhausted, I still had energy to burn.

I walked into the storage room, picked up the box that sat on a bureau by the door—the one I used to cast off my excess magic.

I walked into a spot clear of secretaries, bureaus, and baroque headboards, put the box on the floor, and sat down in front of it, legs crossed. I put my hands on my knees and closed my eyes, tried to clear my brain of the jumble of thoughts and emotions: the violence of our capture at the camp, Ezekiel's slap, the sharp pain that still smeared my abraded wrists, the possibility of Liam . . .

Eyes closed, I reached inside, using that sixth magical sense to find the particles of it, burning into the part of my brain that controlled anger and violence. I let myself feel them, the foreign pin-points of magic, spearing into places they shouldn't be and lodging there. Waiting.

I grabbed handfuls of them, felt them prickle against my grasp like a handful of hornets. I imagined squeezing them into filaments, just as I'd done in Algiers, and could actually feel them coalescing inside me, cold and heavy and faintly alien. Disconcerting as that was, I made myself keep a grip on them and opened my eyes to fix my gaze on the box.

I blew out a breath, forced myself to concentrate, and pushed those filaments toward the box, one slow and steady inch at a time. Sweat *plinked* from my forehead onto the floor with the effort of moving the magic, condensed and heavy as it was. Energy waning and my arm shaking with exhaustion, I gritted my teeth and made a final shove, let the box's lid fall down. It settled back onto the base with a satisfyingly heavy *thud*.

Exhaustion settled into bone and muscle where magic had been. I closed my eyes, rolled my shoulders in relief.

I'd told Liam I was doing everything I could to avoid becoming a monster.

Tonight, I'd kept that promise.

CHAPTER THIRTEEN

A nother dawn, another cooing pigeon, another beckoning from an angel: *HQ. Noon.*

I guessed that filled in part of my day.

I tested my ankle, found it only vaguely achy. That was good enough. I dressed and came downstairs to hear voices in my store, the clink of glasses on wood.

"What are you going to do about Claire?"

I stopped on the staircase at the sound of Gavin's voice. And I nearly turned around to go upstairs again to give them their privacy, until I heard what came next.

"There's nothing to do about Claire," Liam said, the words clipped.

"You two have a connection."

"*Sa fait pa rien.*"

"Bullshit it doesn't matter," Gavin said.

My chest hurt at the fact that Liam had apparently spoken those words—even if in Louisiana French—but I wasn't going anywhere. Not when he was actually talking about it, about what was between us and where we stood.

"'It doesn't matter' doesn't put that hangdog look on your face, or hers." There was a pause. "Is this because of Gracie?"

This time, Gavin's voice was soft, comforting. I hadn't heard him talk about Gracie before, their younger sister who'd been killed by wraiths. But from the tone in his voice, he was affected, even if he didn't talk about it.

And for a long moment, Liam didn't answer.

"Gracie has nothing to do with it."

"*T'a menti.*"

"She doesn't," Liam insisted. "I'm a hunter, for God's sake. Claire's a Sensitive."

"And you're both adults," Gavin said. "You pick your bounties, and she trains so she stays out of trouble. She'll be fine."

"And do you know that? Can you be sure that something won't happen? That the magic won't win? Jesus, Gavin. You've seen what it does to people." He went quiet. "You haven't seen her near the gate. You haven't seen her face. The horror in it, when she thinks they might take her."

I put a hand on the wall, the plaster cool beneath my fingertips, reaching for Liam, the effort just as fruitless as if I'd been in the room.

"She used magic the first time I saw her. Not very well, but there you go." There was faint amusement in his voice. "She'd come back here to grab her go bag—she actually had a go bag packed—so she could get out before Containment found her. It wrecked her, the fear that she might be locked up in a prison for reasons she can't control."

"It wrecked her, or it wrecked you?"

Silence fell.

"I'd be the one to take her in, Gavin. I couldn't let her go in with anyone else, which means I'd have to be the one to put her into the nightmare. To make sure her worst fear comes true. I can't be with her one minute and take her in the next."

"She knows how to judge risk, Liam, how to handle herself. Look around you, for Christ's sake. So, is the problem that you don't think Claire could handle it? Or you don't think you can?"

"You don't get it."

Gavin laughed heartily, but there was no joy in the sound. "I get being interested in someone you can't have," he said, probably thinking of Nix. "I've been there. It's brutal. But that's not what this is. I love you, big brother. And I hear where you're coming from. I hear it, and I can see it in your eyes and in hers." Another pause. "Claire's a strong woman with good friends. And among them, Malachi."

Liam growled.

"Growl all you want," Gavin drawled. "But he's helping her. And he likes her enough to keep helping her. He won't let the magic take her. Hell, he might take her himself. He likes the look of her; you can tell that."

I rolled my eyes. I didn't think he was right about Malachi, but he certainly didn't have any sentimentality about it.

There was shifting of wood and fabric. One of them was standing up. I grimaced, turned to the side so they wouldn't see me if they walked near the stairs.

"So you think about that," Gavin said. "You think about whether you're being the honorable one, or whether you're just protecting yourself. And you think about who's protecting her."

"Can I be the one that tells you to fuck off?"

Gavin sighed. "Why do all our conversations have to end like that?"

"Because you enjoy getting under my skin."

"I do. I really, really do. And I'm really, really good at it." More shifting. "I'm going to head outside, see what you did to my truck."

"It's my truck," Liam said.

"It used to be my truck, and I'm curious to know what those shit-heel xenophobes did to it. If Claire magically produces bacon and cinnamon rolls, let me know, because I am all in for that, and that protein bar I just ate was mostly raisins and condensed sawdust."

"At least you got raisins."

There were steps across the store's creaking floor, and then the front door opened and closed. I didn't know if I felt better or worse having heard them talk. Knowing that Liam wrestled with the situation made me want to talk to him, comfort him. But that wasn't going to change anything, which just irritated me further.

Well, whatever I felt, I was going to have to feel it in the store proper. I couldn't stand on the stairs for the rest of the day.

Might as well get it over with, I thought, and trotted down the stairs. It was already warm in the store, so I pulled my hair into a knot while I walked. It gave me something to do with my hands, and I decided it made me look nonchalant.

Liam looked up. "Good morning. You appear to be in one piece."

He sat at the table in a fitted long-sleeved T-shirt with the sleeves pushed up, the *Times-Picayune* newssheet on the table in front of him beside a glass of iced tea and protein bar wrapper. There was more dark stubble across his jaw. He'd gone from more handsome to more dangerous.

"You appear not to have destroyed my store in the night," I said, trying to keep the mood light. And then I nabbed half of his protein bar.

"Hey, that was my breakfast."

I chewed. It definitely could have used raisins. "Hey, it was from my kitchen."

"Payment for guarding your store. And your ass."

"Mmm-hmm. I thought I heard voices in here."

"That was Gavin. He's outside looking at the truck."

"Is he doing any better today?"

"As well as he ever does. How's your ankle?"

"Much better," I said. My face was still a little sore, but my wrists looked much better. I'd taken off the bandages, and the salve had done a pretty good job.

Liam had covered the cut on his forehead with a bandage, and looked whole otherwise. Good. One less thing to think about.

"Any word about Camp Couturie?" I asked. "Whether they found Ezekiel?"

"I haven't heard anything," Liam said, flicking the paper. "And this is literally last week's news."

I said a silent prayer for Gunnar's safety, then walked into the kitchen, poured the rest of the tea into a glass. "New rule!" I called out. "The person who finishes off the tea has to make the next pitcher."

He looked amused when I walked back into the room, and glanced at my glass. "I'd say that's you."

"Malachi left a message. He wants to meet at noon."

"I'll pencil him in," Liam said, and flipped the newssheet over.

"Did you want to look for Reveillon today?"

He looked up at me. "Are you up for that?"

"I'd rather be doing that than sitting here, waiting for something to happen."

His expression darkened. "It's going to happen regardless—at least until Containment breaks them."

"Or breaks Ezekiel. He's the head of the monster," I said. "Cut it off. Disable it."

"Or he's the head of the hydra," Liam said. "Cut it off, and another springs up."

"That is not a pleasant thought."

"No," he agreed. "It isn't."

The bell rang. Mrs. Proctor came in, her arm in Gavin's, her tiny figure tucked into a polished plum-colored suit with matching square-toed pumps. A small hat with a spill of plum-colored lace was perched on the side of her silver hair, and complemented her dark skin. Gavin towered over her by nearly two feet.

Tadji walked in behind them, her hair a cloud of ringlets today. She'd paired a camouflage vest and tank with jeans and lace-up military-style boots. Where Mrs. Proctor dressed for prewar church Sundays every day of the week, Tadji was the model of the postwar cool girl. And they both looked perfect despite what was probably wilting heat outside.

"Prince Edward in a can," Gavin said, patting Mrs. Proctor's hand. "That's a good one, Mrs. Proctor."

"Mrs. Proctor," I said with a smile. "What can we get for you today?"

She gave Liam the side eye. "Oh, a little of this and a little of that."

"I believe she mentioned baking soda," Gavin said, gently extricating himself. It required some moves. She was a spry little thing, was Mrs. Proctor.

"I'll just get it myself," she said, and walked across the store in her plum skirt and jacket and matching shoes and handbag.

"She is turned out today," Tadji said.

"She's a flirt, is what she is," Gavin whispered. "She grabbed my ass on the way over here."

"It's a nice ass," Tadji said.

"Well aware. I work for it, and I'm proud of it. But that's not the point. In addition to the fact that she's practically a hundred—"

"Ninety-eight," Tadji and I said together.

"Well, she may be a young vixen, but she's still not my type."

Since she kept peeking around the corner to look at him, that wasn't a concern of hers.

"That is . . . unsettling," Tadji whispered. "I'd prefer she not sexually harass the customers. Let me help you, Mrs. Proctor," she said, more loudly, and walked forward.

"There's a Containment agent outside," Gavin said. "Said he's here to take a look at the truck."

"Gunnar came through," Liam said, and headed for the door to chat with the woman in fatigues, clipboard in hand, who stood on the sidewalk outside.

"Did you get an earful?" Gavin asked when we were alone.

I looked back at him. "What?"

"This morning, when you were listening from the stairway."

I could feel my cheeks warming.

"He's right," Gavin said with a grin. "You can see every expression on your face. I wasn't actually sure if that was you—I just heard the creak on the stairs. But thanks for confirming it for me."

"I didn't mean to intrude."

"But you couldn't turn away."

I lifted a shoulder. I couldn't really argue with that.

"No harm, no foul," Gavin said, patting my arm. "Brother o' mine isn't exactly chatty about his feelings—or free with them. He's guarded, careful, and honorable to a damn fault."

I couldn't help snorting. "And you're the sexy rogue who leaves a trail of hearts behind him?"

He smiled wolfishly, rubbed a hand over his abdomen. "I am a sexy beast. But the broken heart is sometimes mine."

I almost patted his arm supportively, but I didn't want to encourage him.

Mrs. Proctor bought two boxes of baking soda. No sugar, no vanilla, no flour. Just baking soda. Either she was building a science fair volcano, or she'd been so awed by the brothers Quinn that she wasn't thinking straight.

"Are you sure that you need all this?" I asked her for the third time.

"I'm sure," she said with a grin, looking over the counter at Gavin. He'd moved behind it to stand with me so she couldn't grab his ass again. Of all the people in the Quarter, she wasn't the one I'd expected to be an incurable flirt. I guessed she just hadn't yet seen what she'd really wanted.

"Would you like to walk me out, dear?" Mrs. Proctor gazed at Gavin over the bag I'd given her.

"I—sure," he said, and squeezed my butt on the way around the counter.

"I should get a little fun, too," Gavin said, and began an exceedingly slow walk back to the front door. Mrs. Proctor was making the most of the opportunity.

There were no other customers in the store at the moment, and Liam was still outside with Containment. Good. That gave me a chance to do something else that needed doing.

"And the shelves are clean," Tadji said, walking back and putting the feather duster on the counter.

"Appreciate it. Um, can we talk for a minute?"

Her eyebrows lifted, but she nodded. "Sure. Actually, I've been wanting to talk to you, too. But this was your idea. You can go first."

"No, that's okay." I hadn't yet decided exactly how I was going to say what I knew needed to be said. "Go ahead."

Tadji nodded. "So, I guess I wanted to acknowledge that Royal Mercantile is important to the Quarter, to the people who've stayed here and stuck out life in the Zone. And for a long time, the store was your life. And that was fine. But now, for lots of reasons, you have other things to think about. And that's fine, too." She linked her hands in front of her. "You need someone to help. I'm that someone. I want a job. And a paycheck."

That made it easy, since I was going to make the same offer.

I wasn't swimming in money; dry goods weren't exactly a high-margin business. On the other hand, it was easy to be frugal in the

Zone. There wasn't much to spend money on. Regardless, she was already doing the work; she should absolutely get paid for it.

"Done."

"Well," she said. "That was easier than I thought."

"That's what I'd wanted to talk to you about."

Her gaze narrowed. "And you made me do the asking?"

"You said you wanted to talk to me."

"I guess I did." She frowned. "The thing is—you're a little possessive about the store."

I had that coming. "Listen, that day, after the attack on Devil's Isle—"

"I picked a bad time to change things around, disrupt the balance."

"No—well, yeah. Not because of the attack. The store was hardly the important thing there, but it made me think about some things. Face some things emotionally that I hadn't really wanted to think about."

I told her about it. About my regrets, my jealousy, my "safe space."

"Then I'm here at the right time," Tadji said. "Because there's an entirely new world opening up for you right now. A dangerous and occasionally sickening and cruel world, but a world filled with Cajun bounty hunters and lively conversation about peanut butter."

"You do make it sound so glamorous, what with the peanut butter and all." I tilted my head at her. "Are you sure this is what you want to do? I didn't think 'retail merchandising' figured into your five-year plan."

It had been a very detailed plan. With spreadsheets and colored tabs.

"I've been thinking about that," she said. "Someday I'm going to finish my dissertation research, and then what? I'm going to leave the Zone and try to get a job at some college, telling people how dangerous and mysterious the Zone was? Don't get me wrong—I love what I do, what I study. But for all its issues, I don't want to live anywhere else." She pressed fingertips to her chest. "It gets into your heart."

"No argument there."

"As for right now, I want to keep interviewing people, learning about their language. I think I can do that here: I can help run the store while you're doing your thing, and I can talk to people. There's really no better place to do that. Unless that's a problem for you."

"I want to be in a footnote."

"Done," she said with a grin.

"How much do I pay you?"

"I don't know," she said. "I didn't think we'd get this far. I figured there was a chance you'd boot me out for asking."

"Never," I said. "Think about what you want salary-wise and let me know." I had no idea what the going rate would even be. Even prices were wonky in the Zone.

She held out a hand. "Deal."

We shook on it, but I didn't let her go. "Your skin is crazy soft. What are you using?"

Tadji smiled slyly. "I've been mixing up this concoction with olive oil. If you can get me some more, I can make you some . . . and some to sell."

"This is clearly the beginning of a beautiful entrepreneurial relationship. Although," I said, frowning as something occurred to me, "as keen as I am on bringing you into the biz, people might ask questions if I'm not here."

"They aren't asking any fewer questions when you leave the store locked up for a couple of days."

I couldn't argue with that.

"We'll think of an answer. We'll make it work," she said with a nod. And for the first time in a long time, I felt like I had a partner.

"I actually have a first task for you," I said, and told her about the orders for Lizzie. "But I'll walk you through ordering and all that jazz. Oh, and you can take all the early shifts so I can sleep in."

"No dice."

"Worth a shot. I will give you a handy Royal Mercantile apron." I stepped back, frowned down at the rows of shelves beneath the counter, remembering that I'd lost two of them when we left Camp Couturie. "I just have to remember where the extras are."

"Those are the ones with the pockets in front?" she asked, moving her hands in front of her thighs to mimic their location.

"That's them."

"Good. I really like those."

"About you being gone . . . ," she began, then paused. "It's going to get worse, isn't it? All of this?"

Tadji had a bad history with magic, a childhood that had made her wary of it. She'd recently begun to come to terms with that, and with the family who'd instilled that wariness in her. So I wanted to lie to her. I wanted to tell her everything was fine. But shielding her from the truth—keeping her from preparing herself—wasn't going to help.

"It's going to get worse," I said.

She nodded gravely, as if trying to adjust her expectations.

"I don't know how much worse," I said, wanting to give her some hope. Because what was the point of living here without it, full heart or not? "It depends on how fast Containment can find Ezekiel and shut down Reveillon. Maybe they found him overnight at Camp Couturie."

"And if they didn't?"

"These are bad people, Tadj, especially Ezekiel. They're believers, and they're believers who are willing to be martyrs. They're violent, they're dangerous, and they believe they are absolutely right. They won't stop until this is done—whatever that means. So if you see any of them coming, you run in the other direction. Walk right out the back door, go to the Cabildo—to Gunnar or to Burke—and don't look back."

"You'll be careful, too?"

I pulled her into a hug. "With friends like you guys, how could I not be?" I just had to hope we could all keep one another safe.

Liam strolled in a little while later, sweat beading across his brow. It was a hot day, and he'd been monitoring whatever the Containment agents had been doing to his truck outside.

"You want to take a field trip?" he asked when he'd grabbed a bottle of water from the fridge. "Take a look at that address?"

It took me a moment to realize what he was talking about. When I did, I stared at him suspiciously. "To Mid-City? Yeah."

He nodded but looked over the store, then took a step closer. "Tell Tadji we're going to check something out, if you want, but skip the details. Just in case."

I frowned at him. "Just in case what?"

He leaned down. "Just in case this is something your father only wanted you to know about."

"I trust her," I said, irritation blossoming.

"It's not her I worry about," he said, gaze still and serious. "But those who'd use her to get the information."

That lifted the hair at the back of my neck. I hadn't even thought that far ahead—of the possibility it was a building that would matter to anyone other than my father. That would matter to Containment. Considering that possibility made me want to visit it more—and absolutely not mention it to Tadji.

"And I'm going to have Gavin stay here with her while we're gone," he said.

I frowned. "Stay here with—" I began, then realized why he'd suggested it. "In case they hit Royal Mercantile. You don't think Containment got him."

"There's a chance he ran after we left. And even if he didn't, the camp is big. It would take a lot of hours and a lot of manpower to clear the entire camp. As for the store, Ezekiel took his first shot at Devil's Isle. I don't think the store is high-profile enough for Ezekiel."

"Even if he's now pissed at me?"

"Even if."

I looked over the store. "We could close it up. Lock the doors and wait for all this to be over."

"I don't think that's necessary," Liam said. "And we won't be gone long. Gavin will keep her safe, Claire. He knows how to handle himself."

I nodded. "What should I tell her?"

"The truth," Liam said. "So she's prepared, just in case."

Damn it, I thought, and went to find her again.

"Tadj," I said, and her dark hair popped up behind a bookshelf she was swishing with a feather duster.

"Liam and I have to run out."

She nodded. "No problem."

"Liam's going to have Gavin stay with you while we're gone."

She figured it out faster than I had, and her eyes went wide. "You think they'll come here?"

"Liam doesn't think so. There'd be no political benefit to hitting the store. But better to be safe than sorry. If you're not comfortable with it, we can close down. The Quarter will live without us for a few days."

The door jangled as Gavin walked in again, and Liam stopped him. After a moment, Gavin looked over at us, nodded.

Tadji looked at me, chin lifted. "No," she said. "We're not closing the store. We're not going to cower from bullies."

"If you need to go," I said, giving her a quick hug, "just go. You're more important to me than the store."

Tadji grinned. "I'm sure that's at least sixty percent true. Go do your thing. We'll be fine."

I wouldn't have called myself especially religious, but for the second time that morning, I offered up another silent prayer for a friend.

"I hired her today," I said as we left the store and walked back into punishing humidity.

"About damn time," Liam said. "How much are you paying her?"

"We haven't gotten there yet." I stopped short on the sidewalk, staring at Liam's truck. The glass had been repaired, dents from gunshots flattened and filled. It didn't look good—Liam's truck would never look good—but it certainly looked better.

"Bulletproof glass?" I asked, walking toward it and tapping a finger against the back window.

"No. The Commandant wouldn't spring for that," Liam said irritably, opening his door.

"Still, it looks pretty good. And they made fast work of it." If Containment hadn't been involved, it probably would have taken weeks just to get the correct windows.

"I can't complain about that," he said, and started the engine when I climbed in, closed the door.

It shut on the first try, which had us both staring at it.

"Huh," he said.

"Yep. No bulletproof glass, but a functioning door's a nice thing."

He didn't argue about it but headed to the edge of the Quarter and then north to the address my father had left behind.

I had no idea what we'd find when we got there. But I hoped some questions would be answered.

CHAPTER FOURTEEN

Mid-City had been one of my favorite neighborhoods in New Orleans. Like the Quarter, it had kept a lot of its unique architecture, although the war had destroyed many of those buildings.

We'd rolled down the windows. The breeze carried the scent of smoke, which grew stronger the farther north we drove, until the air was hazy with it. Then we saw the plume of smoke rising into the sky about half a mile uptown.

"I want to check that out," Liam said, and I nodded my agreement as he turned toward it.

We didn't get very far. Dark Containment vehicles blocked the street two hundred yards from the inferno that engulfed a Containment precinct office. Even that far away, the heat that rolled off the fire was absolutely brutal.

Liam pulled up to the blockade, leaned out the window. "Hitchens!" he called out, and an agent turned around, nodded at Liam, and jogged over.

"Hey, Quinn."

"The hell happened?" Liam asked as Hitchens passed a hand over his damp forehead.

"Reveillon. They went on a spree overnight. Torched four buildings owned by PCC or Containment."

"Damn," Liam said. "Any injuries?"

"I've heard a dozen with smoke inhalation, burns, but no deaths. Reveillon left its calling card—painted 'Traitors' on the street in front, just in case we were confused."

One of Ezekiel's favorite words.

If Reveillon had been setting fires overnight, Containment clearly hadn't gotten them all. And if there was some sort of coordinated arson, Containment probably hadn't gotten Ezekiel at Camp Couturie.

"Assholes," Liam said.

"Agreed," Hitchens said, then slid his gaze to me, back to Liam. "You working the Reveillon bounty?"

"Yeah," Liam said. "Claire, this is Tucker Hitchens. Claire Connolly. She runs Royal Mercantile."

"Sure, sure," Hitchens said. "I know it. I don't live in the Quarter, so I don't get down there, but I know it."

I lifted a hand, offered a smile.

Another agent called Hitchens's name, and he tapped the doorframe. "Gotta get back. Take care of yourself out there."

"You, too, Hitch."

The man ran back to his comrades near the vehicles.

"Ezekiel's still free," I guessed. "And he's pissed."

"Yeah," Liam said. "And New Orleans will pay the price." He put the truck in gear. "Let's get going. I don't want to be far from the Quarter for too long."

I didn't argue.

New Orleans was relatively flat, so we drove to a spot where the buildings had mostly been destroyed, climbed into the back of the truck, then onto the roof, to get a look at the city.

"Four," Liam confirmed, shifting his gaze from each of the four plumes that rose into the sky at what looked like random spots across the city. Except they weren't really random, at least not politically.

"'And the nations were angry,'" Liam said quietly. "'And thy wrath is come.'"

"The Book of Revelation," I said, and he looked surprised that I'd recognized it. "My dad loved horror novels, and he thought Revelation fit the genre."

Liam smiled a little. "Possibly sacrilegious, but it works." He climbed smoothly down into the back of the truck, offered me a hand, helped me step down gingerly beside him.

"Come on," he said. "Let's go take a look at your father's mystery building. Maybe we'll find a magic carpet that will transport us all into Happy Land."

A boy could dream.

We drove back to Carrolton, Liam slowing as the numbers ticked down to the address we were searching for.

My stomach knotted uncomfortably . . . and then I just stared.

It was an Apollo station—an old-fashioned gas and service station probably from the 1950s. There was a rectangular building with two garage doors and a roof that swooped dramatically to one side. The Apollo trademark—a giant, sun-shaped sign—still stood in front of the building like the standard of another era. The modern, angular numbers on the side of the building said we had the right place.

Liam pulled the truck beneath the overhang in front of the building, which had probably shielded gas attendants from torrential southern downpours once upon a time.

"A gas station," he said, glancing through my window at the tidy white building.

"Yeah." It was all I could gather the energy to say. I'd expected something more. I didn't know what, exactly, but something that would tell me about my father, about the secrets he'd been keeping.

Instead, we'd found . . . a gas station.

"Hold on," Liam said, as if he could sense my disappointment. "Let's take a look."

We climbed out of the truck, stood for a moment in the quiet. A dog barked somewhere in the distance, but there were no other sounds of life in the neighborhood. It was creepy to hear that absolute silence, but also comforting in a way. There were no people here, which meant no war and no Reveillon. Just nature drawing its green blanket back over New Orleans.

"The building's in good shape," Liam said, walking around to join me on the passenger side. "Surprisingly good shape, all things considered. Either it wasn't hit during the war or it's been taken care of since then."

He stopped in front of the door, put his hands on his hips as he surveyed the building, then looked back at me. "You've never been here?"

"Nope."

He nodded, put a hand on the doorknob before I could get there. "Wait," he said, and looked around. "Let's do a perimeter check first."

I nodded, followed him to the side of the property, where weeds were tall in the cracked asphalt. There was a drive all the way around the building, a utility box, a locked security door. On the far side, windows coated in white paint.

"I don't see anything telling," I said as we walked around to the front again.

"It tells us no one has tried to break in. Given the looting during the war, it means this building was exceptionally lucky, or someone protected it, at least for a while. The locks are rusty," he said, nodding toward the front door. "That tells us no one's been through the front door, either."

He put an ear to the door, then tried the knob. It didn't budge.

"I don't suppose you know how to pick a lock?"

"I do," he said. "But I don't have any tools on me." He looked back at the truck, frowning. "And none in the truck, either."

"I could open it," I said. I'd shifted a dozen magical tumblers in order to lock the Veil into place. I could probably handle a commercial dead bolt.

Liam looked back at me, then behind me, gaze shifting around us. He walked to the canopy that covered the spots where the gas pumps had been, looked up and down, then back at the roof, the light poles, the streetlights, before returning.

"I think you're safe for that," Liam said. "I don't see any monitors or cameras that could have eyes on us. But even if there is a monitor somewhere, and it goes off, we'll hear Containment coming." Containment tended to roar toward magic with lights and sirens. "And that assumes they've got any personnel who could respond to a call right now."

"The fires," I said, and he nodded.

"Ezekiel knows how to use his people. The border attacks show he knows how to keep Containment spread thin."

"And if they do get here?"

Liam smiled. "We tell them the truth—we're on a bounty, which we just verified with Hitchens. We found a wraith, and he went into a frenzy that triggered the monitor."

That was plenty close enough to the truth.

"All right, then," I said, and crouched in front of the door. I felt suddenly self-conscious doing magic in front of him after last night, after the conversation this morning he didn't know I'd heard.

Maybe I could use that, I thought, shifting to my knees and closing my eyes. Malachi had told me to figure out how to use my emotions to help fuel my magic. This was a good chance to try it.

I let myself be frustrated, let myself open to emotions I'd rather have pushed away and pretended didn't exist. And by doing that, I acknowledged they had weight and power, and substance of their own in that weird space where magic existed.

Experimenting, I let them twine together, let the magic and the emotions braid themselves along the filaments of power, enhance them, direct them. To my surprise, the emotions contained it, a lasso around wriggling prey, and directed its movement. The magic still fought back, tugging against the line, but it was in my grasp, instead of the other way around.

It was the first time I'd set a limit on the magic itself, as opposed to trying to use the magic—its wildness and madness, its forcefulness and strength—to manipulate an object.

Hope filled me.

Maybe Malachi had been onto something.

Before I lost the edge and the grip on the filaments of power I'd created, I linked them together, imagined sinking them into the tumblers, letting them feel their way through the lock. I couldn't actually see their shift, the rise and fall of the pins, but I could feel them with that indefinable sense.

And then they fell into place, and the lock opened with a *click*.

Still on my knees in front of the door, I opened my eyes, the frissons of magic still sparking in the air like dust motes in a shaft of light.

I stood slowly, expecting to feel the magic rush suddenly back into the vacuum I'd created. But there was nothing but the sound of the breeze in the long and waving grass.

I could feel Liam's gaze on me, and looked at him, saw the interest in his eyes, the pride. There was reluctance behind it, sure. Considering what I'd done in the full light of day, I could understand the uneasiness.

The moment passed, and Liam looked back at the door. He held up a finger, signaling me to wait, then pushed it open.

A dusty breeze spilled out, the air cool enough to make a mist of the humidity at our feet. "The air-conditioning works," I whispered. But there were no other sounds, no other smells, no obvious dangers.

When we were certain no one would rush the door, Liam took the first step inside.

I moved to follow him, but the sudden vertigo made the ground shift at my feet, and I put a hand on the doorjamb to steady myself. Maybe I'd have to get used to this new way of wrangling magic, or its aftereffects.

I walked carefully inside, closed the door behind us—and kept a palm on its cold, metal surface to give myself a chance to regroup.

Liam flipped a switch on the wall. There was a momentary buzz, and overhead lights illuminated the space.

"*Merde*," he said, staring at the room.

Silence fell heavy around us.

"Lock the door," Liam said after a moment, and I reached out and flipped the lock. I wasn't entirely sure what we were looking at, but I was pretty sure we didn't want anyone else walking in.

The interior of the building had been rehabbed, stripped down to concrete floor that had been refinished and glossed and bare walls. There was a small kitchenette along the wall to the right, and a spiral steel staircase that rose to a second floor toward the back.

There were shelves along the other walls. And in the middle of the large space were long tables, stacked with objects, like some kind of homegrown museum.

I walked to the closest table, glanced over the objects that filled it. A mask, a dagger, and a book wrapped in black leather. A set of small glass bottles. A large blue-black feather and a carefully folded triangle of white cloth. And that was just a sampling. All four tables, all four shelves, stored the same varied assortment of things.

"Magic," Liam said.

"Yeah," I said with a nod, lifting my gaze to the shelves, and realizing exactly what my father had done. "I think this is an archive of magic."

Magical objects—books, weapons, charms, herbs, statues—filled the room, all of it as contraband in the Zone as magic itself. They hadn't actually been magical until the Veil had opened, spilling the Beyond's energy into our world. But after that happened, Containment feared Paras could use the objects against humans. And considering New Orleans's fascination with ghosts, vampires, and voodoo, there'd have been a lot of them to use.

I picked up a walking stick, similar to the dozens still stocked at Royal Mercantile. Most of the walking sticks in the store had a secret. If this one was here, it probably had a secret, too.

I picked it up, unscrewed the brass end cap. The wood didn't want to give, and it took a few attempts, but I finally managed to pry it away. I held out a hand, upturned the stick. A small purple bag, a symbol crushed into the old and stiff velvet, fell into my palm.

"Gris-gris," I said, holding it up so Liam could see. A walking stick with a voodoo charm tucked inside.

I put the pouch and the stick on the table, wiped dust and sweat onto my jeans, but couldn't erase the tingle of magic. They might not have been magical before, but they were certainly magical now.

"If this is your father's building, then it's probably your father's archive."

But from where? The Magic Act was broad; Containment confiscated everything that could arguably be magic. They saw crystal balls in glass paperweights, summoning guides in books of ghost stories.

"When the act passed," I said, "my father cleaned out the store of everything they said was illegal, gave it to Containment. But it was all innocuous."

Still, I remembered standing with him, watching as Containment burned a pile of books and voodoo "implements" in Congo Square.

"They shouldn't do this," he'd whispered, gaze on the licking flames while others cheered. "These things are harmless."

"These things are dangerous," I'd said, parroting what they'd told us at school.

"People are dangerous. Guns are dangerous. Knives are dangerous." My father had been tall, with brown hair and dark eyes. When he'd looked down at me, he'd seemed unbearably sad. "This is a reaction to fear, to the attacks. Even when we're afraid, we still have to think through what we're doing. We have to consider the consequences."

We'd walked away from the fire then, left the crowd to its bloodlust.

"He was in love with New Orleans," I said. "And he loved objects—was fascinated by their meaning, their history, their symbolism. That's why I stayed here and kept the store." I looked back at the table. "If any of these belonged to him, he didn't tell me about it. He certainly didn't tell Containment about it."

"If he'd gotten these things from anyone else, surely they'd have come back," Liam said. "Cleaned up, or added things, or taken them back."

I nodded. It was a miracle the place hadn't been looted. I swiped a finger of dust off the table. Everything looked carefully arranged—carefully curated—but the dust said they hadn't been touched in a very long time.

I looked back at Liam. "It's cold in here, and nothing looks dirty, moldy."

"Dehumidifier and air conditioner," he said. "Although how that's been operating for seven years I have no idea. Parts break over time, especially metal parts in New Orleans."

"Maybe someone checked on it in the meantime."

"Or maybe it was magicked. This was a big risk," Liam said, flipping through a book before sliding it back onto a shelf again. He looked back at me, his blue eyes blazing. "He put you at risk. If Containment found this now, they'd destroy it. And then they'd destroy you."

I walked across the room, stared up at the golden shield that hung from posts there. It was a weapon of the Consularis, heavily engraved and inlaid with metals and symbols in a language I didn't understand.

I reached out and traced a finger across a deep diagonal dent that ran across the middle of the shield. The metal vibrated softly beneath my fingertips, like an engine hummed beneath it. Magic, alive and well seven years later.

"The walls have to be shielded," I said, pulling back my fingers and rubbing the sensation from my fingertips. "Wraiths would be swarming outside if they weren't. They'd be drawn to the magic." Maybe that was why I'd felt vertigo when I stepped inside.

Liam nodded. "Maybe the same person who shielded the store. More confirmation of your father's involvement."

Yeah, it was. And I wasn't sure how I felt about that.

"I'm going to look around," he said, and walked to the staircase.

He took a testing step, bouncing slightly to be sure the steel was sturdy, then circled up into the second floor.

I walked to the kitchenette, opened the refrigerator. It was cool, but empty. Immaculately clean, as was my father's way. The cabinets were glossy red and slick to the touch. They held a few white cups, a few white plates. The cabinet below it had a small set of pots and pans, still unmarked and unused.

Waiting for someone to use them. Waiting for someone to make this a home.

"There's a loft up there," Liam said, footsteps clanging on the metal treads as he came downstairs again. "Bed, bureau. You find anything?"

I closed the cabinet, frowned. "A few cups, a few bowls, a few pans." I looked back at him. "This place is outfitted like a guest-house, but it doesn't look like anyone stayed here."

Liam nodded, walked to a door on the other side of the room. "Up there, either. It looks untouched. Maybe your dad wanted a hole in case you had to run."

"Because he was a Sensitive." Because my very existence—through no fault of my own—was illegal in the Zone. And the possibility existed that someone would figure that out. He probably felt the same.

"Yeah," Liam said, and opened the door, then closed it again. He must not have found anything interesting.

From my spot in the kitchen, I looked back over the space, realized the tables were perfectly aligned on a couple of large woven rugs, which were placed perfectly parallel to each other, about five feet apart.

This had been a garage, I thought. Maybe it still worked like one. I walked to the far wall, looked over a light switch plate with an awful lot of wide buttons, and pressed one.

"Winning," I said as the metal plate beneath two of the tables began to rise, lifting them into the air and revealing the empty space beneath.

"Clever girl," Liam said, walking toward it. He gave the steel rod that supported the plate and tables a solid look before moving to his knees beside it. "And what do we have here?"

"What is it?" I asked, jogging toward him, my eyes widening as he moved aside to let me look.

"Supplies," he said. The lights above us pooled into the space below the lift, showing crates, boxes, and barrels of food and supplies. Water, dehydrated potatoes, cans of soup and broth, bags of rice and beans.

My stomach growled, and I put a hand against it to silence it.

"Is half of my protein bar the only thing you've eaten today?"

"It was *my* protein bar," I reminded him. "And yes, but I'm fine. That was a covetous growling."

Liam made a sound of doubt and sat back on his heels. "There's got to be a way to get down there. A door, some stairs to the lower level."

He stood up, offered a hand to help me to my feet. When he pulled me up, we scanned the walls.

"There," I said, pointing to the narrow door in a corner of the kitchen.

We walked to it, opened it. A narrow set of stairs led into darkness.

Liam found another light and flicked it on, illuminating another set of stairs in corrugated metal. Another testing step—it was wise never to trust old metal in a subtropical zone without testing it first—and we descended.

The air was even cooler down here, the dust just as thick. The scents were different. The first floor smelled more like an antique store than a gas station—dust and must and fiber. The basement smelled more like a museum. Clinical. Sterile.

Everything was organized—cans on shelves, bags on pallets, life vests and backpacks hanging from a pegboard. Stacks of first-aid kits. Bundled and wrapped sleeping bags. Dozens of cases of bottled water, also still wrapped in their plastic sleeves. In one corner, a humming dehumidifier.

My father had collected food, water, and supplies the same way he'd collected magical supplies.

"This isn't a guesthouse," Liam said, trailing fingers across the front of a row of canned soups.

"No," I agreed. "It's a bunker."

His voice was soft, and I could feel his eyes on mine. "Did your father ever mention it?"

"No," I said again, and could hear exhaustion in my voice. I was tired of developments and revelations, and my anger at my father was growing with every one of them. Growing every time I had to wonder why he hadn't told me about this place, whatever it was.

I walked to the pegboard, unzipped one of four matching camo backpacks. Inside was a bottle of water, two flares, a small first-aid kit, a plastic bag of protein bars. It was a go bag, not unlike the one I had stashed in an armoire in the second-floor storage room. Just in case.

I'd asked him about leaving. One night, when we sat huddled in the downstairs bathroom, all the lights off, all the doors locked, as sirens screamed outside, I'd told him it was insane to stay.

"We can't abandon her," he'd said. "We can't abandon New Orleans."

"I'd rather live somewhere else than die here." I'd been seventeen, and convinced I knew everything.

"We don't just quit," my father had said, putting an arm over my head as shots of magic crackled outside, vibrant green light flashing in the sliver of space along the bottom of the bathroom door. "We don't just walk away."

Instead, he'd made a plan to stay in New Orleans, with enough supplies to last at least a little while.

There was a tall, metal safe in the corner. It was dark green, with the manufacturer's name across the front in pretty gold script. I'd seen a safe like that before—there was one in the back room of the store. Empty now, but meant to hold weapons.

I walked to it, Liam's footsteps falling in line behind me, and turned the heavy handle, and the door swung open. Closed, but not locked. And inside, two rifles, two shotguns, two handguns that I guessed were nine millimeters, or something like that, and several cartons of ammo.

"He was prepared."

"For war," I said, touching a finger to the cold metal barrel of a rifle, then closing the door again.

"They're yours," Liam said carefully, glancing down at me. "You could take these with you—or one of them. Or anything else in here."

I turned back to the room, crossed my arms as I looked at it all. "It's mine if we assume it was my father's."

"You'd know him best."

"I thought I did," I said, and looked back at him. "What am I supposed to do with this, Liam? What am I supposed to think?"

Outside, while using my magic and then while seeing Liam's reaction to it, I'd felt more myself than I ever had. Like, for the first time, I really and truly fit within my own skin, not trying to make myself fit in someone else's. Not just Claire of Royal Mercantile, but *Claire*.

This—this castle my father had built and furnished—made me feel like a stranger all over again.

Liam searched my face. "He didn't tell you about any of it."

I shook my head.

"I'm sorry."

I nodded, walked to the army green cot across the room, sat down. "Me, too." I looked up at Liam. "I feel like I have to keep grieving for him all over again, that every time I find out something like this, I lose him all over again. Lose the person he was."

"Yeah," Liam said with a sigh. "I understand that." He walked closer, stood in the middle of the room with his arms crossed, chin down.

"Helluva thing. So what do you want to do?"

I looked down at the floor—more polished concrete—while I considered. We could use the supplies, sure. Everything in here could be used, sold, distributed to those who needed it. But I thought of the prediction I'd made to Tadji earlier today, of the fact that an army was actively trying to dismantle that organization that remained in the Zone. It wouldn't be wise to burn through supplies we'd almost certainly need down the road.

I thought for a moment but couldn't find anything that would be gained from telling anyone else about this.

"I'm not going to tell anyone. Containment would either destroy the objects . . . or try to use them against the Paras." They'd become more flexible on that as the war had continued. "I'm not going to start a war against Containment, but neither am I going to hand them the weapons to use against someone else."

Maybe that was irresponsible of me. Maybe I should have handed it all over to Containment for the good of the cause. But Containment's "cause" was Devil's Isle. That didn't seem right, either.

Liam nodded. "Agreed. What about Gunnar?"

That answer was easier. There was too much here that could be used against me, against my father. And since I trusted Gunnar completely, used against Gunnar.

"No," I said. "I don't want this to become his problem."

"And the food? The supplies?"

"We don't have a lot these days, but we have what we need. I told Tadji today that I thought this was going to get worse before it gets better, and I think it will." I looked around again, shook my head. "I don't think we should touch it. Not now. Because there might come a time when we need it more."

That neatly sidestepped the issue of whether I wanted to use it, the fact that I felt uncomfortable even thinking about it. It might have been my father's . . . but he hadn't given it to me. And that made me want to touch it even less.

My gaze settled on a pink footlocker across the room. "CC" was painted in green across the front. It had been mine, a Christmas present that I'd filled with dolls and books and mementos. And occasionally pretended was a boat.

Hope flared. Had he saved that for me, so I could have my own things here, my own space?

I rose and walked to it, flipped up the gold latches, and opened it.

It was empty, except for a single photograph.

I stared down at the lithe woman with the long red hair who stared back at me.

She was tall and slender, her long arms and legs covered by a simple wrap dress, sandals on her feet. Her hair was long and straight and vibrantly red, set off by golden skin and green eyes. She stood beneath a live oak, one hand braced on the rough bark, limbs and Spanish moss reaching down around her. The sky was blue and dotted with cotton clouds, sunlight dappling through the leaves to cast shadows on the ground.

She looked like the redheaded woman I'd seen at the Memorial Battle.

I flipped the photograph over, but it was blank. No name, no year, no indication of where the picture had been taken or by whom.

"Claire?"

I could feel Liam suddenly behind me, his body big and warm.

"Is that your mother?" he asked when I didn't answer.

"I didn't know my mother," I said, barely holding back tears I didn't want to shed. "She died—had a bad strain of the flu when I was only two. There weren't any photographs of her in the house, so I'm not even sure what she looked like."

I looked back at Liam. "This looks like the woman I saw at Memorial."

He took the photograph, stared at it. "I didn't see her—the woman with red hair." He looked up at me, then back at the photograph again. "She looks like you."

I nodded. But if this was my mother, I didn't know then, and I didn't know how I could know it now.

"Do you want to take this?" he asked, offering it to me again.

I didn't know the answer to that. I didn't know if I should drop it back into the trunk—the trunk with my name on it, that carried no memories of me or anything else—or take it with me, because maybe I could use it to figure out who she was.

"I don't know." I didn't want to take it. But I also didn't want to leave it here. And I was too angry and sad to make a decision about anything.

"I'll take it," Liam said. "I'll put it in the truck, and it will be there when you're ready."

That small kindness nearly did me in, but I forced myself to hold it together. We had bigger problems right now—bigger dangers—than my personal drama.

"Okay," I said, and climbed to my feet.

"Let's go back to the store," Liam said, putting a hand against my back.

"Yeah," I said, and turned my back on the spoils my father had gathered.

Whatever this was, it wasn't home. And I was ready to go back to mine.

CHAPTER FIFTEEN

We went back to the Quarter with more questions than he'd come with. Why not tell me about the Apollo? Why not give me a chance to get there if something had happened to him?

Because maybe it hadn't been meant for us. Maybe he'd built it, prepared it, for her, for the woman in the photograph. Maybe he'd been biding his time until he could get to her.

"You all right?" Liam asked when we'd put some distance between us and the station.

"I don't know. I'm confused and sad and suddenly the owner of what is probably the biggest cache of magical artifacts in the Zone."

"If not the United States," Liam said with a smile. "In a manner of speaking, you hit the jackpot."

"If we ignore the contraband part."

He waved that away. "I'm sure Containment wouldn't care. It's only a few things. A few hundred very illegal things."

"Quit trying to cheer me up."

He slid me a quick glance. "You'd rather wallow?"

"At the moment, yeah, I would."

Brow furrowed, he futzed around under his seat. "I may have a cassette of depressing violin music in here somewhere."

"God," I said, rubbing my hands over my face. "Could you have picked a trainee with more drama? I'm sorry."

"No," Liam said. "Don't ever apologize for who or what you are. A lot of people would have walked away from New Orleans, from Royal Mercantile. You built something, Claire. You are heart and recklessness and fire. The drama just came along for the ride."

This time, I couldn't keep the tears from falling.

"Your eyes appear to be sweating," Liam said, and handed me a tissue he'd scrounged from under the seat.

"Shut up," I said, but I was half smiling when I said it. "And thank you."

"Anytime, Claire. Anytime."

There were several customers in the store, but Tadji gestured us to the back room as soon as we walked in.

We found Gunnar at the table, bottle of Scotch in front of him and fury written in every feature. Gavin stood nearby, arms crossed and watching.

"Hey," I said, glancing between them. "What's wrong?"

"I am in a fighting goddamn mood." He poured a finger of amber liquid into a short glass. "I had to walk away for a few minutes, or I was heading for court-martial."

Liam stood beside his brother. "What happened?"

"They're gone. Ezekiel, the arsenal, anybody else strong enough to fight. They cleared out the camp before PCC could be bothered to send anyone over there."

Liam blinked. "What do you mean, 'before PCC could be bothered'? Why did they wait? They had our firsthand reports."

"They had your reports, and they had a bunch of red tape handed to them by some legal eagle in PCC who decided we didn't have jurisdiction at the camp."

"I don't understand," I said, taking the seat in front of Gunnar.

"Camp Couturie was a federal refugee camp on city property," Gunnar said. "It apparently took a lot of red tape for FEMA to set up the camp in the first place—back when FEMA was still in charge—and all that goddamn red tape had to be untangled so that we could walk into Camp Couturie to search for Reveillon, even with a warrant."

"Jurisdictional bullshit," Gavin said.

"A-fucking-men," Gunnar said. "By the time we got our teams in, they'd probably been gone for hours. And it took hours more to search completely. We found a few perfectly legal weapons and a handful of people who had no interest in joining him."

I looked at Liam. "And that's why they only sent one vehicle after us. They were letting us get away."

"Damn," Liam said with a nod. "Ezekiel had decided to run, and they used the other vehicles to evacuate the camp."

Guilt settled heavy in my belly that we'd been the reason they'd run, had slipped Containment's grasp. But we'd been the only ones willing to check out the lead. Containment should have taken the tattoo, the possibility of Camp Couturie, more seriously.

"Do you have any idea how many Reveillon members were there?" Liam asked.

"Based on the last population estimate, and the count we did today, about a thousand."

Silence fell as we considered that.

"There can't be that many gullible people," I said. "People dumb enough to buy in to his nonsense."

"Not necessarily dumb," Gavin said. "Just gullible and angry."

Gunnar nodded. "Nailed it in one. You're on a roll today."

"I'm more than just delectable good looks."

"They've probably split up," Liam said. "Safe houses or camps across the city so they don't attract too much attention. They might have done the same with the arsenal."

"Every Containment officer who isn't working in Devil's Isle is searching the city," Gunnar said, pouring another shot. "And that's only the first issue in this shitshow of a day."

I took the shot before he could drink it, winced at the heat, and waited for the warmth to settle. Not my poison of choice, but beggars couldn't be choosers.

"We saw the fires," Liam said.

Gunnar nodded, poured another drink, downed it. "We lost two in the fires to smoke inhalation. We also lost records, equipment, stockpiles of water—we keep it all over the city, just in case. But things could have been even worse. Fortunately, Malachi spotted one of the fires, just after dawn. He pulled a couple of napping agents out of the building, triggered the monitor so Containment would respond."

"Clever," Liam said.

"It was. The fire was too big for him to stop, and was raging by the time our people got there. We'd have lost two more men if he hadn't intervened. Unfortunately, that wasn't the end of the violence. One of Burke's convoys was attacked outside the city, near Ponchatoula."

"They nearly made it to New Orleans," Liam said.

"Nearly," Gunnar agreed, misery in his eyes. "But not nearly enough."

Liam sighed. "How many?"

"Four." Gunnar ran a hand through his hair. The anger had burned off into guilt and grief. "Four more agents lost."

"They're spreading Containment thin," Gavin said.

"They are. We know it, but we can't do anything other than what we're doing. At least not unless PCC can get some troops across the goddamn border. That would require identifying the PCC leak, which PCC denies it has."

"The brass taking heat?" Liam asked.

"The president is pissed. Congress is pissed. The Joint Chiefs are pissed. And everybody is blaming someone else for this absolute clusterfuck."

"That's what it's all about, isn't it?"

We all looked at Gavin.

"Blame," he said. "That's what Ezekiel is doing—making promises about the future, blaming the past and present on Paras."

"Yeah," Gunnar said. "And he's doing it damn effectively." He looked at me. "Tell Malachi that Ezekiel is in the wind. And that he has my personal thanks for stepping in when he saw the fire."

I nodded. "We're meeting him at noon," I said, and checked the wall clock. It was nearly time to leave. The Apollo had taken a good chunk of the morning.

"So, what do we do now?" I asked.

"We hunt," Liam said darkly, deadly intent in his eyes. "We find them, and we take them down."

We didn't have time to throw out a plan before the air raid siren began to ring again.

"Shit," Gunnar said, and we followed the crowd out the door. Royal was empty except for the flock of pigeons that lifted into the sky across the street, startled by our outburst.

Smoke lifted inside the walls of Devil's Isle. And for the second time in as many days, we ran toward the prison.

Gavin stayed at the store, so Gunnar, Liam, and I did the running.

The sirens grew louder, the smoke more intense, the ache in my ankle stronger the closer we got to the fence. The gate was closed and guarded, so something had happened inside, not at the gate.

"Report," Gunnar asked, flashing his ID as the gate swung open.

One of the guards who stood inside nodded. "A Reveillon fugitive blew the riverside warehouse."

We followed Gunnar into the neighborhood and two blocks past the gate, where flames shot from the roof of a long, narrow building. A dozen Containment officers stood nearby while firefighters worked to contain the blaze.

Reece stood across the street, hands linked behind his back. He looked like a soldier at parade rest, but for the tension around his eyes.

"Reveillon?" Gunnar asked when we reached him, and the sirens finally quieted.

Reece nodded. "Molotov cocktail. Fire was started by one of the fugitives." He gestured to the opposite corner, where a woman in dirty linen kneeled on the sidewalk, her hands behind her head. She was flanked by particularly pissed-looking Containment officers.

"Only one building affected?" Gunnar asked.

"That we've seen, yes," Reece said.

Near the fires outside the gate, TRAITORS was scrawled in spray-painted letters across the front of the building.

"It can't be a coincidence they set similar fires outside Devil's Isle and inside Devil's Isle today," I said.

"Is there any evidence Reveillon has been talking to the fugitives in here?" Liam asked.

"Not that we're aware of," Gunnar said.

"Maybe they planned ahead," Reece said. "Both knew today was the day."

Liam's gaze lifted to the faint streaks that marked the sky outside the prison. "Or the fires outside were the signal—a sign the fugitives should act. What was in the building?"

"Storage," Gunnar said. "Paper files, mostly. It's barely guarded, because there's literally nothing in there that anyone could use."

"The building wasn't staffed?" I asked.

"No," Reece said. "And no injuries reported."

Reveillon liked drama, which made me wonder why they'd bother torching an unstaffed storage building. It would be inconvenient for Containment, sure, but that was all.

"So there's not really any point in burning it?" I asked.

Liam put his hands on his hips, glanced around, squinting in the sunlight. "Maybe this fire was an answer to Ezekiel's signal. Not an attack per se, but a way to get a response over the walls."

"Signaling what?" Gunnar asked.

"That the fugitives are alive, that they're ready to start some plan of their own . . . or that they're starting."

"Starting what?" Reece asked.

Like instant confirmation Liam had been right, a scream split the air to our left, and then a gunshot did the same from our right. Two more gunshots fired somewhere in front of us.

Liam put out a hand in front of me, like a parent protecting a child in an imminent car crash.

Gunnar pulled a communication unit from his belt as Containment agents around the building looked around, trying to figure where to go and what to do.

"This is Landreau!" he called out, gaze on the towers that marked the corners of the prison. "What the hell's going on out there?"

The response was staticky, but clear enough.

"Attacks . . . Reveillon fugitives . . . All positions report . . . All positions report!"

"To your positions!" Gunnar yelled, and the agents immediately pulled weapons, began to head in all directions. "Reveillon is attacking Paras!"

"Not Paras!" the voice shouted over the comm unit. "Humans."

My stomach twisted as I glanced at the letters etched by fire into the side of the building: TRAITORS.

I thought of our time in Camp Couturie, in Ezekiel's tent. He'd called me and Liam the same thing, said we were betraying our fellow humans because we supported Paranormals. Because we supported Containment.

"Containment agents killed," I said. "Humans attacked. Ezekiel is targeting humans he believes are traitors to his cause." I looked at Gunnar. "How many humans live in Devil's Isle?"

"Only a handful," he said, frowning. "A few agents, a couple of people who staff the clinic." And then he paled. "And Liam's grandmother."

Fear coated my belly. Reveillon knew Liam lived in Devil's Isle. If the fugitives had seen him, followed him, or even just asked around, they might have learned about Eleanor, or even seen her.

Fear and fury crossed Liam's face in equal measure. "I'm going."

"I'm with you," I called out, and fell into step when he dashed in the direction of his grandmother's town house.

"Reece?" Gunnar asked, pointing at us, and got a nod. When Reece fell into step beside us, Gunnar yelled at two agents nearby. "Smith and Valentine. Go with Reece, Claire, Liam to the civilian's home."

Inviting Containment into Eleanor's home wasn't a great idea—she had magical objects, and she had Moses. But it couldn't be helped. We'd just have to do our best to keep things from getting worse.

The town house was only a few blocks away. Unfortunately, after the mile-long run to Devil's Isle, my ankle throbbed like a bad tooth.

We passed two clusters of people along the way, Containment agents administering help to wounded or Paranormals who screamed in a language I didn't understand. A man was on the ground near one of them, arms and legs covered in pale linen and unseeing eyes open to the sky. He was a Reveillon fugitive, and I couldn't muster up any remorse that he was dead.

By the time we reached Eleanor's block, it was empty of guards and people, and much too quiet.

The gate swung open in the breeze, and the door was cracked. There was no sign of Foster, or the Containment guard Gunnar had promised. Liam didn't waste any time running inside. I didn't waste any time following him, the others' footsteps echoing behind me.

Pike and a man I didn't know, probably the guard, lay on the floor, eyes closed.

I cursed Ezekiel under my breath. But Liam had already disappeared up the stairs; he'd need backup, so I had to delegate.

"Reece, please," I said, pointing to them, and headed for the stairs.

While he crouched by Pike, checking his pulse, I took the stairs two at a time, and could hear Foster's low and warning growl echoing down from the second floor.

I rounded the corner, stopped short in the threshold of Eleanor's room.

It had been ripped apart—paintings on the floor, rugs pulled up from the hardwood floors, objects from Eleanor's large bookshelf tossed around. Eleanor lay on the floor near the windows, her petite body looking impossibly frail. Moses crouched in front of her, ferocity in his expression.

And in front of them were two Reveillon members—a man and a woman in their dirty linens.

She stood on Eleanor's high-backed chair, cornered like a treed raccoon by a snarling and snapping Foster.

Liam had already engaged the man, and they exchanged blows on the other side of the room.

Fugitives momentarily contained, I ran to Eleanor. But Moses still crouched protectively in front of her, his horns gleaming like lacquer as he watched me with murderous eyes.

"Moses," I said, firmly, even while my heart was frantically thumping. "I need to check Eleanor."

He bared his teeth, his pupils narrowing to slits.

I didn't know what would bring him back, remind him that I was a friend. And since Eleanor wasn't moving, I didn't think I had time to figure it out.

"Fine," I said, taking another step closer. "Gore me if you need to. But she needs help, and I'm going to check on her."

Mustering every ounce of confidence, I walked past him like this was just business as usual.

I knelt beside Eleanor and put a hand against her forehead, then her neck. Her forehead was cool, her pulse slow but steady. There were bruises already gathering at the thin skin on her arms, and a lump on her forehead. We needed to get her to a doctor—or get a doctor to her, although Lizzie probably already had her hands full . . .

I looked up, around, spied her shawl on the back of her overturned wingback chair, then jumped up and grabbed it, offered it to Moses. "I don't want her to go into shock. Can you cover her with this?"

I hoped that allowing him to help her would help him in turn, bring him around.

Sure enough, the red haze in his eyes seemed to dim as he swung the blanket over her, tucked it in.

"Thank you," I said. "Thank you for protecting her."

He gave me the tiniest nod, which was progress as far as I was concerned.

Maybe thinking I'd dealt with Moses, the female fugitive made a move to get down, but Foster jumped, nipped at her leg. She cursed at him, kicked wildly. Foster was smart enough to avoid her feet, and jumped in front of her while trying to sink teeth into her shins.

Much as I wanted him to bite her—and as much as she deserved it—I didn't want him hurt in the process.

"One minute," I said to Moses, jumping to my feet and walking to the chair where she perched. "Foster, *sit*," I demanded, in a tone that said I was the alpha female.

Surprising both of us, he sat down, ears back and teeth bared, as he watched our mutual enemy.

The woman looked from him, to me, and her eyes went sly. She had a military look—short hair, cut cheekbones, serious eyes—and I recognized her. She was the other woman who'd walked beside Ezekiel at the protest, who'd been in the lead with him as they moved down Bourbon Street. I wondered if there was a reason for that—and if that reason was why he hadn't made her carry explosives.

She stepped down from the chair, fury in her eyes. *"Traitor."*

"You guys do like that word, don't you? Ironic, though, since you're the one who walked into someone's home and attacked her. You think that makes you a savior? You'd be wrong."

"She's a traitor." Her eyes narrowed. "And I know what else she is. I've seen them come and go, the Paranormals. I know why she's here."

Part of me wanted to be afraid for Eleanor—fearful this woman had somehow figured out her magic—but that seemed unlikely, so I didn't have to fake my confusion. "What else is she?"

"A Sensitive."

I rolled my eyes. "No, she isn't." She wasn't—not technically, anyway.

"You lie to protect them, but that doesn't matter. We know now. Ezekiel knows now."

Every cell in my body wanted to stop the action in the room, run to Liam, and relay that Ezekiel now believed Eleanor was a Sensitive. That Liam's grandmother—a woman Ezekiel already believed was a traitor—had magic. Instead, I had to play it off.

"Since you're wrong, he'll be sorely disappointed," I said, trying to sound bored.

"You're lying. Why else would she live in this hellhole, near *them*? Why else would they visit her, talk to her, if she wasn't like them?"

"Did it occur to you that maybe she likes talking to Paranormals? That they like talking to her?"

"That would make her a traitor like you. You'll end up on the wrong side of history," she warned. "We'll end this reign of terror, and we'll end it now."

"You know, the last time someone decided to mow down people to create a new world, they ended up in Devil's Isle."

Logic evaded her. "You're helping Paranormals destroy the Zone."

I gestured to the room she'd trashed. "*You're* destroying the Zone, literally. You're killing people, destroying more of a city that can't afford it."

"We're working for a better world."

I thought of Eleanor on the floor, of Moses in shock, of the screams and gunshots, of the fires and lost Containment agents, of the death and fear and pain.

And I couldn't help myself. I balled my hand into a fist and rammed it into her pretty face.

She hadn't expected me to do it, and hadn't even raised her guard. She wobbled, and then her eyes rolled back. She hit the floor with a heavy thud.

"Bitch," I muttered, then shook my hand, tears springing to my eyes. I'd known it was going to hurt, but not this much. It felt like I'd rammed my knuckles into a steel panel. *"Ow."*

There was a crash of wood. Liam's man had fallen backward onto a low table. On his back on the floor, his eyes fluttered closed.

Chest heaving, Liam lifted his gaze, searching for the other agent, found her sprawled out. He looked at me, the hand I cradled, and a smile crossed his face.

"Did you knock her out?" he asked, walking toward me.

"Yeah." I opened my hand, flexed my fingers, which shot pain through them. "Maybe not my best idea."

"Reckless," Liam said with a shake of his head, but the comment didn't diminish his smile. He held out his hand, and I placed my fingers in his. He touched each bone gingerly, as if checking for breaks. "Right cross?"

"Sure?"

"I think you're all right. Bruised it, but I don't feel anything broken." He turned to Moses and his expression became serious again. He crouched beside him and Eleanor, put a hand on Moses's arm. "Status?"

"Fuckers moved fast. Fast and quiet. We didn't even hear Foster, Pike, or the guard make a noise, and then suddenly they were upstairs."

"They could be ex-Containment or ex-military," I said.

"Yeah," Liam said with a rueful nod. "And that's not real comforting." He squeezed Moses's arm. "You kept her safe. I owe you for that."

"Kept her safe? She's lying on the floor, unconscious."

Eleanor opened one eye. "I'm not unconscious. I was just pretending."

"You were *what*?" Moses turned his angry stare on her. "You think I have time for nonsense like that? For pretending? Scare a body to death. Half to death, anyway."

"Reckless," Liam said again. "Both of them. Where are you hurt?"

He put a hand behind Eleanor's head to help lift her up, but she winced, shook her head.

"Chest. My ribs. But only when I try to breathe," she said, trying for a smile.

"Guy knocked her down," Moses said. "Knew she couldn't see— at least not the way humans usually do—and pushed her right out of the chair. Kicked her, the asshole."

"I try not to use such language," Eleanor said. "But he was definitely an asshole."

Liam closed his eyes on a laugh. I tried to bite one back, as a laugh seemed really inappropriate under the circumstances. But Eleanor turned her pale gaze toward me, fumbled for my hand, squeezed it.

"Laugh," she said. "Always choose to laugh."

"And give 'em a good right cross," Moses said, pointing at me. "Yours isn't too bad, girl."

Well, that was something, anyway.

Liam situated Eleanor on her small bed while Moses and I put away Eleanor's magical effects. He slipped into the next room when the agents came upstairs. There was no point in complicating things further.

Reece walked inside, Smith and Valentine behind him.

"Pike?" Liam asked quietly, to avoid disturbing Eleanor.

"He's been taken to the clinic," Reece said, "along with Agent McNally. He had a bump on the head, as far as I could see. The fugitives must have surprised both of them."

"They'd need some skills for that," Liam said.

"She has the look of ex-military," I said, gesturing to the woman whose eyes rolled back as Smith turned her over, cuffed her.

"That was my thought, too," Liam said. "They'd have needed skills to stay hidden for so long. Maybe disgruntled war vets."

Valentine cuffed the man, and with the help of a couple more agents, the no-longer fugitives were taken downstairs.

"She thinks your grandmother is a Sensitive," I said quietly.

Liam's expression stayed calm, but his eyes tightened almost imperceptibly. He wondered why I was bringing it up in front of Reece. But I had a plan.

"I mean, she's obviously wrong, but she thinks that's why your grandmother lives here. She said Ezekiel knows it."

Reece looked at Liam. "Why does your grandmother live in Devil's Isle?"

"Because I live in Devil's Isle. I wanted her close, because I thought I could keep her safe that way." Liam's tone turned snappish. "I was obviously wrong about that, and I don't like being wrong."

Reece nodded, and his empathetic expression seemed sincere. "She'd have been targeted today as a human living in Devil's Isle, even if not a Sensitive."

"She's not a Sensitive. If she was, I'd have gotten her out of here a long time ago." He'd basically done the same for me by not taking me in.

"That would be illegal," Reece said.

"It would," Liam said. "And I'd have done it anyway. Containment's handling of Sensitives is moronic and shortsighted. Lizzie's a very good physician. But not allowing Sensitives to deal with their magic—to avoid becoming wraiths—is unconscionable."

I wondered if it took willpower not to look at me when he said that. Because I had a hell of a time keeping my gaze on Reece.

Before Reece could respond, there was a thump and cursing downstairs. Reece took a heavy breath. "I'll go escort our Reveillon friends to the brig in the Cabildo, make sure they're safely put away."

"Thank you for your help," Liam said, and Reece nodded before leaving us again.

When the front door had opened and closed again, Liam glanced at me. "'She thinks your grandmother is a Sensitive'?" he repeated.

"Containment could hear it either from us now, or from the fugitive during interrogation when we aren't there to respond. If we get it out here, talk about it, it lessens the impact."

"She's right." Eleanor's voice was quiet but clear.

Liam moved to the bed, put his hands on his hips as he looked down at her. "I guess you're still awake."

She stared blankly toward the ceiling. "Of course I am. I'm entitled to listen when people are talking about me in my own home."

Liam smiled a little. "Fair enough."

She looked in my direction, smiled. "That was a very clever plan."

"Thank you, Eleanor."

Liam shook his head at both of us, and then his expression went serious again. "Eleanor, I think Reece is right. I think it's time to get you out."

Eleanor sighed heavily. "I'm not sure I'm in a position to disagree." She looked toward Liam. "But I'm not going without Moses."

"Bullshit," Moses said from the doorway, then strode toward us with his stiff gait. "You will damn well go without me. You will go today." He looked up at Liam. "You'll take her out today."

"Moses, now—"

He reached Eleanor, put a stubby hand over her delicate one. "I'm just one of the crowd, Eleanor. One of the Paras incarcerated here. That girl may have been wrong about you being a Sensitive, but the truth won't matter much. Not if Ezekiel wants to believe it."

"Exactly," Liam said. "Which is why we need to get you out."

"I'm a grown woman fully capable of assessing risk," she said. "I lived through the war, after all."

"Eleanor—" Liam and Moses said simultaneously, prepared to make their arguments.

I held up a hand. "Stop arguing. We've established Eleanor is amenable to leaving, but she won't leave without Moses."

I thought of what Malachi had said, of the importance of giving Paranormals some authority over their own lives, and looked at him. "If we could figure out a way—if we could make it work—do you want out?"

He looked at me for a long time in silence that Liam and Eleanor didn't interrupt.

I wondered what he was thinking about, what considerations he was weighing. The stability of prison versus being out there on the run? The freedom of it, faced against the possibility of being dragged back into Devil's Isle?

And there was something more there. He looked at me, into me, like he was assessing, evaluating. Like a man who wanted to offer up his hope—a delicate and fragile thing—and wanted to be sure the recipient could care for it.

"Yes," he said, and I nodded.

"Then we'll figure out a way," I said. And that was that.

It took nearly half an hour, but Lizzie eventually arrived in scrubs marked with stains I didn't want to think too much about.

"Sorry it took so long," she said, stepping into Eleanor's room and pulling clean gloves from her pocket, slipping them on. She nodded at me, Liam, Moses, then walked to Eleanor.

"Some of our human staff members didn't come in this week. Too worried to step into Devil's Isle."

"Looks like they had cause," Liam said darkly.

"True, but a pain in the ass nonetheless." She looked back at us. "Why don't you give us a few minutes for the exam?"

"I'll make tea," Moses said, and hopped down from his chair, headed toward the door again. There must have been a kitchen in there.

"You make tea?" I asked him, and grinned at the middle finger he threw back at me.

I really, really liked him.

Liam and I obeyed Lizzie's subtle order and went downstairs, where Foster waited patiently.

I sat down on the floor, focused my attention on Foster's apparently enormous need for scritches. Liam walked to a window across the room, arms crossed as he looked outside. Guilt was etched clearly on his face.

"You couldn't have known this would happen," I said.

He looked at me, obviously pained. "I did know. We talked about her needing protection last night."

Last night, when he'd stayed with me instead of coming back to Devil's Isle. When he'd trusted Gunnar and Containment with his grandmother's welfare.

"In that case, I'm sorry," I said.

He looked back at me, eyebrows lifted, and challenge in his expression. He looked like a man ready for an argument. "For what?"

"For this. For putting your family in the line of fire again."

Anger fired in his eyes again. "What is that supposed to mean?"

I curled back from that fire. "I don't know. Maybe if I hadn't asked you to go to the Apollo, you'd have been here, things would have been different."

"Because you're the boss of me? Because I don't make my own decisions?"

"Well, no. Of course not."

"No," Liam repeated. "Of course not." He moved closer, and it took a moment to realize that fire wasn't anger, at least not at me. His gaze locked onto mine, and the moment seemed to snap into place, like gear teeth settling together. "I make my own choices. I make my own decisions. You aren't to blame for any of them."

"You should stay here overnight," I said. "You'll feel better. I can find someone else to stay at the store, or I can find someplace else to go."

The Apollo would be an obvious choice, but I didn't want to think about that right now, about my father and his secrets. There was enough to deal with in front of me.

"They'll look for you," Liam said, shaking his head. "And they'll look for me. We might as well be in the same place together. I have friends. Bounty hunters that I trust, who mistrust humans as much as they mistrust Paranormals."

"So they wouldn't be swayed by Reveillon?"

He nodded. "Yeah."

"And speaking of which, how do Cajuns say 'coward'?"

Liam smiled. *"Capon."*

I nodded, remembered hearing him say that word before. "Ezekiel is a *capon*. Won't do his own dirty work."

"God's own truth," Liam said. "He's also a horse's ass."

Also the truth.

"Moses," Liam said, looking at me speculatively. "Do you really think it's a good idea to get his hopes up? To tell him we can break him out of Devil's Isle?"

"Why is that getting his hopes up?"

Liam blinked at me. "Because we're in a neighborhood-sized prison with high walls, guard towers, a new gate, and agents with very big guns?"

"I'm not saying it won't be hard. I'm just saying there has to be a way." I looked up at him. "If we don't get him out, Eleanor won't leave. And if Ezekiel knows . . ."

His face went fierce. "I'll carry her out if I have to."

I petted Foster, hoping it would calm me as much as it seemed to calm him. Unfortunately, it didn't.

"This place is death," I said, wrapping my hands around my knees. "For Paras, for Sensitives, for wraiths. And not just because of Reveillon. Because there's no trial, no parole, no early out for good behavior." I looked at Liam. "Every single one of them will die here."

"We can't change the law," he said. "And we can't take down Containment on our own."

"I know. And I know we can't get everyone out. It's not possible—not right now, not with the Magic Act. But maybe, if we could just help one person—one person Containment thinks is dead anyway."

He looked at me speculatively. "I'm listening."

"We have Delta. We have Sensitives, Paranormals, bounty hunters, researchers. If anyone could figure out a way . . ."

There had to be one. Because I was done with violence, done with double standards.

I was done with Devil's Isle.

"Shit," Liam said. "I forgot about Delta. We missed our noon meet."

I'd forgotten about it, too. "We'll head to the church when we're done here. Maybe they'll still be there."

Liam nodded. "They may have heard what happened, assumed we were dealing with it. News travels fast among them."

It always did. Paranormals had networks we didn't even know about. And maybe that was something we could use.

Fifteen minutes later, there were footsteps on the stairs, and we jumped to our feet.

"She'll be fine," Lizzie said, pulling off latex gloves. "A sprained wrist, two bruised ribs, and a bump on the head we don't think is a concussion, but she still needs to be monitored. It will not surprise you that she doesn't want to go to the clinic."

"I'm going to have a friend stay with her."

"Good," Lizzie said. "I'll send Victoria over here as soon as she can get away." Victoria was one of Eleanor's regular nurses. She checked her watch. "I need to head back, free her up."

"Maybe I could help," I said, and they both looked at me.

"What?" Lizzie asked.

Guilt must have made me suggest it. Why else would I volunteer to help in the very place I dreaded going most of all? The place I'd be sent if I didn't manage my magic?

But the words were out, and she needed help. Besides, if I was fed up enough with Devil's Isle to bitch about it to Liam, I might as well walk the walk. Otherwise I was just a hypocrite.

"I could help you at the clinic," I made myself say. "If you want. You're short-staffed, and my store happens to be well staffed right now. I could come by tomorrow morning, play candy striper for a little while." If that was still a thing.

I looked at Liam. "You'll want to check on your grandmother anyway. Maybe Gavin could stay with Tadji at the store?"

Liam watched me silently for a moment. I wondered if he was thinking about his talk with Gavin this morning. But whatever he was thinking, he didn't show it. "Fine by me if it's fine with Lizzie."

When I looked back at Lizzie, her gaze was still on Liam, eyes narrowed speculatively. "You did pretty good after the bombing," she said.

"I can follow directions," I assured her.

Liam snorted, but Lizzie ignored him.

"I know you can." Her tone softened. "That would be great."

I nodded. I'd made the commitment. Now I just had to figure out a way to get through it.

"I'll send someone back," she said, then headed out the door.

"I'll need a little time to make arrangements for the guard," Liam said into the silence. "Before we go to Delta."

"Sure. I want to go to the store anyway."

"How will you get back?"

I looked down. "I will use these sticks attached to my hips."

His gaze darkened. "You're hilarious. There are killers out there."

"Just like there were seven years ago," I pointed out, and got a dour look for my trouble. "Look, my right cross notwithstanding, I can admit I'm not great at hand-to-hand. I may not even be very good at retail. But I can be very sneaky when necessary. It was a skill I learned early."

"Your father?" Liam asked.

I nodded. "I wasn't going to win a battle with a Paranormal weapon, and I wasn't yet a Sensitive. He wanted me to be able to shoot when I had a weapon, and run when I didn't."

"You weren't very good at running away the night we met," he said with the hint of a smile.

And wasn't that a perfect and depressing metaphor?

"If I'd made it out of the store," I said, "I'd have disappeared, and you'd never have seen me again." I meant it as a joke, but the thought—the possibility our paths wouldn't have crossed—made my chest ache with sadness.

Liam ran a hand through his hair, looked back at the stairway, toward the grandmother who needed him. I could see the dilemma in his eyes. That he cared that much about me—that he was torn—meant a lot.

"She needs you more than I do right now."

Liam looked back at me, eyes wide with surprise.

"It's okay," I said. "Stay with her until you're sure she's safe."

Something deep stirred in his eyes. "Be *canaille*."

I lifted my eyebrows at the word I didn't recognize.

"Careful," he said with a sly smile. "Sneaky. Quiet as a mouse."

I'd lived alone in the French Quarter for nearly seven years. I knew how to be invisible.

I walked quickly and quietly back to the gate, passing Containment's fire brigade, which shot water at the storage building while Gunnar and Reece looked on. Warm rain began to fall as soon as I made it outside the fence, lifting the scents of swamp, water, and smoke into the air.

The rain kept people indoors, so I crept alone through the Quarter. By the time I got back to the store, the rain had stopped and I was drenched, but I hadn't seen a single other person.

Gavin stood on a ladder in front of the store in jeans and a WHO DAT? T-shirt, futzing with something on the underside of the wrought-iron balcony. The bruise around his eye had begun to turn that ironically sickly green of healing.

"Are you breaking my place?"

He made an amused sound. "Your manager asked me to take a look at the bracket. She said the balcony squeaked in this corner, had a little give. I'm making sure the ironwork is still in good shape." He adjusted something with a wrench, climbed down the ladder, used a corner of his T-shirt to dry his sweaty face. Beneath it, I'm happy to report, his body was as fantastic as his brother's.

"And is it?"

"This one is. Bolts needed a little tweaking, but it's fine." His expression went serious. "You want to tell me what happened out there?"

I told him about Eleanor, about the attack, and our possible next steps.

"You haven't talked to our friends yet."

I shook my head. "We were supposed to meet at noon. We missed the meeting."

He nodded. "Go when Liam comes. I'll stay here."

"I appreciate it. She means a lot to me, as does the store."

"It's no problem. I mean, I'd rather be out there mixing it up, using my considerable strength." He flexed an impressive biceps. "But one does what one must do."

I put a hand on his arm, squeezed supportively, and appreciated his good humor. "Your sacrifice is noted."

He was chuckling when he moved the ladder down to the next bracket.

Inside, the store was dark, the new-to-me air conditioner silent. Unlike in Devil's Isle, which had some kind of special generators that weren't affected by my magic fluctuations, the power was out here, and heat and humidity had begun to collect in the store.

Tadji stood behind the counter, finishing up an order for a customer. I waited until she was done, then told her what had happened.

"I'm glad Eleanor and Moses are okay." She glanced at the agents who came in the door, headed to the rack of walking sticks, joked around about which one they'd buy.

Tadji leaned closer. "Is he thinking about getting her out of there?" she whispered.

"He is. Has some convincing to do," I said, opting not to mention Moses until there was a possibility we'd be able to pull off an escape. No point in dragging her into possible treason yet.

Because dragging her into treason after that would be fine? I wondered ruefully.

"You should get out of those clothes," she said, and plucked at her own shirt. "It's humid enough in here."

I took her advice and, when I reached the bedroom, let my soaked clothes fall heavily to the floor. I pulled out another T-shirt and jeans, hung the wet ones up to dry.

When I went downstairs again, I found a new shipment of boxes on the table in the back room. I wanted some quiet, and some thinking time. Unpacking stock was the perfect way to deal with that.

I pushed open the curtains and opened the windows. There wasn't much of a breeze through the back courtyard, but at least the air circulated. By the light of the open window, I began opening boxes.

I lost myself in work, counting soap and lightbulbs to ensure their numbers matched our invoices, restocking the shelves, breaking down the boxes for recycling when I was done.

I put aside a bag of sea salt for Lizzie. I could take it to her in the morning, when I walked willingly into the Devil's Isle clinic again. Nervous as I was about going, it was hardly a sacrifice for someone with freedom.

The shadows and light on the floor shifted as I worked, time slipping past. When the store quieted, Tadji came back, looked at the empty boxes I'd stacked, then at me. "Are you okay?"

I stopped, hands on the corners of a box, and looked back at her. "I'm tired. Emotionally, mentally."

She crossed her arms, nodded. "Yeah. I feel the same. And I think Burke does, too."

I cocked my head at her. "How is Burke?"

"Right now, trying to keep his people safe—the caravans that travel through the Zone, the agents who work in Devil's Isle. Frustrated that he can't do more. But I don't think that's what you meant," she said, leaned against the edge of the table. "We're taking it slowly. Very, very slowly."

"Because you aren't sure of him?"

"Because I'm not sure of anything right now. Because he's not in my five-year plan."

I smiled at her. "In fairness, neither was retail."

"Right?" She paused. "I'm still not sure if this is a long-term thing. I guess I thought there'd be timpani drums, and I'm not hearing any timpani drums." She looked at me with speculation in her dark eyes. "Not like I imagine you hear."

"They are drums of sadness and despair," I said, breaking down the box and putting it in the pile. "So don't feel left out."

She shrugged. "I don't know. I just kind of assumed that when the big-time love happened, I'd get the timpani drums and the orchestra and the chorus."

"What do you get?"

Her brow furrowed as she considered. "I don't know. I like spending time with him. I'd say we're friends."

"It's only been a few weeks. Maybe something more can grow."

She nodded. "Or maybe it can't. And for Miss Type A, that uncertainty kills me."

I smiled. "Yeah, waiting it out isn't really your style."

"Maybe we should do one of those friendship pacts. If we're still alone in fifteen years, we marry each other, settle down."

I looked her up and down. "I could do worse."

She rolled her eyes.

"When Liam gets here, we're going to meet our friends. Gavin can stay, but it might be safer if you go home, out of the Quarter. Once word spreads about the attack, there probably won't be many people shopping anyway."

"Then maybe we need to change that."

I lifted my eyebrows.

Tadji shrugged. "I don't know. I've been thinking—it's like we're letting Reveillon set the pace. Tell us how to live in our city, how our city should be run. I think we should fight back."

She held up a hand when I started to argue. "I don't mean with weapons. That's not my gig, and I don't want it to be. I mean in terms of presence. Maybe it's time we set the pace. We should get people into the Quarter. To live, to talk. To watch for these cowards who think genocide is the solution to their problems. Maybe, if we're out there, if we're engaged in our city, we screw up their plans a little." She lifted a shoulder. "Just an idea."

"I think that's a really good idea."

She brightened. "Really?"

"Girl, you know you're brilliant. It's not your first good idea. And yeah, I think you're right. I think they're capitalizing on fear, on our memories of war. But if we stay home, if we stay inside, we help them win. It's a lot easier for them to march down an empty Bourbon Street than one that's full of people."

She nodded decisively. "Since you're on board, I'm going to make some signs for the windows, spread the word." She grinned. "I could probably just tell Mrs. Proctor and let her do the rest. The woman does not hold back information."

"No, she doesn't. You want information to spread, she'd be a good vector."

Liam appeared in the doorway, glanced at Tadji, at me.

"Hey," Tadji said. "How's Eleanor?"

"Resting comfortably," Liam said. "Thanks for asking."

She nodded.

"Did you get any information about the other attacks?" I asked.

"There were two others," he said. "One fugitive started the fire, two were at Eleanor's, and two more attacked humans. One of Lizzie's nurses lives on the north side of the prison. She was shot, but she'll be fine. One civilian volunteer was inside Devil's Isle, leading a literacy class. She was killed."

"They kill indiscriminately," Tadji said.

Liam nodded. "They've apparently decided everyone not in their group is supporting Containment, and therefore an enemy, a traitor."

"At least they've gotten all five fugitives contained now," Tadji said.

Liam nodded. "Assuming the original count was correct, yeah. If

Containment miscalculated—and there was a lot of chaos during the blast; the cameras were toast—there are more waiting for another opportunity."

"We need to get to our meeting," I said.

"How long has the power been out?"

Tadji glanced at the wall clock. "About an hour and a half."

Liam blew out a breath. "If the power doesn't come back, we'll be walking."

I nodded. "Yeah."

"Do try to keep Claire injury free for once," Tadji said, walking into the store again.

"You say that like I have any control over what she does," Liam called out over his shoulder, then looked at me.

"I'm getting Eleanor out tomorrow, one way or another, and whether she wants it or not. But she won't leave without Moses, and he won't leave her side."

"Loyalty goes a long way," I said. "So we better figure out a way to help both of them."

CHAPTER SEVENTEEN

We had to wait another half hour for the power to come back, for Liam to be able to start the truck. Enough time to unpack the rest of the stock, add the boxes to the recycling pile in the alley for Containment pickup. And let the pain in my ankle dissipate.

When the lights buzzed on again, we drove to the church, parked up the block to keep Containment patrols, Reveillon, or anyone else from getting suspicious about vehicles outside a seemingly abandoned church.

The rain had cleared, leaving the western sky brushed with brilliant streaks of orange and pink, like paint carefully daubed across a canvas. The neighborhood was quiet and Reveillon free.

We knocked on the door and were admitted by Burke. He nodded, waited until we were inside, then closed the door firmly, snapped new locks closed behind us. Someone had moved chairs and a table into one side of the room and lit taper candles in tall brass candlesticks.

Erida stood near the table, arms crossed. She wore white trousers and a sleeveless top in the same fabric, her long hair waving over tan shoulders. She looked effortlessly beautiful—the kind of woman who was gorgeous enough to have stepped off a movie set.

Her gaze slipped to me, and again there was something unpleasant in her eyes. It disappeared quickly, but it was definitely there.

That made two times this woman I'd never met before had given me some Solomon-worthy stink eye. If circumstances had been different, I might have asked her about it. But I wasn't going to waste time trying to prove myself to a woman I didn't even know.

A door opened, closed again, and Darby appeared in the back doorway, followed by Malachi. His wings were already hidden, and he was dressed in jeans, a T-shirt, and a slim running jacket in a slick fabric. Burke wore his fatigues and looked tired and a little demoralized. Even Darby, who was smartly dressed in cuffed jeans and a boatneck shirt that fit her Marilyn Monroe–meets-librarian style, seemed to have lost her usual perkiness.

"I guess we don't need to apologize for being late," Liam said as we walked to the table.

"We're all late," Burke said. "You were at Devil's Isle?"

Liam nodded.

"I told them what happened," Burke said. "We've been helping the Joint Ops team search for Reveillon's main camp, if there is one."

"Technically," Darby said, pulling off a Loyola cap and ruffling her dark hair, "Burke has been helping. I'm just secretly along for the ride, since I'm still persona non grata as far as Containment is concerned."

"You find anything?" Liam asked.

Burke shook his head. "There are more signs around town, more painted-over billboards. No obvious settlements."

"So they're scattered," Liam said.

"That would be my guess. Probably all across the city—they can spread out Containment's response that way, wreak havoc over a larger area." Burke looked at Malachi. "You have any better luck?"

We all looked at Malachi, and I only just realized the grim set of his features.

"What's wrong?" I asked quietly, but he looked at Erida, kept his eyes on her face.

Malachi pulled off his jacket, revealing a bloody stain on his T-shirt that still looked fresh.

"Oh my God!" Darby said, running forward. "What happened? I mean, other than the fact that you've been shot," she added at his dry look.

"I encountered a herd of them. A dozen young humans, all male, some with guns. They wore street clothes but made their Reveillon chants. They roamed the neighborhood like vigilantes looking for their presumptive traitors."

"You engaged them," I said while Darby went into the back room.

Malachi looked at me. "I did."

"Was that a wise decision?" Liam asked.

Malachi slid his gaze to Liam, and there was nothing especially friendly in it. "In my position, what would you have done?"

Since they were both as alpha as they came, Liam inclined his head, acknowledging the point.

Darby rushed back in, first-aid kit in hand. "Let me take a look at that. Shirt off."

"It just grazed me," he said. "That's unnecessary."

When Darby just stared at him, Malachi pulled the T-shirt over his head.

I wondered if Liam was aware that he'd moved incrementally closer, as if there was a real risk I'd jump on Malachi when his shirt came off. His body, while perfectly honed, wasn't the surprise. It was the scars across his chest and abdomen, where it looked like he'd been slashed or burned over and over again.

Consularis Paras had been forced to fight. Malachi had told us he'd been able to overcome the compulsion, but not before waging some war. I wondered if those scars were from that fighting, or because of his time in the Beyond.

Darby didn't seem surprised by them but moved him closer to the candlelight, made him sit on the edge of the table.

"I could turn the overhead lights on?" I offered.

"Better if they're off," Burke said. "It attracts less attention, which seems better."

"I can manage," Darby said, frowning as she used snips to trim a piece of gauze. "Not my first rodeo."

I guessed we all had our war experiences.

"So, what happened with the humans?" Erida asked as Darby worked.

Malachi's expression remained stony. "I attempted to teach them manners and fair play. Most of them scattered when they realized it wasn't going to be a fair fight." He smiled, but the look was more scary than joyous. "I left a few unconscious, so I activated the magic monitor and left them for Containment."

"Nice," Liam said, and this time Malachi did the inclining.

"So, what's the plan?" Darby asked, closing the kit when she'd finished bandaging Malachi's wound. "We can't just stand around and watch them destroy the Zone."

"We actually have a request," Liam said. "Two of the Reveillon fugitives attacked Eleanor and Moses today; they think she's a Sensitive. Which means Ezekiel thinks she's a Sensitive."

"They'll try for her again," Burke said, and Liam nodded.

"Eleanor won't leave Devil's Isle without Moses. So we need your help. We need to break him out of Devil's Isle."

The church was absolutely silent.

"You want to break a Paranormal out of Devil's Isle?" Darby asked.

"Yes," Liam said. "Moses. She won't leave without him. He wants to go. So . . ."

"And how do you propose to do that?" Malachi asked.

"That's partly why we're here," I said. "We were hoping you'd help us."

Silence hung heavily in the room.

"You're talking about treason," Burke said quietly. "I shouldn't be hearing this. I mean, I'm not going to leave. Not when it's getting interesting. But I shouldn't be hearing it."

"I hear you," I said, and I looked around the room. "Each of us is a potential prisoner. Burke and I, because we're Sensitives. Malachi, because he's Consularis. All of us because we're sympathizers, because we've worked and communicated with Paras, helped them. We could all be arrested right now—so let's not pretend this is the first time we've broken the law. And let's not use that as an excuse."

I looked at Burke. Every Sensitive had a unique power. I could move things. Burke could make himself invisible. "Could you escort Moses out using your invisibility? I mean, make him invisible, so he basically walks out of Devil's Isle?"

Burke frowned, shook his head. "The magic makes me invisible, not anyone else. And I'd set off the magic monitors."

"But your clothes disappear," I pointed out. "They aren't inherently magic." Quite the opposite, since they were Containment fatigues.

"They become part of me, is my understanding of the magic. The problem is, I can't expand the magic beyond that to encompass someone else."

"Perhaps you could do something about that." We all looked at Erida, who was watching Malachi. Then we all looked at Malachi.

"Could you?" I asked, and thought of our practice at Algiers Point, the way he'd used his magic to make that pinecone heavier.

"Enhance Burke's magic? Magnify it so we can make someone else invisible, too?"

He frowned. "I've never tried to apply it to a Sensitive's power before." He looked at Burke, considered. "If I was close enough, and we moved quickly enough."

"How quickly?" Liam asked.

"Minutes?" Malachi suggested. "He's still a Sensitive. We don't want to overexpose a Sensitive to magic."

Burke crossed his arms, worried his lip with two fingers. We'd all play our parts, but Burke would be taking a big risk. After a time, he looked at Malachi. "We'd have to try it out. Make sure this could actually work."

"I have no objection to that," Malachi said.

"Okay," Burke said. "But that still doesn't address the monitors. If they go off, Containment will close the gate, and none of us will be going anywhere."

"I think we can deal with the monitors," I said, and glanced at Liam. "Moses is very, very good with electronics."

"A lot of moving pieces," Darby said. "You have to turn the monitors off. Malachi has to be in the right place to affect Burke. Burke has to concentrate on his magic."

"We could take Eleanor at the same time," Liam said. "That way, Claire and I are with you just in case something happens."

"And if we manage to pull it off?" Burke asked. "To get them out. What then?"

I looked at Malachi. "When Containment first established Devil's Isle, started moving Paras into the prisons, I bet you had a way to get Consularis Paras out of the city and into the bayous."

Malachi watched me carefully for a moment. "There were routes to be followed."

"Then we use that tactic here. If it's what they want to do, we could move him—or both of them—from one way station to the next. We could use Royal Mercantile, since it's the closest stop to the prison. Then Royal Mercantile to here."

"To the bayous," Liam said, nodding. "That's a possibility. There's the cabin at Bayou Teche. I haven't been there in years, but it's a possibility. There'd need to be arrangements. Her medical care, getting supplies to them."

"We have mechanisms for supply drops," Malachi said. "If Moses is with her, and considering her magic, there are procedures we can use. They are our people, too." He glanced at me. "If that's what they want to do."

Treason had never felt so good.

We talked for three hours. Debated, reassessed, and tried to plan for every complication, because the plan was already dangerous enough.

"Burke will meet Liam and me at Eleanor's house at noon," I said. "That's when the guard shifts change, which gives us a little flexibility. Malachi will direct his magic from a high point outside the gate. We'll use a utility cart, drive Moses and Eleanor out of Devil's Isle and to the store, where they'll wait until the coast is clear. Gavin will drive them to the church, where Darby will be waiting."

She nodded.

I looked at Malachi and Erida. "And you'll get them to the Quinn place at Bayou Teche."

"We will," Erida said.

"I haven't told Gunnar," I said, apropos of nothing, but because it was bothering me. "I don't think I will."

"Because you don't think he's trustworthy?" Darby asked.

"Because I know he is, and that puts him in an impossible spot. He can't do his job and ours, too. And frankly, we'll probably need him in that spot before all this is said and done. But I'll have to tell Tadji," I realized. "I can't take them to the store—put her in the middle—and not give her the truth."

"She comes from a long line of trustworthy people," Malachi said, probably thinking of Tadji's mother, who'd been instrumental in closing the Veil. "And she has a healthy fear of magic."

"We all fear a lot of things these days," Liam said. "And speaking of which, we should get back to the store." He glanced at me. "I'll drop you off, and then I want to check on Eleanor and Moses, make sure the new guard has arrived."

I nodded.

"I can meet Claire at the store," Malachi said. "Work with her on her magic until you return."

I wasn't sure what response Liam had expected to get, but he didn't seem thrilled by Malachi's offer.

"Don't you and Burke need to practice?" I asked.

"We do," Burke said, rising and pushing back his chair. "But I need to make some arrangements of my own, if I'm going to be running around Devil's Isle. Actually," he added, glancing at me, "if it's all right with Claire, we could practice in the store, since it's insulated."

"That's fine by me," I said. Better than fine, as it would give me the chance to watch them practice together. The more I learned about magic, the better for all of us.

"Did you want a ride back to the store?" I asked Malachi, and he shook his head, unfolded his wings. Candlelight gleamed through them, making him seem a creature of light. "I have my own means of transportation."

He nodded at each of us, then disappeared through the back of the church.

"Does he think they won't see him?" Liam asked quietly. "Or does he want the fight?"

"Both," Erida said. "He is who he is, and prefers not to pretend otherwise. That's why Devil's Isle is anathema to him. Containment wants Paranormals to be humans—magicless, impotent."

Yet another reason for doing what we'd planned to do. Maybe we could start a change.

It was late when Liam dropped me off. Malachi already stood beneath the balcony, waiting for us, and the store was dark but for a small lamp behind the counter.

"I'll be back," Liam said, and I wasn't sure if it was a promise or a threat.

"Be careful," I said, and watched the truck's lights disappear down Royal.

"Let's get inside," Malachi said, waiting until I'd walked into the store, then closing the door behind us, flipping the locks.

I walked to the counter, looking for the note that would assure me Tadji was safe, and found it beside the receipt pad.

Late. Exhausted. Gavin's going to bunk at my place until Burke arrives. Stay safe.

Good. One less thing to worry about.

"I want something to drink," I said, and glanced at Malachi, who was picking through a box of colored duct tape, staring like they were exotic jewels. He browsed the objects here just as he'd done downstairs. And in much the same way as Nix, the Paranormal who'd betrayed us, had once done.

"Would you like anything?"

He shook his head, so I grabbed a bottle of water, found him waiting at the bottom of the stairs.

"Shall we see your magic?"

"Lead the way," I said with a flourish.

I followed him to the second-floor storage room. He flipped on the light, moved immediately to the box of cast-off magic.

"Good," he said, fingers skimming, but not quite touching, its surface. "You've been casting off."

"I have plenty of incentive," I said. "I've been working on using my emotions to control my magic. How did you know I'd be able to do that?"

Malachi smiled. "I didn't."

"You didn't?"

Malachi just shrugged, a surprisingly human motion. "Magic isn't inherent for humans, and I haven't communicated with many Sensitives regarding their abilities. I wasn't entirely certain what would happen." He cocked his head. "What did happen?"

"Insulation, I think. I can use the emotions to surround the magic, coax it to do what I want."

He looked intrigued. "Can you show me?"

"I can try." I'd used anger before, but didn't feel especially angry right now. I felt unsettled. Unsettled and guilty and impatient. That was a different kind of emotion, but maybe still powerful enough to make the magic work the way I wanted it to.

I looked around, considered my box of magic. I narrowed my gaze, focused my concentration on it, gathered up the guilt and sadness I'd felt in Devil's Isle today. Where the emotion I'd used before had been frenetic, tightly wound, this was more like a slow syrup. So when I pulled magic from the air, it was like dragging the ropes of magic through liquid, slowing their vibration, corralling their fire. I uncoiled those ropes toward the box, wrapped them around it again and again, until I'd given over enough magic to lift it.

Even then, it was difficult going. The box was heavy with magic. My own fault, for pouring so much into it. But if that was what I had to do to stay alive . . .

Sweat beading in the room's still, warm air, I lifted the coils of magic and the box wobbled into the air, a few inches, then a foot. I let it hover for a moment, concentrating on keeping it even, level, and still. Sweat slipped down my back at the effort; it was small, but it felt as heavy as Malachi had in Algiers.

Fingers clenched in concentration, I shifted the coils again, slowly lowered the box back to the bureau. It landed with a heavy *thud* that shook the bureau beneath it.

"Gotta work on sticking the landing," I said, breathing heavily now.

Malachi stared at the space between me and the box, as if he could see the invisible threads of energy that had bound us together. He glanced back at me. "There is sadness in the air, and it weighs on the magic."

That described it exactly, so I nodded, trying to get my breath back. "So the effect will be different for different emotions?"

Another nod.

He looked for another moment, then walked to me, around me, behind me. I could feel the warmth radiating from his big body.

"I'm going to test you," he said behind me. "Use your emotions, if you find it necessary, to maintain balance."

Before I could argue, he wrapped his arms around me and twined our fingers together. Warmth pulsed from the connection of our bodies, loosening tension and clearing away worry and fear.

I floated on the sensation, my eyes drifting shut. I leaned back against him, my head falling against his broad chest.

Here in the cocoon of magic, he smelled of evergreens and fresh air, like the Blue Ridge mountaintops on which the angels had famously trumpeted during the war. Even if my heart was occupied by Liam Quinn, unobtainable or not, Malachi's power and magnetism were undeniable.

And then his lips were at my temple, his breath steady but faster now, and it relieved me to know I wasn't the only one being affected by the magic, by the spill and spin of it around us, heady and powerful.

I was being seduced by magic.

Realization dousing me like cold water, I pulled away, put space between us, and then looked back. He watched me, gaze even.

"You did that on purpose."

His expression didn't change. "Yes."

I swallowed. "Why?"

"To gauge your emotional reaction . . . and because I wanted to see what it felt like."

My gaze snapped back to his, and he stared at me with that same expression of perplexed fascination. The expression of a Paranormal trying to puzzle out a human, or of a man trying to puzzle out a woman?

Danger, was the word that came to mind. Glorious and intriguing and mysterious danger. A kind of danger I hadn't faced before—not exactly. Prejudicial or not, I knew enough about Paranormals to be wary, and to think that catching feelings for an angel would leave me the fallen one.

I was human and could feel attraction, but I wasn't enslaved by it. Maybe that was a lesson he needed to learn, too.

His expression blanked again as the mood in the room shifted. "You have feelings for him," he said, apparently finding it unnecessary to say Liam's name.

And yes—I had complicated feelings for Liam Quinn, and he'd probably say the same thing about me. But . . . "It doesn't matter," I said.

"Why?"

"Because he thinks he might be the one who has to take me into Devil's Isle. Because he's being honorable."

I could hear the bitterness in my voice. Malachi apparently had, too. "You're better than that, Claire."

I looked back at him. "Meaning what?"

"You'd be quick to dismiss a man's honor? You've seen enough to know how often humans and Paranormals alike disregard honor for desire, for gain, for money." He took a step closer, his gaze demanding. "Would you rather he be someone he's not? Someone unconcerned about the future? About you? About your freedom?"

I didn't like his answer. And I didn't like what it made me feel about myself. "No. But it still isn't fair."

"Life rarely is, in your world or mine."

I nodded. "What are relationships like in the Beyond? Do you have courtship? Romance?"

He looked surprised by the question. "Of course. But not like those here, which are . . . complicated. The Consularis pride themselves on stability."

I thought of what Lizzie had told me. "And rules, I understand."

Malachi nodded. "We value social order."

"And the Court doesn't?"

His smile wasn't especially cheerful. "All creatures value order; it is an inevitable part of existence. The only thing that differs is where they place themselves and their allies within that order."

I couldn't argue with that, since it was precisely Ezekiel's plan. Maybe not his entire motivation—to put himself in charge—but certainly to get Containment out of control. And I'd need to be more prepared for that than I was now.

"Let's practice again."

His eyebrows lifted.

"Not that kind of practice. Let's work on insulating my magic. On improving my control."

"All right." He walked to the other end of the room, smiled cannily. "Lift me up."

I managed to get Malachi about four inches off the floor twice. By then, my legs were wobbling with exhaustion and excess magic—which seemed like a dangerous combination.

I cast off again, looked up at him from my spot on the floor. I felt like I'd run three marathons, and probably looked it. He'd been shot, and still looked ready and able to lead a war.

"Magic is exhausting," I said. "Can't I just shoot them?"

"What if you don't have a gun?"

I held up a fist. "Right cross." Although the thought of it sent phantom pain through my knuckles.

"And if that's not enough?"

"What if there's a magic monitor?" I countered.

"A gun will kill," Malachi said. "But a gun won't fight magic." He checked the nearest grandfather clock of the several in the room. "Burke will be here soon. But it's important that you learn to use your magic even when tired."

"I know, I know. Less than optimal conditions."

He nodded, managed a smile. "One more round."

"Fine," I said. "But help me up." I held out a hand.

He'd just crossed the room and pulled me to my feet when Liam's voice rang in the doorway. "Am I interrupting?"

I looked back. Liam's gaze was on the man whose hand still held mine, and there was nothing especially polite in it. It looked hostile, and it looked like jealousy.

I didn't really feel bad about that.

Malachi and I stepped away from each other.

"Your grandmother?" I asked.

"She's covered for tonight, and ready to leave tomorrow. As is Moses."

"Good," I said.

Liam nodded, but his gaze stayed on Malachi. Malachi, who knew exactly the lay of the land, stepped beside me. Now who was toying with whom?

"You appear to be covered, too. Burke's here," Liam said, without waiting for a response. "He's getting water. He'll be up in a moment."

"Great," I said, and looked back at Malachi. "One more round?"

"I think you could use some rest," he said, and Liam glowered until Burke walked into the room.

I didn't really feel bad about that, either.

I'd wanted to watch Burke and Malachi practice, but I was exhausted. So I left them to their work, and went downstairs to get my own water.

Liam sat at the table, his .44 in front of him, along with oil and a cleaning rag. He glanced up, watched me move into the kitchen. "How was the lesson?"

"Educational, just like last time."

When I looked up from the fridge, he stood in the doorway. "He's manipulating you."

"I know." *And I'm not the only one being manipulated*, I thought. Malachi knew where I stood, and knew where Liam stood, and was manipulating Liam with emotion the same way he manipulated me with magic.

"You know? If you know, then why are you letting him do it?"

I took out a bottle of water, slammed the door. "I'd remind you that it was your idea to walk me into Devil's Isle and introduce me to a Paranormal who could teach me how to use my magic."

"Not *that* Paranormal."

"Why? Because he's hot?"

Liam glowered.

"Who else can do it? Erida? I don't even know her, and she already gives me dirty looks. Nix? No, because she's a traitorous bitch."

"Burke," Liam suggested.

"So the blind can lead the blind? I don't need another Sensitive. I need a Paranormal who understands magic, who knows that it's a living, breathing thing."

"Yeah, he knows exactly what he's doing."

Liam had made his boundaries clear, and even Malachi had demanded that I respect that line. Both of them were right. But I had a line, too, and Liam was getting perilously close to it. I walked to him, looked up into his fiercely blue eyes. "He knows what he's doing, and so do I. No one is naive here, Liam. We're all doing the best we can under crappy circumstances."

Liam shook his head, looked away.

I took a breath. "I said you didn't trust me. That was wrong of me, and I'm sorry. I know you trust me, and I know it isn't that simple."

He blinked, and just like that, the wind went out of his sails. "Damn it, Claire."

The frustration rang in his voice. I was glad I wasn't the only one.

"Good night, Liam," I said, and slipped around him, leaving him alone in the near dark.

CHAPTER EIGHTEEN

The building was empty of men and angels when I woke, and there weren't smoke rings or scorch marks in the storage room. But I found a note from Malachi confirming that the plan was a go.

I was in a pisser of a mood. This was going to be a big day—a dangerous day—and everything felt unbalanced. Liam and I had fallen into a good rhythm. But last night, things had shifted again.

The store was open when I went downstairs, my ankle pain free as I walked and took in the scent of lemon in the air. Tadji stood at the counter, polishing it with furniture spray.

I grabbed a bag of coffee beans from a basket along one wall, then headed into the kitchen. Tadji followed me.

"Liam went to Devil's Isle," she said.

He was going to get Eleanor and Moses ready, I guessed as I opened the bag and poured the beans into the grinder. I mashed the button.

"If you're making coffee, shit's about to get real."

We didn't get coffee regularly, so I didn't let myself drink it very often. Last thing I needed was another addiction to something I couldn't have. Considering what we'd be up against today, I made an exception.

"Real as it's ever been," I said, scooping grounds into the filter. "Is anyone else in the store?"

"Not right now. Why?"

"Go lock the door, flip the sign. We need to talk."

She looked surprised by the secrecy, but not the request. By the time she came back, the pot was burbling and I was sitting at the table.

"All right," she said, taking a seat across from me. "Don't soften me up. Just get it out there."

"I'm going to help Delta break Moses out of Devil's Isle. We'll bring him and Eleanor here, and then they'll be escorted out of the Quarter, and eventually to a safe house."

She stared at me. "And when is this going to happen?"

"Today. Around noon."

"Because of the attack yesterday?"

I nodded. "Liam wants to get Eleanor out. Reveillon thinks she's a Sensitive, so it's likely they'll try again. And she won't leave without Moses."

Tadji nodded, looked down at the fingers she'd knitted together on the table, picked nervously at her thumbnail. "Fucking humans and fucking Paranormals and fucking magic."

"Pretty much, yeah."

She looked up. "I guess I had it coming when I signed up to cover your ass in the store."

"You probably should have seen it coming," I agreed with a smile. "But I don't want you to do anything you're not comfortable with. If this is more involved than you want to be, you could focus on interviews for a few days, or maybe go visit your mother."

She put both hands flat on the table, and leveled me with a look that would have frightened a Seelie. "However ungraciously I may have been dropped back into the world of magic, I'm in it. I'm not saying I'm ready to actively participate—but I'm certainly not going to hide behind your skirt. Besides, I'd like to meet Eleanor Arsenault." Her eyes gleamed. "Do you think I could interview her?"

"I don't think she'll be here that long. We're a fast food drive-through within the larger escape plan. But I'm sure, when she's settled, she'd love to talk to you. I should have hooked you two up before." But Tadji shook her head.

"That would have required me going into Devil's Isle. No, thank you."

"Ironic that you say that, because I'm about to walk willingly in there. I told Lizzie—she's in charge of the clinic—that I'd help her today."

Her eyes widened. "Isn't that where the wraiths go? And the Sensitives?"

"It is. It's the right thing to do."

"You better have two cups of coffee."

I rose to walk back into the kitchen, nearly screamed when I saw Erida in the back doorway. "Jesus, you scared me. What are you doing here?"

Her perfect eyebrows lifted. "I am here to protect you and the store until the package arrives."

I hadn't done the math, or thought about the fact that Gavin, Liam, Malachi, and Burke were all occupied. I'm glad someone had.

"Thank you," I said. "I appreciate it very much. Tadji, this is Erida. Erida, Tadji. We're just making coffee. Would you like some?"

She might have been a goddess of war, but there was no mistaking the lust in her eyes.

It was early, and Devil's Isle was quiet. A few crowing roosters, a woman hanging brilliantly colored laundry on a line, a child eating what looked like a granola bar on a stoop while raised voices discussed something in the house behind him. There was no sign of any remaining Reveillon members, and the storage building was now a dark, wet husk.

I used my pass to walk through the Devil's Isle gate, let the guards inspect the box of supplies I'd bought for Lizzie. And then they pointed me to the palest person I'd ever seen, except calling her "pale" didn't really cover it. Although there was a gauzy white cast to her skin, it was completely translucent.

She was tall and slender, with short, pale hair, a sharp chin, and lavender eyes. She wore pink scrubs like the ones Lizzie favored, and she carried a large, nylon bag with a physician's caduceus embroidered on one side. Medical supplies, probably.

"Claire," she said, stepping forward. "I'm Vendi. Lizzie asked me to meet you."

"Hi," I said, resituating the box and offering a free hand.

"Would you like me to take that for you?"

I offered a smile. "I'm good, thanks."

She gestured the direction to take, and we walked down the street, past piles of debris from the bombing and the reconstruction.

"Would you like to get the question out of the way?"

"I would love to," I said, "except I have no idea what to say or ask. You are an anatomical wonder."

She snorted. "That's one of the nicer things humans have said about me. We're referred to as Xanas in the Beyond. We live in darkness, so our skin never developed pigment."

I nodded. "And you're a physician at the clinic?"

"Nurse," she said. "And office manager and general person-who-makes-things-happen." She glanced at my parcel. "What's in the box?"

"A few things Lizzie asked me to bring. Salt, some hard candies. It's what I had on hand."

"Nice. And are you here because of guilt or court order?"

The question had me blinking, and it took a moment to realize it wasn't meant to be rude—or not entirely—but practical. Those were probably the two main reasons the clinic got volunteers.

"No court order. Ten percent anger, maybe sixty percent guilt."

"What's the other thirty percent?"

Being a Sensitive. Proving to myself that I could handle my magic, part of which seemed to be acknowledging the clinic's existence, dealing with that.

"That's more personal," I said. I could feel Vendi's curious glance, but I wasn't about to spill my secret to a stranger.

When we turned down a side street, I looked around in confusion. "This isn't the way to the clinic, is it?"

"We won't actually be at the clinic today," Vendi said. "After yesterday, it's tight quarters in there."

"Okay. So what will I be doing?"

She smiled. "You'll be making home visits with me."

"Oh," was all I could think to say. I'd happily deal with not going to the clinic, but I'd have to reconfigure my expectations.

"That a problem for you?"

"No. Will it be a problem for Paras? That I'll be walking into their homes?"

"We'll find out," she said. Which didn't instill a lot of confidence.

Our first house was a Creole cottage, the walls bright pink with white-shuttered windows. The paint on both was peeling, but there were potted plants on the small porch and a few worn toys near the door.

"You can leave the box on the steps," Vendi said, pointing to a spot.

I put down the box and stood behind her, trying not to fidget while I waited. I had no idea what I was going to see or hear inside, which made me equally uneasy and excited.

Vendi knocked on the door. "It's Vendi from the clinic," she said. "I'm here to check on Thora."

The door opened and we were swept inside on a wave of chatter and noise. Three small girls with squat bodies, smooth, green-gray skin, and dark hair surrounded us, talking animatedly to Vendi in an unrecognizable language. They looked like goblins from a child's book of fairy tales, but they darted and chatted just like children.

The cottage was small, and the front room was an equal cacophony of sounds, of scents, of colors. The air was fragrant with something smoky and warm, and the walls were covered in posters of American movies, record covers, flags, and Mardi Gras beads. Every other surface was equally colorful—rugs on the floor, blankets and tapestries across couches, cloths on tables.

"Vendi!" A man of short height, wide girth, walked into the room, his skin the same color as the girls who flitted around Vendi.

"Hello, Nedra," Vendi said, offering her hand. "This is Claire. She's helping me today."

"A guest!" Nedra said, and led me to a chair covered in quilts and blankets. I sat down, and a thimble-small glass of liquid was thrust into my hands.

"Appa," Vendi said. "A traditional greeting beverage."

I sipped it, was pleasantly surprised by the peachy flavor and warm burn. "That's delicious, thank you!" But I put a hand to my throat when the burn only intensified. Suddenly, it was like drinking Tabasco sauce.

"That has a kick," I wheezed as Nedra took my glass, placed it on a side table.

"Like a mule," Vendi agreed. "One is usually enough."

A woman walked in, smaller than Nedra, larger than the girls. She used a cane, favored her left side.

"Hello, Thora," Vendi said. "How are you feeling?"

"Good," Thora said, her voice lightly accented. "It aches today."

Vendi nodded, guided her to a chair. After pulling on gloves, she began to remove bandages from Thora's right leg.

There was a horrible gash that reached nearly from knee to ankle, the edges red and swollen.

"Cold iron," Vendi said, glancing back at me. "A wound she received seven years ago. If it doesn't kill, it permanently injures."

I didn't know what to say. Both sympathy and apology seemed indulgent. So I nodded and did what I was here to do. "Can I help you with instruments or anything?"

Vendi shook her head. "I've got this," she said, and applied a salve to Thora's still-wounded leg, replaced the bandage. "The salt didn't help?"

Thora shook her head. "Not with the pain."

"Claire has brought us some new salt, so maybe we'll get lucky."

Thora looked at me, nodded. "It is appreciated."

Maybe thinking I had connections, Nedra looked at me. "You know about this Reveillon?"

"I know some."

"Tell us about it."

I glanced at Vendi, who smiled. "Tell them what you think they deserve to know."

If I was here—and the possibility existed that I would be—I'd want to know every single damn detail. So I gave them the truth.

"There's a small army of humans who believe magic is ruining the Zone and everything in it. They believe the only solution is to kill all Paranormals, dismantle Containment, and kill every human who's involved with Containment or Devil's Isle."

The questions started immediately, were thrown at me like

darts. How many were there? Was Containment trying to find them? Would there be more attacks?

Vendi whistled shrilly, which quieted the noise.

"I don't know much," I said, "except that everyone is looking for them. They've hurt a lot of people, and they want to hurt many more. I think it's fair to say they're Containment's priority."

That didn't stop the questions, of course. I didn't know how much I could or should say, but I tried to keep to the basics, repeating the company line. And when I realized I was repeating the company line—the Containment line—I stopped.

I held up a hand. "I don't work for Containment. I own a store in the French Quarter, about a mile from here. We sell food and supplies. But I know people who work for Containment. Maybe you could give me a list of questions, and I could make sure my friend gets them? I could ask him to make sure you get the answers."

"Paper," Nedra said, clapping his hands together. "And a pen! Find them!"

We went from cottage to cottage, from Para to Para, meeting individuals and families, checking the conditions of some who were ill or injured, making sure others were getting sufficient nutrition. Every family received an allotment of food and Devil's Isle tokens, but they hadn't all adjusted well to human food.

Vendi seemed comfortable in every home, able to navigate each family's unique culture and circumstances. She didn't hesitate to direct them to me when they asked questions about Reveillon. Some were as gracious as Nedra's family had been. Others were quiet, suspicious, obviously angry. I wasn't sure whether that was because some were Consularis and others Court of Dawn or if my being human made them equally cross.

"We're done," Vendi said after a few hours, when we'd made our way down one side of the street and back again. "I'll take the box to Lizzie, and you can be on your way."

"Thank you for the experience," I said, handing it over. "It was very educational."

Vendi smiled. "Good. You did a passable job for a human."

I decided to take that as a compliment.

I crossed the neighborhood to Liam's building and went up the stairs to his apartment, then knocked on the door.

And when no one answered, I knocked again.

The door swung open, and a woman stared back at me.

She was trim and about my height, with short, dark hair in a bob that angled down toward her sharp cheekbones. Her eyebrows were dark slashes, her eyes luminously hazel, her lips a bee-stung pink against pale skin. She wore a white tank top and jeans, showing off the black and silver tattoos that covered her arms and chest.

She looked me over, one perfect eyebrow lifted in amusement. "Yeah?"

"Who's at the—" Liam began, then stepped into the doorway, pulling a T-shirt over his planed abs, then running a hand through his hair to straighten it again.

"Door," he finished, stepping beside her.

I wasn't entirely sure who this woman was, or why she was answering Liam's door while he was getting dressed. Nor was it any of my business. But that didn't stop the hot spike of jealousy that buried itself in my chest. I *felt* like I had a claim on him, and a better claim than the woman draped casually in the doorway.

My first thought was that she was revenge for Malachi's maneuvering the night before. That Liam, in some kind of "I'll show you" rage, had found a woman, come back to his apartment, and given her a very nice wake-up call. And that made me absolutely furious.

"Claire," Liam said, "this is Blythe."

Wait. I'd heard that name before . . .

She smiled lazily, draping herself in the doorway. "Pleasure."

"Sure," I said.

"Come in," Liam said, and Blythe turned to the side, hands in the air, and waited for me to pass.

The memory surfaced—the first time I'd met Eleanor, she asked about Blythe, who I'd assumed was Liam's girlfriend. He hadn't said anything about her then or since, and I'd never seen any sign of her.

"Claire owns Royal Mercantile," he said, closing the door again. "Blythe is a bounty hunter. She's also the woman I hired to keep an eye on Eleanor and Moses."

Of course she was, I thought, and felt a stirring of relief. That explained why she was standing in Liam's doorway. Except . . . "If she's here, who's at Eleanor's?"

"Gavin," Blythe said. "He relieved me a few hours ago."

"He'll go with us back to the store," Liam said. "He wanted to be along for the ride, just in case. How was the clinic?"

"I never got there, but the home visits we did instead were fine."

"You want something to eat?" Liam asked. "Something to drink?" He looked at me while he asked, but it was Blythe who walked to the kitchenette on the other end of the room.

"I'd love something—thanks," she said.

She pulled a bottle of water from the fridge, bumped the door closed while she uncapped the bottle and took a drink. "So, this is Saint Claire?" she asked, crossing her arms as she leaned back against the window ledge.

Slowly, I turned my gaze to Liam. "Saint Claire?"

"My words, not his," Blythe said, pushing off the window. "She's pretty," she added, looking me over.

"She's in the room," I pointed out.

"*Blythe*," Liam warned, but she ignored him, smiling as she walked toward me and sized me up again.

"It's all right, Liam. We're both grown-ups. Aren't we, doll?"

"Yes, we are," I said, and took the bottle from her hand, drank, and handed it back to her. "And I prefer Saint Claire to doll."

Blythe smiled appreciatively. "Well played."

I ignored the compliment, slid my glance to Liam. "Are you ready? It's time to go."

"Ah yes," Blythe said. "Time for the big, noble plan." She walked to the bar, picked up a worn leather jacket that had been tossed onto a stool and exchanged the water for rum. "That would be my cue to exit."

I found it curious that he'd told her. But then again, he'd trusted her with Eleanor.

"You aren't going to help?" I asked.

She pulled on the jacket, raised flat eyes to mine. "I work for a living, and I like working and living. I'm not out to make an enemy of Containment. But you two have fun."

She walked to Liam, pressed a kiss to his cheek. It looked chaste enough, but the fingers she dug into his chest said she was ready and available for more. "Maybe next time," she said to him with a wink and disappeared, closing the door behind her again.

The silence that fell between us prickled against my skin. I was bristling when I looked back at him. Claim or not, I didn't like being baited.

"She seems . . . ," I began, but couldn't think of a very nice adjective.

"Blythe is very good at her job," Liam said, but his voice was tight and his jaw was clenched in irritation. She hadn't just been baiting me; she'd been baiting him. Teasing him, maybe, about our relationship.

"Is she trustworthy?"

"Interpersonal skills aside, I trust her completely."

I'd let him do the trusting. "Good," I said, and walked to the door. "Because Malachi left me a note this morning, and we're a go."

I stopped and put a hand on his chest, batted my lashes the way Blythe had. "Maybe next time," I said, then walked into the hall.

"Saint Claire, my ass," was all I heard muttered behind me.

By the time we walked outside, an oversized golf cart was parked in front of Eleanor's house. Three rows of plastic, cushioned seats for our treasonous pleasure.

Inside, Foster guarded the first floor. He padded slowly and carefully into the living room when Liam opened the door, verifying us before trotting forward to say hello.

It hadn't occurred to me that we'd be leaving Foster alone in the house, and the thought of him pacing around an empty house made me unbearably sad.

"Gavin's going to take him," Liam said, crouching to scratch Foster's chin. "He'll be okay alone for a few hours until we can get Mos and Eleanor settled."

"Good," I said, when Foster padded to me, brushed his muzzle against my leg like a cat. "I'm glad. Maybe he can teach your brother some manners."

Liam snorted. "He fought a goddess of war, and lived to tell the tale. There's no saving him now."

We took the stairs to the second floor and the hallway to Eleanor's room, which had been mostly reset after yesterday's incident.

She sat on the bed, her delicate feet propped on a chair, all of her covered in a blanket despite the heat.

She looked a little better than she had yesterday. Still pale, and with a wrap around her wrist, but some of her color had come back. Her cheeks were pink with what looked like excitement.

Moses stood in the middle of the room, an old-fashioned buckle suitcase on the floor beside him, its leather a vibrant, pukey green.

Liam walked to Eleanor, kissed her forehead. "Where's your other grandson?"

"Making lemonade," Gavin said, appearing in the kitchen doorway. He walked to Eleanor, handed her a glass.

"Thank you, darling. Claire, how are you this morning?"

"I'm good, thank you. How are you feeling?"

She smiled cheekily, an expression she'd probably passed on to Liam and Gavin. "Truth be told, I'm very excited about our adventure."

I nodded. "I'm excited, too." Nervous as much as excited, but there was no point in telling her that. No point in making her carry both my fear and hers.

"What's that?" Liam asked, pointing at Moses's suitcase.

Moses looked down at it, brow furrowed. "My valuables. The stuff I managed to salvage from the store after it burned to the ground." He stuck up his chin. "If I can't take them with me, I'll just risk it. I'm spry on my feet."

I doubted all three and a half feet of him had ever been spry.

"And you didn't think your running around carrying a suitcase would look suspicious?" Liam asked.

Moses narrowed his eyes. "You sayin' I can't be careful? That I can't dodge and weave with the best of them?"

"I'm sure you can," Liam said. "But today we're on a mission with a short trigger. If the guard at the gate decides he wants to search the suitcases, I imagine he'll have a few questions about what's in it and why Eleanor's carrying it. And that will slow us down."

Moses growled.

"You can't take the suitcase this trip," Liam said firmly. "But—but," he added, when Moses bared his teeth, "if you leave it here, I'll come get it later, make sure it gets to you. That way, I'm the only one taking a risk."

Moses didn't look convinced, and he moved a step closer to the avocado monstrosity. I couldn't exactly blame him. His opportunity for freedom, or what he could find of it in a world where his very existence was illegal, meant leaving everything behind.

"How about this?" I said. "You can have an unlimited credit at the store for anything Liam loses or breaks."

Moses looked suspicious. He was a retailer at heart, and probably thought the offer sounded too good to be true. "You got cable? Wires and such?"

I smiled. "Dozens of spools."

He considered. "Okay, yeah. That would work."

"Crisis averted," Liam said, moving the suitcase to the far wall under Moses's gimlet stare. "Is Malachi in place?"

Malachi walked into the room in jeans and a fitted white T-shirt. "Yes, he is."

We stared at him. The Consularis general had apparently walked right into Devil's Isle. Of course, getting into Devil's Isle had never been the hard part. The trick, as we were about to prove, was getting out again.

"How the hell did you get in here?" Liam asked.

"I walked in," he said simply, stepping toward me with a warm smile, then looking at Liam. "We practiced last night, and we believed we managed to sync my magic and his invisibility. But we wanted a test inside the gates, just in case."

The air shimmered, and Burke appeared beside Malachi.

Eleanor gasped, her eyes seemingly focused on middle distance as she looked at the magic only she could see. "How marvelous! You have such beautiful magic, both of you. A beautiful copper, which split into gold and blue when you separated. Absolutely stunning."

"Malachi and Will Burke," Liam said.

"A pleasure to meet you," Burke said. "And thank you."

She nodded regally. "It is truly my pleasure, young man. You are doing a very good thing for a very good man."

Moses actually blushed.

Liam frowned, crossed his arms. "What did you learn with your testing?"

"We need proximity," Malachi said. "Being outside Devil's Isle—outside the wall or above the grid—isn't enough. If I'm inside Devil's Isle, and nearby, our combined magic can encompass us both."

"We need it to encompass all three of you," Liam pointed out.

"We can do it," Burke said with a grin, then looked at me. "We hid half the stuff in the storage room last night."

Too bad I'd been exhausted; I'd have liked to see that.

"Don't worry about the magic," Malachi said. "I also managed to keep us shielded from the monitors. But movement makes that tricky, and I'd rather not rely on it." He looked at Moses. "Monitors?"

"A cinch," Moses said, waving off the concern. "Come into my lair."

We followed him into a small room two doors down from Eleanor's, where he'd cobbled together mismatched parts to create some kind of computer. The contraption—boxes and keyboards and monitors joined together on a low table in the middle of the room—had a central monitor that glowed with green print.

I didn't bother to ask how he'd gotten the gear. Moses was re-sourceful.

He walked to the system, tapped the keyboard mounted beneath it. A list of words in the same bright green scrolled across the screen.

"I accessed Containment-Net. *Again*." He said the word with total boredom, as if he'd been given the dullest possible assignment. "Popped into the magic monitors, and I'm ready to set them all in neutral mode. The lights will stay red, like they're armed and ready, but they won't actually detect anything. But," he said, looking back at us, "the monitors are tested and, if necessary, reset every twenty minutes. When they are, they'll be put back into active mode. When I hit this"—he pointed to an enormous red button that looked like it had been borrowed from a toddler's toy—"we have twenty minutes to get somewhere safe, or stop using magic."

"So when we go, we shouldn't stop," Gavin said.

"That's the ticket." Moses hopped off the stool, toed a bundle of wires aside. "And you'll probably want to get this equipment out of here in case anyone comes sniffing around."

"We'll take care of it," Liam said.

We went back into the main room, and Liam lifted Eleanor into his arms like she weighed nothing. Which, if not actually true, was pretty close to it.

"That's my strong boy."

He smiled. "My grandmother made sure I cleaned my plate at every meal."

"Growing boy needs a good meal and a watchful grandmother."

"You need to stay nearby," Burke said to Moses. "And it's better if you're actually touching me. It makes the illusion easier."

Moses groaned. "I'm not gonna hold your hand like a kid."

"You don't have to." He pointed at his fatigues, which had large pockets on the legs. "Just grab a pocket. That's good enough. You stay on my right, Malachi will stay on my left, and we'll make it work."

Moses clapped his hands together. "All right. Enough chitchat. I am itchy for freedom."

We all looked back at him.

"No? I thought 'itchy for freedom' was a good one."

"No," we said simultaneously.

"How about 'let's get this show on the road'?"

That worked well enough.

Moses hit the timer. Liam carried Eleanor downstairs while Gavin picked up her suitcases. When we reached the front room, Liam looked at Burke, Moses, Malachi. "If we need to stop, touch my shoulder or Claire's."

"Got it," Burke said. He nodded, and Moses grabbed one of his pockets. They both looked at Malachi.

"Ready," Malachi said, and touched Burke's shoulder.

The ignition of magic changed the pressure in the air. The three of them shimmered—as if their bodies were composed of a thousand tiny mirrors shifting forward in sequence—and disappeared.

Liam let out an audible breath of obvious relief.

It was only the first step, but at least we'd gotten there.

Unfortunately, the building's front steps proved trickier. There was plenty of grunting as Moses, Malachi, and Burke maneuvered their way to the cart, but they managed it.

Gavin loaded the suitcases and took the driver's seat. I took shotgun and Liam and Eleanor took the second seat. Our magicked crew took the back bench.

Gavin looked back at his grandmother. "Ready?"

"Ready," she said with a decisive nod, and Gavin led us toward the Devil's Isle gate.

"Did I mention there's coffee at the store?" I said into the nervous silence, trying to keep the conversation light.

Liam lifted his eyebrows. "Actual coffee?"

I nodded. "I opened a new bag. Figured we could use a pick-me-up, what with Reveillon and the late nights."

"Tadji's probably already got plans to pipe the scent out to the sidewalk," Gavin said, rounding the corner, "lure in more customers like a siren."

"She is weirdly good at the merchandising thing."

"She interviews people in the Zone for a living," Liam pointed out. "She knows who they are, what they respond to."

His tone was relaxed, his gaze on the cottages and buildings we passed, and anyone who hadn't known him well would have assumed he was taking in the view. But I could see the tension in his body, the strength in the arm he'd banded around Eleanor's shoulders. Her head was back on the bench and she was smiling, her eyes closed as she absorbed the sunshine. I wondered how long it had been since she'd left the house.

When the vehicle slowed, I looked back at the street . . . and the barrier of Paras who stood in front of us.

CHAPTER NINETEEN

Solomon stood in the middle of the street, hands in the pockets of a very bad pin-striped suit. Was he trying to emulate a stereotypical mobster? If so, he was pulling it off pretty well.

While I thought he looked ridiculous, I still understood the danger. Liam and I had been attacked by Solomon's thugs on my first trip into Devil's Isle. As far as I knew, that business had been concluded, but Solomon was still a bully. And the four very large Paras who stood around him looked like they were, too.

"Son of a bitch," Liam muttered. "I don't recall that we have any business today," he added, expression cold and hard as Solomon walked toward the cart.

"I should think not, since it looks like parade season in New Orleans. Is it Mardi Gras Day, and nobody told me?"

Liam looked bored. "It takes more than one cart to make a parade."

Solomon's eyebrows lifted, and he slid his gaze to the empty space behind us. *Shit*, I thought, and cold sweat trickled down my back, even as heat and humidity pummeled us.

He took a step closer, and so did his people, closing in around us. "You may be able to fool the humans, Mr. Quinn, but you don't fool me." He sniffed the air, his large nostrils expanding. "I can smell my repugnant little cousin a mile away." I guessed Solomon was aware that Moses hadn't died in the explosion.

I could practically feel Moses baring his teeth at my back. But he maintained his control, just as he was supposed to.

Liam rolled his eyes. "Solomon, we're in a hurry. Claire's got to get back to the store."

"It's shipment day," I confirmed. "If I'm not there to accept it, I get dinged by Containment."

By my calculation, it had taken seven slow minutes to get to this point in the neighborhood. That meant we had thirteen minutes to get out of Devil's Isle and all the way back to the store—nearly a mile away.

"And FYI," I added, "there's a Containment agent on the corner watching you." I pointed to the woman on the corner, saw her gaze slip from Solomon to the magic monitor. The light was red. But Solomon could have been doing all the magic in the world, and that wouldn't have changed.

Solomon looked pissed at my interruption. And also probably because I'd cried wolf about Containment the last time we interacted.

"Cross my heart," I said, and made the motion. "Maybe one of your fine colleagues could look?"

Solomon snapped his fingers behind him, and the man directly behind him glanced around.

"Five o'clock," he confirmed. "Dame."

Seriously, had they learned about humans by watching 1940s mob movies? Give 'em spats and tommy guns and they'd be all set.

"So," Liam said, drawing Solomon's attention again. "Since you stepped into my path, if you could tell me what you want and be on your way?"

Solomon grinned, and much like Moses's attempts, it didn't look quite natural. "Cash," he said, "is universally accepted."

Liam rolled his eyes dramatically. "Cash for what? Because your cousin has a stench that is apparently following us around the Marigny?" He pulled at his hem as if fanning fumes from his shirt.

Solomon stepped closer. He was shorter than Liam, but carried fifty more pounds, and a lot more ego. I didn't know if he'd earned it.

"You think we don't know something's coming? Bombing, fire, attack, all by outsiders. Something is happening out there, something Containment hasn't handled. We don't like it." For the first time, there was a strand of fear in Solomon's eyes.

Liam watched him for a long time.

"Reveillon is big," Liam finally said. "Ezekiel has an army. If you can stock some food and water, put it away, you'll want to do that."

Solomon nodded, then squinted and glanced behind us again. "And as for today's business?"

"We just gave you advice," Liam protested.

"That's appreciated," Solomon said. "But it doesn't affect this transaction."

Damn it, we were losing time.

"Twenty Devil's Isle tokens," I offered, and Solomon's gaze snapped to mine. "And you walk away right now."

Solomon's grin was feral. He thought he'd found a mark. "Thirty."

"Twenty-five." I glanced behind him. The Containment agent, ten or fifteen yards away, was beginning to walk toward us. "And you head off the Containment agent. And if you say no," I threw out, heading off his argument, "I'll give them to your cousin."

I could practically hear seconds ticking down in his silence.

Solomon growled but nodded. "When do I collect?"

"I'll get them to Liam. Liam will get them to you."

"In that case," Solomon said, as the Containment agent began to move closer, "it's been a pleasure doing business with you." He turned. "Agent Correlli! A pleasure to see you as always."

Liam gave the agent a friendly wave, rolled his eyes dramatically to signal his frustration with Solomon. But to his credit, Solomon kept her occupied while we continued down the street.

"He'd have taken twenty," Liam said when Solomon was well behind us.

I grinned. "I'd have paid him thirty. This way, we both go away satisfied."

We just had to be sure we could go away quickly.

Gavin looked bored when we approached the gate and flashed his pass at the guardhouse.

The guard nodded. "Agent Landreau told us to expect you and Mrs. Arsenault." He lifted fingers to his forehead in a small salute. "Pleasure knowing you, ma'am. Best of luck out there."

"Thank you," Eleanor said with a regal nod.

The gate began its crawl open again, and we drove through. And I didn't breathe again until it closed again behind us.

We cruised down Royal, but as we neared the store, we found a cluster of people standing outside, murmuring and chatting animatedly.

"Shit, shit, shit," Liam muttered, echoing my thoughts. "What's happening?"

Someone had seen Malachi, had been my first thought. Or maybe Broussard was causing trouble.

Gavin pulled the cart into the alley beside the store, behind a dark luxury sedan with tinted windows.

Liam sighed. "And where did you get the car?"

Eleanor gave Gavin a sour look. "Gavin Arsenault Beauregard Quinn."

"Beauregard?" I said, grinning at him.

"It's a family name," Gavin said. "And I'll hear nothing else about it."

"The car?" Liam prompted.

"Borrowed. I left an IOU and everything."

Liam rolled his eyes. "Stay here," he said to the rest of the group as he and I hopped out of the cart.

We walked around to the front of the store, where the windows and door had been covered with white sheets. Tadji had painted PRE-PARING FOR GRAND REOPENING in large golden letters across the one that hung in the left-hand window. Cheery big band music piped from the store from a speaker Tadji had propped outside.

"Oh my God, she's a genius," I muttered. She'd figured out a way to give us almost complete privacy. The sidewalk stragglers couldn't see through the sheet, and they wouldn't hear us talking over the music.

The dozen customers in front of the store shouted questions as we walked to the door.

"Are you remodeling?"

"Was there a fire?"

"Will there be door prizes?"

The door slitted open, and Tadji peeked outside. "I heard the crowd, figured you were out here." She scooted aside just enough for Liam and me to slip inside.

"Sorry for the delay, everyone!" I said, offering them a wave. "I think you'll decide the wait was worth it!"

I didn't wait for responses, but closed and locked the door again.

"I'll get them in through the back door," Liam said, jogging to the other side of the store.

Malachi, Burke, and Moses shimmered into view inside the store just as the monitor across the street turned off, blinked twice, then settled again into red.

We'd gotten very, very lucky.

Having done her duty by keeping an eye on the store, and apparently not in the mood for company, Erida slipped out the back. Burke settled Eleanor at the table while Moses inspected the store, peering into baskets and surveying shelves. Royal Mercantile was three-for-three on captivating Paras.

"I was pacing the floor," Tadji said, bringing mugs and a fresh pot of coffee into the front room. "My hands are still shaking."

"Then maybe I should take that," Burke said, intercepting her and taking the carafe.

She nodded, handed out mugs.

"Introductions," I said. "Tadji, you know Malachi, and this is Eleanor Arsenault and Moses. Eleanor and Moses, my friend Tadji."

"A pleasure," Eleanor said. Moses's face was buried in a gilded manuscript on a bookstand, but he lifted a hand.

"That might be the best you get from him," Liam said. He ran his hands through his hair, linked them atop his head, grinned hugely. "I cannot believe we just pulled that off."

Gavin looked at Tadji, pointed to the window. "That was a stroke of genius."

"It really was," I said, embracing her until she squeaked.

"I thought, in case things didn't go smoothly, you might need some time to regroup. Unfortunately, they are going to expect something pretty spectacular when we open the doors again. Which I'm working on." She gestured to the markers and clipboard on the counter. "Everything on your end went well?"

"Well enough," Liam said, pouring coffee into mugs and passing them around the table.

"It didn't occur to me that Solomon could sense Moses," Malachi said.

"I'm not entirely sure he did," Liam said, "versus making a very lucky guess. And that's my bad, too. I hadn't thought to plan for Solomon, who is a chronic pain in my ass. I should have."

I left them to discuss the irritation that was Solomon, walked to Moses. He stood in front of the rack of walking sticks, pulling each one out, inspecting it, sliding it in again.

He glanced up at me. "So this is your place."

"It is. What do you think?" It was suddenly very important to me that he like my store.

He looked around. "Humans make a lot of things out of wood."

"Yeah, Nix said the same thing."

Nodding, he walked to a box of doorknobs, picked through until he found one with a cut-glass handle that gleamed in the light. "That's a nice bauble."

"Why don't you take that?"

Moses looked at me suspiciously. "Why?"

"Because it would be a favor to me," I said, and suddenly realized that this fabulous person was about to disappear from my life. If not forever, then for a very long time. "Like, something to remember me by."

Moses snorted, but tucked the doorknob into a pocket of his baggy pants. "Shines pretty good."

"That it does," I agreed.

"I guess we should go over there before they start hollering," Moses said.

"I guess we should," I agreed, but crouched down and hugged him before he had a chance to escape. "Thank you for everything. If it wasn't for you . . ."

"Don't say it," he said, and embraced me back, his arms squeezing tightly, but only for a second. Moses released me, and sarcasm was back in his tone and expression quickly enough. "No need to get all emotional. This is temporary."

He walked back to the group, waved his arms. "Just temporary. This will all be worked out soon enough, this Containment and Devil's Isle nonsense." He looked at Malachi, and his eyes narrowed dangerously. "Right?"

Malachi didn't miss a beat. "I'll do everything in my power to make it so."

"As to things in my power," Gavin said, putting a hand on his chest and gesturing to the store's back door. "Your chariot awaits."

Malachi took shotgun in the black sedan, and Gavin held open the car's back door while Moses climbed inside. Then he looked at his grandmother. "We'll come see you as soon as we can get clear here."

She nodded. "I know you will." She glanced in our general direction, her eyes even paler in the afternoon sunlight. "Thank you for everything you've done. For everything you sacrificed."

She put a slight hand on the car to balance herself as Liam helped her lean into the backseat.

But then she sucked in a whistling breath, fingers clutching at the car's roof as she stared wide-eyed at something only she could see. And there was horror in her gaze.

Liam looked around, but it was quiet except for the rustle of pigeons above us.

"Eleanor!" Liam said, and scooped her up when her knees trembled and she began to slide to the ground. He carried her around the corner to the courtyard behind the store, set her carefully on the bench.

Liam crouched in front of her. "Eleanor. What's wrong?"

"So much darkness," Eleanor muttered, eyes blindly searching as she reached out, gripped Liam's hand. "I see so much darkness."

"It's a rose, a blooming rose." She swallowed hard, put her free hand against her chest. "Not a flower. Power. Darkness. But spreading."

"I'll get some water," Tadji said quietly, and went back into the store.

Burke kneeled beside Liam, his eyes wide with concern. "Tell me what you see, Eleanor. Is it magic?"

"A flower. Oily. So dark. So fluid." Her breath shuddered in, then out.

Tadji came back, offered Liam the cup of water. He handed it to Eleanor, whose hands shook as she sipped from it.

"I've seen dark magic before," she said, her voice so quiet, so delicate. "But not like this. Not this kind of darkness." She turned her gaze toward Liam. "My book?"

That was her coded record of all the magic she'd glimpsed, organized by color.

"The book is in your suitcase," Liam assured her. "It's in the car. Where did you see this magic?"

She shook her head, took another small sip, then gestured toward the north. "There? I don't know how far away. I don't know if it's still there. It was a stain—a smudge, and then it was gone."

But it had been there. And I didn't want to know what we'd find.

We let Eleanor catch her breath. And when her complexion had lost some of the peaky haze, Liam carried her back to the car again.

"You don't need to carry me," she said.

"You could probably outrun me in a marathon," Liam said. "But I won't have a chance to carry you for a while, so you're doing me a favor."

"From ornery child, you've grown into a wonderful man."

I snickered. "He's still ornery, Eleanor."

"About damn time," Moses said from the backseat, and offered Eleanor a cellophane-wrapped peppermint and a small bottle of water. "Refreshments?"

The question made her smile, just as he'd intended. "No, thank you, kind sir. But I believe I'm ready to get out of the city."

"Je t'aime," Liam said, and pressed his lips to her forehead. Then he closed the door, and moved to Gavin's open window.

"Be careful," Liam said.

"Walk in the park," Gavin said, but his expression said Serious Business.

"I'll go back to the Cabildo," Burke said as Gavin drove down the alley. "Tell Gunnar that there might have been some kind of attack. Maybe he can pull a patrol from one of the other quadrants, have someone take a look."

I looked at Liam. "Magic doesn't sound like Reveillon."

"No," he agreed. "It doesn't. But that doesn't make me feel any better."

For a long time, Tadji, Liam, and I sat silently at the table, the store quiet behind the sheets that still covered the window.

We'd managed to get Eleanor and Moses out of Devil's Isle, but Reveillon was still out there. And now we had to wonder what Eleanor had seen.

An hour later, Gavin returned, confirmed they were safely in Darby's, Erida's, and Malachi's hands. They'd stay at the church until darkness fell, then head toward Bayou Teche. Once at the cabin, Erida would stay with them until they were set up and she was sure Reveillon wasn't a threat.

An engine rumbled, drew nearer. We peeked through the window. The crowd had disappeared, and we watched Gunnar and Burke hop out of an enormous Hummer.

Gunnar walked inside, offered the keys to Gavin. "It's all yours."

Gavin's eyes narrowed. "I'm suspicious of this gift."

"It's not a gift," Gunnar said. "We've got every agent patrolling the city, the hinterlands. Because of the border skirmishes, PCC hasn't been able to send anyone else into the Zone. We're as short-staffed as we get. See if you can figure out what Eleanor saw. And if you see any Reveillon bastards, take them out."

The words were harsh, but so was Reveillon.

"Come to papa," Gavin said by way of agreement, gaze on the gleaming vehicle. "The rational part of my brain says this thing is too big for scouting. Too big and too noisy." He grinned. "I'm just going to consider that a challenge to be overcome."

"You do you, little brother," Liam said, and clapped him on the back.

"Happy hunting," Gunnar said, and Gavin gave a cheeky salute, walked outside, and began to caress and whisper to his new toy.

"You might want to sterilize that thing when you get it back," Liam said.

"Already on the agenda."

"I'll go with Gavin," Burke said, then glanced at me. "Maybe we'll bunk here tonight, if that's all right with you. I'd feel better if we were together."

Tadji nodded, wrapped her arms around herself. "I'd rather not be alone."

"It would be convenient for me, too," Gunnar said. "And better than the barracks."

"They smell like feet," Burke agreed.

I wrinkled my nose. "That is disgusting. And bunking here is fine," I said. "There's a bed down here and one in the storage room. We'll make it work. And I have a request for you," I told Gunnar, and grabbed the questions I'd written down in Devil's Isle. I offered it to him.

He looked it over, then up at me again. "What's this?"

"I helped Vendi with home visits this morning. The Paras had some questions about Reveillon. I know they aren't constituents; they're prisoners. But they're under attack. They deserve to know what's happening. They deserve answers."

Gunnar watched me for a moment, then added the list to his folder. "I'll see what I can do," he said, then rubbed a hand over his face as if he might break up his obvious exhaustion. "I'm going back to the Cabildo."

"We should plan some kind of meal when he gets back," I said, realizing most of us were probably running on fumes. I glanced toward the kitchen. "Except I'm pretty sure we're nearly out of food. You people have been using my store like an all-you-can-eat buffet."

"I can probably get you an industrial can of beans," Burke said with a smile.

"I don't want your government beans," I assured him, then walked to the window, looked outside. It was sunny, at least for now.

"We'll go to the garden," I said, and glanced at Liam. "I wouldn't mind a few minutes of peace and quiet and weed pulling. And since you did so well with the beets, you can go with me."

"I want nothing to do with beets because they are disgusting," he said. "But since it's a good idea that we stay together, I will sacrifice."

"So noble," Tadji said, reaching over to squeeze his hand, give him a solemn look.

"But I'm not pulling weeds," Liam said. "I have too many memories of pulling weeds at Eleanor's house."

"Because you liked to garden?" Burke asked.

"Because Gavin and I had 'behavioral issues,' or so she said."

"Yeah, that makes more sense." I grabbed the canvas-lined basket that held my gardening supplies from behind the counter, handed it to Liam. "Let's go rustle up some grub."

The Quarter's community garden sat on the top floor of the old Florissant Hotel. The deck, which had once been home to a luxurious pool, bar, and tropical garden, now held small plots of dark earth used by agents who lived in the barracks and by the few civilians who still lived in the Quarter. My plot was on the northernmost corner of the building, and was currently overburdened with fall vegetables. I hadn't been here to harvest in nearly a week.

I gathered the vegetables that were ready to eat, put the rest in the compost pile. Liam weeded without a single complaint, so I didn't argue when he took a break to look out over the city. I joined him at the roof's edge, took in the slate roofs of the Quarter's remaining buildings, the tall and glowing walls of Devil's Isle, the empty shells of skyscrapers in the CBD. And behind it all, the dark ribbon of the Mississippi River.

"Do you believe in fate?" Liam asked.

Not a question I'd have expected Liam Quinn to ask. "I think we are who we are, at least to some degree, within some kind of limit. I mean, I'm not going to become a trapeze artist."

He smiled quizzically. "Was that on the list?"

"Briefly," I admitted. "I went to a circus when I was a kid—this artistic carnival that set up in Audubon Park. The acrobats were gorgeous women in stockings and satin costumes with sequins, and I thought they were the most beautiful creatures I'd ever seen. They flew like birds, and I wanted to be one of them."

He smiled. "Since I haven't seen you in a satin costume, I'm assuming it didn't pan out?"

"No. The carnival came back the next year, and they held a class where you could climb up the trapeze ladder and take a turn on one of the trapeze swings. You're hooked up to harnesses and there was an enormous net, but you'd still get the experience of flying. They strapped me into the harness, and I climbed up the ladder, hand over foot, and got to the little pedestal where they push you off. And then I looked down—all the way down."

"And that was the end of that?" he asked.

I grinned, remembering. "I climbed right back down that ladder. My father wasn't thrilled he'd lost his deposit."

"But probably happy you weren't going to run off and join the circus."

"True. Heights don't bother me as much now, but my life on the flying trapeze is behind me." I looked at Liam. "Do you believe in fate? Or would you like to tell me an embarrassing story of your childhood so we're even steven?"

Liam stood up, stuck out his chest. "I've always been a brave and resourceful lad."

I snorted. "I bet."

Before he could elaborate, the sky opened, and rain began to fall in sheets that left us instantly soaked to the bone.

"I guess I won't need a shower," Liam said, scooping back his wet hair. He was somehow sexier in the rain, as if the rivulets of water had sharpened the lines of his face, the strong cut of his jaw, made his blue eyes shine like sapphires against his coal black hair.

"Me, either," I said. I smiled, but stiffened when he brushed a lock of hair from my face.

"Saint Claire of the Florissant," Liam said as rain streamed down his face.

The moment lingered and stretched, as they always did when we faced each other across this same chasm. But once again, the chasm defeated us.

"Let's get out of the downpour," he said.

And the rain continued to fall.

CHAPTER TWENTY

Burke and Gavin were back by the time we walked, drenched, into the store again. They were only slightly less damp than we were.

"This doesn't bode well," Liam said as we approached them. "Do we have time to dry off before you tell us what happened?"

"It will be a quick update," Burke said. "We think we found what Eleanor saw. There was a murder in Congo Square. A Paranormal."

The store went quiet, an implicit moment of silence.

"Who?" Liam asked.

"No one I know or have seen before," Burke said. "He had wings, but he looked like he'd been living on the street for a while."

Liam frowned. "A homeless Para? That's a new one."

"PTSD hits Paras as well as humans. He could have suffered a break during or after the war. It would have been easy for him to hide his wings. People might have thought he was human, maybe mentally ill."

"How'd you know he was Para?" I asked.

Burke said, "The killer cut off his wings, and wrote 'Cleansed' on the brick by the body."

"Reveillon," Liam said, and they nodded.

"It was a gory scene," Gavin said, pushing a hand through his damp hair. "One of the worst I've ever seen, including during the war. That must have been what Eleanor saw."

"The blossoming blood," I said quietly, and Burke nodded.

"He had golden eyes like Malachi," Burke said. "Open and staring at the sky, like he was waiting to be called home." He looked away, shook his head. "It's a damn waste, and a damn shame."

"We happened to run into two Containment agents who were on their way back to the barracks," Gavin said. "Had them stay with him until we could tell Gunnar, send a pigeon to Malachi."

"I'm sorry you had to see that," Tadji said, putting a hand over Burke's. "And I'm sorry it happened, and I'm sorry Eleanor saw what she did. The world is just completely screwed up right now."

"Yeah," Burke said, lifting their joined hands to his lips, pressing a kiss to them. "Let's be glad we've got friends and a safe place to sleep."

Because not everyone was so lucky.

We were starving, but not really in the mood to eat. So we opted for sustenance, came up with canned white beans with onion from the garden, corn bread from a mix, and the last of the iced tea. The greens we'd gathered would take a while to cook; we'd eat them tomorrow.

We ate in silence as steady rain turned into a storm, each roll of thunder shaking the old glass in the store's windows. But they'd survived tropical storms and hurricanes; they'd manage a good wet-season soaking.

"I'll take care of the dishes," Burke offered when we were done. "I don't mind."

"I won't say no to that offer," I said. "I hate doing dishes."

We took the dishes and leftovers into the kitchen, blew out the candles. And then there was a knock on the door.

"No," I said. "I am not accepting any more death or drama today. Just no."

"Maybe Ezekiel wants to turn himself in," Gavin muttered. "Excuse me," he said in an exaggerated drawl. "I have come to my senses, and genocide is a nasty, nasty business. Please take me to the Cabildo."

"Your impressions are as bad as your hand-to-hand," Liam said, walking to the door. "He doesn't have an accent." He peeked through the sheets that still covered the windows, then unlocked and opened the door.

A very young Containment agent in a dark shirt, skirt, and tidy heels blinked up at him. Behind her, Royal Street glimmered wet in the soggy moonlight. "I'm looking for Liam Quinn?"

"That would be me," Liam said.

The woman pulled a dark folder from her leather portfolio.

Damn it. I also preferred not to accept any more Containment folders this week.

"Agent Landreau requested I deliver this to you. He's not able to get away from the office. He asked that I wait until you read it, get your answer."

I rose, walked to the door to stand behind Liam while he read the sheet of paper inside the folder. It was a Containment form, with PARANORMAL RECOVERY in gothic letters across the top. It was a bounty.

"The wraith in the Lower Ninth has been spotted again," Liam said, scanning the document. "And a group of Reveillon members have been wandering the neighborhood, harassing residents and causing trouble."

The same group Malachi had run into, I wondered, or a second asshole brigade?

"Containment doesn't have the people to deal with it," Liam said, and the agent nodded. He closed the folder, handed it back to her.

"Agent Landreau said to find either, or both. Your work would be appreciated either way. Oh, and I was to tell you to keep Claire out of trouble."

"Acknowledged and accepted," Liam said, then offered his thanks and closed the door. "Saddle up, trainee," he said, glancing at me with resignation. "We're back on the clock."

We drove back to the Lower Ninth, found Reveillon had been busy with billboards. We saw a dozen along the way, all in the signature yellow and red paint.

New Orleans was beginning to feel like a city under siege.

"He's appealing to a lot of people," I said. "A lot of angry people."

"Yeah," Liam said, sliding his gaze from a CLEANSE NEW ORLEANS billboard back to the dark street. "And people who can't think for themselves."

When we reached the neighborhood, we drove for nearly an hour through darkness, past lots still vacant since Katrina, up and down streets that dead-ended at the Industrial Canal Levee.

I wasn't an experienced hunter, but Liam was. That we'd spent two unproductive evenings looking for a wraith in an area with a lot of open and visible ground wasn't a compliment to either of us.

And then I glanced out the side window, and my heart went cold. "Liam, stop the truck."

Tension snapped his body into fight-ready form, and he did exactly as I'd asked, pulling the truck into the quiet side street, idling the engine. "What did you see?"

"A group of people in the middle of the street, pale clothes." I glanced at him. "Maybe that Reveillon fabric."

His expression went hard. "How many?"

"It was a really quick glance. Maybe half a dozen? More than five, fewer than ten."

Nodding, he reached over and opened the glove box, pulled out the .44 and a box of bullets that hadn't been there before. "Let's go take a look."

"You sure you can shoot that thing?"

"Maybe not as well as you," he said, climbing out of the truck, tucking the ammo into his pocket, holding the gun at his side, finger away from the trigger. "But I'll do my best."

Side by side, we slipped back to the street we'd passed, edged around an empty house still marked by a Katrina X-Code, and looked at our foes.

There were eight of them—men in pants and shirts of stained homespun fabric, standing in the middle of a street beneath the sweeping branches of live oaks that were decades older than they were.

"Cleanse the Zone! Cleanse the Zone! Cleanse the Zone!"

Most of them were chanting; all of them watched avariciously the person who writhed at their feet.

It was a boy, I thought, based on the glimpses I got as the men moved around him. Small and slender, with pale skin and ratty clothes. They kicked him viciously, laughed at his obvious pain as he contorted.

"You are filth!" screamed a man of thirty-five or forty. "Garbage! Should have stayed where you came from!"

The boy screamed, the sound a barely human, high-pitched shriek that ripped through the air like lightning. It wasn't the sound of a normal human.

"*Shit,*" I murmured, all the air rushing from my lungs. He wasn't a child—not anymore. He was a wraith, his essence winnowed down by magic to his single, overriding obsession: find more magic. It was the curse of the Sensitive; we had magic because we absorbed it. And if we weren't careful, we'd become nothing more than vessels for that need.

"Liam."

He just nodded, watching them with an intense but otherwise blank expression. He must have thought of Gracie while staring at this boy, who couldn't have been more than eleven or twelve. This child had lost his life to magic in a very different way, but he'd lost his life all the same.

Liam pulled the keys from his pocket, slipped them to me. "Get the truck. Pull it up to the corner, headlights on bright."

"It will blind them," I said, understanding.

"For a moment, anyway. Cowards that they probably are, I'm guessing one or two will make a run for it, and the rest will stay because they're already pumped for a fight."

"This may be the same group that Malachi engaged. They may also be pissed."

"They aren't the only ones. I don't want to shoot them—maybe they're redeemable assholes—but I will if I have to. Otherwise we need to get them down and waiting for Containment. There are zip ties in the truck."

"Did some stocking after Camp Couturie, did you?"

"It seemed wise. Bring those with."

I nodded. "If you can get them away from the wraith, and he senses me, he'll move toward me."

In truth, he'd try to attack me. He'd sense the magic I'd already absorbed, and he'd want it. He was small, but he'd be strong and probably as vicious as the humans who'd attacked him, if not by choice.

"You can handle him? We only have to hold them off before Containment gets here."

"Containment?"

Liam pointed to the blinking green light on a pole halfway down the block. "They've been signaled. Poor little bastard wandered into a neighborhood with a working monitor."

"Are there cameras this far from the Cabildo?"

"Not usually. Monitors are cheaper, and they don't have the staff to watch feed from every block in New Orleans." He looked back at me. "Containment won't be here fast; they don't have enough people for it. But they will be here eventually."

So don't do anything to get yourself arrested, he meant.

"I can handle myself," I assured him. "You've got the tranq kit?" That was the easiest way to keep a wraith from injuring himself or anyone else.

"Also in the glove box."

The wraith screamed again.

"*Go*," Liam said, and I ran back toward the truck, climbed inside, and got it moving. I made a U-turn in the street, came slowly back around to the corner, and when the gun fired, I roared around it and flipped on the lights, silhouetting Liam's strong body.

"You a friend or foe?" asked the man who'd stepped in front of the others. He was tall and lean, with a shaved, pale head.

Two of the others were pinning down the wraith. A couple looked scared. Wise decision on their parts.

"Neither," Liam said. "I'm a bounty hunter, and he belongs to me."

The Reveillon member stepped forward, hands on his hips. "I don't give a shit who you think you are. We are Reveillon. We are cleansing this city from garbage like him. And since you profit from the system, from garbage like you, too."

"Do you know any bounty hunters? Do you know the kind of shit we put up with? The kind of shit we're equipped to handle?" Liam's tone had gone hard and glacier-cold. Bounty hunters had reputations for being badasses, and he was no exception.

"I've got people and guns," the guy said, "and if you're smart, you'll get the hell out of our way."

Two of his friends stepped forward, showed the guns stuffed into their waistbands.

Liam lifted the .44 and cocked it as I stepped out of the truck.

"Oh, you brought your girlfriend," the man in front said. "Big fucking deal."

"*Capons*," Liam spat, his gaze narrowing on the man who'd challenged him. "You want to go? Let's go. I've had one hell of a shitty week, and a workout might make me feel better."

"Fine, asshole," the man said, stepping forward. "Let's go."

Liam had seen enough death, destruction, fear, and hurt from Reveillon. He was ready for a fight, and I wasn't going to take that away from him. So I took the gun he held out to me, kept it trained on the other guys.

Liam and the guy with the big mouth lunged at each other, piled into a grappling mess that hit the ground, started to roll.

While they battled, one of their crew slunk off into the darkness. The two men with guns moved toward me, leering smiles on their faces.

"You a traitor, too, bitch?" asked one of them.

"The only traitors in this town are Reveillon," I said, holding up the .44. "I'm the one with the very large gun."

"What?" said the other, elbowing his buddy. "You going to shoot us?"

I smiled mirthlessly. "Unless you put the guns on the ground by the count of three, yeah, I am. *One*."

"Bullshit," said the first guy. "You ain't gonna shoot nothing."

"*Two*."

They cursed, drew their weapons. One of them held his gun sideways like a moronic movie villain. Were all the assholes in New Orleans watching the same bad shows?

"And three," I said pleasantly, and fired a shot between them. The one on the right scrambled to get away but tripped on the pockmarked asphalt.

The one on the left, all bravado, took another step forward, gun now shaking in his outstretched hand.

"Morons," I said, and aimed at his feet, preparing to fire again.

I'd just taken a step forward, gun trained on him, when the wraith bounded out the darkness, screaming with the wrath of an angry god.

His hair was short and pale, his fingers tipped in nails sharp as diamonds. He fell on top of the man with the gun, and they hit the ground together. The man screamed and kicked, pushed back against the wraith's rubbery skin but couldn't dislodge him. The wraith clawed at his clothes, his skin, as if they held back the magic he needed.

"Help me!" the man screamed.

I moved but was still ten feet away when the wraith dug those nails into the man's stomach, filling the air with the scent of blood.

"Jesus," said the other man with a gun, the one who'd scrambled away from my first shot. He aimed his gun at the wraith, started firing. He'd grazed the wraith, twice, missed on every other shot. But the wraith hadn't even noticed. He was busy on the ground, searching for the magic he could feel in the air.

My magic. And my problem to handle.

"Hey!" I screamed. The wraith's gaze snapped to me, the eyes staring blankly, hungrily. He lumbered to his feet and darted awkwardly toward me, limbs angular and pinched.

"That's right," I said, walking backward toward the truck, keeping the light in his eyes, hoping it might slow him down.

He lunged, fingers catching my forearm and scraping painfully down. I kicked, made contact with his shin. He hit the ground but scrambled up again, grabbed at me again. His eyes were dark and empty, his hair as white as snow, his arms skeletally thin.

When my heart ached with pity, I had to remind myself he wasn't a child. He wasn't an innocent. He wasn't a Sensitive. Not anymore.

Ignoring the mental warnings, I tucked the gun into the back of my waistband and grabbed his left wrist, pushed his arm down to pull him off balance. His arm was thin enough that I could nearly make a fist around it. He screamed furiously, clawing at my hand to free himself from my grasp, then lurched forward, leading with pointed, bared teeth.

"Shit!" I said, letting go and jumping back to avoid his snapping jaw. He came at me, mouth nearly foaming in his hunger for magic I probably needed to cast off. I wasn't sure even Malachi could have given me such a solid incentive.

I moved backward to stay out of his grasp, hit the truck's front grill, realized my opportunity. I feigned right and, when he jumped forward, dodged left. He hit the grill, screamed from the contact with hot metal.

I plunged the tranq into his shoulder.

He screamed, spasmed one last time, and went limp. I caught him as he fell, lowered him carefully to the ground, cradling his head so it wouldn't crack against the asphalt. He was a wraith, but he was what I could become, and he'd become that monster much too soon.

The wraith out of commission, I stood up again, looked at the scene.

Liam had twenty pounds of hard muscle on the man, and probably a lot more legit fighting experience, but they were still going at each other. Liam, a satisfied grin on his face, was leading the man into making stupid little jabs, which would only wear him out.

Liam was toying with him. Not that I couldn't sympathize.

Behind him, there was one dead Reveillon member on the ground, two whose gazes were transfixed on the man the wraith had disemboweled.

I pulled out the gun, walked toward them. "I'd suggest you hit the asphalt, faces down."

"Fuck you, bitch," one of them said, but his teeth chattered with fear.

Liam stepped beside me, breath heaving. "You moron. Now you've insulted her." Liam walked forward, kicked him square in the balls. The man went down to his knees with a groan, eyes rolling back.

"Thanks, I guess, for protecting my honor?"

"Anytime."

Keeping the gun on the second guy, who wisely lifted his hands into the air, I pulled zip ties from my pocket as Liam turned the guy onto his stomach, pulled his hands behind him.

He took one, fastened the man's wrists together, then stood and wiped sweat from his brow. "You'd make a pretty solid bounty hunter."

I flipped the gun around, offered it to Liam grip-first, and looked down at the warp and weft of scratches along my arms. "Thanks. But I have a job."

The cavalry arrived, two fresh-faced Containment agents who looked barely older than the wraith on the ground. Containment was down to the newbies. Everyone else was in Devil's Isle, searching the streets for Reveillon, or already fighting them.

"They're all Reveillon members," Liam said. "They were attacking the wraith."

Their gazes tracked from humans to wraith. "And the Para. Did you kill it?" one of the agents asked.

"It's 'him,'" I corrected. "Not 'it.' And he's a wraith, not a Para. They're different." At least to me. "And no, we didn't kill him. We tranqed him."

"Licensed tranqs," Liam said. "We'll take him to the clinic. Can you handle these three?"

"Sure," the other agent said.

"In addition to the one who didn't make it, four more ran away." Liam pointed. "They headed that way on foot. They're cowards, so you might still be able to grab them."

"Sure," one of them said, and pulled a comm unit from his belt.

"In that case," Liam said, "we'll be going." He didn't wait for them to argue but walked to the wraith and picked him up. He looked even more frail being held by Liam, his arms drawn up like a bird's wings.

"There's a blanket behind the seat," Liam said, gesturing to the truck. I grabbed it, spread it onto the bed. The wraith probably wouldn't care, but that Liam had thought to do it tugged at my heart.

He placed the boy carefully on the blanket, then used tie-downs to create a kind of cage that would keep him from rolling through the truck. It wasn't a pretty solution, but he wouldn't be able to attack us en route, or escape to attack anyone else. However pitiable he was, that had to be the priority.

"I didn't know it could happen to a child," I said as Liam backed the truck onto the main street again, headed toward Devil's Isle. I sat halfway turned in the seat, watching him dutifully.

"He's the youngest I've seen. By far."

"He could have learned balance, to control it. He shouldn't have gotten that far." I looked at Liam. "Is it ironic that we're taking him into Devil's Isle? Or just cruel?"

Liam kept his eyes on the street. "There's no other place to take him, Claire. No one else equipped to handle him."

The breaking of this small boy was only one of the million tragedies, big and small, that the world had seen since the Veil opened. But this hurt as much as any of them.

The Devil's Isle guards were silent when Liam carried the boy through the gate. The houses we passed were equally quiet.

"Lizzie!" Liam called out when I opened the clinic door for him.

She walked into the room a moment later. Her pink scrubs were wrinkled, her face sweaty, locks of hair in damp curls around it. She peeled off dirty gloves, tossed them into a waste can. "It's been a long night already. And it looks like it's about to get completely demoralizing."

She walked to us, checked the boy's pupils with a penlight, then sighed. "How old is he? Eleven?"

"About that," I said as Liam handed the boy over to the orderly who followed Lizzie into the room.

"That's a kick in the teeth." She looked back at us. "Any sign of his parents?"

"No," Liam said, and described where we'd found him, and how. "It's possible they were nearby, but it doesn't look like he's been in a stable home for a while."

"No," Lizzie agreed. "He looks feral. We'll match against missing persons, just in case," she said. "If his parents are alive. It's possible he's an orphan, has been living on the streets for a while." She looked up at me. "Want me to tell you if we find them?"

I nodded. "I'd appreciate that."

Lizzie nodded. "Thanks for taking care of him. I hear you did pretty well on the home visits."

I smiled. "For a novice, maybe."

Lizzie smiled. "That's pretty much what Vendi said, which is high praise. Now get out of here so I can do my job."

The store was locked and quiet when we returned, everyone asleep. Gavin was curled into a chair in the front room. Burke and Tadji had hung a sheet across the hallway to the back room, and I assumed they were sleeping. I didn't want to check.

I went upstairs and changed into a tank and shorts, brushed the day's knots from my hair. I heard Liam step into the doorway. "You need sheets or pillows or anything?"

"No," he said, and when I glanced, I saw that he looked at me like a man with a long-denied thirst.

My heart pounded in silent answer.

"You look like a fairy queen," he said. "Radiant and otherworldly."

I smiled. "I'm exhausted and pissed off."

"You did good tonight. You handled yourself. You handled the wraith." He smiled. "You handled Lizzie."

"I tried."

Liam shouldn't have walked toward me. He shouldn't have cupped my face, stared down at me with adoration even I could recognize, and he probably didn't want to feel.

"It would be so easy for you to run," he said. "To walk away from all this and spare yourself the emotions, the fear, the danger. But you don't. And you don't stand by. You jump in with both feet." He smiled, his eyes glimmering like jewels. "You are so brave."

"Reckless," I said with a smile.

"Reckless," he agreed.

"Doubt is part of life," I said. "And so is hope. Life is about taking chances. You just have to hope that the chance is worth the risk."

I dug fingers into his shirt, rested my forehead on his chest. I should have done the hard thing—the smart thing—and walked away, left us both in peace. But it was too late for that now.

"I don't care about tomorrow, or the next day, or the next. I just care about right now, about me, about you." It was only half a lie, and it was half a lie I could live with. And when he looked at me, I knew he knew it.

I put a hand on his face, knew where we were heading. "Tonight, you'll make me feel whole. You'll keep me safe."

His groan was deep, elemental, utterly masculine.

"I want to be home," I said. "And I'm home when I'm with you."

With those words, I sealed our deal.

He swept me up and into his arms, carried me to the bed. I let myself be carried. I let myself rest against the warm solidity of his body, surrounded and safe, and for the first time in years, content. Maybe this would be the end of us, maybe it wouldn't. But for tonight, neither of us would be alone.

He placed me on the bed as if I were a delicate antique, began to pull off his T-shirt, but I shook my head.

"Let me do it." I wanted to unwrap him, reveal him, one bit of cotton and denim at a time.

Smiling with obvious satisfaction, he put his hands down. "Go ahead."

I pulled up the hem of his shirt, revealing flat abs, strong chest, broad shoulders. He lifted his arms, let me pull the shirt over his head.

While he watched with avaricious eyes, I let my fingers trip and skim over hard and chiseled muscle, honed from sweat and effort. Every inch was strong and taut, every muscle firm, and he shivered under the slip of my fingers.

I let my eyes skim to his impossibly gorgeous face. Piercingly blue eyes, generous mouth, the dark slashes of eyebrows. "You are the most beautiful man I have ever seen in my life."

Those eyebrows popped up. "That's quite a compliment, Claire Connolly. Thank you."

"You're welcome, Liam Quinn."

I didn't have even a moment to wonder what would come next. He climbed above me, roped arms balanced on either side of my head, and stared down at me reverently. "You are the most beautiful and haunting creature I have ever seen in my life. And in New Orleans, that's saying something."

I grinned at him. "Your accent gets stronger when you're flattering me."

He leaned down, lips to my ear. *"Tu es belle."*

I understood the gist of that well enough.

"And it's my turn," he said, and skimmed his strong hands along my ribs, sliding up the thin cotton tank as we moved.

A hand across the flat of my stomach, then my breasts. I closed my eyes and arched into his hands.

"Nearly delicate," he said, his hands on my breasts, soothing and stroking and inciting at the same time, and then his mouth. I arched against him, moved my body against his. My heart wanted to revel in each touch, but my body wanted him to hurry.

He pulled the tank over my head and lowered his body to mine, then kissed me. Softly, at first, then demanding, teeth and tongue challenging me to take, to give, to meet him breath for breath. I slid my hands into his hair, thick and dark, and tugged him closer until his body aligned with mine, his arousal impressive between us.

"Jesus, Claire," he said, burying his face in my neck. "I feel like a teenager."

I smiled. "Good. Because I've been feeling that way for a while now."

He pressed soft kisses to my neck, my collarbone, then down to my breasts again, where his long fingers, equally gentle and strong, teased and incited.

I opened my eyes to stare into his, found him staring back at me as his lips and fingers moved across my chest. *"Ma chère,"* he said, and moved down my body, slipping away shorts and panties until I lay on the bed, bare to him.

"Ma chère," he said again, and kissed each inch of my legs in turn, until he'd worked his way to the center of my body, until his mouth found me and drove me relentlessly to that first, shimmering crest.

"Liam," I said, tangling my fingers in his hair. I sat up to capture his mouth, busied fingers at his belt, then the buttons of his jeans.

Buttons. So many buttons.

"Never wear these again," I teased against his mouth, and almost cringed at the suggestion there'd be more days, more nights like these, when I'd promised him tonight was enough. But his eyes stayed closed, his lips open and nearly panting when I found him, stroked.

His chest heaved as I found my rhythm and his dark eyebrows knitted together with passionate intensity. Until his eyes flashed open, stared back at me, and he kissed me fiercely, teased my tongue with his. "I don't think I can wait any longer."

"Then don't wait."

He stripped off the denim, then his boxer briefs—his naked form an image that I knew would sear itself into my mind—and levered his body over mine again. His hand cupped my face, and I pressed my lips to his palm, kissed the pounding pulse in his wrist. Liam watched my eyes, my mouth, as he moved into me, filled me, and began to rock our bodies together.

"Claire," he said quietly, lifting my hips to drive farther, teeth nipping as he moved. I rolled my hips against him and he groaned, said my name again.

"That's my girl," he said against my mouth, and quickened his rhythm, pleasure building like a hot star in my core as I did the same, balancing movement for movement, each thrust with a swivel of my hips.

Liam shifted away, then shifted me, realigning our bodies so he curled behind me, surrounded me, and moved inside me again, our legs entwined, his hand between mine, stroking with each beat.

I stretched against him, arching to bring our bodies together, waiting while the star warmed, expanded, exploded, taking us both over the edge.

CHAPTER TWENTY-ONE

It was still dark when I woke to birds chirping merrily in the courtyard below. I expected Liam to be gone when I woke, for the sheets to be cool, and the third floor to carry only the faint smell of his cologne.

But I woke in his arms. The room had warmed in the night, and the air had gotten stickier, exacerbated by the fact that our arms and legs were tangled together.

I wasn't sure what was happening, or if some tide had turned. If he'd reached peace with our situation—with the possibilities that stretched in front of us—or if we were just ignoring them.

I was fine with that, I thought, closing my eyes and nestling closer. His arms came around me, hand stroking my back. I was fine with not planning, not thinking, not talking about it. I was fine with just being, with the possibility that this was only for today.

That was still half a lie. And I could live with that, too.

I woke again when sunlight streamed into the room. I slipped out of bed, leaving Liam tangled in the sheets, an arm thrown over his head, his lashes dark crescents against his skin.

I made it downstairs before anyone else was up, found Gunnar at the table, already sipping coffee, a folder in front of him.

I searched his face. Gunnar was a brave man, a strong man, and an honorable man. He wasn't the type to be afraid; he was the type to act. But right now there was fear in his eyes. And that was terrifying.

"What's wrong?" I said.

He glanced up at me. "Why do you think something's wrong?"

"Because you have a folder. Nothing good happens when a Containment folder comes into this store. And because you look exhausted and worried." I pulled out the chair beside him.

"It's been several weeks since I've had a facial."

"It's been *always* since you've had a facial." I reached out, took his hand. "Tell me."

"Good morning," Gavin said, walking out of the kitchen with a hunk of last night's corn bread.

"Is everyone here?" Gunnar asked. "I might as well give the news to everyone at once."

"Tadji and Burke are in the back." The stairs creaked, and Liam walked into the room, pulling on a snug Royal Mercantile T-shirt.

I wanted to close my eyes and pump my fist with victory. Assuming it was a victory. Wasn't it a victory? It meant something. It was a signal, or a sign. Or he just needed a clean T-shirt . . .

But it didn't matter, I reminded myself. I had no claim on him; that was the deal we'd made last night. And, more important, one of my best friends was sitting at my table looking completely worn down and tense. This wasn't the time to worry about relationships.

Gunnar, on the other hand, seemed grateful for the visual distraction. "Damn," he whispered. "He fills out that shirt very nicely."

"He looks better out of it," I murmured, and Gavin snorted.

"That's my girl," Gunnar said.

Liam walked toward us, expression solemn. "What's happened?"

Burke and Tadji pushed back the curtain and joined us. Tadji's eyes widened for a moment at Liam's T-shirt, slid to me. I just shrugged. I'd made my choice, and I'd live with it.

"What's up?" Burke asked, moving to the table.

"We questioned the Reveillon members you found last night. They are cowardly assholes, and sang like canaries. After some creative interrogation techniques," he added, and flipped open the folder. "And we learned who he is."

Inside the folder was a photograph of an average-looking guy with pale skin and dark hair. It was undeniably Ezekiel—the heavy brow, heavy jaw, full nose. There was nothing evil in his eyes. Nothing I could see that indicated he'd gone bad—or would.

"His name's Chip Alexander Thompson," Gunnar said.

"Called that one," I said.

"He's from Oregon. His parents own a logging company."

"His parents have money?" Liam asked, turning the photograph to give him a better view.

Gunnar nodded. "Plenty of it. He went to USC. Graduated with a degree in cultural anthropology, got a wild hair about saving the Zone. We think he came in with his sister. She was declared missing by their parents a year after they left."

I frowned. "Did they file a missing person report on him?"

"Just her."

"So they knew he was alive. Maybe they wondered if he'd had something to do with it."

"War on Paranormals is a pretty big leap from wanting to just save the Zone," I said. "What the hell happened in the meantime? What militarized him? Was it the sister?"

"Best we can trace, he came into Louisiana about a month before the war ended. Told people he'd had a vision 'bout how the Zone could be revived. About how the soil could be remediated, and people could live here again. He went to Camp Couturie, told people about his plan. At first, his plan was positive and proactive, and then he got frustrated. Started talking about conspiracies."

"And there are probably a lot of people in Camp Couturie who buy into that," Burke said.

Gunnar nodded. "People get sick and tired of being sick and tired, and they look for answers, whatever the source. He told people wraiths existed because Containment wanted them to, that Containment's plan was to develop warriors—soldiers who could battle the Paras if the wall fell again."

I sniffed. "If that was true, surely we'd have gotten some on-the-job training."

"No shit," Burke said.

"There's something off about him. Something not quite right emotionally. He's really moody—was moody that night in the camp. Unstable. And we already know he's violent." I glanced at them. "It's not hard for me to believe he had something to do with her death."

"Me, either," Gunnar said. "He's sadistic, and he's decided most everyone in the Zone—except for his core group—is his enemy. I asked them about Eden, about the tent in Camp Couturie."

"What did they say?" Liam asked.

"A man lived there; his name was Louis. He played guitar, blues mostly, and was pretty renowned around the camp for it. Apparently, Ezekiel demanded he stop or donate his talent to the cause. Louis refused." Gunnar's eyes went hard as obsidian. "One night, Ezekiel's men dragged him out of his tent, took him to the fountain, and shot him."

I swallowed hard. "It was his tent."

Gunnar nodded. "Ezekiel's violent, will kill anyone in his way. And that's where we are today." He paused, as if preparing himself.

"Reveillon is preparing an attack," he said. "They're going to try to take out Devil's Isle—Containment and Paranormals—in one, broad-based assault."

Silence fell like a mist across the room.

"When?" Liam asked.

"Within the next forty-eight hours."

We just stared at him.

"You're sure that information's reliable?" Burke asked.

"The members Claire and Liam captured last night and the fugitives from Devil's Isle confirm. The bombing at the gate was supposed to be the first wave of an ongoing attack. He'd hoped for enough damage that the rest of his people could just walk in—but his reinforcements didn't show. We've been keeping them busy at the borders and on the main roads, which is some consolation."

"Did you find a leak in PCC?" Liam asked.

Gunnar's smile was grim. "We did. He's awaiting arraignment for treason. Unfortunately, while he's no longer in a position to give out information, Ezekiel's apparently tired of waiting and ready to move. They also said he's been acting more erratically over the last few days."

That was a lot of specific information given by people who wouldn't be forthcoming.

"Creative interrogation techniques?" I asked.

Gunnar's face was completely neutral. "In the interest of public safety."

Considering what they'd done, I wasn't going to argue with that.

"How many people does he have?" Liam asked.

"The military can't fly over the Zone—it's too dangerous if the grid fails. But based on satellite images, we think about two thousand people."

"*Mais,*" Liam said.

Gunnar smiled. "I've always loved that word, *mais*. It says so much in so few syllables."

"*Mais*," Liam and Gavin said together.

"So, are the army, the marines, whatever, sending in troops?" Tadji asked.

"They've been trying to send in troops since the bombing," Gunnar said. "PCC is pushing again for troops from Jackson, Birmingham. But we don't know if they'll get here in time. I think we have to assume they won't."

That explained why it didn't look like Gunnar had slept.

Tadji sat down heavily. "Ezekiel's bringing war, and no one will come to fight it?"

"Containment's still here," Gunnar said roughly, and I guessed he'd said that today more times than he'd cared to. Then he held up a hand, rubbed the other across his face. "Sorry, sorry. Long night."

"You're still tracking them with satellite?" Gavin asked.

"As we can. And we're still running scouts through town," he said, propping an elbow on the table and running a hand through his hair. "But that hasn't been successful so far. They're operating like nomads, moving from place to place. We don't have the manpower to track them."

"So what do we do?" Tadji asked. "We can't just sit around here, waiting for someone to show up to kill us. Waiting for his army."

"You can evacuate," Gunnar said, three heavy words that people in the Zone had heard time and time again, at least until they'd closed the borders to keep violence and magic from spreading.

"And your more realistic option?" I asked. "Because you know people won't leave. The ones who are here already decided not to go."

"We can use the rest of you in Devil's Isle. Not to protect the prison," Gunnar said, holding up a hand to anticipate the likely argument. "To protect the Paranormals. It's by far the best place we've got to keep them safe."

"Have you asked them if they want to stay?" Liam asked.

Gunnar's face went tight. "They are prisoners of war. Regardless of what they want, there is nowhere else we can take them and come close to guaranteeing their safety." He didn't sound happy about that.

He looked at me. "We're going to offer a town hall meeting to talk about what's happening, explain the process. Maybe answer some questions," he added grudgingly.

"Good," I said. "That's really good."

"Reveillon will be gunning for them," he continued. "Our plan is to move them to the center of the Marigny. That creates a perimeter Reveillon will have to cross to get to them—in addition to the walls of Devil's Isle itself. Containment and whatever branches show up to fight will stay within that perimeter, keep them back until they can be defeated or contained." He looked at us. "We could use volunteers to assist in the process of moving them—getting them into the temporary shelters we're setting up now. And when Reveillon comes, helping protect them.

"We know that's not your job," he added. "It's Containment's. But Reveillon knows what it's doing. It's been building a network for years, working to spread us out to create the perfect opportunity to decimate the remaining Paranormals. If the military caravans can't get through, it's all hands on deck."

I looked around, checking the faces of my friends, then looked back at Gunnar. "I think I speak for everyone when I say that we'll do what we can, but we won't fight for Devil's Isle. We won't fight to save a bad system. We'll fight for the Paras who were brought into this world against their will, for the Sensitives who weren't given a chance to survive. We'll fight for them."

Liam nodded. "Agreed."

"Agreed," Burke said, and looked at Tadji.

"Agreed," she said.

"Agreed," said Gavin.

Gunnar looked at me for a long moment. "Understood," he said, and offered his hand.

As we shook, I wasn't sure if I was making a deal with Gunnar or with Containment. And considering the circumstances, it probably didn't matter much.

"There's one more thing," Gunnar said. "If they march through, they might try to take the store."

Tadji crossed her arms. "Over my dead body will they step one foot in my store."

I didn't mean to grin, but I couldn't help it after the "my store" comment.

"It's going to sustain damage," Gunnar said. "That's inevitable, especially since Ezekiel knows who Liam, Claire, and Eleanor are. There's a hurricane moving toward the city, and it's not going to let walls stand in the way of destruction and chaos."

Tadji looked at me. "We wanted to rally the community. I say we rally them, just like I planned. We'll take down the sheets and open the doors. Use this place as a community checkpoint. I know it's dangerous," she added. "But it's better than locking up and leaving it alone for Reveillon to come knocking."

"That's good," Gunnar said. "I can probably spare an agent, someone who can help with the public."

I held up a finger. "Not Broussard."

That was where I'd put my damn foot down.

We fueled up and strategized, pulled the sheets down from the store's windows. Gavin took the Hummer out on patrol. Burke agreed to update Delta, enlist them to do what they could. Tadji found a round tin of Danish cookies for us and the onslaught of curious and worried customers she was expecting.

"I'll have to apologize for the lack of progress on the reopening," Tadji said dourly as we worked together to fold one of the sheets.

"I think war trumps reopening," I said. "They'll understand. They'll still complain, because they're people, but they'll understand."

Gunnar walked in with a woman I didn't recognize. Slight, with pale skin and blond hair. She had a button nose and wide mouth, and hazel eyes that looked around the store curiously.

"This is Agent Alice Colfax," Gunnar said when they reached us. "She's PCC Logistics and Community Relations, and she's been seconded with Containment for the last sixteen months. She loves red beans and rice, is a helluva bowler, and is available to Royal Mercantile today to answer any questions customers may have." Gunnar glanced at her. "I forget anything?"

She frowned, considering. "I love broccoli, I'm allergic to cats, and I run a five-minute mile."

Tadji blinked. "Like, on purpose?"

Colfax smiled, shrugged. "I like a challenge."

"Then you've come to the right place," Tadji said, gesturing her to the counter. "Let me tell you about Mrs. Proctor."

I couldn't help laughing.

I found a couple of Containment surplus knapsacks, loaded them with bandages, water, protein bars, the tokens I owed Solomon. Tadji offered me a pencil, a small notebook.

"Just in case you hear anything interesting," she said, and tapped the larger versions she'd put on the counter. "Use of language in wartime, new curse words, that kind of thing."

"Always a linguist," I said, giving her a hug.

"But of course." She pressed a kiss to my cheek. "Be careful out there."

"Be careful in here. And if worse comes to worst, leave the store. Go to the Cabildo, or your house. Just get someplace safe. I love this place, but you're the most important thing in here."

"What she said," Liam said, giving her a hug, too. "We'll be in touch when we can."

"I'll walk you as far as the Cabildo," Gunnar said when we headed to the door. "I need to talk to the Commandant. Then I'll find you in Devil's Isle."

"How long do we have?" Liam asked.

"Based on the satellite images, estimates of troop movement, less than twenty-four hours. If they're smart, they'll stay dispersed, attack from all sides, with maybe the strongest force at the gate."

"They're going to use the C-4 from Camp Couturie," I said. "They'll try to tear down the walls."

"They will," Gunnar agreed. "The walls, the Cabildo, the barracks. We've put up extra security as we can. But without backup, if the caravans can't get through, we won't have enough people to keep them from hitting all targets."

"There will be loss of life," Liam said.

"Yeah," Gunnar said. "Lizzie's getting the clinic ready. They'll have to triage as they can. This really is all hands on deck."

We reached the Cabildo, the beautiful building at the head of Jackson Square, the only building that had survived of the three that had once stood there.

Gunnar reached out, gave me a hug, then offered Liam a handshake. "Try to keep her out of trouble."

"I'll do my best."

"I don't need a minder."

They both just looked at me. Which wasn't especially flattering.

Knapsacks on our backs, Liam and I walked the rest of the way to the Devil's Isle gate.

I wanted to say something, to breach the companionable silence and ask about us. I didn't want last night to have been my only night with Liam. On the other hand, I couldn't fault him for who he was, or blame him for taking me at my word. I'd told him there'd be no expectations. That's how it would have to be.

"And once again," I said, feigning cheerfulness I guessed both of us needed, "I walk into Devil's Isle, and hope I walk out again."

"We'll walk out again," Liam said, and took my hand. "Together."

Okay. That was something. I'd take it.

Two dozen volunteers—some Containment agents, some Devil's Isle staff, some civilians—gathered near the old, open-air Marigny Market Building. Captain Reece had apparently volunteered to lead this part of the preparation. He stood beside a large map tacked to a rolling board.

"What's the plan?" an agent asked.

Reece pointed to a map and a red square drawn around several blocks in the middle of the neighborhood. "We want to move everyone in this area. That will allow us to create a second safety perimeter around the residents. Every resident or family unit has an assigned spot or unit. We're going to help get them there in as orderly and efficient a manner as possible."

There was something off about calling prisoners "residents," even if I understood the reason for it.

We were split up, assigned to "resident groups." Mine was a group of adults and children a dozen in number: an extended family, as far as I could tell. The adults, whose pale and hairless skin, spotted with light orange, marked them visually as Paranormals, didn't speak English.

They carried only a few necessities—a bag of what food remained in their homes, diapers for children, their Containment-assigned papers—for the walk down to the emergency barracks.

I did a final sweep of the small house, found rooms with brightly colored paint, toys and games that looked completely foreign, an impressive garden of herbs and vegetables. And when I stepped onto the threshold again, I squinted at the bright light.

A tiny hand took mine. "There's going to be another war."

I looked down. The child couldn't have been more than six or seven, a wisp of a thing with the same pale and spotted skin as her family. She wore pink overalls and a matching headband over her smooth head, and her voice carried a subtle New Orleans accent, probably because she'd learned English from the Containment agents and workers.

"Maybe not a war," I said. "But probably a fight."

"How come?"

"Because sometimes people make very bad decisions."

"Humans, or people like us?"

Wasn't that the big question? "As far as I can tell, pretty much anyone."

"That's pretty stupid," she said, then clamped her free hand over her mouth. "I'm not supposed to say 'stupid.'"

"I won't tell," I said with a smile. "Because you're absolutely right."

"Okay!" she said in a loud whisper her mother—and anyone else in a ten-foot radius—could plainly hear.

We joined the flood of Paranormals making the same walk

deeper into the prison. Some looked worried; some looked unfazed. Others looked downright pissed. I couldn't fault them for that.

The building to which we'd been assigned was an empty room with dozens of rows of cots. The family I'd helped move nodded at me, then walked off to find their designated spot.

Nedra, Thora, and the girls took a set of cots in the opposite corner, the girls bouncing on their temporary canvas beds with visible excitement. Nedra and Thora shared a look of obvious concern, then pressed their palms together before organizing their area.

It was an internment camp inside an internment camp. And that didn't make me feel any better about Devil's Isle.

I walked to Reece, who stood at the end of the building, watching the "residents" find their new home. "Do you think we can keep them safe?"

It took a long time for him to answer. "I don't know. But today, we have a common enemy. And it's our obligation to try."

I couldn't argue with that.

There were a few thousand Paranormals in Devil's Isle, and it took hours to get them moved, situated. There were disputes to address—not enough beds, not enough blankets, too close to the exit, not close enough to the restrooms, and the occasional missing pair of shoes or bag of rice.

The sun was setting when the volunteers were dispersed. By that time, Containment had created its security perimeter, arranging people and concrete bollards in a ring around the square of buildings.

I found Liam waiting outside. We walked together back to the gate, where the front perimeter of the ring was being assembled.

Nearest the gate, agents sat on the sidewalk beneath the eaves of the market building. Inside were dozens more agents, a scale model of Devil's Isle, cases of bottled water, and a kettle of soup over a flaming propane tank.

Containment had been busy.

"I guess that's dinner," Liam muttered, sniffing the air. "Or laundry."

Gunnar stood near the scale model, answering questions. We waited until he acknowledged us, just so he'd know we were there, then grabbed bottles of water and prepared to wait for instructions.

There was commotion outside, snarky comments and raised voices, including one that was much too familiar.

Liam must have recognized it, too. "Son of a bitch," he said, and we followed him outside.

Moses stood between two Containment agents, their hands on his shoulders.

"What the actual fuck?" he said, shaking them off.

"Is there a problem?" Gunnar asked, stepping into the fray.

"This Para won't go about his business," the agent said.

Gunnar lifted his eyebrows. "Moses?"

Moses shrugged himself loose of the agents, stepped forward. When they moved to follow, Gunnar held up a hand to stop them.

Moses had come back to Devil's Isle.

"I don't like the idea of you all being out here without me," Moses said. "I got pretty good skills."

"I don't doubt it at all," Gunnar said, and glanced at the agents who'd manhandled Moses. "A militia of murderers and traitors to this country and to humanity is coming to kill you, to destroy the city we've saved, and to kill every Paranormal inside it. Does it seem wise to you to turn down anyone—anyone—who wishes to stand up with us? Who wants to fight with us?"

The agent wet his lips, looked away. "No, sir."

"No," Gunnar said. "It does not." He looked out over the crowd of agents who'd gathered to watch. "Anyone wants to join in this fight, we say yes. I don't care if you object to their height, their religion, their preference in bourbon, or whether they came from Boston, Bermuda, or the Beyond. They want to fight, they get to fight. Is that understood?"

"Sir!" the agents shouted.

Gunnar acknowledged with a nod. "Now, if you don't mind, I'm going to get back to planning this war we'll soon be fighting." He glanced at Moses. "Can Claire and Liam get you settled?"

"Course," he said.

"You rock my world," I whispered to Gunnar.

His expression was bleak. "It's do or die now, for all of us. And I hope to God we know what we're doing."

"I like that kid," Moses said as Gunnar walked back into the market. "He's got spine. Don't always agree with him, but there you go."

When Moses looked back at Liam, Liam's expression had gone stone cold.

"What the hell are you doing here?" he whispered. "You should be long gone by now."

"I walked back."

We stared at him. "You walked back. From Freret to the Quarter." Liam blinked, obviously dumbfounded. "And then you just waltzed into Devil's Isle?"

"I did. And my feet are killing me."

We looked down at his calloused toes. They looked pretty much the same as before, as much as I was any judge of things.

"Let me ask another way," Liam said, one bitten syllable at a time. "You walked back from Freret to the Quarter without a disguise? In full view of everyone?"

Moses's eyes went mean. "What's wrong with the way I look? Least I'm not some gangly, pasty asshole."

I couldn't help the snort.

"Not the time," Liam said. He didn't look at me, but the stern tone was clearly aimed in my direction. He was absolutely livid. I understood the emotion—the frustration over the risk we'd taken to get Moses out. On the other hand, if we could get him out once, we could get him out again.

"Look," Moses said, looking at Liam, then me. "You did me a solid by getting me the hell out of here. I appreciate that. But that was before I knew a goddamn army was on its way." He kicked at the ground. "You think after all that teary good-bye shit I'm going to leave you here to fight alone?"

War could make enemies of allies. I guessed it could also bring allies back together.

I put a hand at Liam's back. Whatever "we" were, that seemed to ease the tension. "Moses, you want water or soup?"

Moses sniffed the air. "I could eat some soup."

Moses wasn't the only one who joined us. Civilians came from the Quarter, from Mid-City, from Tremé, with food, weapons, and supplies. They'd seen Ezekiel's signs, and word had spread about the coming battle. New Orleans was still their home; Paranormals or not, they didn't want anyone tearing up the city they loved.

Some came with feathers and beads, with the traditions of the Mardi Gras Indians.

Tony Mercier, tall and lanky, had dark skin and short, cropped hair, and a patch over one eye. He'd fought with a company from the Lower Ninth in the war and now led the Vanguard, an organization of New Orleans veterans. He'd brought a dozen of them with him tonight.

His suit was in his signature color—feathers of deep, buttercup yellow, layered from head to feet. There were hand-beaded panels on his chest, shins, and arms that showed victory scenes from the Second Battle of New Orleans. The ensemble was topped by an enormous headdress that stretched nearly three feet over his head.

His costume was the largest, the most impressive, because he was the Vanguard's big chief. His lieutenants also wore feathered suits, but no headdresses. And there was nothing remotely decorative about their weapons—guns, large and small; knives; swords; and pretty much anything else.

This, I thought. This was why we'd stayed in the Zone. Because for all of New Orleans's problems, its issues, its inequities, the people of this city rallied. We were the community, the unity, that Ezekiel wanted, but that he and Reveillon would never understand.

Gunnar met Tony proudly, offered a hand. "Chief Mercier. It's a pleasure to see you here."

Tony smiled. "We're actually helping another chief tonight," he said, and moved aside.

Every observant agent went to immediate attention as the Commandant stepped beside him.

He had dark skin, nearly shorn gray hair, and very serious, dark eyes. His lips were generous, but slightly downturned at the edges, as if he was deep in thought and unhappy with the results of it. Gunnar had called it his "resting bitch face," and I thought he had it right.

He wore the dark Containment fatigues, with stars along the shoulder to demonstrate his rank. His black boots were shined to a high gloss, his shirtsleeves rolled halfway up his forearms, as if he was ready for work. He looked as regal as the Vanguard's big chief, shoulders high and back as he looked down at us from his six feet and change.

"Sir," Gunnar said, offering a salute. The Commandant responded in kind.

"Gunnar." He looked at me, at Liam, at the assemblage of agents around him, his gaze falling on Moses, who was working on his third (or maybe fourth?) cup of thoroughly boiled soup.

"Moses," he said. I guessed I shouldn't have been surprised that Moses knew the Commandant, and vice versa.

Moses waved with his spoon. "Commandant."

"It appears the rumors of your death were exaggerated."

"I heard about that," Moses said. "Crazy thing, as I do appear to be alive and kicking."

"I'm glad to hear it." The Commandant looked at Gunnar. "Take all comers?"

"That's my theory, sir. Subject to your veto."

The Commandant smiled slyly back at Gunnar. "That puts me in a very nice box, doesn't it?" he asked, too quiet for the rest of the agents to hear.

Gunnar's face stayed expressionless. "You taught me strategy, sir."

"And to play poker, apparently. Nevertheless, I would tend to agree with you." He looked at Moses. "As I am bound by the Magic Act, I cannot provide you with a weapon. However, as you are a citizen of a foreign land, and the Zone is a territory of no particular state, it could be argued that you're in a bit of a no-man's land legally, and the Magic Act couldn't apply to you."

"Magic is illegal, and isn't supposed to exist, but I exist, therefore . . . ?"

"Something like that," the Commandant said with a smile. "But if you were to find a weapon through no act of my troops and use it against Reveillon, I don't believe there'd be anything to complain about."

"Could I find a grenade launcher?"

"Don't push it."

The Commandant made a speech about duty and honor, with plenty of metaphors about ass-kicking and victory. And then he moved into the market to discuss strategy with his team.

Burke joined us, and he, Liam, and I took seats with the rest of the soldiers outside the market, and then squished together beneath the eaves when the sky opened and poured down, bringing misery and mosquitoes. Moses hovered around the soup pot.

"Next time we have a war," Liam said, "let's do it in the desert."

"A-fucking-men," Burke said, wiping his face with an already-damp bandanna. "I'd take a little dry heat over this goddamn swamp."

"You love this goddamn swamp," I pointed out. "That's why you're sitting in the rain, swatting away mosquitoes big enough to wear pants."

"I think a mosquito just carried off Rogers!" came a woman's voice from the darkness. The troops around her chuckled.

Time passed as we waited, nerves and adrenaline battling against boredom and fatigue. I'd seen war, and I'd been dragged into it, but not as a soldier. Not someone stuck in the long wait before a battle, where tension and hyperawareness became just as monotonous as actually paying attention.

"Ladies, gentlemen, and unaffiliated, I believe I have something to cure what ails you."

I smelled the coffee before I looked up, saw Gunnar and another agent carrying trays of foam cups.

"Twice in a week," I said, climbing to my feet as he held out the tray. "You are my personal hero." I took the cup of caramel-colored coffee and milk, the warmth driving away some of the chill in my fingers.

This was coffee with chicory, a New Orleans and wartime tradition. When coffee hadn't been available, chicory root was boiled to make something coffeelike. And even when coffee was available, we used chicory to enhance the flavor.

"So far," I said, "the coffee served in the pouring rain before a battle with crazy cultists over the future of the Zone is the best kind of coffee."

"I don't think that will fit on the mug," Gunnar said. "And let's hope this is the only time it needs to be served."

Truer words.

"I wish I had a burger to go with this," Burke said, and his stomach rumbled for emphasis. "Little tomato, little red onion, some mustard, some bright yellow American cheese."

"Heresy," Liam said. "You need all that stuff on a burger, it's not a very good burger."

"Burgers and chicory coffee is heresy," I said. "This calls for croissants. Beignets."

"With mountains of powdered sugar," Burke agreed.

"There's more slop in the pot," Liam said. "You can help yourself to it."

"You're ruining my fantasy, Quinn."

"Probably not the first time that's happened," Moses muttered, then let out an "oof" when Liam punched him in the arm.

"When all is said and done," I said, "when we're all safe again and no one is marching toward us with an army, we'll have a party. And we'll have burgers—real, actual burgers."

"And fries," Liam said. "Hand cuts."

"Crinkles!" someone called out to our right. "Crinkles are the only way to go."

"Crinkles are for babies, Rogers!" someone else called out. Rogers was having a rough go of it.

"We'll do both," I promised, loudly enough for poor Rogers to hear. "We'll throw a block party at Royal Mercantile. And the drinks will very much be on the house."

That got about as much applause as you'd expect.

CHAPTER TWENTY-TWO

Reveille played just before dawn to the collective groans of everyone who'd finally managed to drift off and grab a few minutes of sleep. I'd drifted off twice against Liam's shoulder, his hand on my knee. Moses was on my other side; Burke was on Liam's.

At first, when the trumpet sounded, I'd thought it was just something that happened in Devil's Isle in the morning. But then I saw the knot of officers—including Gunnar and the Commandant—talking in front of us, their expressions grave.

I blinked myself awake, watched them for a moment, then glanced at Liam beside me. "Hi."

"Morning." He gestured toward the market. "The soup has been replaced by what smells like something Londoners would serve nineteenth-century orphans."

"I'd rather watch that, I think." I pulled up my knees, nodded to the cluster. "How long have they been talking?"

"Long enough that it seems serious."

And that wasn't the only serious thing to see. As sunlight began to shift through Devil's Isle, Malachi walked toward the market.

"Damn," whispered a female agent somewhere down the line.

"Why do women always stare at him?" Moses asked grumpily. "He's just a guy with wings attached to his back."

"It's not just the wings," someone else said. "And it's not just the women."

I bit back a snort. It was the wings—and the golden armor, shield, and staff, the brick red leather that he wore beneath it. He looked like the warrior he was.

He left his wings unfolded, a reminder of who and what he was, and a demand that Containment acknowledge and deal with it. It was unspeakably brave, and terrifyingly dangerous.

Tony walked out of the market, foam cup in hand, still dressed in his feathered finery. "I think my feathers just got upstaged," he said, to the chuckle of the agents along the building.

Liam, Moses, Burke, and I stood up, walked to Malachi. He nodded at each of us, let his gaze fall on Moses, where it went steely.

"Tough crowd," Moses said, shuffling his feet. I guessed Malachi hadn't approved of Moses's plan to come back to Devil's Isle, or hadn't known about it.

"We'll discuss it later," Malachi said.

"I guess I'll do the introductions," Gunnar said. "Commandant, this is Malachi, of the Consularis army."

"Malachi," the Commandant said. "As I suspect you are not here to surrender yourself to Containment, what brings you into the District?"

"War," Malachi said. "We have a common enemy."

"Humans?" the Commandant asked, an obvious test.

Malachi, of course, wasn't flustered by the question or the insult. "Those who make war for the sake of making war. Those who kill to prove a point. Because they would destroy New Orleans and those within it. I've come to care for both. And they have no more right to kill than the Court did in the first instance."

The Commandant nodded. "And when the battle is done?"

Malachi's eyes steeled. "I did not make war against you willingly, and I will not be punished for the crimes of others. I will help this fight, but I will not be held afterward. And I will do everything in my power to subvert the operation of this prison."

If the Commandant found the plan or the frankness surprising, he didn't show it.

"He's right."

Eyebrows raised, the Commandant looked at Gunnar.

"I'll stand for the Zone," Gunnar said. "For the rule of law. But I won't stand for lies, not anymore. We can't pretend the world is as simple as we want it to be, as black-and-white."

It seemed the entirety of Devil's Isle went silent as the Commandant looked at his second-in-command. "And if I ask for your resignation?"

Gunnar pulled out his badge, offered it. "Then it's yours. I'm standing inside Devil's Isle. Landreaus have stood for this city for a very long time, and we'll do so again today. And when it's all over, if you want to keep me here, I probably won't be able to stop you. But that's fine, because this is the right thing to do. The right course of action, and you will never tell me differently. Congress will never tell me differently."

Silence fell again as the Commandant and Gunnar stared at each other.

"As it turns out," the Commandant said after a moment, "I happen to think you're right." He looked at Malachi, offered a hand. "We'd appreciate your assistance, sir."

"We will help," said another voice. Nedra walked toward us, a dozen Paras behind him. Men and women, pale skin and light. Horns and feathers. Pointed ears and hair flowing like water. Some tall as trees, others small as flitting birds, with wings that moved with gossamer speed. Those, I'd bet, were peskies. Liam had called them, I think, "irritating little assholes." But as long as they were fighting for our side . . .

"We won't sit by while our families are targeted," said a slender woman nearly seven feet tall whose coal black skin sparkled like granite beneath the overhead lights.

The other Paras murmured their agreement.

"You know how to protect yourselves?" the Commandant asked. "How to fight?"

"They do," Malachi said. "I give you that assurance from one commander to another."

The Commandant nodded, then looked out over his people— human and Paranormal.

"I will be frank," he said. "There were more skirmishes overnight. Reveillon killed twenty more people. Some agents, some civilians. The power grid is down across the southern half of the Zone, possibly from sabotage by Reveillon. The feds can't move in personnel except on foot until the grid's up again, however long that may take."

"So what does that mean?" one of the uniformed agents asked.

"It means we're on our own," the Commandant said. "It means this battle is ours to win or to lose. We expect they will begin their attack today, and it appears we will face it alone."

He let his gaze fall to Malachi and Moses, to the human soldiers assembled along the front, and to the dozens of Paranormal men and women who'd joined the line in the night, who were willing to fight.

"It seems today that we—humans and Paranormals—have a common enemy, the humans who would destroy us all." He looked at Malachi. "I won't insult you with promises about what will happen when this is over and done. But I give my word that I will do what I can to seek rights and protections for any who fight with us, and fight honorably."

It wasn't a promise of freedom. But it was, at least, a step in that direction.

"As a show of good faith," Malachi said, "let me offer information." He glanced at the Devil's Isle map.

"Please," the Commandant said, and we walked inside.

"I have seen their advance from the air," Malachi explained, and began to point out the operations. "There are four groups, from what I've seen. One coming in from the river, one from the east in Chalmette, one north from the direction of Camp Couturie—or what remains of it—and one from the approximate west, near Metairie."

"How many?" Gunnar asked.

"At least a thousand. Probably three hundred in each ground group, a hundred more on the river. I expect there are more on the perimeter waiting to be called up if necessary."

Liam put a reassuring hand at my back, and I instinctively leaned back into it, grateful for the comfort.

"That's better intel than we've gotten all week," the Commandant muttered. "Artillery? Ordnance?"

"They have several vehicles, which appear to be military. They're in that green shade human militaries seem to prefer." There was bafflement in his tone, which caused me to bite back a smile.

"Several large vehicles with mounted guns," he added. "Several more with covered beds."

"Those could be carrying people, weapons, or C-4," Gunnar said.

Malachi nodded. "He appears to be a very organized commander. Or there are enough ex-military members of his organization to teach him what he doesn't know."

"There are rumors he's growing erratic," Gunnar said. "At least, that's what the Reveillon members we've captured so far have reported."

"That will serve us," Malachi said.

"Do we target him?" the Commandant asked.

"The center cannot hold," Gunnar said.

The Commandant slid his dark eyes to Gunnar. "Elaborate."

"If he falls, they fall apart. They're committed, yes. But as much to Ezekiel as to the idea. If we can take him out, the rest will lose focus, separate."

"Or we create a martyr," another adviser said, "and they fight even more fiercely. That's the risk when dealing with a cult of personality."

"We have to take him out either way," I said, and didn't feel an ounce of guilt about it. "He's a delusional serial killer with an army, and he's coming with weapons to kill us."

A *boom* echoed across Devil's Isle, the ground quaking with it. Orders were shouted, and men and women began running to their positions. Adrenaline stalled by so many hours of waiting began to course through me.

"Report!" the Commandant shouted, and a man ran to him.

"Explosion at the Marriott," the agent yelled. "Grenade, by preliminary reports. The building was empty."

The store was between the Marriott and Devil's Isle. And from the look on Burke's face, he knew it, too.

"They want to draw us off our positions," Gunnar said. "We are not going to do that. All positions hold or advance as assigned." He looked at me, and his expression had turned to stone. This was a soldier's face, a battle mask. "Can you take him out?"

Could I kill in cold blood? he meant.

I looked at Liam, thinking of the confession I'd once made, of the Valkyrie I'd killed in the home I'd shared with my father, of the two Paras I'd killed after that. I didn't want to kill. I didn't want to *have* to kill. But these people were determined to bring war to our doorsteps, to kill innocents to satisfy one man's ego. I'd do what was necessary to protect them.

"I can do what needs to be done," I said.

Gunnar looked at me for a moment, then nodded. "Get back to the shelters."

We nodded. "We'll do our best," I said, and the company split apart to take their posts.

"A minute," Liam said, and took my hand, led me to the end of the market. "If this goes sideways . . ."

"It will go sideways," I said. "It's pretty much destined to go sideways. Our job is to keep it from going too much sideways."

"Then, just in case that happens . . ." Liam took my face in his hands, kissed me until my body had melted against his. When my breath was heaving, he pulled back but kept his hands on my cheeks. His lips were swollen, his eyes dark with desire, with possessiveness, with grief.

When I nodded my understanding, Liam dropped his forehead to mine, and we stood there in silence for a moment.

When I lifted my face to his, he took my hand, pressed it to his heart. "This is yours," he said. "Whatever else is between us, whatever else happens today, it's yours."

Hand in hand again, we walked to our positions, to protect those who'd once waged war against us, because enemies made strange allies.

When Liam and I reached the low, rectangular building, another *boom* shook the Marigny. This time the quake was strong enough to put us both on the ground. Air raid sirens began to wail, the sound nearly deafening.

Paranormals began to scream inside, and the nurses and civilian staff did their best to keep them calm.

"The gate's been breached!" shouted the radioman over the cacophony of noise. "They're coming in!"

We waited for what felt like an eternity as the fight raged in front of us, and Containment fought back the Reveillon onslaught. We tried to stay alert, our gazes scanning the streets, looking for Reveillon members who made it through the perimeter. Wondering if they would come in a swelling wave, a tsunami of violence, or one or two at a time as they pierced Containment's resistance.

The sound of battle gradually grew louder, closer.

I glanced at Liam, found his gaze on me. He nodded. "You find him, he tries to hurt you, take the shot."

No need to ask who "he" was.

Two Reveillon members emerged from an alley across the street; at the same time, a woman's scream erupted to my right, her language unfamiliar.

"I've got her," I said, and Liam nodded.

"Go!" he said as he moved to meet the Reveillon members, eagerness in his eyes.

I moved to the corner, then looked around the edge of the building. Three Reveillon women who'd pinned a Para woman—curvy and lavender-skinned—against a brick wall. All three had handguns, and a stripe of blood stained the Para's cheek.

I stepped forward, lifted the pistol. "Back away!" I ordered, and waited until they looked back at me.

"Move along, traitor," said one of them, before immediately turning back to her imagined prey.

"I'm not the traitor here, but I am one helluva shot. You head back to the gate, or I can put holes in your very nice linen clothes." My hands were shaking, but I sounded like Eastwood, so I was fine with that.

She turned back to me again. "And we shall cleanse the earth with blood," she said, and lifted her gun.

I gave her a quick look. She had nice nails and shoes without a single scuff. She wore the same pale pants and clothes as the other Reveillon members, but hers were clean and pressed. Five bucks said she'd never fired a weapon before, had probably never even seen combat until she signed on with Ezekiel.

"There's always one," I muttered, and aimed at her right arm, fired.

She jerked back when the bullet hit, dropped the gun, grabbed her arm, and hit the ground screaming, "You bitch! You *shot* me."

"Yeah, that's what war does to you," I said, and kicked away the gun she'd dropped, keeping my weapon trained on her while I crouched to grab it. "All three of you move back, and step away from the woman."

Ignoring my orders, one woman ran forward to the one I'd shot. The other ran at me, gun in front of her and screaming like a banshee.

My instinct was to run, so I had to force myself to stand and face her, to raise my gun again. I fired, hit her in the thigh. And when she went down, she went down hard.

"You fucking bitch!" she screamed, wailing and clutching at her leg. "You shot me. You fucking traitor."

"Not a traitor," I said. "And unlike you, not an asshole." I looked up at the third woman, the one who hadn't yet advanced.

I'd expected her hand to shake, or to see some hesitation in her eyes. But the hand that lifted the gun was steady, and her eyes were flat with anger.

"You're ruining this. You're ruining our chance at something different. They ruined our lives. They ruined the Zone."

Unlike her flashier friend, this woman looked genuinely angry, genuinely sad, and one hundred percent more willing to die for what she believed in.

"The war ruined the Zone," I said. "But the war's over. We're trying to make it better, and Reveillon is trying to destroy it altogether. Right now you can drop the gun, and I won't have to shoot you. Or you can stand there, and I'll have to. Because you chose your side, and I chose mine."

Without a word of argument, she crumpled to the ground.

I blinked.

I didn't think I'd been that compelling.

And then I looked behind her at the Para with the brick in her hand. She blew out a heavy and shuddering breath.

"Well," I said, looking at the Reveillon women on the ground, "that was very well done."

I helped the Para back into the shelter, then moved outside again to rejoin Liam, but he was gone. The building was quiet, the sounds of fighting echoing from somewhere to the east.

Liam wouldn't have left his post without a reason. Either someone was hurt or someone was here . . .

I walked to the intersection and scanned the streets, caught sight of him turning a corner. I ran forward, skimming the building and peering around the edge of the building.

Ezekiel and Liam stood in the middle of the long, narrow park in the middle of Devil's Isle, ten feet between them, and a cluster of Reveillon members around them.

Ezekiel wore clothes that were clean and pressed and free of blood or dirt. He stayed clean, even as he demanded others kill in his name.

There was a streak of blood on Liam's face. With dark scruff along his jawline, his shirt torn and battered, and his eyes gleaming with battle, he looked like a warrior of myth, an Irish prince whose kingdom was on the line.

I crept closer, looking for a spot where I could aim, get a clear shot. And that's when I saw it—that look in Ezekiel's eyes. The hatred, sure. The anger. But also the hunger.

It was the same hunger I'd seen in the eyes of the young wraith we'd taken back to the clinic. The hunger for power . . . and the hunger for magic.

Malachi's words echoed in my head, as clearly as if he'd been standing beside me. *You have to be prepared for the unexpected.*

Ezekiel was a Sensitive, and he was well on his way to becoming a wraith.

I suddenly understood the killing of the angel in Congo Square, why Eleanor had seen the stain of magic. Ezekiel had been wraith enough to kill the Para, to destroy his body in the futile attempt to get at his magic.

She'd seen Ezekiel's dark power, the spilling of the angel's blood.

All this time—all this hatred—and Ezekiel had the same power and magic he'd railed against. Did he hate magic because he had it, or in spite of it? Did he hate us because of his own self-loathing, or was he in denial that he'd become his own enemy?

There was nothing more dangerous than a man who couldn't recognize his own hypocrisy . . . unless it was the followers who'd realized he was a hypocrite. I was close enough to shoot Ezekiel, but, like the adviser had suggested, that might just create a martyr.

I needed to destroy the illusion he'd created first. That might make his followers turn against him, and that might just end the war.

Gun at my side, I walked through the circle of Reveillon members and onto the grass. Their gazes flicked toward me—Liam's with concern, Ezekiel's with excitement.

"Well, well, well. Claire Connolly. You two enjoy rescuing each other, don't you?"

I gave him a confused stare. "I don't see that either of us needs rescuing."

Ezekiel smiled wildly. "You're traitors who we've surrounded. This is over, although I'll allow you to confess your sins before you go, if you'd like."

"Would you? How thoughtful. What sins would those be?"

Liam watched me carefully, obviously trying to figure out what I was planning.

I moved a step closer to Ezekiel, just close enough to let him get another whiff of the magic he'd sensed in Camp Couturie—but hadn't recognized. And just as I suspected, hunger flashed in his eyes again.

"Son of a bitch," Liam muttered. He'd figured it out, too.

I kept my gaze on the killer. "A very wise man told me that the center cannot hold."

"Meaning what?" His voice was hoarse with wanting, and he swallowed thickly.

"Meaning, if you confess your sins, what happens to those who follow you?" I took a step closer, gazed into his ravenous eyes. "If you tell them you're a Sensitive?"

His expression went cold. "Traitor. Harlot."

"Maybe. But that doesn't change the fact"—I took two steps back—"that you have magic."

The Reveillon members looked back and forth between us, debating who to believe.

"I don't have magic!" Ezekiel screamed it, then ripped open his shirt, revealing a network of scars across his abdomen and ribs, some of them fresh. "Those demons were excised."

Rage bubbled in me, rage that the refusal to deal with Sensitives had led to this, that he'd actually cut himself in some delusional attempt to rid himself of magic. And by doing that, by deciding he'd been cured of it, he'd eliminated whatever chance he'd had to learn to cast it off, to find the balance that would have saved him.

"The demon is excised!" he repeated, his eyes belying the words.

"Let's test that theory," I said, and reached into the magic still spindling inside me.

"Claire, no!"

Liam knew what I intended, and his voice was tinged with concern. Containment would come to know exactly what I was, and I'd have to face the consequences of it.

He was right. It was a risk. But I was tired of hiding. I was tired of pretending to be something else. This was necessary to show what Ezekiel really was, and I'd be damned if cowardice steered me away from it.

I shook my head but didn't take my gaze off Ezekiel. "It's time, Liam. It has to be. That's how this ends."

As if he sensed the magic I gathered, Ezekiel's eyes went almost slack with desire. I wrapped fury—tinged with pity—around those threads of magic, and used them to whip a machete from a Reveillon member's hands, sent it spinning at Ezekiel. He ducked, and it hit the oak behind him, shattering splinters into the wind.

Before Reveillon could object, could curse my name and my magic, Ezekiel screamed, the sound as horrible as any wraith's. And as he sang that unholy note, fire burst from his mouth, singeing a line across the grass.

The man could *scream fire*.

For a moment, there was only shock—the Reveillon members horrified by the man they'd believed would lead the charge against magic, and Containment agents baffled by the irony. They'd figure out eventually that Ezekiel was fighting his demon the best way he knew how—by excising it not just from his body, but from *everything*.

I avoided the line of fire, gathered up magic for another shot. Anger gave me control, helped me lift a nearby bench into the air, spin it toward Ezekiel. He hit the ground to dodge it, sang his fire again.

This time, the stream was nearly bullet-fast. I sidestepped, but not fast enough to avoid the knife-sharp pain of fire along my leg. I'd burned myself before, but this was no ordinary fire. It was angry and barbed, as if each lick of flame was infinitely forked to scrape and sear.

Maybe it was time for a different plan.

Ezekiel and I faced each other, the battle still proceeding around us. I stared at him, looking purposefully hopeless, even as I gathered more magic for another shot. Or more precisely, for another volley.

When he opened his mouth to scream, I wrenched my magic against his, wrapped those braided links of power around the stream of fire. Sparks shot up from the conjunction of his magic and mine, as alien power battled alien power.

He pushed, and I pushed back, sweat running down my back, my shaking arms, as I struggled to keep the magic from surging back toward me. Ezekiel was powerful, but I doubted he understood his own strength, knew how to control it. Not after denying it for so long. Still, he warred ferociously, changing the pitch of his magic to change its temperature, its vibration, so I had to counter with moves of my own. It was like controlling a feather in the middle of a hurricane.

I was getting dizzy, adrenaline, magic, and exhaustion taking their toll. One final push, I told myself. One final push, and he'd be down, and the center would be gone. He would be done, and with him, the rest of it.

I gathered every ounce of magic, every frazzled thread of anger and frustration, bound them together with will and resolve. And when that braid was strong enough, tight enough, I thrust it toward him.

Ezekiel went pale . . . and he faltered. Telekinesis overpowered fire, pushing his magic back toward him, into him. It slammed into him like a bus, throwing him back against the live oak behind him, where he slumped to the ground.

I fell to my knees, chest heaving.

Ezekiel shuddered as Containment agents swarmed to him, to the rest of the Reveillon members. But he raised his bloody eyes and smiled at me, the stain of death at the corners of his mouth. "You're too late," he yelled, and pointed at something behind me, his eyes closing as the agents surrounded him.

As the battle exploded again around me, Reveillon members fighting with the agents who tried to subdue them, I looked back.

Liam lay alone on the ground twenty feet away, body shuddering from the force of Ezekiel's magic. A shot meant for me must have ricocheted, or Liam had stepped in to shield me from it.

"Liam!" I screamed, and ran to him, fell down in the grass beside him, fear piercing me as sharply as a Paranormal's blade.

His left shoulder was charred, his shirt singed, but he was still breathing, pulse tapping visibly in his neck, chest rising and falling with each breath. Tears of relief streamed down my face as I gingerly pulled his shirt away from the wound. It would need a thorough cleaning and bandaging, but Lizzie would take care of it. He'd be fine.

He'd be fine. He had to be fine.

My fingers grazed his skin again . . . and that's when I felt it—under and behind and running through those shudders was something foreign, and yet utterly familiar. Liam's lashes fluttered, and he opened his eyes, blinked to adjust, to focus. And when his eyes finally trained on me, they shone brilliantly gold.

He was alive, and he was . . . magic.

I couldn't stop my voice from shaking when I said his name. "Liam."

Eyes still fixed on mine, fear transforming to realization, he grabbed my hand, and magic—power—jumped like a visible spark between us. He clasped my hand hard, squeezed until my bones ached, while frissons of magic shimmered in the air.

"Claire," he said, his voice ragged with magic, with power, and with what looked like the cruel ecstasy of whatever passed through him.

He was like me now. "You were hit by my magic"—I told him, watching waves of it pass through his body—"and I think you have magic now. Like Eleanor."

I returned my gaze to his face but failed to recognize the emotion in his eyes.

"Magic?"

I nodded. "You'll be all right, Liam. You're alive," I said, and pressed my mouth to his. "You'll be all right." I looked around for help, but Containment agents would be useless here. "I'm going to find Lizzie. She'll take care of you. Stay here, and don't move. I'll be right back."

He grabbed my hand, gripped it hard enough to bruise. "No, Claire . . . I can't . . . leave . . ."

I'd thought he didn't want me to leave. "I'll be right back," I assured him. "I promise. I have to get Lizzie."

I searched for five minutes but couldn't find her in the crowd. Afraid for Liam, I gave up and ran back to him. I'd wait with him until someone came—someone would come eventually. He'd be okay until then.

But when I reached the spot where he'd lay, the grass was empty. He was gone, and the Containment agents dealing with the Reveillon members they'd captured there now stared at me suspiciously.

They'd seen my magic.

They knew what I was.

I shook my head, willing myself to stop, to think. That was for later. Liam was now. Where had he gone? Had Lizzie gotten to him first? Taken him to the clinic?

Instinctively, I looked in that direction, found Malachi in the middle of the street. Liam stood at his side, holding his wounded arm. They both looked at me, Liam's gaze steely and somehow alien, Malachi's unreadable.

There in the middle of the street, Malachi stretched his wings and draped Liam's good arm around his neck, as if preparing to lift them both into the air.

But why would he take Liam? Why not just wait for Lizzie to check him out, to take him to the clinic?

I stared at Liam, watched his golden gaze—so much like Malachi's—turn angry, and then turn away.

Realization hit me. Malachi wasn't taking Liam for help, I realized, knees nearly buckling.

He was helping Liam run.

Liam had become magic, the thing he loathed and feared, the reason Gracie was dead. The reason Eleanor was injured. He'd become the enemy he'd been hunting since the war began. Not a Paranormal and not a Sensitive, but certainly not a human.

Liam had become one of the demons he chased, and he was running.

And he was running without me.

zekiel had been a Sensitive, and he'd become a wraith, or close enough that Containment wouldn't care much about the difference. He'd made war against humans, Paranormals, Containment. That I'd helped battle him back would be dwarfed by that simple fact—whatever else I was, I was still a monster. I was a demon not yet unleashed, and Gunnar couldn't protect me forever.

Liam had chosen to run. I no longer had a choice.

Gunnar had been right about Ezekiel. Without his leadership, and with a new understanding of who he was and how he'd lied, the assault lost momentum and the sounds of battle receded again. No longer afraid of losing ground to Reveillon, Containment agents began to gather up their enemies.

Since I'd proven I was one of them, I had to go.

I ran back to Royal Mercantile, past the revelers who'd already gathered in Jackson Square to celebrate with booze and candles and music. Some were subdued and quiet; others sang a raucous version of "When the Saints Come Marching In."

I ran past them, past the Pontalba Apartments to Royal, past the former shops and empty lots, pushing through the stream of humans heading toward the Square to join the celebration.

As much as I wanted to be like them, I wasn't. And I'd made that known to the world.

I was a full block away from the store when I realized how little there was to come back to.

I stopped in front of what remained of Royal Mercantile, stared.

They'd knocked the glass out of the front door, but left the leather strap with the bell. The front windows were gone; glass fanned across the sidewalk like snow. The store had been trashed, emptied. Goods either taken or broken, which was just pointless and wasteful.

I walked inside, right through the door, glass crunching beneath my feet, and stared at the devastation.

I'd known this might happen, was likely to happen. But there was a big difference between knowing it and actually seeing it.

Tadji was sweeping glass and grit in the middle of the store. "Claire!" She dropped her broom, ran forward, embraced me in a hug. "Thank God. You're all right."

I nodded, too numb to react. "Are you okay?"

"I'm good. I'm good." She looked around the store. "I mean, you can see what happened here."

"Reveillon?"

She nodded. "The ones too afraid to actually fight, I think. They broke the windows, took a lot. There were so many of them. I wouldn't let the customers fight. I didn't want anyone else getting hurt, Claire. Not over things."

"Good," I said. "Good. You did just the right thing, because you're right—it's just stuff. It doesn't matter."

Did anything matter now?

"What about Burke? Gunnar? Gavin? Liam? Are they all right?"

Guilt settled heavily in my bones. "I don't know," I admitted. I hadn't seen them, knew only that we'd won the battle, that Liam had gone, and that I had to. Everything else blurred at the edges.

I went to the stairs, took them two at a time to the storage room.

"Claire!" Tadji called after me as I grabbed the go bag from my armoire. She reached the doorway as I stood up again, and she looked down at the bag with wide eyes.

"Claire, stop," she said firmly, holding up a hand. "Stop and tell me what's happened."

"We beat them back. We won. I don't know what will happen with Devil's Isle, with the Paras who helped. But we beat back Reveillon. Ezekiel is dead."

"Then why are you running?"

"I used magic in front of Containment."

She looked confused. "But after all this, after everything, they'll understand now. They'll get it."

I shook my head. "Ezekiel was a Sensitive."

It took a moment for her to understand what that meant, and why it mattered. "Jesus. He was a wraith?"

I nodded. He was close enough to it. "Containment knows he had magic, what he did with it. The destruction and death he brought. To beat him back, I had to show him. But they won't change their mind about Sensitives. Not now."

Reveillon was mostly vanquished. Paranormals had shown they could be helpful.

We would be the new enemy.

Tadji shook her head. "Things will change, Claire. They will. Gunnar will see to it. Gunnar will help them understand."

Gunnar would do what he could within the limits of the law.

"They might change someday," I said, "but they aren't going to change today. And I can't become a prisoner. I have to go," I said, and walked past her. I took the stairs again, went to the kitchen.

Reveillon had been here, too. They'd cleaned out most everything that wasn't nailed down.

I pried up a loose floorboard, pulled out the linen pillowcase that held my emergency stash of rice, beans, onions, and water, checked to make sure nothing had spilled out. I rose, handed it to her.

"What's this?"

"Food for you and Burke. Go back to your house and stay there. Gunnar or Gavin will look for you, find you."

"I don't understand, Claire," she said, taking the pillowcase and putting it on the counter. "I don't understand what's happening. Where's Liam? He won't let you go without him. He'll want to be sure you're all right."

"Ezekiel's magic struck him."

Tadji pressed a hand to her mouth, horror in her eyes.

My voice sounded far away, tinny. Was I in shock? "He's alive," I said. "But . . . the magic changed him. His eyes . . ." I swallowed hard, willed myself to stay strong. "They turned golden."

"They turned—" she began, stopping as she realized the implication. She lowered her hand. "He has magic."

"He went with Malachi. He went without me. I think maybe that he thinks he's a monster. Or, I don't know . . ."

"No, Claire. He must not have seen you. He'd have known that you'd come back here. He's probably on his way."

"He saw me. I watched him leave." *He turned away from me*, I wanted to say. I wanted to scream it. But those words were too unbearably sad to voice. So instead, I let silence drop heavily between us.

"He's gone," I made myself say. "That has to be okay, or I'm not going to make it." I swallowed a sob that wanted to choke me. "So I'm going to focus on what's next. I'm going to run. And then I'm going to get them out. The Sensitives, the Consularis Paras. I don't know how, and I don't know when, but I'm going to get them out. I can't do that if I'm in the clinic."

"Where are you going?"

There was one place I could still go—the place only Liam knew about. And wherever he was right now, whatever future he was facing, he wouldn't tell. He didn't want to think about me.

"I can't tell you. If I don't tell you," I added when I could see her preparing to argue, "you won't have to lie for me."

I went behind the counter, took the gun and ammo from the safe, put them in my bag.

"What about the store?"

I zipped up the bag, looked around at the remains of Royal Mercantile, of my family's legacy. My gaze fell on the cuckoo clock at the other end of the counter, its pieces still in organized piles. But it was just a thing, like everything else in the store.

I looked back at Tadji. "Give Lizzie whatever she can use. You take the food—hand it out in the Quarter if you want, or take it home. Make sure Mrs. Proctor has what she needs. Tony, maybe, if he needs something. Board up the rest of it. Just lock it up."

She looked horrified.

"I'm not worried about the store, Tadji. I'm worried about you, about Gunnar, about Burke and Liam and Eleanor. About Moses and Malachi. Royal Mercantile existed before, and it will exist again. If it can't exist right now, so be it."

"How are you so calm about this?"

"I'm not calm. I'm angry and I'm afraid that I'm losing everything that means anything to me. Liam . . ." I looked at her and couldn't stop the tears that filled my eyes. "I love him, Tadj. I didn't mean to, not with everything . . . But I do."

She came to me, put her hands on my arms. "If he has magic, if he is magic, that's not standing between you anymore."

"He ran, Tadji. He ran from me, and I don't know if he's coming back."

"And what about you?" she said. "Are you coming back?"

"I don't know. When I can. If I can." I shook my head. "I don't know."

Tadji lunged forward and embraced me hard enough that I could feel the sobs that racked her as she stroked my hair.

"I thought we'd be done with it, with all of it," she said. "When the fight was done, when Reveillon was done, we'd rebuild again, and I'd work in the store, and Liam would fall in love with you, and that would be that. We'd make our way, just like we made our way before."

Don't you dare break, I told myself. *She needs you, so before you walk away, you damn well better not break here and now.*

I pulled back, brushed the tears from her cheeks. "We'll make our way, Tadji. We did before, and we will again. But it will have to be a new way. If you need me, if there's some emergency, get a message to Malachi. He may be able to find me." If anyone could find a cache of magical objects, it would be him.

Gunnar stepped into the store. He looked a little banged up, but he was on his feet and moving. Relief flooded me. And then fear and regret.

"Thank God," he said. "I couldn't find you—"

"How's Gavin?" I asked. "And Burke, Moses, Lizzie, Tony—is everyone all right? I came back fast, and I didn't see . . ."

I knew only about Malachi. About Malachi . . . and Liam.

"Tony took a hit from a machete, but he'll be fine. Moses is still eating soup, I think. Gavin and Burke are helping Containment gather up the rest of the Reveillon members. Lizzie's at the clinic. A battalion from Birmingham made it through, and they're on their way." He nearly smiled, but that hope faded when he looked at my face, then down at the bag in my hands. "Where are you going? And where's Liam?"

I couldn't stop the tears that welled again. "He's alive. Tadji can tell you the rest. I have to go. You know I do. I go, or you stay and arrest me."

"I won't arrest you." His voice was fierce.

"If not you, then Broussard, or Reece, or the Commandant, or someone else. It doesn't matter who. Someone will be here to take me in. After Ezekiel, Gunnar, you know they have to. It might be a nicer, kinder Devil's Isle, but it will still be Devil's Isle."

I could see he wanted to argue but knew there was no argument to make. "Where will you go?"

"I can't tell you. There's a place I can go, and I'll be safe there. But I can't tell you where it is."

Rage, fear, and understanding seemed to cross his face in turns.

"Plausible deniability, Gunnar. You know it's better that way."

His lips tightened, but he nodded. "How will we know you're safe?"

"I'll get in touch when I can. Keep Tadji safe. And yourself."

Gunnar nodded, his own eyes reddening. "I love you, Claire. Please be careful."

I could only nod, and made myself put on a brave face for both of us. "I love you, too, Gunn. Maybe this will only be temporary," I said, thinking of what Moses had said, the irony of our positions. He'd come willingly back into Devil's Isle; I was running away from it.

Gunnar walked me to the door, leaving Tadji in front of the counter. I glanced back at her, offered a small wave. She nodded, brought fingers to her lips as her eyes filled with tears.

Everything was changing. The life I'd built for myself, dragged for myself out of war and misery, even if it was a small life, had been mine. I'd had my place, my friends, my routine, my preconceptions of who I was, who my father had been, who Paranormals were. And now that was all gone. Every bit of it dashed.

The rose-colored glasses had been knocked away and trampled underfoot.

But I'm alive, I reminded myself. I was alive and outside Devil's Isle, where I could change things. For now, that was what mattered. That was what had to matter.

The sun was setting as we walked outside.

And to our left, still a block away, three Containment agents walked down Royal, heading for what remained of Royal Mercantile. Captain John Reece led the charge, and they all had weapons strapped to their sides.

Gunnar's gaze sharpened, and he turned toward them, shielding my body with his. "Go, Claire. Now. Out the back."

I slipped into the alley as he called out, "Captain Reece. What can I do for you?"

It was three miles to the Apollo. I walked slowly, stayed in the shadows and stopped every few blocks, waiting for a car to pass, or a spotlight to swing by, scanning for Reveillon members still on the loose, or for the Sensitive who'd shown her magic.

When I reached the station, I waited behind the fence of the empty house next door for fifteen minutes, figuring anyone who'd tracked me that far would have shown themselves. But the silence was broken only by the hum of crickets, the breeze through palm leaves.

I jogged to the door, magicked the lock, and slipped inside, locking it again behind me.

I stood in the silence for minutes—five or ten—sure that Liam would walk out of the darkness and find me, that we'd comfort each other, that he'd realize we could finally be together.

That we were the same kind of monster.

But the building was utterly and completely silent. There'd be no homecoming. Not now.

I dropped my bag to the floor and followed it there, sliding down to the concrete. I cried until my eyes burned and my chest ached. I cried for the souls we'd lost that day, for the humans who'd sought salvation in hate and violence, and who'd paid the price for their choice.

I cried until I was exhausted of tears and emotions. And then I scrubbed my face with my hands, pushed my hair from my face, and took a deep breath.

There was no point in wasting the energy on regret.

Liam would come around. He had to.

I lifted my head, glanced at the space and the objects that filled it. There was so much magic, so much potential here. And plenty of irony, I thought, that not only had Containment failed to grab me, but they'd managed to send me into the largest surviving cache of magic in New Orleans, maybe even in the Zone.

I walked to the closest table, picked up a book of voodoo and hoodoo rituals.

I could organize these things. I could catalog them. And I could learn to use them.

I just needed a plan.